PRAISE FOR
Darkness, My

"*Darkness, My Old Friend* is deeply p
undeniable momentum. Lisa Unger's entnralling cast of characters pulled
me right in and locked me down tight. This is one book that will have you
racing to the last page, only to have you wishing the ride wasn't over."

—Michael Connelly

"Lisa Unger is one of my favorite authors. She gets better and better
with each book."

—Karin Slaughter, *New York Times*
bestselling author of *Fallen*

"Lisa Unger's writing has the gift of rhythm. She has created a melody that
traps readers with heart-stopping stories that only Unger could write. The
characters are profound and reveal the hidden side that exists in all of us. This
is a magnificent, well-told story, full of revelations about human nature."

—Javier Sierra, *New York Times* bestselling
author of *The Lost Angel*

"Gripping psychological thriller . . . as much about uncovering the past
as it is about accepting the future."

—*Publishers Weekly*

"Unger has a sure touch with teenage characters and their parents, exploring
the sometimes painful territory without falling back on stereotypes. She also
shines a light on marital bonds, some strong, some broken, some unhealthy.
Her story's roots are in those family relationships, which any detective will
tell you account for plenty of homicides. Unger gives us one other important
element: characters to root for as well as against. She's definitely one of
my new favorites."

—*Charlotte Observer*

"Verdict . . . one of Unger's best thrillers yet."

—*Library Journal* (starred review)

"As all of the characters' story lines come together in the thrilling conclusion, the reader may stay up all night to finish. This is a fast-paced page-turner with compelling characters who draw you in."

—*Parkersburg News and Sentinel*

"Good reading, canny characterizations."

—*Cleveland Plain Dealer*

"Unger raises questions of faith, memory, sacrifice, and love in her latest novel. It has a gripping plot, fast-paced action, and characters that seem so real they almost leap from the printed page. *Darkness, My Old Friend* is a great follow-up to her previous novel, *Fragile*."

—*Tucson Citizen*

"Readers will find themselves drawn to the author's mastery of characterization and her psychological penetration. As in *Fragile*, Ms. Unger is especially adept at delineating the emotionally troubled depths of rebellious adolescents. Frustrated, despondent parents are drawn equally well. The recovery from a kind of safe paralysis to dangerous action that brings Jones Cooper back to his essential self is handled with insight and skill. The author makes Eloise Montgomery's uncanny talents vivid and credible, while she handles the control freak-psyche of Kevin Carr with a sure hand."

—*Florida Weekly*

"This is one of Lisa Unger's best novels, with a complex plot and a great cast of characters. You'll fly through it to find out what has happened."

—*Daily American*

"Reading *Darkness, My Old Friend* feels a bit like moving to a small town like The Hollows. First you get to know the locals, slowly but surely, and then once you're familiar, you start to notice the oddities and peculiarities of the place, wondering what secrets it's hiding. The book might not be explosive or edgy, especially not at first, but it does steadily build suspense in a way that might be even more effective."

—Bookreporter.com

lisa unger

darkness, my old friend

a novel

broadway paperbacks
new york

BROADWAY

This is a work of fiction. Names, characters, places, and incidents either are the product of the author's imagination or are used fictitiously. Any resemblance to actual persons, living or dead, events, or locales is entirely coincidental.

Published in the United States by Broadway Paperbacks, an imprint of the
Crown Publishing Group, a division of Random House, Inc., New York.
www.crownpublishing.com

BROADWAY PAPERBACKS and its logo, a letter B bisected on the diagonal,
are trademarks of Random House, Inc.

Originally published in hardcover in slightly different form in the United States by
Crown Publishers, an imprint of the Crown Publishing Group,
a division of Random House, Inc., New York, in 2011.

This book contains an excerpt from the forthcoming book *Heartbroken* by Lisa Unger. This excerpt has been set for this edition only and may not reflect the final content of the forthcoming edition.

Library of Congress Cataloging-in-Publication Data
Unger, Lisa, 1970–
Darkness, my old friend : a novel / Lisa Unger. — 1st ed.
p. cm.
1. Missing persons—Investigation—Fiction. 2. Women authors—Fiction.
3. Psychics—Fiction. 4. Police chiefs—Fiction. I. Title.
PS3621.N486D37 2011
813'.6—dc22   2011009973

ISBN 978-0-307-46518-4
eISBN 978-0-307-46519-1

PRINTED IN THE UNITED STATES OF AMERICA

Book design by Lynne Amft
Cover design by Mumtaz Mustafa
Cover photography by Felicia Simion/Trevillion Images

10 9 8 7 6 5 4 3 2 1

First Paperback Edition

For
Joe, Tara, and Violet

I am blessed that my brother is also my dear friend,
That I can think of his wife as my sister,
And that their darling daughter is a lovely flower
in the garden of all of our lives.

part one

gone

*"Fools," said I, "you do not know
Silence like a cancer grows."*

—Simon & Garfunkel,
"The Sound of Silence"

prologue

Failure wasn't a feeling; it was a taste in his mouth, an ache at the base of his neck. It was a frantic hum in his head. The reflection of failure resided in his wife's tight, fake smile when he came home at the end of the day. He felt the creeping grip of it in her cold embrace. She didn't even know the worst of it. No one did. But they could all smell it, couldn't they? It was like booze on his breath.

Traffic on the highway stuttered. He tried to breathe through the trapped-in-a-box feeling that was expanding in his chest, that too-familiar tightness of frustration. He looked around at his fellow commuters, wondering why none of them had taken to screaming, or banging on their dashboards. How did they do it day after day? Killing themselves for pointless jobs that ultimately lined someone else's pockets. Then they sat in an endless snaking line only to get home to a ceaseless litany of needs. Why? Why did so many people live like this?

This weekend is your very last chance to take advantage of the absolutely rock-bottom prices at Ed's Automart. No job? Bad credit? Nothing to trade in? No problem. We can help!

Kevin Carr snapped off the radio, that schizophrenic rant of criticism and demands. *Eat this. Buy that. Need to lose weight? Whiten your teeth? Bacon double cheeseburger. Personal trainer. Foreclosure auction on Sunday.* But the silence that followed was almost worse, because all he could hear then was the sound of his own thoughts—which sounded suspiciously like the radio, only there was no "off" button.

Around him the herd of commuters—some carpoolers, but mostly solitary drivers like himself—gripped their wheels and stared ahead. No one looked happy, did they? People weren't singing along with the radio or smiling to themselves. Plenty of people were hands-free talking, gesticulating in their conversations as though there were someone sitting beside them. But they were alone. Did people look gray and angry? Did they seem unhealthy, dissatisfied? Or was he just projecting? Was he simply seeing in the world around him a portrait of his own inner life?

He pulled into the right lane quickly, without signaling, cutting off some asshole in a late-model BMW. The other driver made a show of squealing his brakes and leaning on his horn. Kevin looked into the mirror to see the guy flipping him off; the man in the Beemer was yelling, even though he must have known that no one else could hear him. Kevin felt a rush of malicious glee. It was the first time he had smiled all day.

The phone rang. He pressed the button on his steering wheel to answer, though he didn't like to take calls when he couldn't see the ID screen. He had so many balls in the air he could hardly keep track of them all.

"Kevin Carr," he answered.

"Hey." Paula. "On your way home?"

"Almost at the exit," he said.

"The baby needs diapers. And Cameron feels a little warm. Can you get some Motrin?"

"Sure," he said. "Anything else?"

"I think that's it. I did manage to get us all to the grocery store today." He heard water running in the background, the clinking of dishes in the sink. "*And* we got through it without a meltdown—if you can believe it. Cammy was such a good boy. But I forgot the diapers."

He could see them there. Claire still in the baby carrier mounted on the cart, Cameron trailing behind Paula—pulling stuff off the shelves, clowning around. Paula was always together, with her hair brushed and her makeup done. She wasn't like the other mothers he had seen the few times he'd dropped Cameron off at preschool—circles under their eyes, stains on their shirts, hair wild. He wouldn't allow that.

"Make a list next time," he said.

In the silence that followed, he heard the baby start to mew. The sound of it, that wheedling little cry that would turn to screaming if someone didn't figure out what in the hell she wanted, made him cringe. It was an accusation, an indictment, and a conviction all at once.

"Okay, Kevin," Paula said. Any initial brightness had left her voice completely. "Thanks for the advice."

"I didn't mean—"

But she'd hung up already.

In the grocery store, Elton John thought that it was lonely out in space. Elton sang about how he was not the man they think he is at home. Kevin knew too well what he meant. He wandered the massive aisles. They were stacked with garishly packaged, processed promises—low-fat, no carbs, sugar-free, no trans fats, no cholesterol, ultra-slimming, buy-one-get-one-free, all-natural. In the baby aisle, everything went pink, blue, and yellow, little ducks and frogs, Dora the Explorer, Elmo. He searched for the green-and-brown packaging of the diapers Paula liked for the baby—organic, biodegradable. This was his personal favorite, the whole organic thing. Corporations had been raping and pillaging the environment since the industrial revolution—spewing waste into the air and water, mowing down the rain forests, poisoning the earth. And now, all of a sudden, it was up to the *individual* to save the planet—by paying twice as much for "green" products, thereby increasing the profit margin of the very companies that were responsible for global warming, the almost-total depletion of natural resources, not to mention obesity and all its related diseases. It killed him, it really did.

At the gleaming row of cash registers, the young, pretty girl was free, thumbing through the pages of some celebrity rag. What was her name? He didn't have his glasses on, so he couldn't read her name tag. Tracie? Trixie? Trudie?

"Hey, Mr. Carr. I saw your wife and kids earlier," she said. She dragged his purchases over the sensor. Diapers: $12.99. Motrin: $8.49. Looking at twenty-year-old tits: priceless. He didn't need his glasses to see those.

Paula had nursed Cameron until he'd turned two, just a month before they'd realized she was pregnant again. And now she was going on eighteen months with Claire (though she'd promised him she'd stop after a year). They'd both come to see her breasts as something utilitarian, the way they came out of her shirt without a second thought as soon as Claire started fussing. Gone were the lace push-ups and silky camisoles. Now, if Paula wore a bra at all, it had this snapping mechanism on the cup to unlatch, so the baby could nurse. TracieTrixie-Trudy was probably wearing something pink and pretty, her breasts like peaches, no baby attached sucking away her sexiness.

"You're so lucky," the girl was saying. "You have such a beautiful family."

"It's true," he said. He looked into his wallet. No cash, as usual. He stared at the tops of seven credit cards peeking, colorful and mocking in their leather slots. He couldn't remember which one wasn't maxed out. "I'm blessed."

With a smile he swiped the Platinum Visa and held his breath until the signature line showed on the electronic pad.

Kevin knew what the girl saw when she looked at him, why she was smiling so sweetly. She saw the Breitling watch, the Armani suit, the diamond-studded platinum wedding band. The sum-total cost of the items hanging off his body was greater than what she might earn in half a year. When she looked at him, she saw money, not the mounting, uncontrollable debt his purchases represented. That's all people saw, the glittering surface. What lay beneath, what was *real,* mattered not in the least.

"Did you remember your reusable sack?" she asked. She gave him another beaming smile and shook a finger of mock admonishment at him.

"No, I didn't," he said. Playing her game, he tried to look contrite. "That's all right, though. I don't need one." He picked up the two items and headed for the door.

"You saved a tree, Mr. Carr!" she called after him. "Good for you."

Her youthful exuberance made him feel a hundred years old. Just as he stepped from beneath the overhang, it started to rain, hard. By the time he'd climbed into the car, he was soaked. He tossed his purchases onto the seat beside him. Then, looking in the rearview mirror, he ran his fingers through his dark hair, smoothing it back. He grabbed a towel from the gym bag on the seat behind him and mopped off his suit jacket, the raindrops on the leather all around him.

He turned on the engine and started to shiver. It wasn't even that cold. He just felt a familiar chill spread through his body. He sat, blank for a moment. He just needed a minute, this minute of quiet, before he put the mask on again. He was about to back out and head home. Then, on a whim, he reached under the passenger seat and retrieved the small black bag he kept there. He just wanted to check, just wanted to see it.

He'd had it under there since they drove to Florida and took the kids to Disney over the summer—a trip that cost Kevin more than three thousand dollars between the park, the hotel, and the meals. The whole venture had been a masquerade of normalcy. The endless ride down south was a chaos of Goldfish crackers and juice boxes, the manic sound tracks of Cameron's DVDs, Claire's eternal crying and fussing. They spent their days at the park; Cameron had a good time. But the baby was really too young; what with the incessant heat and the slack-jawed crowds, Claire fussed constantly, driving him nearly mad. He plastered a smile on his face and pretended that he didn't feel like his head was going to explode. When he'd met Paula, she was young and hot, smart and vital. Now she was a mom at Disney, two full sizes bigger. When had her legs gotten so thick? It was then that he realized he had to get out. He couldn't live like this. Of course, divorce was not an option. What a cliché.

He'd gone out one night to bring in a pizza and stopped at one of the many gun shops he'd seen around.

"This is the most popular handgun in America," the dealer had told him. "The Glock 17 fires seventeen nine-millimeter Luger rounds. It's lightweight, perfect for the home. Hope you never need to, but you'll be able to protect your family with this, even without much gun experience."

The dealer, who looked to be in his twenties and had an unhealthy enthusiasm for his work, also sold him a box of ammo.

A couple of days later, the night before they were about to head home, he stopped back and picked it up. Kevin could hardly believe that he was able to walk out of the shop with a gun and bullets, carried in a small canvas bag. In the parking lot, he'd stashed everything under the passenger seat. And there it had all stayed for the better part of six months. Paula never drove this car. Even on the weekends, they always used her Mercedes SUV, because that's where the car seats and diaper bags and all the other various kid gear—strollers, sippy cups, extra wipes—were kept. You'd think she was planning to go away for a month with everything she had back there.

Now he unzipped the small duffel and removed the hard plastic case, opened it. In the amber light shining into his car from the parking-lot lamp above, he looked at the flat, black gun in its case, its neat lines and ridged, ergonomic grip. He could hear the tapping of the rain on his roof, the muted sound of a woman talking on her cell phone as she walked to her car. *I can't believe he would say that!* Her voice echoed. *What a jerk!*

The sight of the gun gave him a sense of comfort. He felt his shoulders relax and his breathing come easier. Some of the terrible tension he carried around all day seemed to dissolve. He couldn't say why. Even if someone had asked, he wouldn't have been able to say why a blessed sense of relief washed over him at the sight of that gun.

chapter one

Jones Cooper feared death. The dread of it woke him in the night, sat him bolt upright and drew all the breath from his lungs, narrowed his esophagus, had him rasping in the dark. It turned all the normal shadows of the bedroom that he shared with his wife into a legion of ghouls and intruders waiting with silent and malicious intent. When? How? Heart attack. Cancer. Freak accident. Would it come for him quickly? Would it slowly waste and dehumanize him? What, if anything, would await him?

He was not a man of faith. Nor was he a man without a stain on his conscience. He did not believe in a benevolent universe of light and love. He could not lean upon those crutches as so many did; everyone, it seemed, had some way to protect himself against the specter of his certain end. Everyone except him.

His wife, Maggie, had grown tired of the 2:00 A.M. terrors. At first she was beside him, comforting him: *Just breathe, Jones. Relax. It's okay.* But even she, ever-patient shrink that she was, had started sleeping in the guest room or on the couch, even sometimes in their son's room, empty since Ricky had left for Georgetown in September.

His wife believed it had something to do with Ricky's leaving. "A child heading off for college is a milestone. It's natural to reflect on the passing of your life," she'd said. Maggie seemed to think that the acknowledgment of one's mortality was a rite of passage, something everyone went through. "But there's a point, Jones, where reflection becomes self-indulgent, even self-destructive. Surely you see that spending your life fearing death is a death in and of itself."

But it seemed to him that people didn't reflect on death at all. Everyone appeared to be walking around oblivious to the looming end—spending hours on Facebook, talking on cell phones while driving through Starbucks, reclining on the couch for hours watching some mindless crap on television. People were *not* paying attention—not to life, not to death, not to one another.

"Lighten up, honey. Really." Those were the last words she'd said to him this morning before she headed off to see her first patient. He *was* trying to lighten up. He really was.

Jones was raking leaves; the great oaks in his yard had started their yearly shed. There were just a few leaves now. He'd made a small pile down by the curb. For all the years they'd been in this house, he'd hired someone to do this work. But since his retirement, almost a year ago now, he'd decided to manage the tasks of homeownership himself—mowing the lawn, maintaining the landscaping, skimming the pool, washing the windows, now raking the leaves, eventually shoveling the snow from the driveway. It was amazing, really, how these tasks could fill his days. How from morning to night, he could just putter, as Maggie called it—changing lightbulbs, trimming trees, cleaning the cars.

But is it enough? You have a powerful intellect. Can you be satisfied this way? His wife overestimated him. His intellect wasn't that powerful. The neighbors had started to rely on him, enjoyed having a retired cop around while they were at work, on vacation. He was letting repair guys in, getting mail, and turning on lights when people were away, checking perimeters, keeping his guns clean and loaded. The situation annoyed Maggie initially—the neighbors calling and dropping by, asking for this and that—especially since he wouldn't accept payment, even from people he didn't really know. Then people started dropping off gifts—a bottle of scotch, a gift certificate to Grillmarks, a fancy steakhouse in town.

"You could turn this into a real business," Maggie said. She was suddenly enthusiastic one night over dinner, paid for by the Pedersens. Jones had fed their mean-spirited cat, Cheeto, for a week.

He scoffed. "Oh, yeah. Local guy hanging around with nothing to do but let the plumber in? Is that what I'd call it?"

She gave him that funny smile he'd always loved. It was more like the turning up of one corner of her mouth, something she did when she found him amusing but didn't want him to know it.

"It's a viable service that people would pay for and be happy to have," she said. "Think about it."

But he enjoyed it, didn't really want to be paid. It was nice to be needed, to look after the neighborhood: to make sure things were okay. You didn't stop being a cop when you stopped being a cop. And he wasn't exactly retired, was he? He wouldn't have left his post if he hadn't felt that it was necessary, the right thing to do under the circumstances. But that was another matter.

The late-morning temperature was a perfect sixty-eight degrees. The light was golden, the air carrying the scent of the leaves he was raking, the aroma of burning wood from somewhere. In the driveway Ricky's restored 1966 GTO preened, waiting for him to come home from school next weekend. Jones had it tuned up and detailed, so it would be cherry when the kid got back.

He missed his son. Their relationship through the boy's late adolescence had been characterized, regrettably, by conflict more than anything else. Still, he couldn't wait for Ricky to be back under his roof again, even if it was just for four days. If anyone told him how much he'd really, truly miss his kid, how he'd feel a squeeze on his heart every time he walked by that empty room, Jones wouldn't have believed it. He would have thought it was just another one of those platitudes people mouthed about parenthood.

He leaned his rake against the trunk of the oak and removed his gloves. A pair of mourning doves cooed sadly at him. They sat on the railing of his porch, rustling their tawny feathers.

"I'm sorry," he said, not for the first time. Earlier, he'd removed the beginning of their nest, a loose pile of sticks and paper that they managed somehow to place in the light cover of his garage door's opening mechanism. Mourning doves made flimsy nests, were lazy enough to even settle in the abandoned nests of other birds. So the garage must have seemed like a perfect residence for them, offering protection from predators. But he didn't want birds in the garage. They were harbingers of death. Everyone knew that. They'd been hanging around the yard, giving him attitude all morning.

"You can build your nest anywhere else," he said, sweeping his arm over the property. "Just not there."

They seemed to listen, both of them craning their necks as he spoke. Then they flapped off with an angry, singsong twitter.

"Stupid birds."

He drew his arm across his forehead. In spite of the mild temperatures, he was sweating from the raking. It reminded him that he still needed to lose those twenty-five pounds his doctor had been nagging him about for years. His doctor, an annoyingly svelte, good-looking man right around Jones's age, never failed to mention the extra weight, no matter the reason for his visit—flu, sprained wrist, whatever. *You're gonna die one of these days, too, Doc,* Jones wanted to say. *You'll probably bite it during your workout. Whaddaya clocking these days—five miles every morning, more on the weekends? That'll put you in an early grave.* Instead Jones just kept reminding him that the extra weight around his middle had saved his life last year.

"I'm not sure that's a compelling argument," said Dr. Gauze. "What are the odds of your taking another bullet to the gut, especially now that you're out to pasture?"

Out to pasture? He was only forty-seven. He was thinking about this idea of being out to pasture as a beige Toyota Camry pulled up in front of the house and came to a stop. He watched for a second, couldn't see the person in the driver's seat. When the door opened and a slight woman stepped out, he recognized her without being able to place her. She was too thin, had the look of someone robbed of her appetite by anxiety. She moved with convalescent slowness up his drive, clutching a leather purse to her side. She didn't seem to notice him standing there in the middle of his yard. In fact, she walked right past him.

"Can I help you?" he said finally. She turned to look at him, startled.

"Jones Cooper?" she said. She ran a nervous hand through her hair, a mottle of steel gray and black, cut in an unflatteringly blunt bob.

"That's me."

"Do you know me?" she asked.

He moved closer to her, came to stand in front of her on the paved drive that needed painting. She was familiar, yes. But no, he didn't know her name.

"I'm sorry," he said. "Have we met?"

"I'm Eloise Montgomery."

It took a moment. Then he felt the heat rise to his cheeks, a tension creep into his shoulders. *Christ,* he thought.

"What can I do for you, Ms. Montgomery?"

She looked nervously around, and Jones followed her eyes, to the falling leaves, the clear blue sky.

"Is there someplace we can talk?" Her drifting gaze landed on the house.

"Can't we talk here?" He crossed his arms around his middle and squared his stance. Maggie would be appalled by his rudeness. But he didn't care. There was no way he was inviting this woman into his home.

"This is private," she said. "And I'm cold."

She started walking toward the house, stopped at the bottom of the three steps that led up to the painted gray porch, and turned around to look at him. He didn't like the look of her so near the house, any more than he did those doves. She was small-boned and skittish, but with a curious mettle. As she climbed the steps without invitation and stood at the door, he thought about how, with enough time and patience, a blade of grass could push its way through concrete. He expected her to pull open the screen and walk inside, but she waited. And he followed reluctantly, dropping his gardening gloves beside the rake.

The next thing he knew, she was sitting at the dining-room table and he was brewing coffee. He could see her from where he stood at the counter. She sat primly with her hands folded. She hadn't taken off her pilled houndstooth coat, was still clutching her bag. Those eyes never stopped moving.

"You don't want me here," she said. She cast a quick glance in his direction, then looked at her hands. "You wish I would go."

He put down the mugs he was taking from the cabinet, banging them without meaning to.

"Wow," he said. "I'm impressed. You really *are* psychic."

He didn't bother to look at her again, let his eyes rest on the calendar tucked behind the phone. He had an appointment with his shrink in a few hours, something he dreaded. When he finally gazed back over at her, she was regarding him with a wan smile.

"A skeptic," she said. "Your wife and mother-in-law offer more respect."

"Respect is earned." He poured the coffee. "How do you take it?" he asked. He thought she'd say black.

"Light and sweet, please," she said. Then, "And what should I do to earn your respect?"

He walked over with the coffee cups and sat across from her.

"What can I do for you, Ms. Montgomery?"

It was nearly noon. Maggie's last morning session would end in fifteen minutes, and then she'd come out for lunch. He didn't want Eloise sitting here when she did. The woman could only bring back bad memories for Maggie, everything they'd suffered through in the last year and long before. He didn't need it, and neither did his wife.

"Do you know about my work?" Eloise asked.

Work. Really? Is that what they were calling it? He would have thought she'd say something like gift, or sight. Or maybe abilities. Of course, she probably did consider it work, since that was how she earned her living.

"I do," he said. He tried to keep his tone flat, not inquiring or encouraging. But she seemed to feel the need to explain anyway.

"I'm like a radio. I pick up signals—from all over, scattered, disjointed. I have no control over what I see, when I see it, the degree of lucidity, the power of it. I could see something happening a world away, but not something right next door."

He struggled not to roll his eyes. Did she really expect him to believe this?

"Okay," he said. He took a sip of his coffee. He didn't like the edgy, anxious feeling he had. He felt physically uncomfortable in the chair, had a nervous desire to get up and pace the room. "What does this have to do with me?"

"You're getting a reputation around town, you know. That you're available to help with things—checking houses while people are away, getting mail."

He shrugged. "Just in the neighborhood here." He leaned back in his chair, showed his palms. "What? Are you going on vacation? Want me to feed your cat?"

She released a sigh and looked down at the table between them.

"People are going to start coming to you for more, from farther away," she said. "It might lead you places you don't expect."

Jones didn't like how that sounded. But he wouldn't give her the satisfaction of reacting.

"Okay," he said, drawing out the word.

"I wanted you to be prepared. I've seen something."

When she looked back up at him, her eyes were shining in a way that unsettled him. Her gaze made him think for some reason of his mother when he found her on the bathroom floor after she'd suffered a stroke. He slid his chair back from the table and stood.

"Why are you telling me this?" He leaned against the doorway that led to the kitchen.

"Because you need to know," she said. She still sat stiff and uncomfortable, hadn't touched the coffee before her.

Okay, great. Thanks for stopping by. Don't call me, I'll call you. Let me show you out. Instead, because curiosity always did get the better of him, he asked, "So what did you see?"

She ran a hand through her hair. "It's hard to explain. Like describing a dream. The essence can be lost in translation."

If this was some kind of show, it was a good one. She seemed sincere, not put on or self-dramatizing. If she were a witness, he would believe her story. But she wasn't a witness, she was a crackpot.

"Try," he said. "That's why you came, right?"

Another long slow breath in and out. Then, "I saw you on the bank of a river . . . or it could have been an ocean. Some churning body of water. I saw you running, chasing a lifeless form in the water. I don't know what or who it was. I can only assume it's a woman or a girl, because that's all I see. Then you jumped in—or possibly you fell. I think you were trying to save whoever it was. But you were overcome. You weren't strong enough. The water pulled you under."

Her tone was level, unemotional. She could have been talking mildly about the weather. And the image, for some reason, failed to jolt or disturb him. In that moment she seemed frail and silly, a carnival act that neither entertained nor intrigued.

The ticking of the large grandfather clock in the foyer seemed especially loud. He *had* to get rid of that thing, a housewarming present from his mother-in-law. Did he really need to hear the passing of the minutes of his life?

"You know, Ms. Montgomery," he said, "I don't think you're well."

"I'm not, Mr. Cooper. I'm not well at all." She got up from the table, to his great relief, and started moving toward the door.

"Well, should I find myself on the banks of a river, chasing a body,

I'll be sure to stay on solid ground," he said, allowing her to pass and following her to the door. "Thanks for the warning."

"Would you? Would you stay on solid ground? I doubt it." She rested her hand on the knob of the front door but neither pulled it open nor turned around.

"I guess it depended on the circumstances," he said. "Whether I thought I could help or not. Whether I thought I could manage the risk. And, finally, who was in the water."

Why was he even bothering to have this conversation? The woman was obviously mentally ill; she belonged in a hospital, not walking around free. She could hurt herself or someone else. She still didn't turn to look at him, just bowed her head.

"I don't think you *can* manage the risk," she said. "There are forces more powerful than your will. I think that's what you need to know."

For someone as obsessed with death as Jones knew himself to be, he should have been clutching his heart with terror. But, honestly, he just found the whole situation preposterous. It was almost a relief to talk to someone who had less of a grip on life than he did.

"Okay," he said. "Good to know."

He gently nudged her aside with a hand on her shoulder and opened the door.

"So when do you imagine this might go down? There's only one body of water in The Hollows." The Black River was usually a gentle, gurgling river at the base of a glacial ravine. It could, in heavy rains, become quite powerful, but it hadn't overflowed its banks in years. And the season had been dry.

She gave him a patient smile. "I don't *imagine*, Mr. Cooper. I see, and I tell the people I need to tell to make things right. And if not right precisely, then as they should be. That's all I do. I used to torture myself, trying to figure out where and when and if things might happen. I used to think I could save and help and fix, drive myself to distraction when I couldn't. Now I just speak the truth of my visions. I am unattached to outcomes, to whether people treat me with respect or hostility, to whether they listen or don't."

"So they're literal, these visions," he asked. He didn't bother to keep the skepticism out of his voice. "You see something and it happens exactly that way. It's immutable."

"They're not always literal, no," she said.

"But sometimes they are?"

"Sometimes." She gave a careful nod. "And nothing in life is immutable, Mr. Cooper."

"Except death."

"Well . . ." she said. But she didn't go on. Was there an attitude about it? As if she were a teacher who wouldn't bother with a lesson that her student could never understand.

She moved through the door and let the screen close behind her. He didn't know what to say, so he said nothing, just watched as she stiffly descended the steps. She turned around once to look at him, appeared to have something else to say. But then she just kept walking down the drive. Her pace seemed brisker, as if she'd lightened her load. She didn't seem as frail or unwell as she had when he'd first seen her. Then she got into her car and slowly drove away.

chapter two

She wrote slowly. Heavily tracing over each of the letters until her pen broke through to the notebook page beneath. Big block letters along the top of her English notebook: THE HOLLOWS SUCKS. It did. It did suck. She hated it. Beneath that she wrote in a loopy cursive, *Why am I here? Why?*

"Willow? Miss Willow Graves. Care to join us?"

She sat up quickly, startled. Sometimes she disappeared into her own head and the world around her faded to a buzzing white noise, only to crash back in some surprising and often embarrassing way. They were all looking at her, the cretins.

She lifted her eyes to Mr. Vance, her English teacher, who was watching her expectantly.

"I didn't hear the question." She felt the heat rise to her cheeks as someone in the back of the room giggled.

"The question was," he said, "can you tell me the difference between a simile and a metaphor?"

She didn't mean to roll her eyes. But sometimes they seemed to have a mind of their own. Mr. Vance crossed his arms and squared his shoulders. A dare.

"A simile is a literary device that compares things, using the connector *like* or *as*. As in 'His eyes were blue and beckoning, like the deep, wide ocean.' A metaphor is a figure of speech that equates one unlike thing with another. For example, 'Her love for him was a red, red, rose.'"

She'd played it vampy, flirty, just to save face. But it came off wrong. From the zombies there was more nervous giggling. *What a dork.* The words wafted up from the stoners in the back of the room like a plume of smoke. Mr. Vance wore a high red blush—anger, embarrassment, maybe a little of both.

When Willow was younger, her mother used to say, *Your mouth is going to get you into trouble, kid.* Then, *That mouth, Willow. Watch your words.* Lately the admonishment came so often that her mother had simply shortened it to *Mouth!*

Mr. Vance *did* have the prettiest blue eyes. He was a preppy, neatly pressed, hairstyled, shiny-new-gold-wedding-band kind of clean. But she wasn't crushing on him or anything. She liked him. Most teachers just found her "challenging," "distracted," "bright but undisciplined," or "difficult to engage." There were as many descriptions as there were parent-teacher conferences, most of them negative.

But Mr. Vance was different. He let her talk, didn't become frustrated by her questions: Wasn't there evidence that Shakespeare really was a woman? Didn't his sister really do all the writing and he just took the credit? Did anyone else find Hemingway flat and inaccessible? Or *Moby-Dick* dull in the extreme? When Mr. Vance had met her mother during the last parent-teacher night, he'd told her that he thought Willow was "gifted" but often bored and "needed lots of challenge and stimulation to really excel." He was the first teacher with whom she had ever really connected. And now she'd fucked it up. Screwed it up. Her mother didn't like it when Willow said "fuck." *Use that imagination of yours, Willow; swearing is for people with small vocabularies.*

"That's right, Willow," said Mr. Vance. He turned his back on her and walked to the front of the room. "That's right."

He returned to his lecture on literary devices, but Willow didn't hear another word, just sulked the rest of the class. Usually she hung around to talk to him after the bell rang, but today he left before she could put her things in her bag. It was familiar, that feeling of having said the wrong thing and driving someone off, that sinking disappointment, that pointless wishing that she'd watched her words.

On her army-green locker, someone had scratched the word *freak* into the paint. They'd done this at the beginning of the year, and she hadn't complained or even tried to cover it. She liked it. The Hollows was a social and cultural void, populated by the petty, the small-minded, the unimaginative; here she *was* a freak and proud of it. She wanted all of them to know that she *was* different. She wasn't a freak in New York City, where she'd lived all her life until her exile to The Hollows six months ago.

She rifled through the backpack and found her cell phone. She dialed and tucked it between shoulder and ear while she bent down to retie the laces on her Doc Martens, straighten out her fishnet tights.

"How's life in the fast lane, kiddo?" her mother answered.

"It sucks." She leaned heavily against her locker and watched the sea of morons wash down the hallway. Lots of giggling and shouting and running, sneakers squeaking.

Her mom sighed. "What's wrong?"

Willow told her about the incident with Mr. Vance. "I was just kidding."

"Well, what do we do when we hurt or embarrass someone we care about?"

"We try to make amends," Willow said. Why had she even called? She could have predicted the entire conversation verbatim.

"Sounds like you know what to do."

"Okay," Willow said. "Yeah."

She tucked herself against her locker. She wanted to ask her mom to come get her. The first couple of weeks, Willow had called and begged to be picked up, and her mother had complied. But then her mom said no more; Willow would have to ride out the school day no matter how miserable she was. And when her mom said no more, she meant it.

"I love you, Mom."

"I love you, too. And, Willow? I know things aren't easy for us right now. But they're going to get better. I promise. Just try to find small ways to be happy."

"I'll try."

"Art class next, right?"

"Yup."

"That should be fun."

Willow hated that forced brightness in her mother's voice. It reminded her that her mother was suffering, too.

"Woo-*hoo!*" she said.

"Okay, smarty." Her mom laughed a little. "Hold it together over there."

After ending the call, Willow traded her textbooks for the art supplies in her locker and slammed the door.

"Nice backpack." The nasty voice carried down the hall, bounced off the walls. Willow turned to see Becka Crim surrounded by her plastic, pretty clones. Their designer bags—Juicy Couture, Coach, Kate Spade—seemed to gleam with malice. She'd bought hers at the army-navy store. It was cool. Too cool for school. Willow flipped them off and kept walking, listening to them all laughing.

"Her love for him was a red, red rose."

She didn't know which one of them said it. But it hardly mattered. None of those morons were in her AP English class, but they'd already heard about what had happened in class. *Perfect.*

The door to Mr. Vance's office was closed. Through the frosted glass, she could see his shadow behind the desk. She felt a flutter of nerves but lifted her hand and knocked on the door, anyway.

"Come in."

She pushed the door open, and he lifted his eyes from the file on his desk, then dropped them again. She hovered in the doorway, unsure if she wanted to go in.

"What can I do for you, Willow?" he said when she didn't enter. He looked at her, brow creased into a frown.

"I came to apologize," she said finally. "I'm sorry. That was stupid."

He motioned toward the chair opposite his desk. As she sat, the bell rang and she heard someone break into a run, a door close. She was late for art class.

"Let me explain something to you," said Mr. Vance. "We're friends, right? We have a relationship of sorts—we talk about books, we spend extra time discussing topics from class."

"Right," she said. On his desk she saw the picture of Mr. Vance, cheek to cheek with a smiling woman she assumed was his wife. Willow had thought his wife would be prettier for some reason, imagined her tall and blond. But she was kind of on the plain side, with mousy hair and glasses. She seemed happy, though. And nice.

"But it's delicate," said Mr. Vance. "Any hint that there's something inappropriate going on and that's my career. Do you understand that? I have a wife, a baby on the way. I need my job, my reputation."

She felt heat flood her cheeks, the threat of tears. "I didn't mean—" she started to say. Then, "I'm sorry."

"You embarrassed me," he said.

She started to apologize again, but her throat closed up. She wouldn't be able to talk without crying. The room was hot, and she suddenly felt too close to Mr. Vance. She stood, just wanting to be away from him, his disapproving stare, so different from his usual smile and mischievous gaze. His face was pale, his mouth pulled taut. They wouldn't be friends after this; she could tell. She bumped the chair as she backed up, and it made a loud scraping sound on the floor. His face softened then.

"Okay," he said. He lifted his palms. "I get it. I put you on the spot. You were trying to save face."

Somehow his knowing that just made her feel worse.

"I'm really sorry," she said, barely keeping her voice from breaking. She wouldn't cry in front him. He was punishing her, and she wouldn't give him the satisfaction of knowing that it hurt. She walked out the door of his office and started jogging, her backpack knocking clumsily against her.

"Look, Willow . . ." His voice carried down the hall. "Do you need a late pass for your next class?"

But the walls, the shame, the smell of cafeteria pizza were closing in on her. She couldn't stand it, being there under the fluorescent lights, in a place where she was a freak, where she couldn't make herself seen or understood. When she turned the corner, she slowed and walked toward her class. But just as she was about to go inside, she saw the exit door at the end of the hall. Light streamed in from the narrow rectangular windows. Without really thinking, she kept walking and pushed out into the cool air of late autumn. For a moment she stood looking behind her at the squat brick building, the olive green doors. Then she moved quickly down the back drive to the side road and kept on going.

She expected someone to come running after her, wanting to know where she was going. No one did. And she just kept heading up the quiet, two-lane road lined with whispering elm trees. She had the giddy, anxious sense of stolen freedom as she made her way along the shoulder. It was only a matter of time in a town this small before someone drove by, saw her, and made a call, a teenager walking away from the school alone in the middle of a school day. Then there'd be trouble. Her mother was going to be upset. But she didn't care. She just wanted to be . . . away. It was a familiar feeling.

She didn't have a plan, wished she'd kept her jacket with her. A stiff wind blew through the trees and brought down a spray of golden leaves that lofted and danced and finally fell to the ground, crushed beneath her thick, black shoes.

She was a year and a day and a hundred thousand miles from *life before.* There were people she could call, her old friends. Some of them had forgiven her; some of them still called and sent e-mails, still commented on Willow's Facebook page. But why bother? Every time she talked to them or saw their updates in her news feed, read their stupid tweets, she felt her exile. She knew that there was no road home again even though everyone, including Willow, pretended otherwise.

There was a book her mom used to read to her, about a boy who got angry with his parents and ran away from home to join the circus. He put his head in a lion's mouth and walked the tightrope. He sailed above the crowds on the flying trapeze, and he danced with the clowns. But at the end of the day when the lights went down and the crowd went home, he found himself alone in a small, dark tent. He closed his eyes and cried for his mother, who, it turned out, wasn't that bad after all—she'd just wanted him to eat his broccoli. When he opened his eyes, it was all a dream and he was safe in his bed, his mom leaning in to give him a kiss on his forehead.

"I ran away and joined the circus," he told her. He told her about the lions and the clown and the flying trapeze. "Even after all that, I just wanted to come home."

"You're always home, because I'm always with you," the storybook mom said. "You can go out in the world and be or do anything you want, but you can always come back to me."

Willow remembered loving that book, always nuzzling in close to her mom at the end. Even now, when it seemed maudlin and contrived, she still liked the idea that you could find yourself at home in your bed, safe and loved and everything okay after all. She used to believe that things were like that, that the world was safe and that there was nothing her mom couldn't fix.

She heard a car coming, so she stepped off the road and into the trees. Fingers of light shone down through the thinning tree cover, glancing off the damp ground. The earth beneath her feet was a soft cushion of fallen leaves and sticks. The air was thick with the aroma of decaying vegetation. She started making her way through the woods.

Better to be off the street; she knew she could walk through the trees for a mile or so and come out onto the dirt road by her house. She'd done it before, even though she'd promised not to. Once she came back here and smoked a joint with Jolie Marsh, the only halfway-cool girl she'd met in The Hollows. But Jolie got suspended for cutting last week; now Willow's mom didn't want her to hang out with Jolie anymore.

There was one thing about The Hollows that Willow didn't mind—the silence of the place. She never realized how loud the city was, how noise invaded every element of her consciousness. *I can think here,* her mother said of The Hollows. She'd get this annoyingly dreamy expression. *I can breathe.* Willow knew what she meant, though she wouldn't admit it. She tended to sulk when her mother started going on and on about The Hollows, how pretty, how quaint, how close to nature she felt, how clean the air.

God, Mom. Give me a break. This place is a pit.

Try, Willow. Just try.

The sun drifted behind the clouds, and the golden fingers withdrew. She was left in a milky slate light. The leaves suddenly just looked brown. She felt the unfurling of regret . . . her stupid mouth in class, her lame apology, and her reckless flight from school. Now there were miles to walk through silence and only trouble waiting for her at the other end.

Then the wash of fear. If the school called her mother, she'd be worried, really worried. Her mom got so upset, her wild writer's imagination spinning every awful scenario in vivid Technicolor flashes. And that's the last thing her mom needed right now.

Willow dug her cell phone out of her backpack. But as she was about to dial, she saw that she had no signal. The Hollows was full of random dead zones, places where cell phones mysteriously didn't work. Jolie had told her it was because there were miles of abandoned iron-mine tunnels beneath the ground. Willow didn't see why that would be a reason. But what did she know? She strongly suspected that the town itself was trying to keep her isolated and alone, just to torture her, to ratchet up her misery. There wasn't even a Starbucks.

She shoved the phone into her pocket, knowing that the signal might return at any time, and she picked up her pace. She looked up at the sky and saw three large birds circling overhead. She stopped to stare at them, watching them aloft in the air, wings barely moving. There were things she'd never seen before that she saw here all the time: deer on their expansive property, wild rabbits, blue jays, cardinals, crows. She liked that about The Hollows, too. Of course, these things—the peaceful silence, the wildlife—hardly made up for the rest of it.

While she was staring up, she started to notice something she'd been hearing in the distance for a while. A kind of rhythmic thumping, something so soft and steady it had taken a while to leak into her consciousness. Willow glanced around to determine the origin of the sound, but it seemed to come from the earth, the sky above. She knew there were some properties that backed up against the edge of the Hollows Wood, and sounds carried.

Jolie said that the old-timers called the acres and acres of trees the Black Forest, even though that wasn't the real name. But the Germans who had settled the town had stories; it was the forest of every fairy tale ever told—filled with witches' cottages and gingerbread houses and big bad wolves. Apparently the Hollows Wood reminded them of that place. And it was a nickname that stuck.

There were a few huge, newer houses sitting on acres of privately owned land that backed up against the edge of the wood—the house that Willow's mother had bought among them. "So city people can feel like they live in the country now," Jolie had said, as if it were something she'd heard and was repeating because it sounded cool. Willow wasn't sure if Jolie knew that she, Willow, lived in one of those houses and whether Jolie was making a dig or was just ignorant. And furthermore, Jolie had never been to the city and she didn't know *any-*

thing about city people. But Willow didn't say so because Jolie was her only friend.

Some of the land belonged to old Hollows families, just shacks in the middle of nowhere. The roads were impassable after the first snow. Many of those folks, kids included, disappeared for the winter. All this according to her pot-smoking, suspended friend, whose family had lived in The Hollows for four generations, her German ancestors actually members of the original settlement.

Ka-thunk. Ka-thunk. Silence. *Ka-thunk.*

Through the trees ahead, she could see the clearing. Once she crossed that, it was just another mile or so and then she'd come out down the road from her house. But instead of walking in that direction, she found herself moving toward the sound she heard, deeper into the woods. She felt that jolt of curiosity, that itch to know something. She loved that feeling, how it took her out of herself, away from her own issues and problems. She felt a hammering of excitement, started moving a little faster. She checked again for a signal on her phone. Still nothing.

The sound grew louder, and she slowed her pace, walked more quietly through the trees. Something snagged her arm. As she drew it back to her body, she felt the smack and sting of an old black branch. Looking down, she saw that she'd ripped the flowered cotton of her Lucky Brand blouse. She put her free hand to her arm, and it came back with a smudge of blood. Her favorite shirt; she got it at the SoHo store on her last visit home. It was like having a little piece of the city with her, something none of the Barbies at school would have. Again that wash of anger with herself. *Willow, if you didn't put yourself in these positions, things like this wouldn't happen.* That's what her mother would say. And she'd be right.

Ka-thunk. Ka-thunk.

She immediately forgot her stinging arm and started moving toward the sound again. When she saw him, she stopped in her tracks. She wasn't sure what she'd expected to find when she followed the noise—some kind of animal maybe, or a swinging door at an entrance to one of those mine tunnels. But she hadn't expected to find a man digging a hole in the ground. *Ka-thunk.*

He was as tall and powerful as the thick trunks around him, his long, dark hair an oil spill over the gray hooded sweatshirt he wore. He was up to the knees of his dark blue work pants in the hole and still digging. She stood frozen, suddenly breathless, but still observing. *Take in the details. Everything tells a story. Zoom in.*

Beside him was a large black bag that looked to be full of tools. A skein of sweat darkened his back. She heard the tinny strains of music. He was wearing headphones, listening to music, blasting loud, loud enough for her to hear at twenty yards. The sky went darker then, and the temperature dropped. Willow was suddenly cold to her core. She started to back away, aware of the sound of her own breath.

He stopped what he was doing, looked up at the sky, took the headphones from his ears, and leaned back, stretching. Willow kept moving away. Then her cell phone started to ring. A blaring Lily Allen track sliced through the natural silence. No, it exploded, ripping open the quiet. He spun, and she saw his pale white skin, his black, black eyes.

"Hey!"

Willow didn't answer; she just turned and started to run. She fumbled for her phone, which was still ringing. It was so loud, piercing. Why did she have the ringer up so loud? But just as she got it from her pocket, it slipped from her fingers. She turned to see him standing, watching her run but not running himself, just following her with those eyes and an odd, almost mocking smile.

She didn't stop for her phone, didn't look back again, just ran and ran and ran, across the clearing, through more trees, until she burst out into the light and was on the road. Only then did she allow herself to stop, bent over against the horrible cramp in her side, the tight breathlessness in her chest. An athlete she was not. She couldn't run anymore; if he was behind her, if he came bursting through the trees, she'd use the last of her strength to scream and claw at him and hope someone heard her.

But there it was again, that Hollows silence—just the singing birds and the cool wind through the leaves. She looked through the trees, and there was no one coming. She was alone—her shirt ripped, her cell phone lost, her chest painful from uncommon effort. Fear drained, leaving her feeling weak and foolish. She started toward home. She wouldn't tell anyone what she saw. She couldn't. No one would believe her, anyway. Because Willow Graves was a liar, and everyone knew it—even, and maybe especially, her mother.

chapter three

Where was she? *God, why did this keep happening?*

She'd heard the house phone ringing and ignored it, determined not to be interrupted from her work by the thousand things that conspired daily to distract her. Then her cell phone started chirping, so she pushed herself up from her desk and found where she'd left it after Willow had called earlier. HOLLOWS HIGH SCHOOL, the screen read, and she answered, heart already in her throat.

"Mrs. Graves, this is Henry Ivy from Hollows High."

She'd met him when she enrolled Willow. The newly appointed principal, he was handsome in a sweet, geeky kind of way. A nice man.

"Is something wrong?" She already felt the swell of anxiety.

"Well," he said. He cleared his throat. "Willow's left the school. She didn't show up for art class, and she was spotted leaving the property about twenty minutes ago."

Fear and anger jockeyed for position in her chest.

"She was spotted and no one went after her or stopped her?" she said.

She didn't like the sound of shrill indignation in her own voice. She wasn't one of those parents who blamed others for her child's mistakes and bad behavior. Still, wasn't it somebody's responsibility to make sure teenagers didn't just walk out of school in the middle of the day?

"Another student spotted her and reported it to my office," he said.

Bethany felt an irrational wave of annoyance for that particular student. *Tattletale,* she thought, rubbing at the back of her head. She took a deep breath against panic and picked up a picture of a tiny Willow running with a big smile and determined eyes over a chalk drawing on the pavement in Central Park. It was so easy then, hand in hand, never more than steps from each other, fretting over nursing and bumps on the head. Now Willow was her own person, out in the world and wreaking havoc.

Bethany sank onto her bed, looked out the window into the trees that surrounded the house. "Was she alone?"

Jolie Marsh, Willow's only new friend, was a disaster waiting to happen. Bethany could just see the two of them sneaking off into the woods to drink or smoke or whatever it was that teenage girls did when no one was looking.

"Yes, as far as I know, she was alone," said Mr. Ivy.

She tried to think of what to say. It seemed as if she were always trying to think of what to say to some school official about Willow.

"I'll head out to look for her." *Again,* she thought but didn't say. It wouldn't be the first time she'd set out to hunt for Willow.

"You'll need to bring her in to discuss this, Ms. Graves. And we'll need to take disciplinary action." His tone was soft, apologetic. Not crappy and judgmental. But he might as well have said, *You're a terrible mother, and Willow is a problem for all of us because of that.* Because that's what she heard, and that's how she felt.

"I will," she said. "Of course. We'll come by your office in the morning."

She hadn't even ended the call before she grabbed her bag and was heading out the door. Behind the wheel of their new SUV, she felt more in control and had a moment of respite from that special panic reserved for a parent who doesn't know where her child has gone. Bethany had purchased a Land Cruiser because she figured they'd need a four-wheel drive for the winter months to navigate the long dirt road to their house. And she wanted as much metal around them as possible, since she hadn't operated a motor vehicle in more than thirteen years.

Of course there was an argument with Willow about it, because there was an argument with Willow about everything.

What about the environment, Mom? Your carbon footprint? Hello.

The environment won't mean very much to us if we're both dead, squashed like beetles in one of those Smart cars.

You're such a drama queen. You do know how to drive.

Just zip it, Willow.

Driving the route between their house and school, Bethany dialed Willow's cell twice and got no answer. Her agitation, dread, and anger ratcheted up with each of the four miles along the narrow, twisting road between school and home, then back again.

Where would Willow go? There was no place to go in this town. Willow knew that better than anyone. But Bethany had thought that's what they needed, after everything they'd been through—a quiet, peaceful place to live. Or maybe it's just what Bethany had needed. Or what she *thought* she needed. Or maybe, as Willow was quick to accuse, the decision to move from Manhattan to The Hollows was one she hadn't thought through at all.

Arriving back at home, she was sure she'd find Willow slumped on the couch, her hand buried in a bag of potato chips, the television blaring. But no, the house was empty. Feeling the space around her expand with her anxiety, she listened to the silence—no siren, no bleating horns, no constant hum of traffic, electricity, elevators in shafts, subways beneath her feet.

She walked up the creaking staircase, an extravagant sweeping turn up the wall leading to a landing.

"Willow!" she called pointlessly.

She walked down the long hall, glancing into the myriad empty rooms occupied by boxes she had yet to touch from the move. She'd fantasized about these rooms—this one would be a gym, this one a library. Downstairs they'd finish the basement and make it a media room. But those plans, so exciting while she was packing up their New York City apartment, now just seemed daunting and unattainable—not to mention silly and naïve. Every little project would take months, cost thousands.

Everybody thinks it's so romantic to move to the country. Oh, the stillness and solitude. And then . . . Unsolicited commentary from her friend and agent, Philip May.

And then what?

And then they're in the country. And oh, God, the stillness! The solitude!

She pushed into the door of her daughter's huge bedroom, amazed at how much clutter and mess had accumulated in the short amount of time they'd been there. Willow's closet was so stuffed with clothes that the door wouldn't close completely. The drawers were gaping, spilling T-shirts, tights, socks, and underwear. There were stacks and stacks of books, a giant television, piles of DVDs. Willow's desk, dominated by a computer screen, had disappeared beneath mounds of paper, magazines, photographs, and sketchbooks. They'd simply moved her old mess from her much smaller room in Manhattan. It had apparently grown to fit the new space.

She sank onto Willow's bed and fought the urge to start poking around. That's when the imagining started. Willow on a train to New York City or getting high in the woods with Jolie or, worse, with some strange boy. Bethany could see her daughter tumbling in the leaves with some pierced and tattooed kid. And then it got even worse: There was Willow, angry and vulnerable, climbing into some stranger's van. Bethany could see the stranger's hands, big and muscular on the wheel. He'd ask her little girl, *Where are you headed?* Bethany had no idea what Willow might say. But it wouldn't matter. The driver of that imaginary van wouldn't care where Willow wanted to go, only where he wanted to take her. Next Willow was falling down one of those mine shafts Bethany was always hearing about. She'd be walking, defiantly miserable, with her iPod blaring, when the earth gave way beneath her.

Willow was alone, in the dark. Hurt, weeping. Bethany could write the whole story—the manhunt, the hotline, the tearful news conference. She could feel the horror, the grief. She could rocket through the seven stages of loss.

The rich and vivid imagining that served her so well on the page was torture in her real life sometimes, if she let her thoughts sweep her away. But she didn't; she knew better. She was always able to keep her feet on the ground, especially for Willow. She didn't have the luxury of hysteria. She pushed out a deep breath to calm herself.

She walked the rest of the house, even climbed up to the attic—which was spacious and studded with skylights. Eventually she planned to renovate it and make it her office. But she wasn't thinking about that as she headed back down to the first floor, out through the sliders to the elevated deck that allowed them to look over the tops of trees to the mountains beyond. It was her dream house, really. But she bought it during the worst time of her life, almost like a consolation prize. And the thought of it *had* consoled her. It was just that the reality of it took more work than she'd imagined. Kind of like marriage. Kind of like life.

She was walking back into the kitchen when she heard the front door slam, Willow's heavy footfalls beating their way down the hall. Such a small girl—legs like reeds, torso as slender as a pencil, ballerina arms—and yet she thundered about the house like a rhino, crashing down the stairs, banging around her room.

Bethany knew she should be angry, furious. She should storm and shout. But instead her own legs felt wobbly with relief. She put the phone back in the charger and rested her head in her arms on the counter, summoning her strength for the battle ahead. When she looked up, her daughter was standing in the doorway. Willow's hair was wild, her face flushed.

"What happened?" Bethany asked. "Where were you?"

She fought the urge to run to her daughter, hold her in her arms and squeeze. She had to at least pretend to be angry, not just afraid and sad and feeling like a complete failure as a parent. Willow dropped her bag heavily to the floor, pulled out a chair from the table with a loud scrape against the hardwood, and threw herself down.

"That place—" Willow began.

"Don't, Willow." Bethany raised a palm, feeling a welcome wave of anger. "Don't tell me how and why you had to leave that horrible place. I don't want to hear it. You are not supposed to leave school without permission. Not ever. Not for any reason."

"But, Mom—"

"There's no excuse for this."

Her words didn't feel powerful enough, sounded lame and weak to her own ears. She'd ground her daughter, but the kid was having trouble making friends here and had no place to go, anyway. Bethany put her hand on her forehead, trying to think of something with some impact. "No Internet for a week," she said finally. "And I want your cell phone."

"But—"

"No. I told you if I ever tried to reach you on that phone and you didn't answer that I'd take it away."

Willow slumped in her seat and blew air out the corner of her mouth, lifting some wisps of hair from her eyes. "I lost it. My phone. I dropped it somewhere."

Bethany looked at her daughter, who in turn was looking at the ripped knees of her fishnet tights. Bethany could see that Willow's knees were skinned, that her shirt was ripped. Worry shouldered anger aside.

"What happened?" Bethany asked. "Tell me."

Willow rolled her eyes. "I came home through the woods."

"Christ, Willow!"

"I got scared and started to run," she said. Willow looked teary and so young suddenly, just like when she was a toddler, in those moments right after a fall and before the real crying started. "I fell and dropped my phone. I was too afraid to go back for it."

"Oh, Willow." Bethany didn't know whether to believe her or not. That was the really sad thing. She just didn't have an instinct anymore about when her daughter was lying. Lord, what she wouldn't give for a glass of wine. She glanced at the clock; it was a few minutes after three. She heard that if you were looking at the clock waiting for the hour to chime five so that you could have a drink, you might have a problem with alcohol. Bethany wasn't sure she believed that. Seemed like there was always someone waiting to tell you that you had a problem with something.

"Really?" she said. "You lost it." Bethany picked up the phone and dialed Willow's number.

"Don't!"

Bethany watched her daughter and held the phone out from her ear against the blasting music that played instead of a ringtone. She didn't hear the phone ringing in her daughter's backpack or on her person, as she'd suspected she would. She practically dropped the phone when a male voice answered. Some unnamed fear pulsed through her.

"Who is this?" she said.

"Who is *this*?" the voice on the line asked. There was something nice about his tone, something soothing. "I found this phone in the woods."

Willow was pale, staring at her with eyes the size of dinner plates.

"Don't tell him who you are," she said. She was standing now, pulling on Bethany's arm. "Mom, hang up!"

Bethany gave her daughter a warning look, and Willow drew back, looking stricken. Then she put her head in her hands. "Mom, please."

"This is Bethany Graves. Can I come and pick up that phone from you? Sorry for any inconvenience. My daughter lost it."

"Sure, of course," said the voice. He sounded as though he found the encounter amusing, which was just a shade irritating. "Or I could come to you?"

"Well, we could meet you somewhere." Nice voice or not, the New Yorker in her thought better of giving some strange man her address, letting him come to their remote house surrounded by ten acres of trees. Peaceful, isolated. Perfect for a writer. *Yeah, and no one can hear you screaming,* Philip had commented when he came for dinner last weekend. The sentence had stayed with her.

"How about the Hollows Brew in an hour?" he said.

"Perfect. Thanks so much." She ended the call.

Then, to Willow, "What is *wrong* with you, kiddo?"

The look on Willow's face made her stomach flutter. It was always like that with them, even when Willow was an infant—what one of them felt, the other felt, too. When Willow was small—yesterday, a hundred years ago—as soon as Bethany opened her eyes in the morning, or at night, she would hear Willow start to stir. If Bethany had been nervous, anxious, upset, Willow was cranky. It was still true. There was no way Willow could feel sad or stressed or afraid without Bethany's feeling the tug of it on her insides.

"Who was that?" asked Willow. Her cheeks were pale, her eyes wide. "The man from the woods?"

"You saw *a man* in the woods?"

"I wasn't going to tell you. I didn't think you'd believe me."

Bethany felt a flash flood of annoyance banked by guilt. Willow was probably right. Bethany might not have believed her.

"Try me," Bethany said.

Willow started talking fast about her teacher, how hurt and embarrassed she was in his office, fleeing from the school, what she saw in the woods. She paced, waved her hands in the air. Bethany just watched in awe, listened to the way she wove the story, told the details—the damp leaves, the sky through the trees. Her daughter was a natural-born storyteller. And this—at her age, anyway—had not proved to be a good thing. When Willow was finished, she collapsed back down in her chair in a dramatic flop, as if exhausted by the events and their retelling.

"Now he knows who we are," Willow said. "What if he was burying a body or something?"

Bethany pulled up a chair beside her daughter, wiped the strawberry blond hair back from her face, squeezed her frail little shoulder. She'd been looking into those dark brown eyes for a million years. The girl around them had grown and changed, but those eyes seemed as eternal as the moon.

"Willow. Really," Bethany said. "Where did you *ever* get such a wild imagination?"

Willow looked at her sharply, incredulous, and then they both started to laugh. They laughed until they were weeping with it, both of them clutching their middles. And Bethany thought how much she loved her wild, defiant child, how she'd failed at almost everything, lost so much, but that none of it mattered because of the one thing about her life that was right.

chapter four

"So how have you been feeling, Jones?"

Useless, aimless, broken, Doc. Really just miserable. Was that true? No, not totally. But Jones felt as if Dr. Dahl would be happier if that's what he said.

"Good," said Jones. "You know. Keeping busy."

"Keeping busy with what?" Dr. Dahl had this earnest way about him. He always accompanied his questions with a hopeful, inquiring lift of his jet-black brows.

Jones offered a shrug, took a sip from the coffee he'd carried in with him. He'd brought one for the doctor, too. But the other man had declined. *I'm off coffee*, he'd said. *Thanks.* This refusal somehow seemed petty and superior to Jones; it made him like the doctor a little less. And Jones didn't like Dr. Dahl very much to begin with.

"The house, mostly," said Jones. "An old house like ours requires quite a bit of maintenance." He paused, but the doctor didn't say anything. Jones felt compelled to go on. "My neighbors have been relying on me a lot lately—watching their homes while they're away, checking mail, helping some of the older people with jobs around the yard. You know." Why did it sound so lame?

Dr. Dahl looked pensive. Jones thought the doctor was a little too pretty, with girlish lashes and smooth skin. Too well maintained. His nails shone a bit, as though he'd had a manicure. Why it should bother Jones that the guy took care of himself, he didn't know. But it did.

"It's been a year since you stopped working," said Dr. Dahl. The doctor's tone implied a question, but Jones knew he wasn't asking. The doctor was making a point.

"About that long, yes." Jones felt his shoulders tighten with the urge to defend himself. But he didn't say anything else. The doctor seemed to wait for Jones to go on. When he didn't: "So. You're a relatively young man. Have you given much thought to what might come next? If you might embark on another career?"

Jones looked around the room, his eyes resting on a tribal mask that hung on the wall. It was the only thing in the space that was not generic, that told him anything about the doctor. In the landscape of gold and cream surfaces, within walls featuring the most banal art images—a sailboat at sunset, a still life of flowers, another of fruit— that mask was the single object that Jones could tell wasn't picked from some catalog. Sometimes during his sessions he found himself staring into its hollow eyes, fixating on its snarling mouth.

"I haven't thought about it much," Jones said. The truth was, he didn't want to think about it. He *couldn't* think about it. He was a cop; that's what he'd always been. He simply couldn't imagine doing anything else. What was he going to do? Go to work in some office, stand around a watercooler and sit in a cubicle? What was he even qualified to do? He didn't say any of this to the doctor.

"What were your interests before you were a police officer?" asked Dr. Dahl.

"Before I was a cop, I was a kid. I went straight from college to the academy. I was on patrol before I was twenty-three."

"So you didn't have any interests?"

"Sports." He was conscious of the fact that he had folded his arms across his chest, was so tense that his shoulders were starting to ache. He tried to relax, let his arms rest at his sides. "I played lacrosse."

There had been other interests; he'd always liked working with his hands, building things with wood. He'd done well in his shop classes, might have gone on to a vocational school if he hadn't developed an interest in the police department, heard that you did better on the job with a degree. Of course, his decision was informed by his crippling guilt, his sick relationship with his mother, his abandonment issues. All things he'd hashed over in this office until his head ached.

He'd been seeing the doctor for the better part of a year—partially (mostly) because his wife insisted, partially because he *was* struggling with the events that had caused him to retire early from the only work he'd ever wanted to do, partially because he knew that there were things going on inside him that weren't quite healthy. But what good was it doing him, really? Did he really feel any better than he had a year ago? He didn't know.

"Anything else?" said the doctor. Jones wondered how long Dr. Dahl had been waiting for him to go on.

"I used to like woodworking. I was pretty good at it."

The doctor sat up with interest, almost looked relieved. For the first time, it occurred to Jones that he might be a difficult patient.

The man can't help you, Jones, if you don't like him, trust him, and open up to him, Maggie had said to him as recently as yesterday.

What if I don't need help?

A sad smile, a hand on his arm. *What if you do?*

"Since you have the time and the freedom, maybe you could think about taking a class," said Dr. Dahl. "It might open a doorway for you."

"Maybe," said Jones.

Something about the idea of signing up for a class made him uncomfortable. He threw the doc a bone and said as much.

"Why do you think that is?" Poor Dr. Dahl was practically on the edge of his seat.

Jones looked out the large window to a parking lot edged by woods. The trees in the valley were a firestorm of orange, gold, yellow, and brown in the light of the waning afternoon. The truth: because he didn't want to be part of a group that was looking for something, people who were seeking. He didn't want to be lumped in with people who were looking to one individual for answers to a question. Come to think of it, it was the same problem he had with therapy. *What quali-fies you to teach me anything?* he often found himself thinking.

But he didn't have the words to say this. He knew it sounded angry and arrogant. And maybe it was that. But it made him feel weak and vulnerable to think about signing up for class, sitting in a room with a bunch of other sad, middle-aged losers adrift in their lives. Be-cause that's who it would be—the retiree, the empty-nester, the newly divorced.

"It seems like a waste of time," he said.

He saw something flash across his doctor's face—disappointment, concern, something. Then the doctor bowed his head slightly. Dr. Dahl put the notebook he'd been holding in his lap on the small table beside him and leaned back in his chair, crossed his legs. Jones recog-nized it as the body language of resignation, surrender. Then there it was: the headache that started in the base of Jones's neck and would reach its clawing fingers over his crown, then start pressing on his eyes without mercy.

"Look, Jones," the doctor said. His voice was soft, and Jones no-ticed, not for the first time, how young the guy was. Maybe he was in his early thirties. "Before our next session, you might want to give some thought to why you keep coming here."

"I don't understand." But Jones *did* understand, and he felt some kind of dark victory, as if he'd won a game he hadn't even realized he'd been playing.

The doctor rubbed his eyes with his right thumb and forefinger. "I mean that I think you're resisting here, purposely not allowing yourself to find a path forward, a way to deal with the traumas of your past, even learn from them to forge a better future."

"I'm here, aren't I?"

The doctor seemed to force a smile, tilted his head a bit.

"Physically, yes, you are consistently here in my office. And you've been quite articulate about the things that have happened to you— your relationship with your mother, the abandonment by your father, the loss of your career. And that's great. That's progress. But now that you need to find a way forward into the next phase of your life, I feel like you're shutting down."

Jones found his shoulders relaxing as he sat forward, preparing to get up and leave. It sounded like the good doctor was getting ready to break up with him; the thought flooded him with relief.

"I don't know what to say, Doctor. I'm doing my best." The lie hung between them, bounced off the walls. "If you don't think you can help me . . ." He let the sentence trail, giving Dr. Dahl the opportunity to fill in the blank and hand Jones his get-out-of-jail-free card. To say something like, *Maybe you'd do better with someone else,* or *Maybe you should take some time off from therapy.*

But he didn't say anything like that. Instead he looked at Jones for a moment. Jones saw what he already knew, that Dr. Dahl was a good man, a kind and compassionate doctor, excited about his work—a lot like Maggie. And Jones felt like a heel, but he stayed silent.

"I'll just ask you to consider one thing before our next session," said Dr. Dahl. "I'm not here to give you answers, to tell you what road to take or what you should do. I am here to help you find those answers within yourself. When you walk in here, I don't want you to give power away to me. I want you to find it right here." He stopped a second and tapped on his chest. "And use it to make your life what you want it to be."

Jones looked away, embarrassed by the other man's obvious passion. He felt heat in his cheeks, a strong desire to leave and not come back.

"Okay," Jones said. He knew that his voice sounded cold and professional, nearly sarcastic for its lack of feeling. "I'll think about that."

A beat passed where Jones looked longingly at his coat on the rack by the door, but where he couldn't seem to lift himself from his chair.

"Fair enough," said Dr. Dahl. But the other man couldn't keep the disappointment out of his voice. Jones didn't look him in the face again as he muttered good-bye, grabbed his jacket, and left.

A few miles away from the office, he drove through at Burger King and ordered a mountain of food—a Whopper with cheese, a large soda, onion rings, french fries, a chocolate shake. The kid who handed him his sack had black-painted fingernails and a face full of piercings—nose, ears, eyebrows, and tongue. Jones dropped his change in the scratched plastic tip cup.

"Hey, thanks so much," the kid said. For some reason his friendly smile and chipper attitude left Jones unsettled, as if he were being subtly mocked. As he pulled out onto the street, the familiar salty-savory smell, that engineered delight, filled the car, and he felt a palpable relief of tension as he unwrapped and bit into the burger. He ate it all mindlessly as he drove, not really tasting it, then sank into the fat-absorption stupor that inevitably followed a large fast-food meal. By the time he got home, he felt vaguely sick but mercifully blank.

chapter five

The cat was missing, and that wasn't really like him. He was fat and lazy, rarely moving at more than a snail's pace from couch to food bowl, food bowl to bed, bed to window seat. Even when he *could* be bothered to heft his frame through the kitty door, he did not, once outside, chase birds or rodents. He observed squirrels and finches, mice and robins with studied indifference. Eloise had never even bothered to put a little bell on his collar, knowing that it was the sun alone that drew him outside. He did not have a hunter's heart. He was a creature designed for, and dedicated to, luxuriating. He cared only to lie on the stone bench by the sundial and let his ginger fur soak up the heat. Then, having reached some unknown limit, he'd trundle back inside and replant himself.

"Oliver," she called. She stood on the back stoop. The wind made the various chimes, hanging from the eaves and trees, sing. Eloise hated the cooling air of autumn. It heralded the arrival of snow and black branches, the death of everything green.

"Oliver."

Eloise felt an anxious flutter as she gazed about the yard and then shut the door. The cat could be under one of the beds or down in the basement. He'd come back when he was hungry, she told herself. Lord knew he couldn't survive in the wild.

Back inside, she heard her cell phone ringing. She walked over to the kitchen table and dug the phone out of her purse, even though she had no intention of answering it. Ray Muldune, the blinking screen informed her. Again. She put the phone down on the table and watched it skitter a bit with its vibrating.

Ray wanted her to tell him things that she couldn't tell him. She was cold, stone cold, except for her dreams of Jones Cooper. This happened sometimes, a mental loop excluding all other signals. That's why she'd gone to see him, knowing full well how he would react to her. She figured she'd get it out, deliver the message. And maybe that's all she was supposed to do. Maybe. She never knew.

Eloise was about to open a can of food for Oliver. Doing so, she knew, would cause him to lumber from wherever he was, near or far. But as she pulled open the cupboard, she heard the crunching of gravel on her driveway. She walked over to the bay window and looked out to see Ray Muldune's ancient Caddy in the driveway.

Her phone issued a single buzz. She pulled it from her pocket.

YOU'RE AVOIDING ME, his text message accused.

"Oh, Ray," she said out loud, though there was no one there to hear her. "You never could take a hint."

Then he was on her porch, his authoritative knock causing the panes to rattle. She went to the door and looked at him through the glass.

"I've got nothing for you, Ray," she said. She didn't move to let him in.

"Okay," he said. He gazed off to the side of the house. He did that a lot, talked to her but looked elsewhere. He did it with everyone, as though he were always scanning the area for threats or problems. "I get it. How about a coffee? You got that for me?"

She felt the smile bubble up from inside her. It was rare for her, a true smile, true affection for another. She and Ray had worked together for a long, long time. He was the closest thing she had to a friend.

She gave him a scowl that she knew neither fooled nor daunted him and let him in. His energy was big, caused her to back up and bow her head. His size—six-four and, he claimed, 210, but she knew better—dwarfed her. His aroma—stale cigar, though he promised to quit—overwhelmed her. And rain. Beneath the smoke he smelled like rain, something pure and fresh from the air. He was losing his hair, a spreading shine on the back of his head, a retreat at the widow's peak. But somehow he was handsomer, more virile than the day they'd met, many years ago. The deep lines around his eyes, the gray in his stubble, only served him. She, on the other hand, had withered and dried, looked ten years older than she was. She knew this because the mirror didn't lie and photos didn't even bother to be kind about it.

Ray wanted to talk. By the time she followed him to the kitchen, he was already in her cupboards, pulling down the coffee can and filters.

She pulled up a chair at the kitchen table and sat. She traced the grain of the wood with her finger. She still wore her wedding and engagement rings, though her husband was long, long gone. She was glad she'd remembered to put her prescription bottles away in the cabinet over the sink. If she'd left them out, Ray would have noticed them, because he never missed anything. And that was a conversation she didn't want to have, not tonight.

Ray made a lot of noise—banging mugs, turning on the faucet full blast to fill the pot, slamming the refrigerator door. That was his way. He was physical, expressing his frustrations through movement. He was also prone to bear hugs and big gestures with his hands. Beside him she felt small and unnaturally reserved, like a plain wooden shack weathering his storm.

"I told you I'd call if anything," she said. "By now you should know how it works."

He stopped moving for a second to look at her pointedly. "I don't know how it works, and neither do you."

"Well," she said. She raised her palms in surrender. "We both know that stalking and nagging don't help."

He grunted and pushed the button on the ancient Mr. Coffee. "Get a new machine, Eloise."

"It still works," she said. "Why should I replace it?" The pot gurgled its agreement.

"Because your coffee tastes like axle grease."

"I'll take this opportunity to remind you that you were not invited for coffee."

He sat at the table, across from her, the chair whining beneath his weight. Then he took a tin of breath mints from his pocket and popped one into his mouth, rattled the box at her. She lifted a hand to decline.

"Seems like 1987 was a hundred years ago," she said.

"Not to our client. To him it was yesterday."

Ray slid forward on his elbows, frowned at her. He thought she'd grown jaded, cold. No, she wasn't that. He stood up quickly then, banged around in the kitchen some more, and then came back to the table with two mugs.

The coffee smelled rank—bitter and acidic. It reminded her she hadn't smelled anything that even remotely stimulated her appetite. She couldn't even remember the last time she'd been hungry.

"You used to care," he said. He put the cups on the table, sat down again heavily.

"I still do."

She wanted to explain to him the difference between apathy and acceptance. She, unlike most, no longer labored under the delusion of control. She had released most of her attachments. And in doing so she had found, if not peace exactly, then at least calm. To others, still grappling with their misconceptions about the world, their relationships, their lives, this could look like depraved indifference. They still suffered. She did not.

"I have nothing for you, Ray." She looked down at the second cup of coffee poured for her today that she had no intention of drinking.

"You're not trying," he said. "You're all wrapped up in this Jones Cooper thing."

"I went to see him."

He raised his eyebrows at her. "Really? You told him?"

She recounted the conversation for him.

Ray shook his head. "That guy is a closed door."

"Yes and no."

"Well, good. Maybe that's what you needed to do. Maybe it will free you up."

"That's my hope. You're not the only person who wants something from me." She found herself staring at the kitty door, willing Oliver to squeeze himself through, mewing for dinner. The sun was getting low. Where *was* that stupid cat?

When she glanced up at Ray again, he looked chastened. "I'm sorry, Eloise."

"I know you are, Ray."

He reached across the table and touched her hand. And that's when she saw it: a flash of light, a breathless run through dead leaves, a spinning fall, then a night sky above the trees. Then there was only the fading wallpaper of her own kitchen, Ray looking at her intently.

"What is it? What did you see?" he asked. His eagerness exhausted her.

"Someone running . . ." She couldn't say more. It just wasn't clear.

"Where?"

She shook her head, her heart still racing. "I don't know."

"But that's good, right? It means you're clearing up."

"I suppose I am."

He was the first one to do that to her, to touch her and make her see. Before him it had always been scattershot—dreams, day visions, breaks in her consciousness. Not all her life. She did not descend from a long line of witches and seers. She was not one of a clan of aunts and sisters, mothers and grandmothers who mixed purple potions and sprinkled stardust spells for love.

No, it was an accident. A terrible car accident that had taken her husband and one of her children, left her in a coma for five weeks, left her with . . . what? On the bad days—and there were so many really, truly bad days—it was a curse. On the good days, it was a gift. For a while she thought she'd lost her mind. And then she'd found Ray.

"Has it occurred to you that I'm a nutcase?" she asked. "That all these years you've been running around according to the rantings of a madwoman?"

Ray gave a little laugh. "So many years and more than twenty cases solved that no one else could have solved. Not crazy. Troubled, maybe."

He smiled at her, warm and sad. Years ago that smile would have had them upstairs tearing at each other's clothes. But that appetite, too, had waned to nothing. If she didn't have to eat to survive, she wouldn't.

He got up, brought the cups to the kitchen, and rinsed them in the sink.

"Call me if you dream tonight," said Ray.

"I will," she said. She felt a weariness settle into her body. "You know I will."

She stood up to gaze out the window and saw Oliver making his way up the yard. She felt a surprisingly strong wave of relief. So she hadn't given up all her attachments. Animals were easy to love, to live with. They wanted so little . . . just a bowl of food and a warm body to sit on, to sleep with, and they were forever loyal. That was about all she had to give.

chapter six

"Why does it get dark so early here?" Willow had perfected the art of the miserable slouch. Her whole body got into it, slim torso scooped, shoulders folded, head bowed. Bethany was pretending not to notice.

"It doesn't get dark any earlier here than it does in the city," Bethany answered.

"Yes it does."

"No it doesn't." She had been trying to keep that annoyed edge out of her voice when talking to Willow. But the kid didn't make it easy. *Everything* was an argument. "There's less ambient light here," she went on to explain. "Fewer streetlights, buildings, cars."

"Tell me about it." Her daughter stared at the window hopelessly, like some character from *The Road* looking out over an apocalyptic wasteland.

Bethany had also promised herself to start ignoring Willow's comments about The Hollows. They lived here now. And that was that. Willow would learn to accept it in time, even love it. *I don't know, I certainly never accepted it when my parents moved me to the burbs in the eighties,* Philip had said. *I never fit in, ran screaming after graduation.* She really needed to stop talking to her agent about these things—he didn't have any children, and the only way he was leaving Manhattan was in an urn.

They drove up Main Street. The bustling town center had sold her on The Hollows before she'd even seen the house. Bethany loved the picture-postcard look of the place—the cute little bistro and the bakery, the yoga studio, and the small art gallery. Just off the square was a pretty church, a decent library. Some of the bigger chains like Crate & Barrel and the Gap had taken up residence among the cute boutiques and the Hollows Brew. But everything seemed to fit together nicely, a happy blend of small and large businesses, all nestled in restored historic buildings.

Mostly, it was peaceful, easy. Even now when Main Street was bustling with people walking home from the train station, doing last-minute errands and shopping before dinner, walking kids home from after-school activities, there was a harmonic aura to the town, none of the frenetic energy of the city at this time of day. And that's what Bethany had needed when she made the decision to move—peace, harmony, a shift to a quieter, more normal life. After the chaos of the last eighteen months, it's what she'd truly believed they had both needed. Willow passionately disagreed.

Bethany found a spot in front of the coffee shop and stopped the engine. She looked over at her daughter to see that she was making no move to exit the vehicle, was maintaining her beleaguered slouch. Willow rested her head against the glass.

"Well, let's go," said Bethany. She made a hoisting motion with her arms.

"No way," Willow said. She turned her body away. Bethany could see her staring at the window of the coffee shop. "I'm not going in there."

"Willow."

"If you want to go have a cup of coffee with the friendly neighborhood ax murderer, be my guest." But Willow had those worried eyes. What she'd seen in the woods had frightened her; she was too cool to admit it.

Bethany supposed it was her fault that her daughter had no qualms about asserting herself in their relationship. A generation ago her mother would have said, *Don't you dare talk back to me. Get your butt out of this car.* And Bethany would have complied, because that's who she was.

But Bethany didn't talk to Willow that way, and neither did any of her friends talk to their children that way. Today it was all about communication and negotiation, at least when it came to the luxury issues—such as whether to wait in the car or not.

She and Willow were close, maybe too close. But that's how it was sometimes with an only child. Their relationship had almost a sibling quality, because they'd always spent so much time together, Bethany's love and attention never diffused by other children. And Bethany had never hesitated to get down on the floor with Willow to color or make Play-Doh animals. She had never been the disciplinarian. That had been her husband's role, once upon a time. Bethany picked her battles.

"Suit yourself," she said. "But do not get out of this car for any reason. Do you understand? I'll be two minutes. I'm just getting the phone that *you* lost."

Willow made a W with her two thumbs, wiggling her figures. Bethany was just hip enough to know that the gesture meant "Whatever." But Willow had a sweet smile that kept her from seeming too awful.

"I'm serious." Bethany took the keys and climbed out of the car.

"Hey, it's cold," Willow said. "Leave the car running."

"Ha," said Bethany. "As *if.* You're cold? Come inside."

"Mom!"

Bethany shut the door on the rest of Willow's tirade, turned to see her mock-shivering in the seat. She pressed the lock button on the remote, even though of course Willow could unlock the car from the inside. She wouldn't be long, just a couple of minutes. She looked back at Willow before she entered the coffee shop. Willow was watching her but quickly averted her eyes.

A little bell rang as Bethany stepped from the damp cold into the warm interior—the aroma of coffee beans, glowing amber lights, the hiss of a milk steamer. She looked around the room, realizing that she didn't know whom she was looking for, precisely. A couple of young girls were giggling by the fireplace, a pile of books and notepads unopened on the table between them. A young mother fed her toddler some yogurt. Willow had described the man she saw as large *(GI-normous)*, with long, dark hair *(like Vlad the Impaler or something)*. There was a man sitting in the far corner of the shop, his head down over a book. He did have long hair, tied back. But wearing wire-rimmed glasses, with a pencil in his hand, he hardly looked menacing.

"Hey, Beth," said the guy at the counter. What was his name again? Todd. That was it. "How's the writing going?"

"Good. Thanks for asking," she said. She walked over to the counter.

"The usual?" Todd asked. This unnerved her a bit about The Hollows. She and Willow had lived here only six months, and everyone seemed to know her name already, seemed to be familiar with her habits and things about her life, her career. *Duh,* said Willow. *They're reading your blog, visiting your website.* Bethany found this surprising, though of course she shouldn't. She was used to the anonymity of New York City—no one knew who you were at the neighborhood coffee shop, and furthermore no one cared. In this little town, people seemed to keep up with one another. Was it weird or normal? Did she like it or hate it, the fact that people knew who she was? She hadn't decided yet.

"Sure. That'd be great," she said. Todd thought her usual was a double espresso with a little splash of half-and-half to take the edge off. And she supposed it *was* her usual at the moment.

"Bethany Graves?"

The man with the wire-rimmed glasses had walked over to stand beside her. Willow was right. He *was* tall, over six feet. But more than that, he seemed powerful, with wide shoulders and thick arms. In his large palm, he held Willow's cell phone. Bethany took it from him.

"Thank you," she said. "I really appreciate this."

She dropped the phone into her bag. And looked up at him to see him smiling. It lit something up on his face. She found herself smiling, too.

"I didn't get your name when we spoke," she said.

"Michael Holt." He offered his hand, and she shook it. His grip was warm and firm. Not too hard, nothing to prove. She couldn't stand a weak handshake—from a man or from a woman. Limp handshakes meant weak spirits. And weak spirits couldn't be trusted. But some men squeezed too hard, putting on a show, wanting you to know how strong they were. If she looked back, way back, she thought of it as the first bad sign about her ex-husband. From their initial encounter, she'd pulled her hand back smarting.

Michael stuck his hands in his pockets and rocked back on his heels a bit. The action made him seem boyish, though she could see more than a little gray in his long dark hair, a cluster of lines around his eyes. She put him in his late thirties.

"I think I scared your little girl," he said. "Your daughter, I mean. She probably wouldn't want to be called a little girl."

"You have kids?" she asked.

He shook his head, casting his eyes down. "Nieces. Twins about that age. Thirteen going on thirty."

Willow was a very young-looking fifteen; it drove the kid nuts that people always mistook her for younger. *There's no rush to grow up, Willow,* Bethany always told her. *Easy for you to say,* Willow would come back. *You're already grown up. Nobody ever tells you what to do.* That's what kids think it means to be grown up, that no one ever tells you what to do. There was no way to tell them otherwise, to explain the price of freedom.

"Well, thanks for this," she said.

"Double espresso, splash of half-and-half. That's $2.09," said Todd.

She pulled a twenty out of her pocket and handed it to him. "I'll take this gentleman's check as well."

"That's not necessary," Michael said quickly.

"It's my pleasure," she said. "I insist."

He looked like he was about to offer more protest, but then he was wearing that grin again. "Thank you," he said.

When Todd handed Bethany her change and she was getting ready to say good-bye, Michael pointed toward his table. "Would you like to join me?"

She sensed that he was just being polite, that he expected her to decline the offer. Bethany glanced out the window to see Willow still slouched in the seat. She had her earbuds in. She was nodding her head lightly to whatever rhythm was playing on her iPod. But she was watching, staring at Michael Holt. Bethany was surprised she'd stayed in the car. She'd half expected to see her daughter lurking outside the picture window, peering inside.

"My daughter's waiting for me in the car," she said. She didn't want to seem rude. But Bethany really didn't talk to men anymore, had decided that she wouldn't bother for a good long time. On the other hand, there was something interesting about him. It wasn't attraction that she felt—not at all. It was curiosity. He was odd. She couldn't say how, exactly. She liked odd people.

They stood awkwardly a second, he looking down at his feet, she looking around the room. Todd was eavesdropping, she thought, hovering near the sink with nothing apparent to do. The toddler at the far table issued a little shriek of delight over something. "Indoor voice," his mother whispered.

"So what were you doing out there in the woods?" she asked. She hadn't moved toward the table. She took a sip of her espresso, peered at him over the cup. "Willow's sure you were burying a body."

He let go of a nervous laugh, which was kind of sweet in its way. He removed his glasses and used the bottom of his sweatshirt to rub the lenses. Bethany found herself laughing a little, too.

"Daughter of a mystery writer," he said.

And Bethany's laughter stopped short.

"How did you know that?" she asked. She took another sip of her coffee, looked back at the door instinctively. She could still see Willow in the car.

"Sorry," he said. He looked sheepish and pointed back to his table at a laptop she hadn't noticed. "I Googled. Actually, I'd already heard about you. There aren't any secrets in The Hollows. Well, at least not when it comes to an author moving into town. And I don't even live here anymore."

Bethany felt herself flush. So they *were* talking about her. She decided right then and there that it *was* weird, and she didn't like it at all. But what could she do? Maybe that was the price of the silence she so prized. Bethany gave him a careful nod.

"I'm sorry," he said again. He seemed to mean it. She thought about thanking him again and excusing herself. But she stayed rooted, that curiosity getting the better of her.

"So what *were* you doing?"

"I wasn't burying a body, that's for sure."

Bethany found herself staring at him as he looked down into his now-empty cup. She liked the gray rivers through his hair, the lines on his forehead. She even liked the rough calluses she saw on his hands, the dirt beneath his nails. He looked real, solid, earthy, like The Hollows itself. When he gazed back up at her, something on his face sent a shock through her. She couldn't have said what it was—pain, sadness, fear? But then it was gone. He had that grin again. This time it didn't seem as sincere and boyish.

"Quite the opposite," he said. "I was digging one up."

chapter seven

Maggie hadn't said much. She was loading the dishwasher, placing the dishes in their little slots, unhurried, never banging anything together. She was always careful like that, slow and easy. Jones was wiping down the table, going over the same area again and again, just to keep moving. Her silence worried him a little, because his wife was not a woman to hold her tongue. She was a talker, a communicator. Of course she was. It was her business to communicate. He found himself rambling a little bit, going on and on about the doctor, and what a fancy-pants he was, and his manicured nails, and could she believe he'd say such a thing. He'd been *there,* faithfully doing the work for *months* and *months.* And maybe he was right, maybe the doctor couldn't help him. But that wasn't about *him,* was it? That was about the doctor.

She came to stand in the doorway between the kitchen and the dining room. She had a dishcloth in her hand. She folded it in half, then folded it again, kept her eyes on it.

"What are you trying to tell me, Jones?" she said.

The light from the halogen bulbs in the kitchen caught on her copper curls. She was wearing her hair shorter these days; it just danced about her shoulders. When he'd first met her, it spilled down almost to the middle of her back. He remembered the first time she'd unfurled it before him, took it down from the bun it had been in and let it cascade around her shoulders. He'd been breathless with desire.

He cleared his throat. "Just that things are maybe not working out with Dr. Dahl."

She folded the towel again, still didn't lift her eyes.

"I mean, you said yourself that if we're not compatible, I should find someone else," he said into the silence that hung between them.

"So that's what you're going to do?" she said. "Find someone else?"

He thought about going for the broom, to sweep up the floor. But Maggie had him locked in *the look* now.

"When?" she asked.

"I don't know . . . in a couple of weeks? Honestly, I think I need a break from therapy. I certainly don't need to be going twice a week anymore."

His next scheduled appointment was in two days. Twice a week was supposed to be temporary, to help him through the initial crisis. But it was overkill, wasn't it? How much talking can a person do?

Maggie sat down at the table. He stayed standing, holding the can of Pledge. The chemical lemon in the air was making his nose tingle.

"What?" he said.

She seemed to have to gather herself together, closing her eyes and issuing a light sigh. Maybe he'd better sit after all. He pulled up a chair, though he would have preferred to walk away and turn on the television, hope she'd disappear into her office. He'd prefer to leave the communicating for a day when he didn't feel so drained. Though he couldn't say when that might be.

"I don't know if you've noticed, but I haven't been sleeping in our bed."

He hunched up his shoulders. "I noticed. The snoring, right? The waking up."

"Yes, partly."

There was a time long ago, when Ricky was a toddler, that she'd stopped sleeping in their bed. Jones would wake up in the night to find her downstairs on the couch or in the guest bedroom. And he'd watch her sleeping, then go back to bed himself. He'd never asked her why, but he remembered that the sight of her asleep alone had frightened him. It reminded him that she was someone separate from him, someone with an inner life to which he didn't have access unless she invited him in. He had that feeling now, that creeping fear. Sitting across the table from him, she seemed suddenly very, very far away. He wanted to reach his hand across the table, take hers. He could say, *Hey, what's going on? I love you.* He could use that soft tone that he knew would put her at ease. But he didn't.

"This year has been hard," she said. "For you. For me."

He watched as she started to twirl her wedding band, the tiny muscles in her hand shifting, her nails pink and square, the milky quality of her skin. He tried to remember the last time they'd made love (a week, maybe two?), the last time they'd had any fun at all (longer than that). He couldn't. In the reflection of the sliding door that led out to the pool deck, he saw himself thick and hunched across from her like some ogre. Beauty and the beast.

"I know it has been," he said. "I'm sorry."

She reached her hand across to him, and he took it.

"You don't have to apologize," she said. "I know you're struggling. But I am, too . . . with the secrets you kept for so many years, with the things I've learned about my own past—with your . . . retirement." She paused before the last word, as if she weren't sure it was the right one. And it wasn't, really. But he couldn't think of a better one.

He found he couldn't meet her eyes. They were the prettiest denim blue; he'd seen them shine with love and anger and fear. He didn't want to see what played out there now.

"There's a space growing between us, Jones. And if it gets much wider, we might not be able to bridge it again."

He shook his head but couldn't find any words. This was something that had never occurred to him, that something between them might break and not be mended. He didn't even know who he was without Maggie.

"Look at me," she said.

And he looked at his wife. She loved him, he could see that. But he could also see that she was sad, almost desperate. In the kitchen the dishwasher hissed. The refrigerator dumped ice cubes into the bin with a *clunk-clunk.*

"What are you saying?" he asked her.

"I'm saying listen to your doctor. He's right. You're stuck in the past, picking at scabs. You need to find a way to create your future. For yourself, for us."

"I'm trying."

"It's easier to wallow, to place blame on the people who caused our pain, to reflect on all our mistakes. It's easier than it is to leave it behind and find a different road ahead where we have to do better."

"You think I'm wallowing."

She closed her eyes a second. "What I'm saying is that who we were *before,* what we were, it doesn't exist any longer. We need to move forward as who we are now, find a new *us,* a new life—without Ricky living in our house, without you as the town cop, without you carrying this secret burden. And if you can't help me to do that . . ."

She let the sentence trail with a sad shake of her head. She looked back at that cloth in her hand, folded it again, smoothed it flat.

Estrangement didn't always break and enter. It didn't smash your windows, come in with a gun and steal your love. It slipped in through the open back door. Under cover of night, it took the little things that you might not miss at first, until one morning you woke up and everything you thought you had was gone.

"Maggie."

She leaned back from the table and looked at him hard. "Do you hear me, Jones?"

"Yes."

"Don't stop seeing Dr. Dahl. Let him help you. Let him help us."

"Okay."

She got up and walked away from the table. She passed through the kitchen, and he heard her walk slowly up the stairs.

He knew he should go after her; he wanted to. He knew he could soothe her, make her feel better. But an odd inertia held him back, made his limbs and his heart feel so heavy. He managed to heft himself up from the table, move down the hallway, and stand at the stairs. From the bottom landing, he could see that the bedroom door was closed. He heard the shower running.

Words were so awkward in his mouth. He didn't know how to use them to express his inner life. It was as if they didn't fit, a language that seemed to work for everyone else but him. He couldn't bring himself to climb the stairs, wasn't sure what he would say if he did go up to her. He'd made so many apologies, so many promises. What was left to say?

He found himself thinking suddenly of the workbench. For Christmas a few years back, after they'd discovered that his cholesterol and blood pressure were through the roof, Maggie bought and had installed in the garage an elaborate workspace, with every possible tool he'd need for the woodworking he used to enjoy. He'd never once touched it; it just sat, collecting dust.

He wandered down the hallway now and went out into the garage. He pressed the button by the door to open up the space to the outside, and he flipped on the light. The garage door clattered open, letting in a rush of cool evening air. The wind outside was wild, sending leaves skittering across the drive.

He walked over to the bench . . . tiny drawers filled with every possible nail and screw, a hammer and a set of screwdrivers hanging, still gleaming. Beside the bench a circular saw, a cabinet with a selection of blades, a power drill with every bit. Everything he needed was there to build anything he cared to build. He just didn't know what he wanted to construct. But for the first time, he didn't feel guilty looking at it; it didn't stare back accusingly, neglected.

As he lifted his hand to touch the work area, the garage flooded with a blinding halogen light, the rumble of an engine. He shaded his eyes against the glare and walked outside. A giant maroon SUV had pulled up beside Ricky's car. The door opened, and out climbed Chuck Ferrigno. He looked a little heavier, a little more haggard than the last time Jones had seen him, not quite a year ago.

"I know," said Chuck when he caught sight of Jones. "I look like shit."

Jones had always really liked Chuck, was glad that the post he'd resigned as head detective at Hollows PD had been given to the other man. Chuck deserved it. He might be the last of the real cops, someone who didn't come to the job because of a crime show he'd seen on television.

"The job takes its toll," said Jones. He gave Chuck a hearty slap on the shoulder as they shook hands.

"You look good, Jones. Rested. Retirement agrees with you."

I'm in therapy. My wife hates me. And I have no fucking idea what to do with whatever amount of time I have left. Oh, and I'm obsessed with death. Wake up every night with the sweats just thinking about it.

"Can't complain," Jones said. "Life is good."

"My wife wants me to retire," Chuck said. He issued a snort of disdain. "I told her she needs to pull down six figures like Maggie and I'll think about it."

Chuck rubbed his forehead, and Jones noticed that he'd lost the little hair he used to have on top. Chuck's crown gleamed in the light over the garage. He still kept that ring of hair around his ears, though, like a friar. Jones thought he should shave it, grow a goatee, make it work for him. But real men didn't talk about hair.

"What brings you out?" asked Jones.

"Ah," said Chuck. He glanced up at the sky, then around the yard, as though looking for something he'd lost. "I need to talk. Have some time?"

Buddy, I've got nothing but time.

"Sure. Come on in. I'll put on some coffee."

Jones was embarrassed to acknowledge a giddy rush of excitement as he led Chuck inside.

He couldn't breathe, but it was okay—a relief even. He almost could believe it, how close was the edge of darkness. One minute he'd been standing on the bank, the great rushing river a roar in his head. Then he saw her, a floating reed of a girl, motionless but for the current sweeping her along. There was no thought. He was only action. He was only the blast of the frigid water all around him. Then there was a blissful silence, a peaceful, all-consuming quiet. He almost let it take him. But then he saw her floating ahead of him. Her hair was a halo. Her arms were outstretched like wings.

Come on, girl. I'll take you home.

Her thin body was in his hands. He could feel her ribs against his palms as he lifted her, kicking them both toward the milky distant light of the surface. How were they so deep? How did they get so far down?

Don't give up.

Then something powerful lifted her from his grasp, and she rose, pulled like a puppet on strings. He watched her go, and as she got farther from him, he felt his will waning. The pull of the cold water was so strong. And now that he had no one to save, his desire to reach the surface was fading. His legs felt heavy, his arms too tired to stroke. So he simply stopped moving, pushing, struggling. It was just that easy.

"Jones."

Maggie. I'm sorry.

Then he was in his own home, lying on the couch. The television filled the dark room with its flickering light. Maggie sat beside him, looking small and pale in her white nightgown.

"You were howling." Her voice wobbled in the sentence; her eyes were wide.

"Was I?" He sat up, wiped some drool from the side of his face. Being embarrassed in front of his wife was a new feeling. He didn't like it, how awkward they were with each other. When had it happened? How long had it taken him to notice?

"I thought it was an animal—in pain," she said. "In terrible pain."

That's not too far from the truth, actually.

"What were you dreaming about?" she asked.

He shook his head. Already the dream was slipping away from his consciousness. "I don't remember," he lied.

He hadn't told Maggie about Eloise Montgomery's visit or her premonition. But obviously she'd unsettled him more than he would have been willing to admit.

Maggie curled her legs under her. He'd decided to sleep on the couch tonight and give her the bed rather than continue to wake up to notice her absence, to lie awake and wonder why she didn't want to sleep beside him.

She was looking at him in a way that he realized had become familiar, as though her husband were a confounding puzzle she was unsure she wanted to solve.

"What did Chuck want?" she asked. "I saw him pull into the driveway."

Jones sat up and turned on the lamp beside the couch, grabbed the remote control, and turned off the television. The stack of files Chuck had left sat on the end table. It seemed like a week ago that he'd been there; it had been only a few hours.

"Do you remember Marla Holt?" Jones asked.

Maggie cocked her head, stared up at the ceiling. "The name is vaguely familiar."

"You were still in graduate school at the time."

Maggie had left for New York City right after high school, earning her undergraduate degree at New York University and then going on to Columbia for her master's in family and adolescent psychology. When her father was dying from lung cancer, she'd returned to The

Hollows to help her mother. During that time Jones and Maggie connected for the first time since Hollows High and fell in love. She came home, they got married, and she opened a private practice. They'd been in The Hollows ever since.

"Maybe my mother mentioned it," she said. There was very little that Maggie's mother, Elizabeth, failed to mention. The former principal of Hollows High, Elizabeth was, in her retirement, an information hub. She would have known everything there was to know about the Marla Holt case and everything else that went on in The Hollows. "But I don't remember the details."

"Marla was a woman in her late thirties with a fourteen-year-old son and a small daughter when she went missing in 1987," he said. "Her husband, Mack Holt, said she ran off with another guy. We suspected foul play, but we could never prove anything. Eventually the Holt disappearance went into the unsolved file."

"It was your case?" She was leaning toward him now. He remembered this—how she'd always loved talking about his work and how he'd loved talking to her about his cases. Her ideas, her psychological insights, her knowledge of human nature made her an invaluable resource. He relied on her so much, for everything. He wouldn't have been half as good at his job without her.

"One of my first after making detective," he said. He got up and bent back to stretch out his spine. He heard a sharp succession of pops, but there was little relief from the ache that had settled there.

"What happened to the children?"

"Funny you should ask. I'm not sure about the girl, but the boy is in his thirties now. And he's still looking for answers."

"He wants to reopen the case?" she asked.

"He's hired the dynamic duo," he said. "Ray Muldune, retired detective, and Eloise Montgomery, psychic sidekick."

Maggie released a long, slow breath, rubbed at the bridge of her nose. Those names were bound to bring up a lot of bad memories.

"She came here today, too. Coincidentally," Jones said. He just dropped it in, so that it would sound casual. "Or maybe not so co-incidentally. Maybe it's part of whatever scam they're running. Who knows?"

She looked up at him, surprise creasing her brow. "Eloise Montgomery came here? What did she want?"

He released a disdainful snort. "She had a *vision* about me pulling a body out of water. She thought I needed to know about it."

He rolled his eyes to further emphasize his skepticism, but he could tell she didn't buy it. She pinned him down with an inquisitive look. He sank into the couch beneath the weight of it. The clock on the DVD player read 12:03.

"How did you feel about that?" she asked.

She didn't fool him, either. She didn't want to deal with how it made her feel, so she was asking him about *his* feelings.

"Annoyed more than anything," he said. "Who does she think she is?"

Maggie wrapped her arms around herself. A lifetime ago Maggie's mother had visited Eloise Montgomery. And the things she'd learned from Eloise had far-reaching impact, the true nature of which was discovered only last year. Jones slid in closer to his wife, dropped an arm around her shoulder, and she molded herself against him.

"So . . . what?" she said. "Chuck had questions about the Marla Holt case?"

Jones shrugged. "He asked if he could bring the files by, wondered if I'd take a look and see what I remembered. Who knows, maybe from a distance something might pop."

"Are you going to do it?"

"If that's okay."

She gazed up at him with something like relief. He felt her body relax under his arm. "Are they paying you?"

"Just barely," he said. "Holt is making noise—calling the chief, writing letters to the mayor. Muldune has been asking for the files.

Chuck held them off by telling them he'd put someone on it unoffi- cially. But with budget cuts they had to let two guys go this year; they don't have the manpower."

"So they want you as a consultant."

He liked the sound of that, couldn't help but smile. "On the cheap and down low," he said.

"I think it's a good gig. Maybe you need something like this."

"As long as it doesn't interfere with my other thriving business— guy around the neighborhood with nothing to do but get your mail."

She lifted a hand to touch his face. He caught it and pressed it to his chest. She gave him a tentative smile, then looked away.

"That reminds me," she said. "You got a call today from a woman by the name of Paula Carr from The Oaks. She got your name from the Pedersens."

The Oaks was a wealthy neighborhood about ten minutes north of the downtown area where Jones and Maggie lived. It was his first call off their street, and it reminded him again of Eloise's visit and her other warning that he was getting a reputation. What had she said? *People are going to start coming to you for more, from farther away. It might lead you to places you don't expect.*

He shared this with Maggie, and she accepted it with a nod but didn't say anything right away. In the quiet, Jones noticed the ticking of that goddamn clock again. He really hated that thing.

"So that could mean Chuck, too," she said. She sounded thought- ful, far off.

He pushed out a nervous laugh. "Yeah, if we're putting weight behind the ramblings of a mentally ill woman."

He felt her snake her arms around his middle and hold on tight. He returned her embrace, leaned down to kiss her soft, open mouth.

"We're not, are we?" he asked. He looked into those deep, sweet eyes.

She leaned up and kissed him again. Was it a little urgent? It sent a jolt through him. They still had it, that heat. It had never once waned in all their years together, even in the hard times, even when they were sleeping in separate rooms. He always wanted her. Always.

"No. Of course not." She stood and offered him her hand. "Come to bed."

chapter eight

Michael Holt pulled into the driveway of his childhood home and cut the engine. The windows were dark, the lawn overgrown. One of the lower-level shutters hung by a single nail, listing to the side. He sat in the warm interior of the car and considered driving back into town and getting a hotel room. The Super 8 off the highway had rooms for sixty-nine dollars a night, including cable television and a pancake breakfast. The billboard had boasted superlatives like CLEAN! and SAFE!—which might not be enough for some but were more than enough for Michael, especially given his current residence.

He thought about his dwindling bank account, though, and the fact that the house—run-down and badly in need of modernization— could sit on the market in a struggling economy for months, even years.

Well, said the agent he'd hired to list the house. The word had sounded more like a sigh coming from her pretty, glossed lips. *We'll see what we can do. Some people are looking for teardowns and handyman specials.* She'd been all smiles in the office. On the property, when he was showing her the house, she'd gone stiff, her smile turning down into a kind of grimace, a look of falsely bright endurance. She'd made polite little noises of dismay. "Um," she'd said in the upstairs bath. "Oh," she'd murmured in the attic. "Wow," she'd said in his father's room. In the kitchen she'd lost her composure. "Oh, my God. How did he live like this?"

"I don't know," Michael had said. "We weren't . . . close."

"Michael," she said finally in the foyer. He'd watched her back toward the door, a beautifully manicured hand to her forehead. "You're going to have to clear out some of this *clutter*. I really can't show it until you do."

Clutter. It was an interesting choice of words. Clutter seemed so innocent—maybe a pile of papers on the desk, or a closet filled with too many old clothes, maybe a mess in the garage. Clutter was almost funny, something that needed to be cheerfully tidied up. It didn't begin to describe his father's house. It was a towering menace of filth. There were the overflowing boxes in the hallways, stacks of newspapers and magazines in the bathroom; Michael's old room was filled with computer parts and old telephones, an unexplainable graveyard of nonfunctioning electronic devices. There was a closet where they'd kept the cat's litter box. The cat was long dead, but the smell of his urine and feces remained. Opening that closet door was to invite an olfactory assault that could bring a man to his knees.

There were shelves and shelves of books in every room, and a cartoon plume of dust flew up whenever one was removed from its place. It was the kitchen, though, that was the dark heart of the house, the smell of decay so oppressive, the buzzing of flies so unnerving that he'd not even set foot over the threshold. And that was just the first floor.

Movement on the property next door caught Michael's eye. He saw Mrs. Miller on her porch, her arms folded across her middle. It was dark, but he could tell she was looking in his direction, wondering why he was sitting there in his car. She was probably wondering, too, about the sign that the agency had placed in the yard today. He'd thought it would bring him some relief to see it there. But instead he felt a familiar dark hollow within him, this terrible emptiness he had carried around ever since his mother had left. It started just below his navel and spread through him like a stain—red wine on linen.

———

"Where's Mom?" It was a hundred years ago that he'd first asked that question, the question he'd been asking in one way or another every day since.

His father, Mack, had stood in the kitchen, scrambling eggs in a scratched-up yellow pan on the stove. His father had seemed to freeze, to hold his breath, when Michael entered the room and pulled up his usual chair at the table. Michael remembered everything about that room that morning. How the sun came in from the window over the sink, and through it he could see the tire swing he hadn't touched in years. How the chair leg always caught on the vinyl tile that was coming up, how there was a cigarette burn in the red-and-white checked tablecloth. He could smell the eggs, cooked too long. His mother wouldn't like the coffee his father had made; it smelled weak. They'd probably bicker about it. *If you don't like the coffee I make, make it yourself.*

"What do you mean, *'Where's Mom?'*"

There was something strange about his father's tone, something taut and foreign; his shoulders seemed to quake just slightly. Mack still hadn't turned to look at him; Michael stared at the back of his father's head, the dark brown hair run through with gray, the eternal plaid shirt, the chinos and brown leather shoes. *What are you wearing, Mack?* His mother's eternal question that wasn't a question but a taunt.

That morning Michael had a terrible headache, a real killer. He'd struggled for the details of the night before but found he couldn't remember. He was supposed to spend the night at a friend's house, but once there he'd wanted to come home. He remembered riding his bike through the quiet streets. He remembered leaving the bike in the drive and coming up the front steps, putting his hand on the knob. But that was the last moment he could recall. As vivid as his memory of that morning was, the night before was still, years later, a total blank.

"Where is she?" he'd asked again.

"She's gone, son. You know that."

His father had turned then, and the man looked as though he'd aged ten years since Michael saw him the day before.

"Gone where?"

I hate you. I hate this place. I hate this life. The words came back, the echo of her desperate shrieking still bouncing off the ceiling and the walls. That's when it started opening in him, that abyss of despair.

A hard knock on the window of his truck snapped him back to the present. Mrs. Miller. He rolled down the window, though he didn't want to.

"Michael," she said. "What are you doing just sitting there like that?"

"Sorry," he said. "Just zoning out. Long day."

"You didn't tell me you were selling." Her breath smelled of something stale. It was hard to see in the darkness, but he knew her hair to be dyed a preposterous shade of orange, her face a cracked mask of deep lines.

He'd always hated Mrs. Miller. It seemed as if she'd been the mean old lady next store forever, the keeper of lost balls, the frowner, the finger wagger, the parent caller. Would she ever die? Or would she just rattle about that house for millennia, torturing generations of neighborhood children?

"Yes, Mrs. Miller," he said. He always tried to be polite. "It's on the market."

She issued an unpleasant snort. "Well, if you don't clean it up, it's only going to attract riffraff."

Riffraff? Did people still use words like that? What did it even mean? He imagined some barefoot, downtrodden family dressed in rags, their belongings in garbage bags.

"I'm working on it, Mrs. Miller."

Mrs. Miller looked back at the house, and he followed her eyes.

"He used to keep it up, before he got sick," she said. There was an accusation inherent in the statement. But Michael knew enough about people like Claudia Miller to ignore the subtext. She didn't know anything about him. And she certainly didn't know anything about his father. No one did.

He opened the car door, and she backed away from him, her eyes widening a bit—at his height, he supposed. He towered over her. She wrapped herself up in her arms. He saw how the threadbare fabric of her housecoat clung to her small, shriveled body; he turned his eyes from her. There was something, not just about her physical appearance, that repulsed him. He started to feel that familiar rise of discomfort that he often had in personal encounters, a desire to flee into the house and close the door. But for a moment she didn't move, and neither did he.

"Mrs. Miller, do you remember my mother?" He had to force the words out.

She looked up at him, startled. A brown paper bag danced noisily down the street, lofting and landing, lifting again in the wind that was picking up. Except for that, the neighborhood was quiet. It always was. No music blaring or dogs barking. People came home and went to work, might be seen tending to their properties on the weekends. But the things he remembered as a kid—the block parties, the gangs of boys and girls riding around on their bikes, playing in one another's yards—had vanished. Each house was a bubble; people kept to themselves these days.

"Of course I remember her." What did he hear in her voice? Disdain? Judgment? *The woman who ran off on her family, the slut? Of course I remember her.*

"Do you remember anything about the night she disappeared?"

Claudia looked down at her feet, continued backing away. "It was a long time ago."

But Claudia remembered. Because everyone remembered Marla Holt. Every little boy thinks his mother is beautiful. But Marla Holt had been truly, luminously lovely. With chestnut hair that flowed like a river around her shoulders, with those dark eyes, with her hour-glass shape, she filled the room when she entered. Men stared, smiled; women looked down at their nails. She wasn't reed thin; she wasn't glamorous. Her face wasn't flawless. Her beauty was something that welled up from inside her, a kind of radiant heat. Even in the snap-shots Michael had of her, he could see it. The camera worshipped the contrast on her face, the black eyebrows and red lips against the pale white of her skin. She complained endlessly about the size of her bottom, the constant maintenance she felt her appearance required—plucking, waxing, moisturizing, and exercising. He'd follow her on his bicycle while she ran around the neighborhood.

"I was designed for luxuriating, not for sweating," she'd pant.

"Come on, Mom. One more mile. You can do it."

As a boy he'd loved his father, of course. But it was his mother who put the stars in the sky.

"You told the police that you saw her leave," he pressed. "That she got into a black sedan parked in front of the house, that someone was waiting for her and they drove off together. You said she was carrying a suitcase."

She stopped moving, gave a single nod. "If that's what I told the police, then that's what I saw." He noticed a tremor in her right hand.

"Do you remember anything else?"

"They were always fighting," she said. "There was always yelling coming from that house. It used to drive me crazy."

It was true. He used to hide under his covers and wait for his mother to come weeping up the stairs and close the door to her bedroom. That was the closing bell; the fight was over, and she was the loser again. His father never came after her. Michael never heard the soft tones of their making up. If they ever did make amends, it was in private.

"Did you see who was driving the car?"

"Such a long time ago, Michael," she said. She shook her head sadly. "I'm an old woman. How can I remember?"

But she did remember, he could tell. She no longer wanted to look at him, was moving toward the safety of her house. Finally she turned and walked rapidly past the line of hedges that divided their yards. From behind the line: "Just don't sell this place to any unsavory types. Think of the neighborhood."

He knew he should move after her, try to get her to say more. But he'd leave that to Ray Muldune; the private detective's services didn't come cheap. And Michael had had enough social contact for one day—first the girl in the woods, then her mother. He had the drained and exhausted feeling that plagued him when he'd been aboveground too long.

Michael was happier underneath the world. This sunlit place above, where normal life was lived . . . now, *that* was scary, that was the place of monsters and nightmares. The modern world and most of the people that populated it made him uncomfortable. The people he knew—friends and acquaintances, if he could even call them that— seemed motivated by things he didn't understand. They said one thing but appeared to be thinking something else, wearing smiles that never reached their eyes. The people he didn't know, those he observed, were what he liked to call busy-addicted, engaged in one task but paying attention to something else—grocery shopping while talking on their cell phones, driving their cars while sending texts. Multitasking, they called it. When did it become a badge of honor to be too busy, to have *too much* to do?

The world was in a fearful rush; he'd never been able to keep the pace. Michael often felt confused, had the vague sense that there was something terribly wrong with him. He wanted to stop and look at the sky and the trees; he wanted to talk to the people he knew and met. But everyone seemed to speed past him, move around him. He was an obstruction on the superhighway of life. And that was on a good day. On a bad day, he felt that at any time strangers might start point-ing and shrieking, identifying him as something unwanted. Sometimes he was nervous to the point of sweating, even in the most mundane encounters—at tollbooths, grocery checkout lines.

But below the ground there was another world. In the dripping darkness of the mines, there was solitude and silence. There he started to relax and expand, to become more fully himself. In that peculiar living darkness, all his senses came alive.

He listened to Claudia shut her door, then turned his attention back to his father's house. For another moment he wavered again about the hotel. But then he started up the cracked and overgrown path. He stood on the stoop a second, took in the rusting letter box, the flickering porch light, and then he walked inside.

He always stooped when he walked through doorways, though he wasn't quite that tall, just over six feet. But he'd hit his head on so many things that others cleared with ease that it was just habit to fold in his shoulders, to bow his head.

He let the door close behind him. He could still hear her voice—her enthusiastically off-pitch singing, her trying-to-be-stern tone, her mellifluous laughter. Long after she'd gone, he'd hear her when he came home from school.

Is that you, sweetie? Are you hungry?

And the sound of her ghost voice caused him to ache inside. After she left, this house was haunted by her, though only in the way all houses were haunted—by echoes and memories, energy trapped in the drywall and floorboards. But that was bad enough. It was reason enough to go away and never come back again, to leave his father to grow old and lonely, to leave him to become sick and to rot like the rest of the debris in the dump he'd made of their home.

The hallway was lined on both sides with piles of newspapers that reached to the ceiling, narrowing the passage by more than a foot on either side. Michael had to flatten himself and turn to make his way sideways down the hall, to avoid touching the wall of newsprint, heading toward the only habitable room in the house.

The sitting room, with her television and shelves of books, the coffee table she'd inherited from her mother, the framed landscapes she'd painted hanging on the walls, remained as he remembered it. The surfaces and fabrics in here were kept clean. The sofa and love seat were free from stain; the dusky pink carpet was still fresh and bright. There was no dust even on the books. The visiting nurse had told Michael that his father had pulled out the bed from the couch and slept on it at night, replacing it in the mornings until he grew too weak to do that. Their wedding picture (did they look stiff and unhappy even then?) sat on the end table, beneath a lamp she'd cherished, with its blue-and-white flowers painted on porcelain. It had shocked him when he returned from his father's hospital room to find this oasis in the center of chaos, this eye in the storm. Michael would have thought the old man had forgotten her or tried to, but instead he'd kept her room like this, just as she'd left it.

He sat on the chintz couch and tried not to smell the old man's sickness. But it lingered, even with all the other competing aromas. It was there—that smell of medicine and washcloth baths, antiseptic and something else, something rotting from within. Or maybe that was just his imagination.

He found himself thinking about Bethany Graves. He thought she had a quiet energy, not unlike his own. She was careful; she listened, then waited a second before she spoke, absorbing, it seemed, everything that he'd said, and maybe what he hadn't said.

"What does that mean?" she'd asked after he told her he'd been digging up a body. He'd seen a glint of curiosity, more than a hint of caution.

"That's what I do," he told her. "I dig up the past. I'm a caver. The Hollows was originally settled as a mining town. There are tunnels everywhere—some of them just exploratory."

"Meaning?"

"Meaning that tunnels were blasted and then for whatever reason abandoned. When you find one, it's like digging up a grave. Traveling back in time."

"I'd heard that," she said. "About the mines around here. Iron, right?"

She seemed interested. But he wasn't a good judge of those kinds of things.

"Magnetite and some hematite," he said. "This town has a fairly rich history. And there's lore surrounding the vein I'm searching for. Two brothers, both looking to strike it rich. One of them did. One of them disappeared."

And what Michael had told her was true. He *was* interested in finding the abandoned shaft where some believed a body might have been buried. It was a story Mack had told him, a tale the old man had supposedly unearthed in his exhaustive research. Michael had never been able to find anything about it in the few history books about the industry and the area. But according to his father's deductions, the tunnel was probably somewhere around where Michael had been digging today. He knew that his father had written about the legend in one of his articles about the area mines, but Michael hadn't been able to find it in the mountain of papers in Mack's office.

His father, a geology professor, had a pet interest in the area mines and their history. He had wanted to document that part of the region's history and wrote voluminously, compiling interviews with the old-timers still living in The Hollows, taking copious photographs, collecting any old documents he could find. He contributed articles to history journals and magazines, had hoped to one day write a book. But it wasn't exactly a sexy topic. Mack was never able to find a publisher, and even interest in his articles dried up over time. But he kept writing.

Michael was sure that if he could dig past the piles of junk mail and circulars and catalogs and bills and bills and bills that formed a literal wall around his father's desk, he'd find those articles, which Michael had always loved reading. They had to be under there. Clearly his father had never discarded anything.

Of course, Michael also had the business of settling his father's estate. He had a meeting with the lawyer, Hank Barrow, an old friend of Mack's. Their recent phone conversation had been grim.

"Your father was a good man, Michael," Hank had said. "But his affairs are a disaster. I'm going to do this work pro bono. After the medical bills, though, I don't know what will be left for you and your sister."

Yet neither of these things was *keeping* him in The Hollows. He'd had a passing interest in that tunnel for years. And his father's matters could be settled from afar. But when he learned from his sister that his father was ill and about to die, that she couldn't (wouldn't) with two children travel home to see it through, something powerful drew him back.

They'd both been estranged from Mack, for myriad reasons. But Michael wasn't drawn home to make amends, or to find peace. He wanted answers to questions he had never dared ask about his mother's disappearance.

"What happened to her, Dad?" He'd asked in the hospital room while his father lay dying.

Mack had looked at him as if through a fog. The hospital room was dim except for the light washing in from the hallway. The man in the other bed was snoring. His father was in a palliative state, only pain relief now. There was no treatment for a body so riddled with cancer.

"You know," he said. "You know."

"No, I don't," Michael said. "She left that night, and we never heard from her again. Not a phone call. Not a card. I've looked for her, Dad, for years. She didn't run off. She never divorced you, never changed her name. She never worked again. Cara's looked for her, too. We've *hired* people to find her."

He locked eyes with his father. But he wasn't sure his father could see him. The old man's gaze was unfocused and watery.

"She may not have loved you," Michael said. "She may have wanted to leave you. But she loved us, Cara and me. She did love us."

"She did love us," his father said. But it was just an echo, a meaningless repetition of Michael's words.

Michael wasn't sure how long he sat there with his father, who looked as shriveled and empty as a corn husk. How long did he just sit listening to his father's rattling breath? Michael dozed in the chair, saw the night nurse come in briefly and cast him a sad smile. She thought him the dutiful son, sitting at his father's deathbed.

But he wasn't that. He was a grave robber, waiting for the night watchman to drift off once and for all. Then, and only then, could he dig his fingers into the earth and exhume the truth.

chapter nine

Willow could tell that her mother liked Principal Ivy. Bethany seemed to have a thing lately for geeky-looking guys.

I've had my fill of cool, Willow. These days it's kindness, honesty, and stability that impress me. Read: boring, snorts-when-he-laughs, totally lame. Not that her mother actually dated. She never went anywhere that didn't have something to do with work. She didn't even seem to have any friends anymore, except her agent—who was so annoying that Willow wasn't sure how anyone could stand him.

Mr. Ivy wasn't a *total* geek. Still, that sweater had to go. Argyle? Really? He could do something about his hair, too. Maybe mess it up a little. That careful look, parted on the side, brushed back from his face—not working for him.

"I know you've been having a hard time adjusting to the move and the new school. So I'm going to be lenient here. Of course, your friend Jolie was suspended last week for cutting school. But that was her third offense. I don't think we have to go there. Do we?"

Willow shook her head vigorously, did her best to seem contrite. She wouldn't really mind being at the house for a week, watching television and sleeping late. On the other hand, her mother would make her life a homeschooling hell. So she might as well just come here.

"We really appreciate your understanding, Mr. Ivy," said her mother. Bethany was doing her good-conservative-mom routine. She was even wearing a skirt.

"Please, call me Henry."

Oh, brother. He had the goofy smile men often had around her mother.

Willow looked around Mr. Ivy's office, blanking out on whatever small talk he and her mother were making now. There was a wall of pictures—Mr. Ivy with various students, accepting an award, dressed in the school-mascot costume, with the Wildcat costume's head tucked under his arm. There was a case of trophies, not for sports but for things like the chess and science clubs and the debate team, dorky stuff like that.

"She's a good student, Mr. Ivy . . . I mean, Henry," her mother said. Could she be any more overeager? "And very bright. But she *is* struggling."

"I know it. I've seen her school record. Her teachers here see a lot of potential, too. Mr. Vance speaks very highly of her, her advanced comprehension and her creative writing. I think we can all work together to keep her on track."

Obviously Mr. Vance hadn't ratted her out for being so inappropriate in class. For some reason that only made her feel worse about it.

"I'm glad you feel that way," said Bethany. She seemed to relax a bit. "I think so, too."

Sitting there looking out the window now at the kids heading to the field for that mundane misery they called physical education but which everyone knew was just school-sanctioned torture for anyone other than the naturally thin and athletic, Willow felt it. As she listened to her mother and Mr. Ivy talk about *her* behavior, *her* schoolwork, *their* expectations, Willow felt the now-familiar dark lash of anger. It turned to something cold and black inside her, and she let herself sink into it.

She'd felt it the first time she realized that her father was gone and that he wasn't coming back. That he'd call when he should, make all the appropriate appearances, send money and gifts. But that he'd *moved on* in a way that fathers weren't supposed to ever move on from their children. And then she finally understood what they'd told her, that he wasn't her *natural* father, not her biological father. They'd carefully explained to her over the years that he was her stepfather but it was just the same, that he *couldn't* love her any more if she had been his real daughter. But that just wasn't true, was it? His love for Willow was intimately connected to his love for her mother. And when he stopped loving Bethany, he'd stopped loving Willow, too. He stopped wanting to be her father.

And on the day that this finally dawned on her, she felt this thing settle inside her—but it wasn't a thing, really. It was this terrible, ugly absence, a hollow. And she didn't fight it off, though something told her that she should, she *should* fight it back with all her strength. But she didn't. She couldn't. It was like drinking something that made you sick but liking the sickness somehow.

Willow had seen Jolie when they'd entered the school. Jolie was leaning against her locker, and she gave Willow that sly smile she had. The smile asked, *Wanna get high, girl?* And Willow did. She *did* want to get high, so high that her whole world was just a small black dot a million miles away. Willow loved that smile of Jolie's. It made so many promises.

"Are you listening, Willow?"

"Yes. I'm listening." But, startled, she'd said it with that sullen snap her mother *hated*. And Bethany's face changed just like that. It went from open and hopeful to tired and disappointed in a millisecond. And probably nobody but Willow would even have noticed. She'd seen that look a lot. She didn't think her mother herself was aware of the expression on her face. It wasn't something she did on purpose, like her stern look or her trying-to-be-patient look. This was the expression that her face took on when all the other masks she wore failed her.

"No more cutting, Willow," said Mr. Ivy. "If you're struggling, having a hard day, having trouble with the other kids, teachers, whatever, come see me. I'll always make time to talk it through."

He meant it. She could see that in his eyes. He wasn't a fake, like her stepfather, Richard, with all his expensive gifts and "heartfelt" apologies. Mr. Ivy didn't want anything in return, didn't have a guilty conscience to be massaged or a skittish ego to be stroked.

"Okay," she said. "I promise I'll do that, Mr. Ivy."

She offered him a shy smile. Embarrassed-but-trying was the look she was going for. Mr. Ivy seemed to buy it, giving her a warm smile and an approving nod. He leaned back in his chair. Bethany released a breath beside Willow.

"Good. Great," said Mr. Ivy.

"Well," Bethany said, slapping her palms lightly on her thighs. "I feel like we've accomplished something."

Lies, good lies, were about more than words. They were about tone, expression, and body language, too. The best lies contain a little bit of truth. Some details, but not too many. More than any of that, though, you had to believe the lie yourself. You had to *be* the lie.

Her first lie had been about a Britney Spears concert. Her father— and of course she'd always thought of him that way then, because she didn't know anything else—was supposed to take her to the concert for her thirteenth birthday. Front-row seats, he'd said. He was trying to finagle a backstage pass from one of his clients, but no promises there.

She'd told *everyone*—and her friends were sick with jealousy, begging to come along. And truth be told, she would much rather have had one of them with her than her father. But he had only two tickets, and Willow's going alone with a friend was out of the question. But her mom took her to Betsey Johnson and bought her a new top, to Lucky Brand for a new pair of jeans. She felt really grown up, and she rarely had time alone with her dad. So maybe it wasn't *that* lame to be going with him.

The night of the concert, Willow and Bethany had pizza while they waited for her dad to come home. They rocked out to the new CD and danced around the kitchen, using spatulas for microphones. He was supposed to be home by seven, but by seven fifteen he still wasn't there. Bethany called his office and then left a message on his cell phone.

"If you're caught up at work, let us know. I'll come get the tickets and take her myself," she heard her mother say. But he didn't call back and he didn't come home. Anxiety gave way quickly to a bone-crushing disappointment.

As eight turned to eight thirty, and eight thirty turned to nine, Willow wept in her mother's lap. It wasn't the first time he hadn't come home when he was supposed to. He had broken other dates and promises. But this was the first time he'd done it to Willow. Usually it was Bethany dressed up and waiting, falling asleep on the couch, the sitter sent home. They weren't worried about him—that's what Willow remembered—didn't fear that something terrible had happened.

In her room she saw a slew of text messages on her phone from her friends. HOW IS IT??? OMG, I'M SO JEALOUS!!! SEND ME A PICTURE OF YOUR OUTFIT!! She could call any one of them and start to cry about her father. No one would judge her; not one of her friends was living with both her biological parents. They were all accustomed to the heart-break and disappointment of divorce, ugly custody battles, blending families. But she didn't call them. Something inside her couldn't stand to lose face that way; she was the one with the perfect family—the famous mom, the successful plastic-surgeon father. She sent a group text: IT'S AWESOME!!! WISH YOU WERE HERE!! PIX TOMORROW!!

Just as she sent it, her mother was standing in the door.

"Willow. I'm so sorry."

"It's not your fault, Mom."

But she could tell by the look on her mother's face that she was taking it on, the way she took on everything. And somehow this just made Willow feel worse. She remembered everything about that night. But most of all she remembered that terrible aching sadness as she lay in bed.

Around midnight she heard her father come home.

"Oh, Christ, Beth. I forgot. I got held up in surgery."

"Bullshit, Richard. Were there even tickets?"

Willow buried her head beneath her pillow against the crescendo of their voices. Then it got quiet for a while. Just as she was drifting off to sleep, she heard the front door slam and her mother start to cry.

The next day Willow told all her friends about the concert—using details she'd gleaned from blogs and videos posted online. No, her dad couldn't get those backstage passes. But she told them how she'd met this really cute guy when her dad went off to use the bathroom. She gave the boy her e-mail address, because she really didn't want to give out her number. His name was Rainer; he believed her when she told him she was sixteen years old. She told her friends how her dad took her out for a burger and a shake afterward and she didn't get home until past midnight. It was the best time *ever*.

And it was all true. She *should* have been there—she could imagine every detail, hear the music, feel the excitement. She *was* there. Her lie told the truth, as it should have been. And there was not a flicker of doubt from anyone. Why would there be?

Somehow, in doing this, Willow felt a little less desperately sad, as though she'd taken back something that had been taken from her. The real truth was just so pathetic. In telling her lies that day, she felt a kind of rare power. She couldn't control a thing about her life, her father's persistent and growing absence, her parents' disintegrating marriage. But she could control its telling.

And she didn't feel bad about it at all, not about the envy she saw on her friends' faces, not even about how she had to tell more lies now to sustain the illusion. The imaginary boy she'd met at the concert she'd never attended? The next day they were asking about him. Did he ever e-mail her? Of course he did.

She didn't know, couldn't have known, that that first little lie would grow and grow. She couldn't have imagined the consequences.

"Willow? Are you listening?"

"Of course," she said. "I *am* listening."

They were both staring at her. She straightened up from the slump she'd unconsciously sunk into.

"I promise. I'm on board. I want to do better."

Willow did want that. She really did. At least in that moment, she wanted to be someone they could both be proud of. She left Mr. Ivy's office feeling good, optimistic. When she gave her mother a hug goodbye and headed off to advanced calculus, she was sure she'd meant every word she said.

But by the end of the day, she was sinking back into that funk. She'd been brutalized in gym class during a game of softball in which she'd tripped and screwed up a triple play for her team. At lunch she'd sat alone to read but had to endure the snickering, whispering stares of the designer bitches. She and Jolie used to have the same lunch period, but Jolie had apparently been switched after returning from suspension. Willow was pretty sure that Mr. Ivy had a hand in it, wanting to minimize Jolie's influence. But when Jolie was there, Willow could handle the harpies better; they were almost funny when Jolie was around to point out their flaws: Lola had a big ass; Stacey was flat-chested; Emma was prone to breaking out. But not really. That was just Jolie trying to be funny. Without Jolie there to take the edge off, Willow was left to fixate on them. What was it? Genes? How did they get such silky hair, creamy skin, perfect bodies? And why did it make them so awful? So mean? Was it just because their beauty acted as a kind of armor? They could hurt others, but no one could hurt them. Whatever flaws they had were on the inside; no one could call those out and make them cry.

In the margin of her notebook, she'd doodled, *Sticks and stones may break my bones. But words can break my heart.*

She'd zoned out in science lab, hadn't done the reading, anyway. The teacher put a zero in the book, and Willow would have to do extra credit to get it removed.

By the time she was at her locker, removing her things to go home, she was barely holding back a flood of angry, frustrated tears.

"Rough day?" The voice behind her was smoky and mischievous, full of invitation.

"No more than usual," she lied. She turned to face Jolie with a smile.

"I saw you come in with your mom. You looked miserable. Still do. Don't let them do it to you, girl. Don't let them bring you down."

Willow shrugged. Jolie chewed at her cuticle, looked at her with glittering green eyes through lashes caked with dark mascara. Willow noticed that Jolie's black polish had chipped to tiny islands in the center of each nail.

"I like your coat," said Willow. It was a vintage black wool A-line with enormous buttons.

"Salvation Army," said Jolie. She did a little spin. "Twelve bucks. Cute, huh?"

It *would* have been cute if it weren't scattered with stains and white pet hair. This could be said of Jolie, too. She had a kind of beauty, but she looked dirty. She had creamy white skin but a constellation of acne on her chin. Her raven hair always looked like it needed washing. Something about her made Willow itchy.

"Let's take a walk," Jolie said.

"I gotta get home. I promised my mom and Mr. Ivy that I'd work harder."

"So call your mom and tell her you're going to stay and study at the library. Take the late bus."

There was that smile. Willow liked Jolie; Willow felt relaxed and easy when she was around, didn't have that need to make things up to feel better about herself.

"Come on," Jolie said. She gave Willow a gentle nudge with her shoulder. "You can study later. There's someone I want you to meet."

So Willow called her mom, who sounded skeptical but just tired enough to let it slide. Then Willow and Jolie hung out in the library awhile. They tried to look studious with their books open, passing notes back and forth, while they waited for Bethany to call and check up—which she did, predictably, fifteen minutes later.

"She's here, Mrs. Graves," Willow heard Mrs. Teaford, the school librarian, say. "Studying hard."

Jolie buried her face in her arms so no one would see her laughing. Then, when Mrs. Teaford was occupied with a flood of students checking out books and asking questions *(what a bunch of geeks!)*, Jolie and Willow slipped off. Running and laughing down the long gray hallway, then bursting through the side doors, the cold air greeting them in a rush, pushing their laughter up into the sky. Willow wasn't even sure why she was laughing, except that she felt good for the first time all day. There was an hour and a half until the late bus; she had that long to be herself. Then she'd go home and try to be what everyone else wanted her to be.

chapter ten

At first glance Jones wouldn't have said Paula Carr was beautiful. She wasn't the type of woman who caused you to do a double take. She didn't invite the three-point appraisal: face, breasts, ass—not necessarily in that order. She was a mom, with a stylish short cut to her brown hair but wearing very little makeup other than a light gloss on her lips. She had on faded jeans, a ribbed turtleneck, athletic shoes—nothing about any of it was sexy or hot. But after twenty minutes sitting with her, listening to her chat nervously, watching her spoon-feed her baby girl, wipe down the counter, hard-boil some eggs, then sit down with some tea for them both after depositing the little one in her crib, he found himself captivated by her—her wide pink mouth, her high cheekbones, the depths of her dark eyes.

"I'm sorry," she said when she'd finally settled. "You're probably wondering why I called and asked you to come here."

He *was* wondering about that. When he'd returned her call, she'd asked him to come by in the early afternoon the next day.

"I'll pay you for your time, of course," she'd said. "My baby will be taking her nap, and my two older boys won't be home from school." She'd spoken in a hushed tone, as though she didn't want anyone to hear—or maybe so as not to wake the baby. He couldn't be sure. He'd called to tell her that he didn't really take care of any properties off his block, but there was something about her voice. By the end of the conversation, he found himself telling her yes, of course he'd come by.

Maggie said, "You never could resist a damsel in distress."

"What makes you think she's in distress? Maybe she just needs someone to water her plants while she jets off to the Caribbean."

"She'd have asked you that over the phone."

Jones shifted off his coat when Paula didn't go on right away. In the sunny dining room, he was feeling overly warm. Paula stared down at her mug, started tracing the rim with one short fingernail. She had a nice big diamond on her left hand. Married, maybe not too happily. He wouldn't have been able to say why he thought this, that she wasn't happy. There was something odd about the house, too. He wasn't able to put his finger on that, either.

"Over the summer my husband's sixteen-year-old son by another marriage came to stay with us. It was supposed to be short-term."

"Okay."

"At first I was pretty anxious about it. I mean, Kevin goes to work all day. So I was supposed to hang out with the kid all summer? I have two other small ones, so I'm pretty much being run ragged all the time as it is. But what are you going to do? His mother was having a hard time; Cole needed his father. So yeah, of course he comes here."

She looked up at the ceiling for a second, and he followed her eyes until he realized that this was something she did to keep herself from crying. When she looked back down, she wore an embarrassed smile but had managed to keep her tears at bay.

"I'm sorry." It was maybe the fourth time she'd apologized for various little things since he'd arrived. She was sorry that it had taken her a minute to get to the door, that she was running behind with the baby's schedule, that she hadn't offered him tea right away. He didn't think someone with so little to apologize for should be rushing to do it all the time.

"You're fine," he said. "Take your time."

She took a sip of her tea. "Anyway, so Cole arrived. And guess what? He's a total doll. All summer he helps around the house. He's great with the kids. After a few weeks, I was leaving him with Cammy—that's my oldest—while I ran to the store with the little one. Cole's mother is a disaster, but she must have done something right, because the kid's a gem."

"That's great," he said. "It could have been a difficult situation."

He still had no idea what the woman wanted. But if he had learned anything over his years as a cop and a husband, it was that women wanted to take a scenic route to the point. If you were smart, you kept your mouth shut.

"Cole was supposed to go back to New Jersey at the end of the summer. His mother was scheduled to pick him up on August fifteenth. But the day came and went; she never showed. The home phone was disconnected. The voice mail on her cell phone was full. The next weekend Cole and Kevin drove out to her place, only to learn that she'd been evicted. All their stuff was gone. And Robin, that's Kevin's ex, had stopped showing up to work a couple of weeks earlier."

"When was the last time Cole talked to his mother?"

"He said she called on his cell phone a couple of days before she was supposed to come, and everything seemed fine."

"And you believe that?"

She shrugged. "I don't have a reason not to believe it."

"So . . . what? Drugs?"

"Honestly, we don't know. Kevin hadn't had much to do with Cole or his mother. It was kind of sad, but she just didn't want Kevin around."

"Why was that?" asked Jones.

There was a quick darting of her eyes. "I don't really know."

But Jones could see that she did know. She knew exactly why.

She took a quick glance up at the ceiling again. Then, "Kevin said that there had been a lot of different men over the last few years.

And most recently the guy Robin was involved with didn't want Cole around. That's why Cole came to spend the summer with us. Kevin just thinks she ran off with whoever that was."

"How would he know that if there wasn't much contact?" asked Jones.

"I'm not sure." She shrugged and gave a little shake of her head.

"And what did Cole say?"

"I asked him when Kevin was at work. And he said his mother had had a few dates here and there, but nothing serious. If she'd told Kevin about a man who didn't want Cole around, Cole had never met him. That's kind of how Kevin made it sound, that Robin had confided in him. Which seems odd." She released a breath, started twisting at her wedding band.

No pictures. That was it. There were no pictures on the walls, on the mantel, on any of the shelves. . . . None of the expected perfect wedding shots and mall portraits of the kids. No vacation snapshots. Also not a speck of dust on any surface, not a crumb on the floor. In a house with three children? He and Maggie had one child, and their home was a veritable shrine to Ricky. When he was growing up, the place was always a mess—never dirty, but cluttered with all manner of stuff—toys, gear, costumes, tents, tricycles, all the paraphernalia of childhood.

"Mrs. Carr," said Jones, "what is it that you'd like me to do?"

"I was wondering if you could help us find Cole's mother."

He started to shake his head, to say he didn't do that type of work. But she misunderstood it as disapproval. She held up her palms.

"It's not about wanting him to go. Don't think that. It's just that he's so sad. So, *so* sad. His birthday was last week—no card, no call." She didn't bother to try to stop the tears this time, just let them fall. She reached into her pocket and pulled out a tissue, dabbed her eyes and her nose.

"Mrs. Carr," said Jones, "the chances are she'll come back on her own, probably before the holidays."

She looked down at the table, then back up at Jones. "The thing is, he's a good boy. She has done a wonderful job raising him. She *obviously* loved him. I didn't know her—Kevin never wanted us to meet. So I don't know, maybe she *is* the type of woman who would abandon her son for some new guy. Or maybe she does have a substance-abuse problem. But maybe, *maybe,* something has happened to her. It doesn't seem right. Does it?"

She was looking at him so earnestly now, had leaned forward in her seat. Mrs. Carr was a genuinely nice person; he could see it in her expression, even in the way she held her shoulders. He'd met all different kinds in his life as a cop. And some people were just bad news— vacant, conscienceless, malicious, virtually brimming with bad intent. The honest people, those who obeyed the law and did the right thing, were common enough. But the genuinely good people, the innocent people like Paula Carr, the ones who thought of others and put themselves last, that was a rare breed.

It reminded Jones of a question asked of him by a troubled boy. *How do you know if you're a good person or a bad person?* He'd done a lot of thinking on that lately. And he wasn't any closer to the answer. But he suspected that for most people there was no way to know until the end of the day. And maybe not even then. Maybe the answer was different in any given moment, from one time to the next. Who was keeping a tally? Who added up your score when the game was over? He didn't even pretend to know.

"Am I wrong in thinking that you didn't want anyone else in your family to know we were talking?" Jones asked.

He saw a flush rise up her neck. "No," she said. "You're not wrong."

"Why is that?"

"Well, first of all, I don't want Cole to feel he's not welcome here.

Also, I wouldn't want to get his hopes up." That was two. Usually there were three things, three reasons. And number three was the real reason.

"And Kevin . . ." She let the sentence trail with a shake of her head, as if she didn't know how to finish. Then, "He just wouldn't like it. Kevin cares about what he cares about, and that's it. He wants Cole to stay here with us. And he doesn't seem to care much about what happened to Robin."

He cares about what he cares about, and that's it. Jones turned the sentence over, listened to the words again in his head. Jones had never met Kevin Carr, but he was pretty sure if at some point they did meet, they weren't going to get along.

"I'm not a private detective, Mrs. Carr."

She cocked her head at him, widened her eyes. "I thought you were."

"Who told you that?"

She pursed her lips, looked down a second. "I got your name from the Pedersens. They said you were a retired cop who did some private investigating now."

He heard the baby murmur on the monitor in the kitchen.

"I am a retired detective, true," he said. "But mainly I just look after people's houses while they're on vacation, feed pets, let in the repairman."

But she didn't hear the second part, or didn't care to hear it.

"Then you *could* make some calls if you were so inclined? Like, you still know people, right? You could do that?"

And for some reason he found himself nodding. Maybe because it was just that she was so young and pretty, so trusting of him. Or maybe Maggie was right about his not being able to resist a damsel in distress. And this one was most definitely in distress, whether over this or something else, he didn't know. But there was something about Paula Carr that worried him. He wouldn't say she had that skittish self-loathing that he'd seen in so many abused women, but there was something—something tense, something anxious.

"I can pay you, of course. I have my own money." She stuck her chin out a little. "I wasn't always just a mom."

He gave her a smile, stopping short of reaching out to pat her hand, which is what he wanted to do. "Nothing wrong with being a mom. It's the most important job in the world."

"Yeah, that's what they say." There was more than a slight edge of bitterness to her words. Then she forced a smile. "Not that I don't love being a mom."

She seemed to drift inward a moment, got that long stare. He felt something inside him shift. He couldn't leave here without helping her, or at least trying.

"So I'll need a couple of things from you," said Jones, against his better judgment. He reached into his pocket and took out a notepad he carried with him everywhere.

She brightened a bit. "You'll do it?"

"I'll make some calls. Really, that's all I can do."

He flipped open the cover of his notebook, turned through the pages: a list for Home Depot, a license-plate number for a suspicious vehicle he'd seen on his block a couple of times, things Maggie needed from the store.

"And your fee?" she said.

"Don't worry about it," said Jones, lifting a hand. He didn't like it when people offered him money. It made him feel cheap. "If I incur expenses, you can pay me back. And I'll check with you before I incur expenses."

"Thank you, Mr. Cooper. Thank you *so* much."

"I'm going to need a full name, last known address and telephone number, and a Social, if you have it. Last employer, any known associates. That should give us a good start."

"Okay. I'll write down what I have." She got up quickly from the table and moved from the room.

"No promises, Mrs. Carr," he called after her.

"I know," she called back. "I know."

And as he put on his coat in the sunny dining room, he thought how natural it all was, this kind of thing. He hadn't realized how anxious he felt on the days that he had nothing to do, how the emptiness of the house and the list of mundane tasks weighed down upon him sometimes. For the first time in a year, maybe longer, he actually felt happy.

chapter eleven

About a mile from the school, down a winding rural road, there was an old graveyard surrounded by a low, crumbling stone wall. Jolie had taken Willow there before, and on that occasion they'd smoked a wrinkled half joint that Jolie had stolen from her brother's jacket. Hazy and giggling, they'd walked among the crooked tombstones looking at the faded names and sad inscriptions:

ANNABELLE LENIK, BELOVED DAUGHTER,
BORN 1912, DIED 1914.
SHE SINGS WITH THE ANGELS.

SAMUEL ABRAMS, DEVOTED HUSBAND, FATHER AND SON,
BORN 1918, DIED 1948.
HE DID HIS DUTY WITH HONOR AND LOVE.

And so many more—inscriptions so worn as to be unreadable, grave sites just masses of weeds. At first Willow found it more sad than eerie, since on that first day it was sunny and hot. Toward the north end, there was an old clapboard house, sagging on its frame, windows boarded, door padlocked. A sign on the door warned that the building was condemned.

"It's haunted," Jolie had told her on their last visit.

"Of course it is," said Willow.

"No, seriously. The night watchman killed himself there."

"Okay."

"Like, two years ago," Jolie said. Willow waited for the mischievous grin to erupt on her face, but it didn't. "They haven't been able to get anyone else to work here. That's why the place is such a mess."

Jolie had kicked a beer can at her feet; it clattered against one of the tilting stones. And just then Willow felt a chill on her neck.

"He shot himself. And the people who tried to take the job after him? They kept seeing him, walking around the graveyard looking for the pieces of his brain." She delivered the information with a grim seriousness.

"Give me a break," Willow said. But the image took hold, and then Jolie was smiling like a maniac. Willow had released an uneasy laugh.

"Give me a break," she'd said again. She'd wanted to leave then, her buzz abandoning her completely.

"It's messed up, isn't it?"

It turned out that Jolie hadn't just been trying to scare Willow. When Willow had returned home that night, Willow searched the story on Google. And everything Jolie had said was true, even down to the fact that no one would work there now and the historic site was falling into disrepair due to late-night vandals. Every time Willow drove by the little graveyard with her mother since then, she held her breath. The dead want to steal the air from your lungs. Hadn't someone told her that once?

Willow wasn't thrilled to be visiting again. She hadn't felt right about it the first time, even before Jolie's grim story. All those lives, reduced to grassy patches that stoned teenagers stumbled over, laughed about. It seemed disrespectful, arrogant, something her mother would frown at—as if their lives would amount to more.

But Jolie liked it there. And so, on this day, when she huddled up on the steps of the old house, Willow sat next to her. She didn't want Jolie to think she was afraid, a dork. Jolie formed harsh, cement judgments: Jayne was a slut; Chloe was an airhead; Ashley was a bitch. So far Jolie seemed to think Willow was fairly cool. Willow wanted to keep it that way.

Jolie produced a roach clip attached to the tail end of a joint and a lighter from her pocket. The air was just cold enough for Willow to feel it on her cheeks and nose, the tips of her fingers.

Jolie offered a shrug of apology. "This is all I could get off of him." Meaning her brother.

Willow didn't care. It took hardly anything for her to get high. Jolie lit up and drew a deep drag, then handed it off to Willow. All she tasted was burning paper, feeling the heat of it on her lips. But she held the smoke in, anyway—only a total dork couldn't hold it in. She felt the burn at the back of her throat. Instead of the warm feeling she wanted, she just started to feel nauseated and remembered that she'd had hardly any lunch. She and Jolie leaned against each other, and through the haze of smoke she saw a dark form moving up the street.

"That's him," Jolie said.

"Who?"

"The guy I wanted you to meet. Cole. He's a friend of my brother's."

Willow watched his slow, rangy approach. It made her think of the way wolves walked, long and easy but full of intent. As he approached, she listened to the song of a chickadee somewhere in the trees above her. Among the chattering, indistinct cries of the other birds, it sounded almost human, someone looking for attention.

"You like him?" Willow asked.

"Nah, not like that. Too young for me."

Willow knew that Jolie went out with older boys, some of them from other towns. Or so she said. She had a look about her, like she already knew things she shouldn't know. That she'd done things a girl her age shouldn't have done. And Willow thought maybe there was something sad about that, even though it made Jolie seem cool and worldly. *Her eyes are old,* Willow's mother had said. And even though Willow wasn't exactly sure what that meant, she sort of got the idea.

"I thought maybe *you* would like him," Jolie said. Her tone was wistful, a note off, as though she were giving something she wasn't sure she wanted to give.

"Why?"

Jolie didn't answer right away, looked down at her slim calves, stretching them out in front of her. She had a long run up the side of her black tights. Then, "Just a vibe I had."

Willow looked into Jolie's eyes, impossibly green in the afternoon sun. They both started laughing for no reason either of them could name.

"He's really nice," Jolie managed between peals of laughter. "Nice like you." The *you* came out in a strangled howl.

Willow doubled over, holding in her pee by crossing her legs. Was it okay to be nice? she wondered even in her hysteria. Was that a good thing? And was she, in fact, nice?

"What's so funny?"

He was a dark smudge against the sun, a shadow. Willow lifted her hand to block the light behind him. And she felt something, a seizing on her insides. If she had made up a boy, from her imagination designed someone who would most appeal to her—and she had done this, so she should know—Willow couldn't have created anyone more beautiful than Cole. She felt all her laughter dry up as she stared at him, and he returned her gaze with a shy smile.

"Are you guys stoned?" he asked.

Jolie pulled herself together long enough to sound indignant. "No," she said. "Of course not." Then she started laughing again.

Cole looked up at the sky. "I'm going to tell your brother that you've been stealing his weed."

"You wouldn't."

Willow could tell by the way Jolie grinned at him and he grinned back that he was already under her spell, dazzled by her very particular kind of magic. When his hazel eyes drifted back to Willow, she wished she were prettier, cooler, a tough chick like Jolie. But she wasn't. She was just Willow.

"Hey," he said. He offered his hand, which she thought was kind of dorky and also sweet. Well mannered, her mother would say. "I'm Cole."

She took his hand and found herself noticing the silver sky, and the gold-orange of the falling leaves, and how hard and dead the ground looked already, even though it wasn't really winter yet, as she glanced around everywhere but into his face.

"I'm Willow."

"That's a nice name."

She started to say something about how it was a family name, maybe her grandmother's, who was a famous dancer in the forties. But that wasn't true. So she clamped her mouth shut against the lie. Dr. Cooper, the shrink she'd been seeing since she moved to The Hollows, had advised, *When you feel that urge to say something that's not true, just try to be silent, observe the feelings that make you want to do this. And remember that you don't have to be anything other than who you are. That's enough.*

"Thanks." The silence that followed felt awkward. She wanted to fill it. "My mom named me after a character in a movie she loved." That was true. And *so* boring.

He nodded carefully. "Cool."

He dug his hands into his pockets, hunched up his shoulders. "So what do you guys want to do?"

"I don't know," said Jolie. "Willow doesn't have much time."

If Willow didn't know better, she'd think that Jolie wanted her to go. Willow pulled her cell phone from her pocket, looked at the time. There was still an hour.

"When I cut yesterday," Willow said, "I went home through the woods. I saw someone out there, digging a hole in the ground."

"You did?" said Jolie. She narrowed her eyes at Willow, gave her a little nudge. "Why didn't you tell me?"

"I'm telling you now."

She enjoyed the way they were both looking at her with keen interest as she spun the tale for them.

"My mom said he's a caver," she said. "There's another word for it, too."

"A spelunker?" said Cole.

"Right," said Willow. "That's it. He told my mother that there's an abandoned mine that might have a body in it. That's what he was looking for."

"I *told* you about the mines," said Jolie. Something in her tone was triumphant and resentful.

"So where was he digging?" asked Cole. "Do you remember?"

She wanted to take them there, to show them something and have it be amazing. But she didn't know if she had time to go there and get back for the late bus. If she was late getting home or had to call her mom, she didn't even *want* to know what was going to happen.

"I can't miss the bus," she said, even though it killed her. "Let's go tomorrow."

"I'll get you home before your mother misses you," said Cole. "I promise."

"He has a car," said Jolie. She gave a pragmatic nod in his direction. Mixed signals from her friend. Did Jolie want her to go or stay?

"A Beemer," Jolie went on. "His dad is rich."

A flush came up on Cole's pale skin. "It's an old car. He's letting me use it until my mom gets back. I'm just staying here with him until she comes home."

The way he said it had a charge; the flush deepened and spread down his jaw. Willow picked up on it right away. It was something bad.

"Where is she?" asked Willow. She immediately regretted asking. She should have kept her mouth shut.

He cleared his throat, looked at his shoes. "My mom is in Iraq. She's in the military."

Jolie narrowed her eyes again, pulled her head back a bit. "I didn't know *that*. How come no one tells me anything?"

"I'm telling you now," he said, echoing Willow. He gave Willow a smile; she knew it was just for her. Jolie started pouting then. Out of the corner of her eye, Willow saw the other girl slump a little.

"Wow," said Willow. "That must be really hard. Really scary."

She couldn't imagine her mom going somewhere like that, being so far away in such a bad and scary place—a place from which she might not return. The idea of this made her think she should go back to school and get on the bus home.

Cole shrugged. "My mom's a badass. Special Ops."

And right then—the way he said it, the way his eyes shifted—she knew he was lying. Takes one to know one. It made her feel sad for him, made her think that wherever his mom was, it was way worse than if she'd gone off to war.

"That's cool," she said. "When does she come home?"

He shook his head. "I don't know."

The wind picked up, and she thought about her mother again and about the promises Willow had made. She stood and shouldered her backpack. Jolie and Cole were both looking at her. They were different from her. Willow was old enough to know that. No one would notice if Jolie or Cole came home late; no one was keeping track of their whereabouts, calling the school librarian to make sure they were where they said they were. She wanted to be like them.

"Come on," she said. "I'm pretty sure I remember where he was digging."

"Really sure?" said Jolie, glancing back at the school. "It's getting late."

"Don't worry," said Cole. "I'll get her home in time."

Willow watched Jolie turn an odd gaze on Cole, while Cole kept his eyes on Willow.

There was a moment where she could have said, *I'll take you tomorrow. But I've gotta go.*

And she could have walked off, and neither of the other two would have stopped her. Jolie and Cole would have passed the afternoon together, because Willow could tell that Jolie liked Cole more than she wanted to admit and that she was sorry that she had invited Willow at all. All of them knew that going home was the right thing for Willow to do. She belonged with her mother, who loved her. And Jolie and Cole belonged to themselves, for whatever reason.

But that moment passed. Willow looked up at the darkening sky and the cute boy who was gazing at her with interest.

And instead of saying what she should have said, she said, "I remember where it is. It's not far. There's time."

She started walking, and the other two followed her into the woods.

chapter twelve

Jones was always getting text messages from his son on the cell phone that Maggie had bought and made him carry. The phone would issue a tone and shudder a little, and then the screen would light up: TEXT MESSAGE FROM RICKY. Often these missives were unintelligible to Jones, containing bizarre abbreviations and acronyms for which he had no reference. HIH, D? MISS U GYS. STDYING HRD. LOL. What did it mean?

What was more frustrating was the fact that at first he'd had no idea how to answer. He could not figure out how to use the keys on the phone to create a message or how to send it. So he usually just wound up calling his son back and talking to him, which was always awkward for reasons Jones didn't really understand. He always felt like he was rousing the kid from sleep, no matter what time of the day it was, or found that he really didn't have anything to say that seemed cool or interesting. Or later he'd send Ricky an e-mail if he couldn't reach him on the phone. But for some reason, uncomfortable phone conversations notwithstanding, Jones felt closer to Ricky now that he was away at school than he ever had when they'd lived under the same roof. Maybe it was just all the different ways they could communicate now. When it came to *talking* face-to-face with his son, he was still hopeless. But he could manage a fairly decent e-mail.

Today the message was, IZ DA RIDE RDY, D? CW!

Jones interpreted this to mean: IS THE RIDE READY, DAD? But CW? *Can't wait,* maybe? Jones didn't know for sure. But he managed to text the letter *y* for *yes* and send it the way Maggie had shown him. A few minutes later, he got a message back: SWEET! Jones laughed a little. Ricky was happy. Happy at school, happy to be coming home for the weekend. Something about that filled him with pride. Jones thought it was an accomplishment to be a happy person, a choice. He couldn't say he'd accomplished the same thing in his own life yet. Not that he was unhappy. Anyway, what did it even mean? To be happy?

He suspected that it was a new idea. That it was very young to think you had a right to happiness, that one might make decisions to that end. Certainly his mother was never happy, never took any steps to make herself happier. As for his father, he had no idea. He didn't know anything about the man who'd left when Jones was twelve; his father had been more or less absent before that.

Lately he and the good doctor had been talking a lot about Abigail, Jones's mother, who had been dead more than twenty years now. The smell of cigarette smoke could resurrect her; he could still hear her voice in his head. *That's what I love about you, Jones,* she'd say right before she'd say something nasty. The day before she had her stroke, she'd complained of a headache. He'd told her to take a Tylenol. She'd said, *That's what I love about you, Jones. You're the soul of compassion.* Possibly those were the last words she'd spoken to him. He couldn't remember. By that time he'd been so worn down by her incessant litany of problems, her endless list of symptoms and issues, her ever-increasing visits to doctors, that he'd barely registered the complaint—or the comment that followed his inadequate response.

"Do you feel bad about that?" the doctor had asked in a recent session.

"No," answered Jones. "Not really."

Dr. Dahl waited for him to go on. Jones shifted in his chair. "I mean, she'd had a symptom a day all my life. She had to be right sometime, didn't she? Eventually she was going to call it."

A slow blink from the doctor. Then, "I meant do you feel bad that those were the last words your mother ever spoke to you?"

The question landed like a shaming slap to the face. Jones felt heat rise up his neck. He found he couldn't answer.

"You spent the better part of your life caring for her," the doctor went on. "You've as much as admitted that you subordinated most of your ambitions and desires for your life because you felt compelled to stay with her."

"It wasn't just that."

"I know. We've talked about the other reasons. Sarah's death and how it haunted you, how you were swallowed by your guilt. But your mother was at least partially responsible for how you handled that situation as well. Let's not forget that you were just a kid. With the right guidance, you might have come through that incident better."

Jones found himself slowly nodding; he kept a neutral expression. *That incident.* It sounded so mild, like a fender bender or a baseball he'd thrown through a neighbor's window, some white lie he'd told. He'd watched a girl die and then left her body alone on a darkening spring night. Sarah's death, his cowardice, all the things that were never revealed until decades later, laid waste to his life, his career. *That incident.*

The doctor was still talking about Abigail.

"You were a good son. Did she ever thank you? Did she ever say anything kind to you?"

It took every inner resource available to maintain a calm façade. The depths were roiling, a potent brew of rage and fear. Jones couldn't even say why, just that it frightened him. He frightened himself. As a young man, he'd been buffeted by these feelings, resulting in bar fights (he'd punched a complete stranger right in the jaw for some comment Jones couldn't even remember), road-rage incidents (he'd all but rammed someone for cutting him off, got out of his car to find a teenage girl crying in the driver's seat), even problems on the job (as a young cop he'd been before civilian review twice for unnecessary force). Oddly, his recall of the particular incidents was fuzzy. But he remembered the feeling that preceded them. It was just like this. It was

Maggie who'd calmed him, who'd saved him from that anger and the damage he could have done.

"I don't think it was in her DNA. Gratitude." His tone had sounded so mild, so easy. "She never had anything but complaints for anyone. I didn't take it personally."

More pointed silence from the shrink.

"And what about your father?" Dr. Dahl continued eventually. Jones had found himself looking at the guy's shoes. Very expensive. He could tell. Probably Italian leather, hand-stitched. It was another mark against the doctor. Vanity. "We don't talk about him very much. It's an area that bears some exploring."

Jones had talked a little about the old man, the familiar story of the cop who drank too much, who was only home, it seemed, to raise his voice about whatever and then was gone for good.

"But there was more to him than that. You can't just cast him as a bad cliché in your life. Maybe you want to find out more about him. Understand him better. You were a detective, after all. You could probably find out anything you wanted to about him."

It took everything Jones had not to leap over the coffee table and start pummeling the guy.

"Our time is up." The doctor shut his notebook with a satisfied slap. "Think about it. We'll pick up here next week."

But they hadn't revisited the topic. In fact, that had been the point at which Jones had decided that therapy was maybe not for him. He had to admit that it was the point where he'd "shut down," as the doctor had accused.

Even now, sitting in the idling car, he felt that ugliness rise within. He realized that just the memory of his conversation with the doctor had him clutching the phone in his hand. His knuckles were white. He forced himself to relax. He still hadn't decided whether or not he was going to keep his next appointment with the doctor. After all, he had this case now. There wasn't an unlimited amount of time to do what Chuck had asked. Maybe he could just *reschedule* the appointment, not cancel it. Maggie didn't have to know.

The house looked as he'd expected it to somehow: brittle, lonely on a small hill. The trees had littered the lawn with dead leaves, and no one was making any effort to stay on top of it. A wind chime hung on the porch, silent in the still air. He got out of his car and walked up the drive. He didn't feel the kind of dread he thought he would. Instead he felt the buzz of curiosity that he'd always loved about the job.

He walked up onto the porch and was regarded by an enormous cat in the windowsill. The cat blinked at him with lazy disdain as Jones raised his fist and knocked three times, not seeing a doorbell. He waited a beat and then knocked again.

Her car was in the driveway, the beige Toyota he'd seen yesterday. If anyone told him after her visit that he'd have reason within the next twenty-four hours to knock on Eloise Montgomery's door, he wouldn't have believed it. He was about to knock again when he remembered his place. He wasn't a cop. She had a right not to talk to him if she didn't want to. But then she opened the door, looking even smaller without her winter coat.

"Hmm," she said. "I wouldn't have predicted this."

"Even psychics don't know everything."

"So true."

She stood back and held the door open for him. He would have expected her to keep him on the porch. He hadn't been very polite with her yesterday. Not polite at all.

"I'm not here about your predictions for my future," he said. He stepped over the threshold; it seemed colder inside than out.

"No?"

"No. I'm consulting for the Hollows PD. I have some questions about your involvement in the Marla Holt case."

She seemed to hold back a smile. "Just to be clear, Michael Holt hired Ray Muldune, who consulted me. My involvement is minimal. I didn't have anything on her until after I saw you yesterday."

Clean hardwood floors, a wall of old pictures, a tidy and sunny sitting room, furniture on feet, doilies on end tables. Just as he imagined it—but somehow not, somehow more run-down, more staid than he expected. She must make money on this racket. People had to pay a fortune to connect with the dead, to answer the questions no one else had been able to answer for them. Had he wanted to see more flash?

"I don't know what you mean by that," he said.

She walked down a long hallway past a staircase and motioned for him to follow. As he did, he noticed the shabby condition of the house—the chipped baseboards, hairline cracks in the wall, flooring in the kitchen coming up, a water stain in the ceiling. If he'd been her friend, her neighbor, or if he'd been taking care of her house while she was away, he'd offer to do the repairs or mention something that might have been beyond his abilities, suggest that she have it looked at. He'd already amassed a book of contacts—carpenters, painters, plumbers—people he knew and trusted, many of whom he'd known since childhood. But he reminded himself that she wasn't any of those things and that he should just keep his mouth shut.

In the kitchen he sat at the table where she motioned for him to do so. The first thing he noticed was the row of medications on the windowsill. The bottles were too far for him to see. But there were too many of them, maybe ten little plastic tubes of varying size with green caps. She sat across from him and blocked his line of sight.

"After I came to see you, I saw her running."

He tried to keep the smirk off his face. "Really. Just jogging by?"

She gave him a flat blink to show that she didn't find him amusing. "Running through the woods. Afraid. Someone chasing."

"Uh-huh," he said. A dismissive, condescending sound, Maggie would accuse. And she'd be right. "I was the detective on her case. It was one of my first. In fact, I'd say it was my first major case."

"And you never solved it. That must have stuck in your craw."

It hadn't, really. He'd never been one to let the job eat at him. He said as much. "Some people don't want to be found," he told her. "It was a lot easier to disappear in 1987 than it would be in 2011."

"What do you remember?" she asked. He was surprised by the question. After all, he'd come here to question *her*. But he didn't mind talking about it.

"I remember that she was a bombshell. Really gorgeous. Too gorgeous for The Hollows. Too gorgeous for Mack Holt. He said she ran off, that he'd suspected she had a boyfriend, and that one night the other guy came and picked her up in a black Mercedes. Holt said she had aspirations to act and model."

He remembered the small house, the boy lurking at the top of the stairs, the smell of cigarette smoke. Holt hadn't reported her missing. It had been a friend from her part-time job at the library.

Jones remembered that he'd thought it strange that she hadn't taken any of her jewelry. He wasn't sure why that struck him. But there had been a leather box filled with all manner of baubles, some cheap and gaudy, some tasteful and on the more expensive side. It would have been easy to grab the box and shove it into her suitcase. But she didn't. Most of her clothes still hung in the closets, organized by color. A few empty hangers waited. Her shoes were in a careful row, a couple of pairs clearly missing. Holt claimed that she'd packed a small bag and announced she was leaving, told him that she'd come back for the children when she was settled. She was sorry. But she couldn't live the life he wanted her to live, a hausfrau, the same day after day. She didn't even love him anymore. Holt had sent the baby girl to stay with his sister, who lived just a few miles away. He couldn't take care of her during the week, what with work and all. Michael was old enough to take care of himself after school. Some of this Jones remembered, some of it had come back to him as he read his own notes. He told all of it to Eloise.

Eloise shook her head.

"No," she said. "That's not how it was. There might have been a boyfriend, but he didn't come for her that night."

"So what happened, then?" He decided to play along. Why not?

"I don't know, but whatever it was had her running through the woods in the black of night. That rarely ends well."

"So she's dead."

"Maybe," she said. "Maybe not."

"But if you're seeing her, doesn't that mean she's gone, crossed over, whatever?"

She offered him a weak smile. "You're talking like a believer. You think I speak to dead people."

"Don't you?"

"I told you that I'm like a radio receiver. I pick up energies, frequencies. Sometimes images, sometimes sounds, sometimes I see people. Always women or girls. Always lost, usually wronged or injured in some way. Not always dead. One girl was found alive in a well. All I could hear was her breathing and the dripping water. She was in shock. Another was being kept in a shed; I just heard her screaming for help over and over. Finally someone else did, too."

"And so in the case of Marla Holt, last night you had a vision of her running through the woods. She was afraid."

"And sad, so terribly sad. I heard voices, too. Male voices shouting."

"More than one?"

"Yes. Don't ask me what they were calling. I couldn't make it out."

"Of course not," he said. Why would she have heard anything that could actually *help*?

"Did you know Marla Holt back then?" he asked. He already knew the answer. It was just his way of coming in soft.

She answered slowly, reluctant. "I baby-sat for Michael and Cara occasionally. Sometimes I cleaned for Marla. That's what I did back then to pay the mortgage. That was a couple of years before she disappeared."

"What do you remember about her?"

"I remember that she was very sweet, a loving mother. Not everyone takes to motherhood, you know. Not everyone likes it. She doted on those children, adored every minute she had with them. She'd call me so that she could get out and get some exercise. She was always very worried about her weight. But she was lovely. You were right. Too lovely for this place."

She said it with more gravity than Jones thought he had. He'd meant that Marla Holt could have been in Hollywood or New York City. Eloise didn't mean it that way.

"She did love her husband," Eloise went on. "At least she did when I knew her. She was always chatting on about him. I think he was some kind of scientist, had won awards, was a professor somewhere out of town."

"He was a geologist," said Jones. "Taught at the college."

"That's right," said Eloise. A little alarm chirped on her wristwatch. She squinted down at it, and then she got up to walk over to the windowsill. She selected one of the bottles and tapped out two pills, filled a glass with water, and swallowed them down.

"Everything all right?" asked Jones.

"Just getting old," said Eloise.

Jones didn't buy that that was all it was, but it wasn't any of his business. He watched her put the bottle back in its row and stare at it for a second.

"So is the Hollows PD reopening the case?" asked Eloise.

Jones shrugged. "I'm not sure what their plans are. Chuck Ferrigno asked me to go over my old files, talk to you and Ray Muldune, see if I remembered anything that asked for looking into again."

"And do you?"

"I remembered that I thought the neighbor was holding something back. I thought it was odd that Marla Holt didn't take her jewelry. It seemed like she'd devoted a lot of energy to collecting and organizing it. It would have been easy to take."

She raised her eyebrows at him. "More odd that she didn't take her children, don't you think? Women don't usually leave without their children."

"Unless there's a new boyfriend, not the stepfather kind."

He tilted back in his chair a bit. On the job he'd seen plenty of women abandon their children. Babies left at the police station, mothers sneaking out of the maternity ward at the hospital, once a baby left in an open locker at the bus station. Probably Abigail would have left him if she weren't so afraid of being alone, if she'd had anywhere at all to go. Not every woman was a natural mother; he was surprised more people didn't realize that.

"Why are you here, Mr. Cooper?"

"I told you."

"But that was only one reason." He'd give her points for intuition.

"Honestly? I'm wondering what your racket is."

She didn't say anything, just held his eyes with that neutral gaze she had. What would it take to really piss her off? Jones wondered. Maggie was always accusing him of trying to get a rise out of people. It wasn't true, generally speaking. He just couldn't stand the fake stuff. Anger was real. Sometimes he liked to see a person get her feathers ruffled, just to see who she really was.

"Yesterday you came to me out of nowhere with dire predictions about my pending doom, among other things. You told me, too, that I was getting a reputation, that people were going to start coming to me for more things. Later that day the Hollows PD asks me to consult on a cold case to which it turns out you and Ray Muldune are connected. I guess I'm not a big fan of coincidence."

She smiled at him, and it was genuinely warm. It lit up her face. He realized that she might have been pretty once, petite and dark-eyed, maybe even pixieish. She might have laughed and been happy in another life. But something had drained all the color from her, cored her out.

"I didn't expect to like you, Mr. Cooper," said Eloise.

In spite of himself, he smiled back. He didn't expect to like her, either. Maybe he did and maybe he didn't. He did find her interesting, though, a curiosity. The pieces of her didn't fit together. He didn't say any of those things.

She came to sit across from him again. "There's no racket. I just say what I see. People can take it or leave it. I get that it's not easy to accept things you can't understand. It took me a full decade to accept what was happening to me."

She gestured around her run-down kitchen, with the old appliances and peeling wallpaper. "As you can see, I'm not exactly living high on the hog."

"Money's not everything."

Eloise sighed then, rubbed her head with a slim thumb and forefinger.

"I think it's time for you to go. You want me to prove to you that I am what I say I am. Or you want to prove to yourself that I'm a fraud so that you don't have to fret about my predictions. But neither one of those things is going to happen today. I'll tell Ray you'll be calling on him. He probably has more to contribute to the conversation than I do."

She rose and walked down the hallway toward the door. After a second, Jones followed. He looked at the photos on the wall, two girls growing up in picture frames—babies in the bath, dance recitals, on horseback, prom. One blond, one dark. One favoring Eloise, one not. There were shots of a much younger Eloise. Jones found himself staring. The woman in the photographs—smiling, vibrant, bright-eyed— bore so little resemblance to the woman before him that out of context he would never have recognized her. There was a candid shot from her wedding; she wore a slim lace gown. Her smile was wide; her eyes were wet. She gripped her happy husband's arm with one hand, a bouquet of roses in the other. Whatever had happened between that frame and the present moment had sucked the life from her. It wasn't just age.

The woman patiently waiting for him at the door was a specter, a ghost by comparison. Jones found himself pushing back an eddy of sadness.

He joined her at the door. She wouldn't look at him, just stared outside.

"If you remember anything about Marla Holt . . ." he said. He let the sentence trail as he stepped onto the porch and took in the ill-kempt yard. He thought about offering to rake her leaves. They were going to kill the grass. And she was obviously not in any condition to be doing lawn work.

"I have a feeling we'll be staying in touch, Mr. Cooper."

"Call me Jones," he said.

"Good-bye, Jones."

He was about to turn back and say something about the leaves, but she had already quietly closed the door.

chapter thirteen

The baby was sleeping, and it was exactly one hour and thirty minutes before she had to leave to pick up Cammy from aftercare. Paula Carr made herself a cup of tea in the microwave, waiting in front of it so that she could turn it off before the buzzer sounded. Then she brought her cup with her to the couch, stepping over the toy truck she'd been meaning to move all day, and sat, releasing a deep breath.

This was the only time she had to think, to breathe and figure out what she was going to do. The rest of the day raced by in a blur of caregiving—breakfast, nursing, dropping off, grocery shopping, nursing, peekaboo, cleaning, nursing, starting dinner, picking up Cameron, snack, bath time, stories, on and on. It was absolutely manic from 6:00 A.M. until 7:30 P.M. She was firm on that bedtime for the little ones. Otherwise she wasn't even a person. Without that time she wondered when she'd ever be just Paula—not Claire and Cameron's mom, Kevin's wife, Cole's stepmother.

Kevin didn't even know that she left Cameron in school for aftercare sometimes. She paid for it out of the account he didn't know she had, either. As she looked out the window to her backyard, she felt a twinge of guilt about it, followed by a swell of anxiety. *What if he finds out?* The leaves were falling from the trees, and the sky was a flat gray.

For some reason, when they'd married, she hadn't closed her savings account right away. At the time there was only a little money in there, just under a thousand dollars. She kept meaning to take care of it, but then she just forgot. Did she *forget*? Or did some small part of her think it was a good idea to have a place, however small, that he didn't know about?

It was perhaps eighteen months into their marriage when she started contributing money to it, money her mother gave her for Christmas and birthdays, money she was able to skim off the household budget. Then, a few months ago, her aunt Janie had died. Janie knew. More than anyone else, Janie knew that something was not right with Paula.

"Are you all right, honey?" she'd ask at the end of their weekly conversations. "Is everything okay?"

"Of course, Janie. Don't be silly," Paula would answer. Because she really *wanted* things to be okay. And more than that, she really wanted everyone else to *think* things were okay. And not just okay, perfect. Perfect marriage. Perfect children. Perfect Paula. She couldn't bear it otherwise. She couldn't stand the thought of people feeling sorry for her, thinking she'd failed. Because, on some level, weren't people a little happier when things were not okay with other people? Didn't it make them feel a little superior, a little better about themselves?

Surprisingly, Kevin had allowed her to take Claire and Cammy to Janie's funeral. She'd figured he would insist on going, or demand that she go alone and come back right away. But he'd seemed to be eager for her to go, to take the kids, stay the weekend if she wanted. It wasn't until later that she'd understood why. He'd waved, smiling in the driveway, and she'd watched him get smaller and smaller in the rearview mirror. The baby started to cry.

"Why is she always crying?" Cammy wanted to know. He glanced over at his little sister with interest.

"She's just a baby," Paula said. "She doesn't have any words yet. She'll fall asleep soon."

"Why isn't Dad coming?" He had that tone. It was pre-meltdown. Wobbly, petulant. Cammy always wanted his dad, even though Kevin was absent, vacant most of the time with the kids, especially the baby.

She wondered why that was, that the parent who gave the least was wanted the most.

"He's busy this weekend," she said, forcing an easy brightness into her voice. "But Pop-Pop will be there to play with you."

"Why is Dad *always busy?*" Now he was staring out the window. When he frowned like that, right before he was about to cry, he looked just like his father.

She drove the two hours to her hometown, stayed with her parents for the first time in years. Kevin didn't like Paula's parents, so their family visits were always quick and perfunctory. They'd meet halfway between their homes, have lunch somewhere. Kevin didn't like her to spend too much time with them, even got angry when he thought she was talking to her mother on the phone too much.

And once she was with them for a while, in their home without Kevin, she understood why. When she was with her parents, she remembered what it was like to be loved and respected. She remembered what it was like not to have every move you made monitored, judged, and criticized. She remembered tenderness, intimacy. She remembered what it was like to be Paula. She expanded, stretched out her limbs from the box she'd been living in. She could breathe.

She'd wept at Janie's funeral, couldn't hide her sadness even though Cameron had his head on her lap and Claire slept on her shoulder. They didn't seem to mind her sorrow, even appeared to understand that it was natural and right to mourn someone's passing. They didn't wail and fuss. Cameron rubbed her leg, and Claire cooed; they were flanked by her mother and father. For the first time in years, crying for her aunt who'd suffered so, and crying for what she'd allowed her own life to become, she felt honest. She felt safe.

After the kids were in bed and her father was firmly ensconced in front of the television, Paula's mother told her about the money.

"Janie wanted you and the children to have what she could give. It's significant. A little over a hundred thousand dollars. But she didn't want it to go to Kevin. She was worried about you, Paula. And so am I."

She started to tell her mother that everything was fine, that she was worried for nothing, that Kevin was just a difficult man to understand but that he was good to them and all was well. Except the words wouldn't come. No more lies. But she didn't tell her mother the truth, not the whole truth. She didn't want her mother to be afraid. Paula just said she was very unhappy and didn't know what to do, but that the money would help her decide. She told her mother about the account that was in her maiden name. She promised he wouldn't find it.

"No one needs to be unhappy anymore, Paula." Her mother said it in a whisper, looking down at the table between them. She looked so sad, older and more tired than Paula ever thought of her.

"What do you mean, Mom?"

"I just mean that you have a *right* to be happy. And if someone is making you unhappy, you have a right to leave. This idea that we hold on to miserable marriages that erode our lives? It's old-school. Life is too short."

Paula was surprised by this; she'd have expected her mother to suggest couples therapy, to try to make it work for the good of the children, something like that.

"You're happy with Dad, aren't you, Mom?" she asked. She had always thought of her parents as being well suited, having a good marriage. It was important to her suddenly that this, too, wasn't some illusion she'd maintained for herself. "You're happy, right?"

Her mother patted Paula's hand. "Happy enough, dear."

Happy enough.

Over the monitor, Paula heard Claire coo. Paula held her breath, waiting for the cry that would herald the early end of nap time. But then she heard the baby sigh, her breathing return to its deep sleep rhythm. Paula felt her shoulders relax. It was a funny, impossible little trap of nature, motherhood. It muddled your brain with floods of hormones and sleep deprivation, kept you constantly busy tending to a million needs, had you forever thinking about the care of others. You could disappear into motherhood, forget completely that once upon a time you were an athlete, a graduate student, that you had ambitions to go into politics, change the world. That once upon a time you wanted to write. And even though motherhood wiped all that away like a cosmic eraser over the chalkboard of your life, it gave you something else—this crazy, blissful, adoring love that splits you open and redefines you from the inside out. Most of the time, in your mommy-addled brain, it seems like a fair enough trade-off. And maybe under normal circumstances it is, if you're happily married, safe in your home. The kids aren't small forever. There's time to work later, when they're both in school. And really, what could be more important and fulfilling than raising kids well?

But that wasn't the problem, of course. Paula wasn't worried about changing the world anymore. Her M.B.A. seemed more like a waste of time and money, something she did to satisfy her own hunger for accomplishment. Kevin had pushed her into it when they were dating. And since he was her boss, too, it had seemed like good advice. He'd implied that it would help when he was campaigning for her to become a partner in the consulting firm he'd formed with a bunch of his buddies from college. At the time business was booming. But now some of the partners were in personal bankruptcy. Major clients had sent their work to India. The company was struggling. And Paula hadn't even pretended to work for them since Claire was born, even though ostensibly there was a job for her in human resources and recruiting when she wanted it. Every once in a while, she did some paperwork for Kevin or made calls on overdue invoices when the baby was sleeping. But all the employees had been laid off. Only the partners remained. She couldn't care less about the company or about her stalled professional life. Those were luxury problems. What she cared about was that there was something wrong with Kevin. Something very, very wrong.

When did it happen? She often found herself wondering. She wanted a moment to point to, a reason. But if she was honest, the signs were there long before they married. They were so subtle, so easily explained away in the blush of early love. At least that's what she told herself. How he always needed to plan everything—first their dates and vacations. It was romantic, wasn't it? Until she realized that she didn't have much to say about anything, even what movie they went to see. Then he started to buy her clothes—gorgeous, expensive clothes. Which was lovely, until she realized he didn't want her to wear her old clothes anymore. Until he suggested that she stop eating bread to fit into a size six instead of size eight. *You're beautiful. I love you. I just want to help you be perfect.* Even when her friends expressed shock and dismay at this type of attitude, she blew it off. It *would* be nice to be a size six for her wedding day. And who needs bread, anyway?

And then her friends weren't good enough. If she encouraged him to see her friends with her as a couple, he'd have too much to drink and say the most awful things to them. *You'd be pretty if you weren't so overweight, Katie. Ever think about joining a gym? . . . You should be proud of your accomplishments, Judy. It's just too bad someone else raised your kids.* If she tried to see them alone, there would be an awful fight when she got home. Slowly her friendships started to drift. Then, suddenly, her family was white trash; they needed to minimize contact. *Your cousin's in jail, for God's sake. Do you want your kids to grow up like that?*

It wasn't until they'd been married awhile, after she'd had the two children he'd demanded they have (two was the perfect number) and she was a slave to the house and the kids she loved more than her own life, that things started to get really bad. It wasn't until she was well and truly trapped that things started to get *scary*.

As of today she hadn't worked out of the home in five years. Kevin had refused to staff her with a client while she was pregnant, relegating her to office work for the company. *You need your rest.* She still drew a salary from the company, which was direct-deposited into an account for which she didn't have a checkbook or an ATM card. He gave her an allowance for the house and the kids.

It was only after Janie died last year that she forced herself to look at what she'd allowed to happen. How she'd gone from an educated, accomplished woman, making six figures before she went to work for Kevin, to a housewife who didn't even have access to the family bank account, whose phone calls to her mother were being tracked by her husband. She was a woman whose whole body flooded with dread when she heard the garage door open at night. She lived in fear of his words, his punishments. And the funny thing was that he rarely raised his voice, almost never put his hands on her. Almost never.

She'd stood up to him once. She had. It was when he told her that he didn't want her to talk to her mother more than once a week. She'd paid him lip service, to avoid a fight in front of the children. But then she'd just ignored his directive. In fact, she'd talked to her mother more often. The night he'd got the bill, he'd come home after the children were sleeping. He'd come in quietly and put the bill on the kitchen counter. He'd reminded her how in college she'd had problems with depression. She'd been in therapy, taken medication. She'd confided in him early in their relationship that she'd felt so much pressure she'd been briefly suicidal.

"That type of mental illness doesn't just go away, Paula. It can come back. You could be a danger to yourself. Even to the children."

What was he saying? That he'd use her history to try to take her children away from her? Or was it even worse than that? Was he threatening to hurt her? To hurt Claire and Cameron? It was such a mind-bending moment that she was speechless with fear and confusion. He slept in his home office that night and left the next morning for work without a word. Why didn't she leave that day? She couldn't answer that question—fear, denial, inertia. It was some insidious combination of all those things.

She asked her mother to call her every day instead. Her mother complied and didn't ask why.

Wasn't there some belief about how if you drop a frog into boiling water, it will jump right out? But if you put it in cold water and turn up the heat gradually, it will allow itself to slowly cook to death? But she wasn't dead yet. She was going to get them all out of the pot somehow.

Before Cole showed up, she'd had it all figured out. Once a year Kevin went away to meet with the other partners at a golf resort in Florida. He'd be gone for four days and come back either elated or in a deep funk depending on how things had gone, what the projections for the year were, whether or not they were going to get bonuses. Her plan was to take the kids and go to her parents' as soon as Kevin left. She was going to tell them everything, the whole truth about the man she'd married. Then she was going to take the children and go far away. She was going to start over and pray he never found them. She couldn't just go to her mom and dad and stay with them. It wouldn't work; he'd come after her. There'd be an ugly battle for the children in the very best case. But more than that, she wasn't sure what he was capable of, what he might do to her, the kids, even her parents. She just didn't know anymore.

That trip was three weeks away. Unless she could find Cole's mother and get him out of the house, she didn't know what she was going to do. She couldn't leave Cole alone with Kevin to bear the fallout of their leaving. But she couldn't take him, either. He wasn't her son, first of all. And he worshipped Kevin like a god.

That was why she'd contacted Jones Cooper. Maybe he could find Cole's mother and Paula could call her, implore her to come back for Cole. If anyone else knew what Kevin was, it must be her.

It was all Paula could do not to throw herself onto Jones Cooper's lap and confess everything to him and ask for his help. He seemed so strong and safe, so *good*. But she couldn't do that. People talk; she couldn't have word getting out, possibly getting back to Kevin. In a small town like The Hollows, there are no secrets once you've opened your mouth. Gossip was viral, infectious. It couldn't help but spread.

The clock was ticking, she knew that. She knew that the company was about to go under. She knew that her husband's moods were growing darker. She'd guessed at his password and logged in to his home computer and had been shocked by the things she'd found there. Kevin was not the man she thought he was. Maybe he never had been. He'd been visiting ugly, hard-core porn sites, guns-and-ammo sites. He'd been visiting sites about postpartum psychosis. She learned that they were drowning in debt. And then Paula found an e-mail correspondence between him and another woman. He was having an affair. The messages were filled with lies about Paula, that she didn't take care of the kids, that she was having an affair, that she was mentally unstable, an alcoholic. It made her wonder about everything he'd told her about Cole's mother, the other women he'd been with before her.

Then last week she took his car to be washed. While she was waiting in line, she started picking up the trash he just left on the floor of the car. She didn't want the people who washed it to think that *she* was a slob who ate nothing but fast food and then dumped the wrappers and empty cups, leaving them littered about the interior. She felt something under the passenger seat and pulled out a black canvas bag. She unzipped it and saw a plastic case inside. Somehow she knew what it was before she opened it. Sitting there, she opened the lid and saw the gun. She felt as if someone had sucked all the air out of the car.

She slammed the case shut and jumped when the attendant knocked on the window. She smiled at him, told him she wanted the Super Wash, and asked him how long it would take. She exited the vehicle with the bag in her hand. Still smiling, she walked inside and paid the clerk. She went over to the window and watched the car get lathered and rinsed, sprayed with wax, and buffed. She wished there were a car wash for her life, something she could enter on a conveyor belt, something that would wash away everything that was dirty and ugly about her life. Where did he get this gun? Why was it in the car? Should she put it back? Should she get rid of it? What would he do if he knew she'd found it and disposed of it? It was a trap, a lose-lose scenario. She put the gun back where she'd found it and drove home. Why hadn't she left that Monday when he went to work? She didn't know the answer to that, either.

What she found so odd about the situation she was in was that on the surface they must seem so normal. She was chitchatting with people at school when she dropped off Cammy and picked him up. She made her daily posts on Facebook, sharing pictures of the family and their various activities. Cammy on his scooter, Claire making a big mess with her mashed sweet potatoes. *Fake*book, a place where people could project the image that they wanted, show only the things they wanted everyone to see, hiding every dark and sad thing in their hearts and in their lives. Or maybe it was just her.

The neighbors must see the handsome Kevin going off to work every morning and coming home in the evenings, bringing in groceries or takeout, grabbing the mail from the box. Saturday night was their date night. They got dressed up and went out to the nicest restaurants, parties in the neighborhood, even into the city. But sometimes on those nights, Kevin wouldn't say a word, checking his BlackBerry while she yammered away like an idiot over dinner. Or he'd dote on her at parties, then rail at her all the way home about how she ate too much or laughed too loud or how her dress was too tight, and was she ever going to lose that baby weight?

It was scary how much people didn't know about one another. For example, no one knew or even suspected that Paula and her children had become a burden, an inconvenience to Kevin and the fantasy he was creating in his mind about his new girlfriend. And that Paula had better find a way to get herself and her children far, far from him and quickly. Otherwise . . . well, she just didn't know what her husband was capable of doing. She just didn't know.

On the monitor, Paula heard Claire start to fuss. She looked at the clock and saw that an hour had passed. It was time already to nurse the baby, pack her up, and go get Cammy. How did the hours, *the days,* pass so quickly? It seemed like some kind of trick. She always had such big plans for nap time. But she so often just found herself blanking out, collapsing into the silence.

When she turned to go upstairs, she saw him standing there. How long had he been standing there like that?

"Kevin," she said. She forced a smile. "You scared me."

"Where are the kids?"

Her hands were shaking suddenly, so she stuffed them into her pockets. It was funny how your body picked up signals that your mind wanted to ignore. She hated herself for feeling as afraid as she did right now.

"Cole's out with friends." She hated the sound of her own voice, so falsely light; the smile she kept plastered on her face actually ached. "Claire's upstairs, just waking from her nap. And Cammy's still at school."

Kevin glanced at the clock. "It's almost four."

"He asked for aftercare today," she said. She was too quick to answer. It sounded like the lie that it was. "So he could play with Nick. I was just heading out to get him."

"Really? Because it looked to me like you were just sitting around on your ass. I'd think you'd use your free time to work out."

Paula didn't say anything, bit back the flood of pure hatred that seemed to come up from her gut and coat the back of her throat with acid. Once upon a time, before they were married, she used to look at him and think how lucky she was. He was so successful, so handsome and charming. She used to think she loved him. But maybe she never did. She didn't know who he was; he'd presented a false image of himself, and she'd been seduced by that. She never suspected how cold his heart was.

She tried to move past him, but he put an arm up to block her way to the stairs. She heard Claire start to cry. Her wails came staticky and broken up over the monitor that was at the end of its range.

"She's crying," Paula said.

"You think I can't hear that? Go turn that thing off."

Her heart was pumping now, adrenaline racing through her system. But she did as she was told. She could still hear Claire crying upstairs, sounding so far away. Her body started to tingle the way it did when one of her kids cried; her breasts were engorged and starting to leak. It was time to nurse. She was glad she'd remembered to put the pads in her bra, so that she didn't soak through her shirt in front of Kevin.

"What are you doing home?" Paula asked.

She wanted to go to Claire, but she stayed where she was. On the bar that separated the great room from the kitchen lay a hammer. She'd been trying to hang a few framed pictures of the kids earlier—there were no photos anywhere. She'd just never gotten around to it. No, that wasn't the reason. By the time they'd moved into this big house that they couldn't afford, she knew they weren't a real family. She couldn't bear the idea of hanging photos that were so fake as to be laughable. But one of her friends, one of her *mom* friends, had made a comment. *You're so smart not to have your walls cluttered with photos! I can't walk an inch in my house without seeing one of their faces!* Which was basically just a veiled way to say she thought it was strange.

"I got an interesting call today," said Kevin.

"From who?"

From where he was standing by the room exit, she knew he couldn't see the bar area. She put her hand on the edge.

"The bank. Your old bank."

She raised her eyebrows. "Oh, really?" But she felt her whole middle bottom out.

"Seems like there's some money there you failed to mention."

She thought about lying, about doing some song and dance. But she decided against it. She just kept her mouth shut, offered a quick shrug. Upstairs, Claire was howling now. She wasn't used to waiting for her mom.

His expression softened then.

"I know that things haven't been great between us, Paula. But how could you keep that from me?" He'd modulated his voice to sound sweet and pleading. She could actually see him tearing up. But those eyes were dead. The game was up; she knew that.

She'd been doing some reading. The sociopath has no real feelings. He does not experience guilt or remorse, love or empathy. He knows only his own needs and goals. But he's a skilled mimic, a brilliant actor. And as easily as sociopaths hide in plain sight, they all have one thing in common: the pity play. When confronted or discovered, they will always try to make you feel sorry for them in order to control you. Paula had read about this in her research. She was fairly sure that's what her husband was. But it wasn't until this moment that she dared to admit it.

"I've given you everything," he said. He took a step forward; she took one back. "I've worked so hard for us. But it hasn't been enough. I've failed. The business is going under. We're nearing personal bankruptcy."

She knew all this. She stayed silent.

"The truth is, baby, we need that money. It could save us."

He couldn't get to it without her. She was certain of that. Husband or not, his name was not on her account, and he did not have access to that money. Otherwise there would be no reason for this show. He'd just have taken it. And if she didn't sign that money over to him, there was only one other way for him to get it. She moved her hand so that now it was resting on the hammer.

"I'm sorry, Kevin," she said. "It was Janie's, and she just wanted me and the kids to have it. That money belongs to my family."

He released a sad little laugh. "But *I'm* your family."

A couple of months ago, he might have been able to manipulate her this way. But not today.

"I know about the debt," she said. "I also know about your affair. I know about the lies you've been telling her about me."

She saw something flash across his face. It was rage. This was the other thing about sociopaths. You are advised not to confront their fantasies—because sociopaths will do anything necessary to protect their self-narrative. All the experts agree that you must get as far away as possible, sever all contact, protect yourself at all costs. Upstairs, Claire had gone quiet. Paula could hear just a miserable whimper. Claire was wet and hungry. Paula needed to get Cameron from school. In another minute she would be late to get her boy. She'd never once been late to pick him up. The thought of him standing there waiting made her sick.

"I don't know what you're talking about," Kevin said. His tone was cloying, his voice just a whisper. "Are you okay, honey? What's wrong?"

He was coming toward her. She tightened her grip on the hammer. And then she saw him pull that gun from his waist. The moment expanded. She was aware of her own breath, the beating of her heart. For a crazy split second, she thought about that game—rock, paper, scissors. They were playing a different version: gun, hammer, toy truck.

She'd been stepping over that little blue truck all day, having added it to her mental model of the room. She'd stepped over it with the laundry basket, the cup of tea. And every time she did, she thought, *I should really pick that up. Someone's going to step on that and go flying.* But she never did get around to doing that.

chapter fourteen

"How's Willow?"

How dare you even ask? is what Bethany wanted to say but didn't. Enduring her ex-husband's weekly guilt call was almost more than she could take this afternoon. She still felt off center after her meeting with Henry Ivy, was regretting her decision to let Willow stay after school to study at the library. She kept watching the clock. She was tempted to call the library again. But she didn't want to be that kind of mom. Once was careful. Twice was paranoid. The late bus would pull up at 4:35. She couldn't quite see it from the house, but she could hear it if the television was off, if she was listening for it. And today she was listening for it.

"She's adjusting."

"Not getting into trouble?"

"It's not really your problem anymore if she is." She couldn't keep the sharp edge from her tone. It crept in against her will, a thug pulling a switchblade, not afraid to use it. Usually he'd snap back and the conversation would turn into an alley fight, dirty and mean, ending abruptly. They'd try again next week, for Willow's sake. But he surprised her this time, by waiting a beat before answering.

"I still care, Bethany. About you. About Willow. Maybe it doesn't seem like it. But I do."

She felt her core melt a bit. And then she got it. What's-her-face—Miss 34DD—had taken a walk. She'd picked up on the fact that all the money and buff good looks in the world didn't make up for every-thing Richard was lacking. Richard Coben looked damn good—even pushing sixty, he was in better shape than most men half his age. That head of prematurely gray hair was exotic, sophisticated. Those icy blue eyes bored into you, seemed to see every romantic dream you ever had. The opening act was spectacular—roses and candlelight, surprise trips to Paris. The girls swooned—Bethany included. But they didn't stay around very long.

"Brenda left?" she asked. They'd known each other too long to beat around the bush.

She heard him sigh. "Yeah. Things didn't work out."

He wasn't a bad man. He wasn't even a dog, really. He was shallow and unfaithful, sure. Work-obsessed, self-involved. But his fatal flaw was that he didn't keep his promises, his vows. He couldn't follow through on the big things. This was disappointing to the girlfriends, painful for the wife, crushing for the child.

Look at this apartment, that ring on your finger, that trip we just took to St. Lucia. Isn't that enough?

It's not nearly enough. It means nothing at all. We don't want or need any of those things. We just want you.

He'd never understood that, still couldn't by the sound of it.

"You know what she called me?" he said. "She said I was an emotional castrato."

"Wow," said Bethany. She was *so* glad she didn't have to keep the smile off her face. "That's a big concept for someone like Brenda. You met her in Vegas, right? Cocktail waitress?"

"Very funny, Beth. And she was a dancer. Not a stripper. A showgirl."

"Oh, my mistake." She walked over to the picture window and looked down over the tree cover. She *could* see the road in patches now that the trees were losing their leaves. No bus yet.

"You have to be very athletic to do that. She's very talented," Richard was saying. She'd heard this tone of petulant defense before. It used to enrage her. Now she just found it sad.

"I'm sure," she said. "And flexible."

She liked Richard much better now that they weren't married, now that he couldn't hurt her anymore. Sometimes, like now, she even found him amusing. She wouldn't say he was an emotional castrato, exactly. That was a bit harsh, if extremely funny. He was more an emotional toddler, clumsy and unaware of himself, seeking to put every shiny, pretty thing in his mouth, ignorant of consequences. No surprise, really, if you met his parents. Joan, his mother, was an overpraising, enabling parent and a doormat of a wife. His father, Richard Sr., acclaimed cardiac surgeon, was a demanding taskmaster, highly critical and distant. He was used to putting his hands inside an open chest cavity and massaging the heart back to life, never missed an opportunity to tell you that. Talk about a God complex. Honestly, Richard could have turned out a lot worse. If he were a sociopath, he might have been a serial killer instead of a plastic surgeon.

"It's not funny, Beth."

"No, I know. I'm sorry."

"Why does everyone leave me?"

"Oh, Rich."

It was true. She *had* left him, but only because he'd given her no choice. Infidelity was a deal breaker, especially when you have a daughter. She couldn't stand to have Willow think that was okay. Plus, he was a terrible stepfather—absent, forever failing to keep promises big and small. Why didn't he know that?

Bethany wished—if *wishing* was the right word for a desire that felt like a burning pain in your chest—that Willow had known her real father. How those two would have loved each other. How different things would have been for her and Willow. She felt a decade of grief and disappointment claw its way up her throat. She couldn't open her mouth, didn't trust her voice. There was a moment of silence between them where she imagined he remembered every harsh word and re-crimination she'd ever hurled at him.

Then, "Are you okay, Beth?"

"I'm okay," she whispered. "I am."

"Can I come see Willow this weekend? I miss you guys."

"Yeah, maybe." She'd ask Willow. It might cheer her up a bit. "I'll call you tomorrow."

She heard the rumble and hiss of the bus, even saw the bright yellow roof through the trees. Richard was going on about how he could come up, bring some stuff they liked from Zabar's. They'd walk in the woods, have dinner in. He wouldn't stay the night, of course. Richard couldn't stand to be alone. They'd see a lot of him until he found another girlfriend. She put up with it because it was important for Willow to see him. He was the only father she'd ever known. Bethany was half listening to him, as she listened to the bus stop in front of the drive. Then it rumbled on its way.

"The bus just dropped Willow off. I'm going to go meet her on the drive so she doesn't have to walk alone. I'll call you tomorrow."

Bethany jogged down the front steps and stepped onto the gravel. It was a long, winding drive. And if she hadn't been on the phone, she'd have driven the Land Cruiser down a few minutes before the bus arrived to wait for Willow. But the walk would do her good. She figured she'd run into her daughter about halfway. But she didn't. She kept walking, hearing in the distance the sound of girls laughing. Willow had probably stopped to chat with the twins who lived on the next lot. Their homes were separated by acres, but the driveway entrances and mailboxes stood side by side. A few neighborhood kids had the same stop—Willow, the twins Madison and Skylar, the painter's son Carlos, and one other girl named Amy or Ava, something like that.

When she reached the street, Madison (or maybe Skylar—who

could tell those girls apart?) and the other girl were chatting and giggling. "He's such a dork. I can't believe it," she heard one of them say. Their backs were to her, so she didn't know which one.

"Hi, girls."

"Hi, Mrs. Graves," they said almost in unison. Madison offered a sweet smile. The other girl looked shyly at the ground. No Willow.

Bethany found herself glancing back up the drive, though of course there was no possibility she could have missed Willow on the way down.

"Wasn't Willow on the bus?" she asked. She tried to keep her voice light, but already she could hear the blood start to rush in her ears.

"No. Uh-huh," said Madison, all blond curls and pink cheeks, wide brown eyes. "I didn't see her when we lined up, either."

Madison might have said something else, but Bethany didn't hear. She was already making her way back up the drive. She was on autopilot as she walked back into the house and grabbed her bag, her cell phone. In the driver's seat, she called her daughter but only got her voice mail. She pulled out of the driveway in the now-familiar trance of anger undercut by worry and headed for the school.

The first time Bethany headed out like this, looking for her daughter, had been in New York City. It was eight o'clock on a winter night. Bethany had asked Richard to leave by then, and she and Willow had been living alone for almost a month. It had all started with that goddamn Britney Spears concert. The lies, the mess that followed—it all began there.

Today, as she drove into the nearly empty school parking lot, she tried not to panic. There were still lights on in the school. She pulled her car over in front of the double-door entrance and got out, phone clutched in her hand. Hollows High was every East Coast public school—a low, long, concrete, flat-roofed structure. And when she pushed inside, a thousand sense memories competed for her attention.

She'd hated high school as much as Willow did, had been every bit as much the fish out of water.

Willow lies because she doesn't feel like who she is inside is enough for her peers. Dr. Cooper had told her this in their last discussion about Willow. Bethany understood; she'd felt the same way as a kid. But she'd channeled that energy into writing.

But I love her so much. She's always been enough for me. She knows that.

It's always our instinct to feel like we've failed when our kids are suffering. But it's not always our fault. She has had experiences that you haven't had any control over. And she chose her own way to deal with them.

Wasn't that just postmodern psychobabble, though? Parents were responsible for their kids, plain and simple. When they were struggling, chances are it had something to do with you. True, it wasn't her fault that Willow's father had died. But she'd chosen badly with Richard. And their marriage hadn't been a happy one. The truth was that Bethany hadn't been really happy for one reason or another for most of Willow's life. That had an impact; it must.

She was thinking this as she walked past the rows of green lockers over the freckled vinyl floors to the office. The lights were on, but the desks sat empty; computer screens were dark.

"Hello?" she said.

"Hello?" answered a male voice from down the hall. A moment later Henry Ivy came walking out. Bethany felt herself blush. He looked so . . . earnest. She hated for him to know how quickly Willow had broken her promises. But it couldn't be helped.

"Willow didn't come home on the late bus."

She didn't want to sound like she was freaking out, but she really was. Her stomach was a mess; she was close to tears.

She remembered how she felt when she'd called Evelyn Coates—was it more than a year ago now?—looking for Willow, who was supposed to be watching movies at the Coateses' Tribeca loft and spending the night.

"Beth," Evelyn had said. She still could recall the immediate pitch of worry she heard in the other woman's tone. "Willow's not here. Zoë's sitting on the couch in front of me watching television."

In that moment she felt a flash of fear and sadness, but also, dare she admit it, hatred for Evelyn and her perfect marriage, her perfect life, her perfect child who was exactly where she was supposed to be.

She'd hopped a cab, and less than half an hour later she was standing in the foyer of the multimillion-dollar loft listening to Zoë confess that Willow had a boyfriend, someone older that she'd met at the Britney Spears concert. Zoë hadn't wanted to lie, but she didn't want her friend to get in trouble, either. So she'd told Willow she'd cover for her.

"But Willow never went to the concert," Bethany had stammered, unthinking. "I don't understand."

"Yes she did. Didn't she?"

"No," Bethany said, still not realizing what she was doing. "Her father got hung up at work and couldn't take her."

More than anything she remembered that look on Evelyn's face—that drawn look of sympathy and concern, really just a mask covering malicious glee, superiority, and gratitude that she wasn't Bethany Graves right now.

"Where was she supposed to be tonight, Zoë? Is she with him right now?"

Zoë shrugged. "I don't know. If she lied about the concert, then she lied about the boy, too. So I don't know where she is."

Bethany realized then that she'd been the one to blow Willow's cover, to unearth whatever lies she'd been telling her friends. As soon as she left, Zoë would be texting, Facebooking, and e-mailing all their shared friends to expose Willow's deceit.

"Where did she *say* she was going?"

"Just out with him. She didn't say where."

"And then she was going to come here?"

Zoë looked down at the floor and shook her head.

"What? She was going to spend the night with *some boy* and come home in the morning?" Bethany didn't like the shrill tone in her own voice, but panic was getting the better of her. Where did her thirteen-year-old daughter plan to spend the night if not at home and not at her friend's loft? And how could Bethany be so ignorant of the fact that Willow was a stone-cold liar?

Another shrug from Zoë. "I'm sorry, Mrs. Graves."

Bethany felt the ground beneath her feet fall away.

Kind of how she felt now standing before Henry Ivy, who had so sweetly tried to help Willow, to cut her a break. "She told me she wanted to stay late to study," Bethany said. "I called the librarian, who confirmed she was there."

"Well, let's go check with Mrs. Teaford," said Mr. Ivy. Just the sound of his voice was soothing. "The library is open until five. Maybe Willow's there, lost track of time."

"Maybe," said Bethany. She felt a surge of hope, which quickly passed as they entered the library. The study tables at the front of the room were empty. The lights over the stacks were dark. Mrs. Teaford looked up from her computer screen; her coat was on, and her bags were sitting beside her. She was ready to go home for the night.

"Oh, Willow *was* here. I'm not sure when she left. Jolie Marsh was with her. Usually they're trouble together, have to be separated. But they were being quiet, had their textbooks open. I didn't notice them get up."

"Don't they need a pass to leave the library?" asked Bethany.

"Not after hours." Mrs. Teaford gave Bethany a politely pitying smile. It was a look Bethany had seen before from school officials, reserved for parents who clearly didn't have control over their children, a mask of empathy that barely concealed disdain.

Out in the hallway, Bethany tried Willow again from her cell phone. Again just voice mail. This bothered her more than anything, because Willow knew she was skating on thin ice with that phone. Bethany had given it back after the incident in the woods, even after threatening to take it away, mainly because she didn't want *not* to be able to reach Willow. But the rule was if Bethany ever couldn't reach her on that phone, the phone would be confiscated indefinitely. Why wasn't she answering? Why hadn't she called? Bethany knew there were dead zones in The Hollows, that cell service was often spotty. But it was almost five. Willow must know that Bethany was sick with worry; by now she would have called with some lame excuse.

"Okay," said Henry. "Let's try to think a second. Where might Willow go? I know that some of the kids like to hang out at the old graveyard up the road."

Bethany remembered Willow mentioning it, that it had scared her a little. She didn't think Willow would go there again. She said as much.

"Well, let's just take a quick ride up there and see."

She hit "send" on the phone again. As she did, she watched a man approach them. He cut a big, dark figure in the hallway, seemed to dominate the space with a slow and easy approach. When he reached them, Bethany thought he looked familiar, but she couldn't place him.

"Hey, Henry," he said, extending a hand.

"Good to see you, Jones," Henry said. He took the other man's hand and patted him on the back in one familiar gesture. "We've got an issue here. I know you need to talk, but can it wait a minute?"

"Sure. Anything I can do?"

Jones Cooper, Bethany realized then, Dr. Cooper's husband. Bethany had seen him working around the yard when she brought Willow for her appointments.

Henry introduced them. She liked his handshake, his barn jacket, and his barrel chest. He had a nice face. *Rugged* was the word that came to mind. *Reliable*.

"We're looking for a couple of kids," said Henry. "Willow Graves didn't come home on the late bus."

She saw a shadow of something cross Jones Cooper's face. It made her own heart start to pound.

"We were thinking of checking out the old graveyard," Henry said. "Just going to head up that way now."

Jones pointed toward the door. "My truck's right outside. I can take a quick run up there with you."

The graveyard was a tired, dilapidated little place, and Bethany could see immediately why Willow hadn't liked it, not that anyone sane had much of an affinity for graveyards. It looked lonely and abandoned, a resting place for the forgotten dead. As they exited their vehicles—Bethany and Henry followed in her car behind Jones Cooper—she could see that the ground was littered with beer bottles and cigarette butts.

"They haven't been able to get anyone to do the job of caretaker here," Henry said. He stopped and peered at a plaque pushed into the stone wall. It was so weathered and calcified as to be unreadable. "It's a historic site. Shame that it's fallen to disrepair."

Fallen to disrepair. As though everything tends that way if we don't hold it back. If we just release our grasp on anything, it falls apart. Jones pushed open the gate; it protested with a squeal. And just then, with the sun nearly gone from the sky, standing in that terrible place, Bethany thought she'd implode with anger and worry and regret. Why had she moved them to this place? She must have been crazy to think Willow would ever adjust to The Hollows. She'd been scared; that was the truth. After that night when she realized how much trouble a girl like Willow could get into in New York City, she wanted her as far away from that place as they could reasonably get. But now here they were, in a graveyard looking for her daughter. She should have known. If you're looking, you can find trouble anywhere. It's waiting—not just on city street corners, in subways, in nightclubs, but on quiet country roads, in a peaceful stand of trees.

Just as she was about to dial Willow again, she saw her daughter emerge from the woods. For a moment she didn't believe her eyes, somehow thought she was willing the vision of Willow and Jolie and some strangely beautiful boy she'd never seen before. They looked ethereal, all of them pale-skinned, dressed in black.

"Mom?" Willow managed to squeeze embarrassment and trepidation into a single syllable. The three teenagers exchanged a look—that too-cool glance, that half smile of rebellion, as if all your parental emotions are ridiculous and contemptible. No, that was just Jolie. Willow looked scared, sheepish. And the boy, Bethany couldn't read his face.

"Willow, get in the car." It was all she could manage—her anger and relief were so powerful she thought she might vomit.

"Mom."

"Get. In. The. Car."

"Where were you?" Henry asked Jolie as Willow made her way to Bethany's vehicle.

"We were just taking a *walk*," said Jolie. "That's not a crime. Is it?"

Jones Cooper hadn't said a word all this time. He'd just stood watching. Now he stepped forward. He had his hands in his pockets, looked unassumingly up at the sky.

"It's not safe back there," he said. He narrowed his eyes at them. "You kids should know that. There are abandoned mines. Some of that is private property, and folks around here aren't too friendly with trespassers." He kicked at the ground, and Bethany heard the tinkle of metal. Shell casings. Once she noticed them, she realized that casings littered the area around them.

"We were just walking around," said the boy. He didn't say it with an attitude. He was confident, but not a punk. Bethany noticed Jones give the kid a hard once-over, taking in the details—denim jacket, some graphic T-shirt, dirty, ripped-at-the-knee jeans that probably cost a hundred dollars, thick leather boots. His blue-black hair was carefully styled and gelled to look like a mess. His eyelashes were so long and dark he looked like he was wearing mascara. But he wasn't. In other words, he was teenage-girl catnip.

"What's your name, son?" Jones Cooper said.

"Cole Carr," he said. The boy offered his hand, and Jones shook it.

"Cole just started here in September," Henry said. "And this is Jolie Marsh."

Jones looked at Jolie. "I know your father."

"Good for you."

Jones raised amused eyebrows at the girl, turned that assessing stare on her. Bethany was happy to watch the girl squirm after a moment and avert her tough-girl glare to the ground. She looked dirty—dirty under her nails, her hair unwashed, stains on her coat. Who was taking care of this kid?

"I just wanted to show them what I saw yesterday," Willow said from the car. She'd rolled down the window.

"What did you see?" asked Jones. No one seemed to question who he was or what right he had to be asking questions. Even Bethany found herself deferring to his natural air of authority. In the car on the way over, Henry had told her that Jones Cooper was a retired detective from the Hollows Police Department, that he was a part-time PI now. She thought she remembered Dr. Cooper saying something about that. He looked the part, especially now that he was asking questions.

Bethany told Jones about Willow's encounter in the woods, about Michael Holt returning her phone and his search for the mine shaft. Jones watched her with keen interest. What she was saying meant something to him; she had no idea what.

"Of course, now I regret ever telling her what he told me," Bethany said. "I should have known better."

Jones gave her an understanding nod, a low chuckle. "Kids."

"Can we go?" said Jolie. "We didn't do anything wrong. We were going to get Willow back for the late bus. It just took us longer than we thought. There's nothing back there anyway. It was a big waste of time."

Bethany heard Willow roll up the window; she turned to see Willow looking angry and sullen in the passenger seat. When she turned back, she noticed Cole staring at Willow and Jolie watching him watch Willow. *Uh-oh,* thought Bethany with a thud of dread in her belly. *The trouble here has just begun.*

chapter fifteen

That day, a lifetime ago now, had started like any other day. That's what Eloise always marveled at. In her life before, there was nothing to indicate that she'd been marked to live the life she was living now. She had been an ordinary girl, born to ordinary working-class parents. She'd married her high-school sweetheart, Alfred Montgomery. She worked as a receptionist at a trucking company, while Al earned his degree at community college. Then she happily gave up her job when her first daughter was born.

Alfred was a high-school math teacher; he never made much. But for the way they lived, it always seemed like enough. It wasn't like it is now, where everyone needs to live like a celebrity to be happy. They were just happy; they didn't know another way to be. She didn't have any angst about staying home with her kids. That's what her mother had done. That's what she wanted to do. Why would she want to punch a clock and sell her time to a company while someone else took care of her daughters? What was so hard about making meals and cleaning house, coloring and singing the ABCs? What was so great about having a career? She never understood all that. The mommy wars? How sad.

"Alfie, did you remember your lunch?"

"Yes, yes. Got it." A quick wave. She could tell by his wrinkled brow that his mind was already on the day ahead. The girls were already in the car. Emily had her headphones on. Amanda had her nose in a book.

This is what she remembered about that morning. Those words hanging on the air that was cool but with an edge of warmth that promises spring. She remembered how he looked back up at her with a smile, embarrassed that his words might have seemed short to anyone but she who knew him so well.

"Thank you, darling," he said. "Yes, I have it."

"That's better."

Alfie. Al to everyone else except to Eloise and her mother-in-law, Ruth. They alone still called him Alfie, remembering the shy, nerdy boy who was always kind and never picked on by the jocks because there was something to him, wasn't there? Something tough beneath those wire-rimmed glasses. Instead they came to ask for help with their algebra.

And it should have been that, the three of them, her husband and two daughters, off to school. Except.

"Oh, no! I need the car," she called.

"What?" he said. "Why?"

"I have my appointment later this morning. Darn it all. Just give me a minute."

They only ever had the one car. He worked fifteen minutes from the house. If she needed the car, she brought him to work, the kids to school, and picked them all up again at the end of the day. She did that maybe a couple times a week, so she could do the shopping or run errands. Or go to the doctor.

"Hurry, Eloise. I have papers to grade this morning before class."

Ten minutes changed her life. She was tempted to say destroyed, ended, ruined, wasted . . . something like that. But no, it wasn't so. Alfie's life ended. Emily's life ended. Her adored and adoring husband. Her pretty, smart, quirky, funny, kind little girl who always smiled even when she was sad. Eloise was left behind with Amanda, her serious, loving, introverted, brilliantly creative younger daughter. The two of them least likely to get back up and live again somehow were left behind to do just that. The two of them who were most likely to want to die for the loss of the others were forced to go on together.

Because Eloise fretted and Alfie laughed it all off. Emily acted out and slept like a log while Amanda quietly worried, lying awake in bed, tiptoeing into the master bedroom to sleep beside her father. It shouldn't have been the two of them left to hold each other up. But it was. After the accident the world went quietly gray. Eloise didn't know how to put the color back in the sky, not for herself, not even for Amanda.

Eloise was in a coma for six weeks, while her husband and daughter both passed and were buried without her. Amanda, who suffered the least of the physical injuries, was cared for by her grandmother, Ruth. When Eloise thought about those six weeks, she hated herself. How could she just lie there, leaving Emily and Alfie to pass without her by their sides? Leaving Amanda all alone with that terrible fear and crushing grief? How could she? It was an unforgivable negligence of duty.

And then, a few months later, the visions came. Amanda was back in school, doing as well as could be expected. Eloise had taken on some cleaning and baby-sitting jobs offered by neighbors. At first they were pity jobs; Eloise knew that. But then her reputation grew—she was good with children, an excellent housekeeper. They would make ends meet fairly well, with Alfie's life insurance, his pension, and the money they'd already managed to save. Eloise always made sure she was home when Amanda got home, that dinner was in the oven and all the lights in the house were on. It was the least she could do. She knew that it was not nearly enough.

It was one of those afternoons, while she waited for the bus to pull up, that she was first struck. That's what it felt like, a blow to the head. A blow that changed the channel she was receiving, from what was around her to something that was elsewhere—another place, another time, another *person*.

Labored, panicked breathing. Dark. The sound of dripping water echoing off stone. And then a horrible keening scream, *Help, help, help me!* It was a loop, replaying over and over. She didn't know how long.

She became conscious again to find herself on the floor with Amanda hovering over her, pale and terrified.

"Mom," said Amanda. Her voice was just a whisper. "Mom."

Eloise struggled up, struggled to shake off her disorientation. This was the last thing Amanda needed right now.

"Honey, I'm fine. I skipped lunch. I must have fainted." Eloise tried for a self-deprecating smile, but she couldn't shake the vision or the fear. What the hell had just happened to her?

Amanda stared at Eloise with wide eyes, her carbon copy as Alfie always said. But no, she wasn't that. She was more beautiful, smarter, and kinder than Eloise could ever have dreamed of being. In her slender, pale face, in her stormy eyes, Eloise saw all their grief and sadness, all their terrible loss. And something else: a simmering anger, a growing rage. Amanda was too young to know how hard and unfair the world could be; she'd suffered too much pain for her fifteen years. And something inside, the child who'd been asked to grow up too fast, was furious.

"I'm okay. Sweetie. Look at me. I'm fine."

Outside, the wind chimes were wild. She heard the cooing of the mourning doves that had come to live in the eaves. She pulled Amanda in close and clung to her, feeling her daughter's arms wrap around her middle and hold on tight.

What had happened to her? Most anyone would question her sanity, would immediately imagine posttraumatic stress disorder or some kind of psychotic break. And, of course, she had considered these things. (The grim diagnoses, the candy-colored rainbow of pills, would all come later.) But even then she knew. She knew she hadn't lost her mind. She was Alice, slipping down the rabbit hole into some other world, a place she'd never even imagined until she was there.

Now she had the Internet, the ubiquitous web of information that linked the whole universe together. Now, when she had the visions, she sat down at her computer and started typing in key words like *missing women* or *missing girl*. If she'd heard a particular bird chirping in her vision or saw a certain type of plant or leaf, heard an accent or a different language, she'd use that. But that took years, decades of instruction and practice to be so mindful in her episodes. At first she was just reeling, terrified, taking on the emotion, the terror. She couldn't think straight; it took hours to get her equilibrium back. Back then she had to wait for the news at six and eleven, hope that whatever she'd seen had made it onto the national broadcast. Back then there wasn't even cable, no twenty-four-hour world news channels at the click of a remote.

She couldn't shake it that first night. And after Amanda went to bed, she turned on the news and watched. She couldn't have said why she did this. But she knew she must. And there it was, a missing girl in Pennsylvania. There was a giant manhunt, a weeping mother begging anyone with information to come forward. *She's in a well. If you don't call now, it will be too late. She's dehydrated and cold. She won't survive the night.* It wasn't a voice—and it was a voice. It was a knowledge that leaked into her consciousness from the air. It had a particular sound—and it didn't.

She picked up the phone and called the hotline number.

A young woman answered. "Do you have information relating to Katie?"

"I think I do."

"Would you like to give your name?"

"No." She said it too quickly. She knew she sounded like a crackpot or someone with something to hide. Possibly she was both.

"Okay."

"I've had a vision." Eloise was shaking from her core. She couldn't keep it out of her voice. It was more like a shiver, as if she were freezing from the inside out. Adrenaline was pulsing through her.

"A vision." It was the first time she heard that particular tone—disbelief, mixing with annoyance, mingling with hope. She would hear it so many, many more times after that.

"Katie is in a well. She has fallen. She's cold and dehydrated. She won't make it through the night. She's not far from her home. I'm not asking you to believe me. I'm just asking you to check."

"Okay."

"She's wearing jeans and sneakers." Eloise had had no awareness of this in her vision. Wasn't even sure why she was saying it now. "And a long-sleeved T-shirt, green and white. It says 'Daddy's Girl' on it." She didn't even know how she knew it. But as she spoke, she was certain it was true.

There was only silence on the line. She heard a muffled voice, someone speaking, a hand covering the phone.

"Hello?" There was a male voice on the line now. "This is Detective Jameson. Can you repeat to me what you just told the hotline operator?"

She repeated the information.

"You need to hurry. Please," she said when she was done. She could still hear his voice as she hung up the phone. She didn't have anything else to say, was unwilling to give her name. She was too naïve to know they had already traced her call, that the hotline was set up for that.

When the phone was in its cradle, she felt a shuddering sense of relief. Only when she felt it did she realize the terrible low buzz of anxiety she'd been suffering. Then she looked up to see Amanda standing in the doorway to the living room.

"Is it true?" she asked. "Is that what happened today?"

Amanda came to sit beside her on the couch. She wore one of her sister's nightgowns. Amanda had been sleeping in Emily's pajamas since her sister died. *It makes me feel close to her.* Eloise didn't mind it. She liked seeing Emily's things animated, as if she were still with them. Eloise hadn't touched even one of Alfie's belongings—his razor, his toothbrush, his slippers under the nightstand. It was as if Emily and Alfie were still here as long as those things remained. Those mundane items tingled with their energy. Even though most days she was just wading through a hip-deep swamp of grief, the sight of something that Alfie or Emily had touched could make her smile.

"I think so. I needed to call. I know that."

Amanda considered her mother in that grave way she had. "What if you're wrong?"

"But what if I'm right?" The answer to that was scarier. This was acknowledged between them without words.

They sat in the quiet dark. The television was on with the sound down, casting its strobe about the room. If Alfie and Emily were there, they'd both be chattering and grilling her about all the details. There would be no quiet, knowing acceptance of the bizarre. Both of them would be skeptical, playing devil's advocate. But they weren't there. And somehow Eloise knew if they were, this wouldn't have happened.

"It's not fair. It's *so* not fair. None of it," Amanda said.

Eloise didn't know if Amanda was talking about Alfie and Emily, or the vision Eloise had had, or that there was a girl fallen in a well whom no one could find. She suspected that she meant all of it. And she was so right.

"No. Life's not fair. We just do our best. Okay? We have each other."

"For now."

Amanda was too smart to be mollycoddled.

But Eloise said anyway, "Forever. We'll be together forever. All of us."

Even though she didn't know if that was true, that's what she said. She knew they were promised nothing. Now was the only gift anyone was guaranteed to receive. She envied people who had faith in the stories of religion, faith in a heaven where all good souls were reunited with their loved ones. Life would be so much easier if she could believe in all that, so much easier to explain to her daughter. But she didn't have that brand of faith.

That night they slept together in Eloise's bed the way they had since she came home from the hospital. She slept well that night for the first time. She didn't wake with pain in her back or her hip or her neck as she often did. She didn't need any medication to get through the night. Amanda slept, too. No nightmares where she experienced the horrible crash over and over, even though neither of them could remember what happened after Alfie pulled from the driveway. Neither of them saw the tractor-trailer that glanced off their car when the driver fell asleep at the wheel and drifted into oncoming traffic. Neither of them remembered rolling five times to be stopped by a great oak tree. Mercifully, neither of them remembered a thing. Except poor Amanda, in her dreams.

In the kitchen the next morning, they turned on the television to watch *The Today Show,* each of them pretending that they both weren't waiting to hear about the missing girl. As soon as the television came to life, they saw the footage of little Katie being lifted from the well on a rescue stretcher, her parents running to her. And Eloise felt joy. Real joy. A thing she'd been sure she'd never feel again. And she felt this until Amanda turned to her.

"Is this why He took them?"

"Who? Took who?"

"Is this why God took Dad and Emily?"

"Amanda—" She didn't know what to say.

"Don't you think that's why? Maybe it's them telling you what they see. You know—from the other side."

Amanda's eyes were welling with tears. "Do you think, Mom? Maybe?"

"I don't know, honey. I don't understand what happened to me yet."

"But it's possible, right? Emily always wanted to help people, right? She was such a good person."

"That's true."

"That would be something good, right?" And then her daughter's face fell into pieces and she started to cry. And Eloise went to her, and they clung to each other weeping in a way they hadn't together. It was cleansing, washing over and through them. As they stood there like that, the phone started ringing. After that it never really stopped ringing.

But that was a hundred years ago, or so it felt. Jones Cooper had left, and Eloise was online, searching for information on current missing women. Oliver sat contentedly on her lap. And although it was a bit of a nuisance to have him there—she had to lift up her elbows awkwardly to reach the keyboard over his ample frame—she didn't have the heart to move him. She cruised the usual news sites, the National Center for Missing and Exploited Children. The Amber Alert site had been a big help in recent years. But today nothing was jogging her frequency; she remained stubbornly tuned in to the present.

Lots of times, after a powerful vision like the one she'd had yesterday, she'd cruise those sites and see a face she recognized. Then she might get another vision. She hoped for that to happen, that it might be someone else. Maybe it was Marla Holt, the woman she'd seen running. She'd assumed it was, and Ray seemed to think so, too. But maybe not. For whatever reason, Eloise really didn't want it to be. She hadn't wanted this case, had tried to convince Michael to let his mother go. But he wouldn't hear her. Something powerful was driving him. She had a bad feeling about all of it. Scrolling through the faces of the missing, though, she didn't see anyone she recognized.

She visited the sites daily. Sometimes later on she'd get a vision or hear something, as if the Internet could connect her to the energy that gave her her peculiar abilities. Then she'd make a proactive call to the authorities. More these days than in the beginning, they worked with her. She had a reputation now. Plus, the whole psychic thing wasn't such an oddity; it was part of the public consciousness. People thought that it was possible, were more open to it. Occasionally they gave her a hard time, were very rude. She didn't care. She just did what she had to do.

Sometimes people called her, finding her through referrals or an online search. Sometimes then the visions came as if in answer to the need. And as often they didn't. People were frequently disappointed in her. They got angry. Eloise understood.

She'd been angry once, too, when Alfie and Emily were taken from her. She'd wanted to lay blame, seek restitution. The anger was a worm inside her, gnawing at the back of her throat, squirming in her gut. She'd wanted the driver of that tractor-trailer to pay. He had a problem with pills, taking amphetamines to stay awake, then downers to sleep. That morning his addiction caught up with him. He'd passed out at the wheel, drifted into oncoming traffic, and sent their car rolling. He emerged from the accident unscathed.

Eloise had wished him dead; she had hoped for him to lose everything he loved—his family, his money, his whole world. She wanted him to know all her pain, times ten. It kept her up at night. Once, before his trial began, she considered buying a gun and bringing it to the courthouse and shooting him dead. The only thing that stopped her was Amanda, her pale-faced angel. Eloise was all she had left. She thought of how her daughter had managed everything with such stoic acceptance. She'd bear that, too, so bravely. And at some point she'd self-destruct and there wouldn't be anyone left to save her.

Then Eloise met him, Barney Croft, the man who'd killed her family. And when she looked in his face, she saw how broken, how undone he was—by addiction, by regret, by his hardscrabble existence. She saw him standing outside the courthouse with his lawyer. The lawyer had his hand on Croft's shoulder. Croft smoked a cigarette. Eloise had been coming in from a crying jag in her car, to listen to the rest of the testimony. She walked over to him; she couldn't help herself. She wanted him to see her. She wanted him to see what he had done to her.

The lawyer saw her first, put up a hand as if to ward her off. Then Croft turned around. She saw the color drain from his face as her own heart started to pound and her throat swelled.

"Oh, Lord," he said. And all she smelled was his cigarette smoke and his misery. "Forgive me. In the name of the Lord, please forgive me." He put his head in his hands then and started to weep, his whole body shaking with it, the cigarette still clutched between his thick fingers.

Maybe that was where it started. Because looking at him, she *saw* how life had ground him down. It dwelled in his ruddy skin and in the deep lines around his eyes, in the narrow gap of his thin-lipped mouth. She *saw* how he drove to support his family, how he took pills to drive longer, to make more. How then he needed more pills to sleep. And how the human body was not designed to live on drugs and bad food and endless miles of dark highways. She saw so clearly how people make the wrong choices for the right reasons and blow everyone up, anyway.

"I do," she said. "I forgive you."

She meant it. The worm in her gut got smaller. At the sentencing she spoke for leniency and offered him her forgiveness in front of the judge and television cameras. The worm grew smaller still. But that's when she started to lose Amanda.

On her desk was a photograph of her daughter, grown now with her two young children, Alfie and Emily (over Eloise's protests—she didn't believe in naming the living for the dead). Amanda was happily married, a successful accountant, a wonderful mother—and living as far away from Eloise as possible, in Seattle.

Downstairs, she heard the door open and close, then heavy footfalls on the stairs. Ray had a distinctive way of entering her home when she neglected to lock the door, as if knocking were beneath him.

"Eloise?"

Oliver jumped from her lap, annoyed by the intrusion. They passed each other in the doorway.

"I hate that cat," said Ray.

"I don't think he's overly fond of you."

He sat across from her desk, put down a paper bag he was carrying, and steepled his fingers. "So."

"Seriously, Ray. What is it with you? Do you think I wouldn't have called?"

"Let's do it, then."

She released a deep breath. She knew he was going to ask her to do this. She hated it. It was painful, exhausting. And, frankly, she didn't know how much longer she was going to be able to do it, to do any of it. Ray was in deep denial, but Eloise knew that her time was almost up.

"What did you bring?"

"Shoes."

Shoes were good, very good. Feet were the place where the body most often connected to the earth, all the energy passing through the soles.

"You should see that place," Ray said. "Holt's father was a hoarder. It's disturbing."

"Is that where he found her shoes?"

"Yeah, the old man kept everything."

"You know the Hollows PD asked Jones Cooper to look into the case."

Ray frowned. "I didn't hear about this."

"He told me today. I thought he'd come to you next."

"Why did he come to see you?"

"He remembered that I cleaned for her, baby-sat for the children sometimes. He wanted to know what my impressions were." That wasn't really true. She didn't really want to get into their whole conversation. She didn't want to tell Ray that she'd shared her vision with Jones. She didn't even know why.

Ray didn't say anything, cast his eyes up to the ceiling. She stared at the bag he'd put on her desk.

"We don't know that my vision yesterday was related to Marla Holt," she said. "It could have been anyone. I was just online, looking. It could be someone else."

"Did you find anything?"

"No," she admitted.

The intensity he'd had yesterday was reduced to embers; he seemed as tired as she felt. He wasn't looking well lately. His wife had left him almost two years ago now. His kids, both living and working in Manhattan, didn't seem to have much time for him. That's what happened when you couldn't join the living. Late to dinner, distracted when you were there. Ray drank too much, got morose about all the ugly things he'd seen and couldn't change. His wife wanted to play golf and vacation in the Bahamas. Ray wanted to dig up graves. Who could blame the poor woman for leaving?

"I heard from Karen," Ray said. They read each other's minds. It was that way with them, even after they'd ended their affair.

"Oh?" said Eloise.

"She's getting married again."

Eloise gave a little laugh. "She must be out of her mind."

Ray smiled, too. "She met a retired doctor. Get this. She met him while she was taking ballroom-dancing classes."

Karen had always been asking Ray to take ballroom-dancing classes with her. He'd never had the time or, he'd confessed to Eloise, the desire.

"I'm sorry, Ray," Eloise said.

He lifted a dismissive hand. "I'm happy for her. She deserves it."

Karen *did* deserve happiness. She'd been a good wife to Ray and a loving mother to their children. She was beautiful and vibrant, a kind person. And Ray had treated her badly; so had Eloise, for that matter. Eloise would have dinner at the Muldunes' on a Sunday, sleep with Ray the following Wednesday. It wasn't tawdry or dirty; it was desperate and sad. But that was so long ago. They were all different people now.

Eloise could see that Ray was in pain—of course he was. Ray had chosen badly, and all the predictable consequences had formed a line at his door. But there was nothing to be done about any of that now. You just open the latch and let it all in—loneliness, regret, a kind of bone-crushing fatigue.

"Okay, let's do it," said Eloise. Maybe it was pity. At least she could give him this.

"Are you sure?" he asked.

"Yes. I'm sure."

She got up from her desk and walked past him. She went to her bedroom and sat on the squeaking old mattress. She pushed off her shoes and lay on her back. Ray stood in the doorway a minute, and she remembered what it used to be like with them. How he'd come to her in the night like this and they'd make love with all the lights on, all their imperfections in plain sight. They saw each other, understood each other. And when they were together like that, the dead and missing, all the people they were chasing, all the gore and horror that obsessed their thoughts, would recede for a while, leaving them with a brief moment of pleasure and comfort in a world that had gone too gray for everyone else.

He walked over to her and stood above her. For a moment she thought he'd reach for her. And she thought she'd let him, thought she'd take him and let him have her. She could see him thinking about it, what it would be like after so much time. Then he looked away from her face and down to her feet. He removed the shoes from the brown paper bag, an old pair of sneakers. Tenderly, he placed one on each of her feet. Then he took a seat in the chair in the corner. They waited.

chapter sixteen

Bethany Graves cooked dinner, because that's what she did. Her world, it seemed, conspired against putting words on the page, her other great comfort. Sometimes it felt like every page was stolen, secreted, managed in spite of all efforts against her. Inspiration was flighty and delicate, and any disturbance could send it squawking off into the sky. But hunger, the need and desire to prepare food, was steady and reliable, a centering ritual that must take place every day.

She couldn't even *talk* to Willow at the moment. Her child sulked in the family room, sitting on the floor, hunched over a pile of homework on the coffee table—even though there was a perfectly lovely desk built into the bookshelves that lined the wall. But that was Willow, always choosing the hard way.

Bethany chopped the garlic with quick, staccato motions on the butcher-block board. She slid it into the olive oil waiting in a pan on the stove and listened to its happy sizzle; she took in the pleasant aroma. Garlic cooking in olive oil, was there anything better? Then, right before it browned, she tipped in the crushed tomatoes. She chopped the fresh basil and brushed it into the pot. Then she stirred, the heat on low. She'd defrosted the meatballs she'd prepared over the weekend. After a few minutes, she placed them into the sauce and covered the pot, turned the flame to a low simmer. She'd start the pasta and toss the salad after a bit. Spaghetti and meatballs, Willow's favorite. She should have made steamed tilapia and broccoli, which Willow hated. But maybe what they both needed was a little comfort.

She doesn't need comfort. What she needs is a good kick in the ass.
That's what her own mother would have said. Bethany and her mother
had never gotten along, right up until the day the woman died.

Bethany sank into the sectional behind her daughter, who didn't
bother to turn around and acknowledge her. This room was exactly
what she'd hoped it would be when she bought the house—a towering
ceiling, a wall of bookcases, a plush cream sectional, a flat-screen television. Outside the window all she could see were trees.

"Your father wants to come this weekend," she said. She was extending an olive branch. They hadn't talked since the screaming match
they'd had in the car. Willow hated The Hollows, hated her life, and
hated her mother, and she had expressed this to Bethany in a furious
shriek that still rang in her ears.

Willow let out a snort. "You mean Richard?"

She took a breath. "Yes. Richard."

"Did his girlfriend break up with him?"

She reached out and touched the back of Willow's impossibly silky
hair. The shades of red and gold were dazzling. It was cut in a funky
asymmetrical bob. She'd always loved the way Willow's hair felt beneath her fingers.

"I'm sorry, Mom." Willow turned around then.

"I don't want you to be sorry, Willow. I just want you to keep
your promises to me."

"I know. I just . . ." Willow dipped her head into her hand.

"I know. You want friends. You want people to like you. That's
why you lie to them, to me. That's why you break all your promises.
We've been through this with the doctors, with each other. I know.
But now it's time to grow up, Willow. You are enough. You are exactly
who you need to be. And anyone who doesn't see that, who doesn't
like you for who you are . . . well, those people are not meant to be
your friends."

Willow worried a thread on her sleeve. Bethany knew that Willow couldn't hear her. At that age nothing your mother said got

through. But Bethany thought that if she kept saying it, one day it would sink in.

"I'm taking away your phone—for real this time—and the Internet access in your room. I'll be driving you to school and picking you up. And you're not going to see Jolie anymore outside school."

Willow looked up with wide eyes. "She's my only friend."

"Friends like that you don't need."

She expected Willow to explode again. But she didn't.

"How long without phone and Internet?" she asked.

"Indefinitely." She kept her voice calm but firm. She wanted Willow to know that she wasn't backing down this time. "You can use the computer in here for research when I'm in here, too. And you can talk on the home phone, of course."

"If anyone calls, you mean." Willow leaned her head back against Bethany's hip.

"I'm sorry, Mom," she said again.

Bethany didn't want to think it, but she'd heard those words too many times from her daughter. They sounded hollow and insincere. She didn't say anything, just kept stroking Willow's hair. It was as soft as it was the day she was born. *It's angel hair,* Willow's father had said. And she had been their perfect cherub, plump and so pretty. It was all so much easier when she was small, even though Bethany hadn't realized it at the time.

"I want you to talk about all this with Dr. Cooper tomorrow. Okay?" she said.

"Okay," said Willow.

"Willow?"

"Yeah."

"Who was that boy?"

When Willow turned to look at Bethany, she wore a wide smile. Bethany felt her heart fill. She hadn't seen her daughter smile like that in so long. It almost brought tears to her eyes.

"His name is Cole. Isn't he *gorgeous?*"

Bethany couldn't help but smile back at Willow. She reached a hand out to touch her cheek. When Willow was small, she used to climb into Bethany's bed at night and lie on top of her, pressing her cheek against Bethany's chest. *I can hear your heart, Mommy. . . . Go to sleep, Willow.*

"He *is* cute," Bethany said. "How old is he?"

"I don't know. He's a junior."

"So what were you guys really doing back there?"

"We really *were* looking for that mine you told me about."

Bethany was kicking herself. She should have known better than to mention something like that to Willow. "Do you know how dangerous those old mines are, Willow? I mean, people die, get buried alive. I'd have thought after your encounter you'd be scared out of there forever."

She had thought that. She'd figured that the silver lining of the whole incident would be that Willow never went into those woods again.

"We didn't find anything," Willow said. "I couldn't remember where I'd seen him. Jolie thought I was lying. She got mad. But I wasn't lying."

"Well, don't worry about Jolie. It doesn't matter what she thinks. It doesn't matter what anyone thinks."

Willow rolled her eyes. It was one of those things that kids never believe. Because to a teenager it's the only thing that matters. Even most adults never learn that lesson.

"Look," said Bethany. "This is what we need to do moving forward. You need to focus on school. I need to focus on work. We'll make friends and settle in eventually."

"What about Cole? What if he calls me?"

"Well, we'll deal with that when it happens. Okay? Just be up front with me, and we'll work something out."

He was going to call; Bethany knew that. He had that goofy look that boys get when they like girls, and he'd been shining it on Willow.

But Bethany was planning to keep her daughter under lock and key for a while. She just didn't want Willow to know that. Willow didn't need an excuse for sneaking around.

"You promise?" asked Willow.

"If you keep your promises to me and do well in school, I'll keep my promises to you."

Willow smiled again. And Bethany smiled back. There was nothing like a cute boy to brighten the mood of a teenage girl. Maybe The Hollows was going to turn out to be the right place for them after all. Willow *was* going to settle in and adjust, even after this rocky, unpleasant start. Bethany *was* going to finish her novel. Even after the events of the day, it seemed possible, even hopeful.

"Mom," said Willow, "you know I don't hate you, right?"

"I know, Willow."

chapter seventeen

At dusk Jones and Henry made their way through the trees. After everyone had cleared off, Jones had asked Henry if he'd like to take a walk. And Henry had agreed.

"It's always a good idea to know what's going on in the woods behind the school," the other man had said.

As they moved deeper in the direction Willow Graves had indicated, Jones was aware of a low-grade buzz of uneasiness. As he'd mentioned to Eloise, Jones didn't think much of coincidence. He didn't believe in it. Didn't like it when it occurred. So, necessarily after the graveyard encounter, he felt annoyed, off center. First there was the boy, Cole Carr. He'd just been talking to the kid's stepmother a few hours earlier, was unofficially going to look for the kid's mother. Then there was Michael Holt, whom Willow Graves had seen digging up something back in the woods. Jones had the cold-case file for Holt's mother sitting on the passenger seat of his car. Willow Graves was one of his wife's patients; he'd seen the girl and her mother, Bethany, several times coming and going from appointments. Then again, The Hollows was a small place. And it had its ways, this town. Jones Cooper wasn't a superstitious guy, but sometimes it seemed like The Hollows had a way of encouraging paths to cross.

Henry and Jones had both walked these woods hundreds of times, in spite of endless parental and teacher warnings about the abandoned mines and condemned structures scattered throughout the acreage. But as kids they all went back there to drink and smoke and make out. They went back there to explore, to escape the eyes of authority, to make believe. There was something about it, the sighing quiet of the old-growth trees, the coolness, the light through the canopy. How suddenly you could come across a sagging barn or an old house. And yes, the mines, of course.

There wasn't a boy in The Hollows who hadn't walked into one of those death traps. Most of them walked out unharmed, he supposed. Now, as a parent and a cop who'd personally pulled two boys from bad falls back here, he found that the thought of kids exploring filled him with dread. But that was the hypocrisy of adulthood: You never wanted the children you cared about to do things you'd done when you were heedless of the fragility of life. He'd been hard on Ricky, too hard, only because he'd made so many mistakes himself as a young man, mistakes for which he'd paid a heavy price, for which others had paid with their lives.

"I haven't been back here in so long," said Henry. "I think you stop doing that when you grow up, you know. Just walking with no destination, just being outside to be outside." Jones was feeling a little breathless from the walk, but Henry seemed energized and light on his feet. He didn't answer Henry, because he didn't want the other man to hear how out of breath he was.

"So what did you want to talk about, Jones?"

Jones came to a stop, pretended to look around at the trees and up at the dimming sky. The air was cool but humid; it felt like rain.

"Actually," he said when he could breathe a little easier, "I was coming to talk to you about Marla Holt."

"Oh," said Henry. A frown creased his forehead. "Really? What about her?"

"Do you remember when she disappeared?"

"I do." Henry rubbed his crown. "It was a long time ago. She ran off. She left her kids and went away with someone."

Above them Jones heard cardinals. They were issuing the danger-alert call, a kind of *shush-shush* sound that cautioned the others to be still or hide. He looked up for the flash of their red feathers, but they'd hidden themselves well. In the sky above, two hawks circled.

"I remember we talked, Henry," Jones said. "You just lived a few doors down from the Holts."

"We did talk," said Henry. He'd folded his arms around his middle. "Quite a bit, as I recall. It was your first case."

"There were rumors back then."

"Yes, I know," said Henry. He looked down at the ground, moved some leaves with the toe of his brown leather shoe. "But Marla and I were just friends, if you can even call it that."

"Refresh my memory."

Henry offered a polite smile that didn't reach his eyes. "We jogged together every so often. I'd met her out on the street one evening. She'd been running ahead of me, turned her ankle, and fell. I helped her get home, and after that we were friends. We ran in the evenings sometimes after her kids were asleep, when her husband got home from work."

"Mack Holt didn't have a problem with that?" asked Jones.

In the early years of his marriage to Maggie, Jones hadn't been thrilled about his wife's relationship with Henry Ivy. Maggie and Henry had been best friends since high school. But Jones didn't have any female friends, and he hadn't understood why she needed Henry. Maggie wouldn't budge. She'd said, *A man who asks you to give up your friends will, over time, ask you to give up other important parts of yourself.* Over the years Jones had come to accept their friendship.

Henry shrugged. "If he did have a problem with me, she never mentioned it."

"Did you have feelings for her?"

Henry rolled his eyes, gave Jones a weak smile. "Come on, Jones. She was a knockout. Everyone had feelings for Marla Holt. But I was—what? Twenty-five at the time, just starting as a teacher at Hollows High. I had no confidence, even less money. She was untouchable. I couldn't believe she'd even talk to me."

Henry started walking again; Jones followed.

"Did she ever confide in you?"

"About what? An affair, plans to run off? No. I knocked on her door for our Thursday-evening run. She told me her husband wasn't home, that she had the baby to care for. We chatted for a few minutes. Then I left."

"I remember there were phone records. You called, or someone called, from the school."

Jones saw Henry's cheeks flush—effort or embarrassment, it was hard to tell. "I *did* try to call her."

"After her husband left for work?"

Henry sighed and shook his head. "She'd seemed odd at the door. Upset about something. And, honestly, I was concerned. Then, of course, a few days later I learned she was missing."

"You were never a suspect, Henry. I'm not grilling you."

"Really? It seemed like you were looking at me pretty hard back then. It doesn't feel much better now."

"You were crushing on her a little bit, right?"

"A little bit, yes. But I wouldn't do that. She was married with children. I'm not that kind of man now. I wasn't even when I was younger."

And Jones knew that to be true. Henry Ivy was a good man. He ate dinner at their house, had cheered for Ricky at Little League, written him letters of recommendation for college. Sometimes he even came for Thanksgiving, when for whatever reason he couldn't make it down to Florida to see his parents. They'd all been friends for a long, long time. But Jones also knew that Henry had always been at least a little in love with Maggie. That he'd never really, as far as Jones knew, had a serious relationship with a woman. And Jones wondered why Henry always wanted the women he couldn't have. Maybe it was just bad luck. But maybe it was something else.

"What else do you remember about her?" Jones asked.

Henry stopped walking again, shoved his hands into his pockets.

"I thought she was the saddest woman I'd ever met. She seemed lonely. But lonely at the core, as if there were no amount of love and attention that could ever make her *not* lonely. Does that make sense?"

Henry's words made Jones think of Abigail. Abigail Cooper, his mother, had been a black hole of need, a space that could never be filled. He'd spent his entire life trying and failing, until the day she died.

"It does make sense."

"I don't know what happened to Marla Holt, Jones."

They were standing before a clearing now. The locals called this place the Chapel. Toward the edge of the clearing stood an enormous, dilapidated barn. It had become kind of a local gathering place. Because of the way the sun shone in from the holes in the roof, creating golden fingers that reached into the darkness, the frescoes of graffiti on the ceiling, it had earned its name. They'd all been in there at one time or another over the years, though the thing looked like it could collapse at any time. Parties, make-out sessions, a few years ago Hollows PD had broken up a rave out here. Even from where Jones stood, he could see that the ground was littered with bottles and cans.

The flecks of gold in the grass were shell casings. People in The Hollows liked their guns; they liked to come out here and fire off some rounds, teach their kids how to shoot a bottle off a wall. It was one of the big tensions in the community, between the wealthy people who had settled here in the last decade and the people who'd lived here for generations.

"What are you looking for out here, Jones?"

Henry walked into the clearing and squatted down to pick up a spent shell. He held it up under the beam of Jones's flashlight.

"I'm a little curious about what Michael Holt was doing," said Jones.

"He's a caver, gives tours around here and in some of the other mining towns. I think he's writing a book."

Jones hadn't heard any of that. "Is that so? Have you ever heard that story about the mine where a body is buried?"

Henry shook his head. "Nope."

"Me neither," said Jones. Jones knew a lot about The Hollows, its past and its present, more than most. "We've both been here a long time. I feel like that's a story someone would have told before now."

"I could do some research," said Henry.

Jones regarded Henry again. "That'd be great, if you have the time," he said.

"Happy to," he said. "As you know, I'm a bit of a history buff, especially about this region."

Poor Henry, thought Jones. He wasn't a bad-looking guy. But he still retained that nerdy aura he'd carried around since grade school.

"Someone needs to take the initiative to get this place cleaned up," said Henry, apropos of nothing. He kicked at an empty vodka bottle. The label was mostly worn off, but Jones could tell that it came from the Old Mill Bar, where they distilled some of their own liquor. It was truly terrible, an instant headache and upset stomach if you weren't used to it. But as kids, they all drank it. The Old Mill Bar was the only place where they could get served. Once upon a time, it was well known that they turned a blind eye to even the least convincing fake ID.

"It's private land," Jones said. "The Grove family owns it and still pays taxes on it—just like the abandoned O'Donnell farmhouse about a mile north from here. It's a mess like this, too."

They left the clearing and walked a little farther west. The girl had been unsure about where she'd seen Holt digging, hadn't even been able to find it herself again. But Jones thought there was another clearing about five minutes from where they stood.

"I'm going to head back, Jones, if you don't want to talk about anything else."

Jones wished he could shake the feeling. He'd had it years ago when they'd talked about Marla Holt. Henry Ivy wasn't being completely honest. There had been five calls from Hollows High over a three-day period. That was more calls than the average person would make if he were mildly concerned about a running partner, wasn't it?

"Just do some thinking for me, will you, Henry? I suspect that the Hollows PD is going to reopen this case. And even if they don't, the Holt kid has hired Eloise Montgomery and Ray Muldune."

There it was. A flash of something across Henry's face, a slow blink.

"Okay," he said. He pressed his mouth into a line, as if he were already working on it, gave a quick nod. "I'll do some thinking."

There was a rumble of distant thunder in the sky, odd for that time of year.

"I hear there's rain coming," said Henry.

"Oh, yeah?" They were both looking up at the sky. The light of the day was almost gone.

"Yeah, they're saying heavy rainfall."

"Well," said Jones, "stay dry."

Henry turned and started to move quickly away. Jones didn't necessarily want to be caught out there, alone in the dark. He had his flashlight, though he didn't carry a gun with him every day anymore. Not that he was scared. But you didn't grow up in The Hollows without a healthy respect for these woods, without those warnings and cautionary tales forever ringing in your ears. You never listened when you were young. But the voices lingered, came back at you when you were, ostensibly, old enough to know better.

It was only when he got back out to the street that Henry realized he'd have to walk back to the school. He'd ridden over with Bethany Graves and had intended to ride back with Jones Cooper. It wasn't a long walk, not even half a mile. But it seemed to Henry that for some reason he always found himself walking back somewhere alone. Not that he was feeling sorry for himself. It's just that it did seem to be the way of things.

He kept to the shoulder of the road in the gloaming. All he could hear were his own footfalls crunching the dirt and gravel beneath his feet. He thought about jogging it, but he was still wearing his work clothes. If anyone saw him, they'd think it odd. And he really didn't need people thinking that. Although, given his being a bachelor past forty-five in a small town, people did think him odd. Or pitiable. Or gay. Which he wasn't.

The night he'd met Marla Holt, it had been spring going on summer. It was one of those nights, the air full of pollen, a little warmer than it had a right to be yet. It was humid enough that he broke a sweat in the first quarter mile. The leaves on the trees around him were that bright, vibrant new green that promised a long, lazy summer. That was one of the many things he loved about being a teacher—he could still feel excited about the seasons. Summer loomed with its hot days and swimming pools, trips to the beach, the vow to make good headway on that novel he'd wanted to write. Fall was the excitement of fresh beginnings, crisp textbooks and notebooks, new book bags and school clothes. The first snow brought the anticipation of the holidays, the Christmas play, and the formal dance at school. He loved all those things, and he'd never lost that, that excitement for the markers of the year. Even though the years hadn't really delivered any of what he'd hoped for or expected. He'd never written that novel. He'd never married or had children. He'd never really done any of the things he'd thought he'd do.

He'd seen her up ahead of him, moving slowly. She wasn't an easy runner, he could see that. Some people, lean and light, with big lungs and small frames, seemed designed for speed. Others, like himself, like the woman ahead of him, had to work for every mile, felt every footfall. He slowed his own pace, because he didn't want to run past her. It was so discouraging when people overtook you, glided by with ease. He hated to hurt anyone's feelings, even someone he didn't know, doing something that most people would do without a second thought. Then, in the next second, he saw her fold to the ground, issuing a little cry of pain and distress. He picked up his speed and came along beside her.

"Are you okay?"

She looked up at him and then back down at her ankle. "Oh, I'm okay. Just clumsy. I fall all the time."

He offered his hand, but she shook her head and pushed herself up. She limped a little circle.

"I'm just going to try to walk it off," she said. But he could see that she was in pain.

"We should get some ice on that," he said. "Keep the swelling down."

"Oh, you're sweet. But I think I'll be all right."

He pointed down the street. "I'm right down the road, let me run and get you an ice pack."

She gave him an embarrassed smile, and he noticed for the first time how beautiful she was. It was more than the sum of her features, her lush body, her creamy skin. It was more than that. She offered him her hand.

"I know. We're neighbors. I'm Marla Holt. Henry Ivy, right?"

He took her hand in his, and he felt a kind of heat rush through him.

"My son, Michael, came to your door the other day," she went on. "You bought some candy from him for his baseball team. I waved from the curb."

"Of course," he said. He did remember her son, who was striking with black eyes and very tall for his age. "Of course."

"I wasn't a sweaty mess then, lying in a heap on the ground." Her laugh was lovely, somehow managing to be self-deprecating and seductive at the same time. He walked her home that night. And then, without a word of arrangement between them, they started meeting out on the street, doing their miles together. It was nice, comfortable. They became friends. He wished it could have just stayed that way.

Anyhow, it was a long time ago. He thought about her now and then, wondering where she had gone and with whom. He hadn't imagined her to be the kind of woman to leave her children. But then again he didn't know much about women, did he?

He walked up the back drive to the school and then returned to his office. There he packed up his paperwork, including Willow Graves's file. He closed and locked his door and started down the hallway. He felt like he'd been walking down these hallways all his life. He was going to head to the gym and then go home for dinner, like most nights.

He hadn't dated in a while. That last woman he'd met on Match .com had turned him off the process a bit. Not that there was anything wrong with her, or with any of the women he'd met through dating services over the last few years. But there *was* a problem with misrepresentation. Henry was always meticulous in his descriptions of himself, his interests, his hobbies, and what he was looking for in a mate. What was the point of lying? What was the point of looking good on the page but not measuring up in person?

On the drive to the gym, he thought about Jolie Marsh, Cole Carr, and Willow Graves. As a teacher, someone used to separating kids in class and in the cafeteria to minimize horseplay and conflict, he knew a bad combination of personalities when he saw one. It was a chemistry thing. Some people were good together, some were bad together. Jolie was a girl in pain, someone who acted out from that place, caused trouble, got herself in trouble. Willow was a pleaser, the perfect sidekick. And Cole Carr? Henry wasn't sure yet. Cole was quiet, not a bad student. He hung out with some bad elements, like Jeb Marsh, Jolie's older brother. Jeb was one of the kids Henry had lost, a dropout working now at the gas station—dealing weed, LSD, and Ecstasy if the rumors were true.

But Cole Carr hadn't been in any trouble at Hollows High. All his teachers said he was smart, did his work. More than one had commented that Cole might be exceptional if he applied himself. But he didn't seem inclined to do that, skated by on the minimum he could get away with. If Henry had to guess, there were problems at home. The boy had that look to him—that lost, sad look Henry had seen before.

He wondered if he'd made a mistake being lenient with Willow, if Bethany Graves had unduly influenced him. He *was* a little starstruck. It wasn't often you met a bestselling author. But it was more than that. She was lovely, everything about her—the sound of her voice, the way she smelled. She was a good mother, gentle with Willow but not weak, not overindulgent. Anyhow, she was way out of his league. Wasn't she? He didn't even like to get his hopes up anymore. When it came to women, he'd learned that the old adage was true: Nice guys finish last.

At the gym he clocked three miles in less than twenty-five minutes, then moved on to weights. The other guys there were all in their twenties, buff and fleshy in the way of youth. Henry knew he was in good shape, that he didn't have anything to be embarrassed about when he took his shirt off. But he still felt like the skinny nerd he was in grade school, the bully magnet. He wondered, did anyone ever stop hearing those taunts? If someone had told him that he'd still feel the sting of those insults in his forties, he wouldn't have believed it. Maybe if he'd left The Hollows. Maybe if he'd left Hollows High, had a different life, the past wouldn't be so present all the time. Maybe.

On the way home, he called Maggie Cooper—his childhood friend and, although she didn't know it, the love of his life.

"I had some issues with Willow Graves today," he told her. Bethany Graves had asked him to call Dr. Cooper and bring her up to speed before Willow's session tomorrow.

"Oh?" said Maggie. "She's been doing well with me. I've felt like we're making progress."

Henry filled her in on the events of the last couple of days—the incident with Mr. Vance, the cutting, the unauthorized trip into the woods.

"We'll talk it out tomorrow," she said.

"Anyway, it looks like Jones is back on the horse," said Henry. "So to speak."

"Meaning?"

Henry paused a second. She must know. Had he misspoken?

"Oh, you mean the cold-case investigation," she said then. "Marla Holt. He's excited about it. I think it will be good for him."

Henry pulled into his driveway. The same basketball hoop he'd used in high school hung above the garage. He'd repainted it recently and put a new net on it. He hadn't used it in ages, though. But for sentimental reasons he couldn't bring himself to take it down.

"He came by asking some questions, wound up coming out to the woods with us to look for the kids. It felt like old times."

"Hmm," said Maggie. It sounded like she had taken a sip of something she was drinking. "When was this?"

"This afternoon, close to five."

"Hmm," she said again. But this time it sounded different.

"What?" he said.

"Oh, nothing. I just thought he had another appointment this afternoon."

"Uh-oh," said Henry. "Did I get the poor guy in trouble?"

He expected her to laugh, but she didn't.

"No," she said. "It's fine."

Jones and Maggie had had their rough patches over their twenty-plus-year marriage. But they were one of *those* couples, so obviously connected, in love, faithful, and abiding, that Henry could barely imagine one without the other—though he had been guilty of wishing otherwise in the past.

She changed the subject. "Did you know Marla Holt?"

"A little," he said. "We were neighbors. We ran together sometimes."

It was then that he realized he'd called his friend to talk about how that wasn't really it, that there was more. He wanted to tell her and hear what she had to say. But the words didn't come. And the conversation wound down into the usual pleasantries, a plan to have coffee at the end of the week, meeting at their usual spot. And then he ended the call, wound up sitting for a while in his driveway, his mind wandering.

Jones had made it as far as the second clearing. There was nothing there to see, so he turned around and was heading back. He kept his flashlight on the ground in front of him. The sky was dark, and the whole world seemed to hold its breath. He didn't hear any birds or the rustling of small animals fleeing from his path. In the summer the night air would be alive with sound.

The abandoned mines were one danger back here. There was a siren song from those dark entrances that young boys could hardly resist. But beyond that there were the residents, the old families who didn't like people trespassing on their land.

The city people who had recently settled in The Hollows referred to them as "mountain people." The term brought to mind unshaven thugs with flannel shirts, riding four-wheelers, with rifles strapped to their backs, a bottle of moonshine between their legs. It wasn't all that. But it wasn't *not* that, either. The families owned huge tracts of land, refused to sell to encroaching developers. These were people who believed Americans had a right to bear arms, who made their own liquor once upon a time; they didn't like trespassers. The biggest problem these days was the meth labs that had replaced liquor stills. During his time on the Hollows PD, they'd dismantled three with the help of the DEA and the FBI. It was a rural problem. The labs emitted such a toxic smell that it required acres to run one with any stealth. There were still plenty of empty acres in The Hollows.

Because Jones had lived so long in The Hollows, he did fairly well with the longtime residents. Chuck Ferrigno, a New York City transplant, had admitted that he wasn't doing so well. Hollows people didn't like city transplants, and they didn't like the police, so Chuck started every local encounter with two strikes against him.

Jones could hear the rushing of the Black River. It was not quite a mile from where he was, but sometimes on quiet nights like this in the woods, sounds carried in an odd way. He approached the Chapel clearing again on his way out, was going to pass right by and return to his car. It was getting late, and he wasn't even sure what he'd hoped to find. But then he decided instead to move into the clearing. He shone his light here and there, wishing again for his gun. He walked around aimlessly for a few minutes, tracking the beam through the grass. He was about to turn and go when the light caught a glint of something.

He knew the clearing well. If he crossed through the tall grass, he'd find the foundation of another old barn, one that had long since fallen or been demolished. There was a rusted-out old car, too, somewhere to the right. He didn't remember a mine shaft, but he wasn't far from a rock outcropping in which a mine entrance had been blown, so that meant that tunnels could be anywhere below him.

As he moved deeper, he could see where someone had cut back the grass, and he followed the swath into the field. It wasn't long before he saw where a hole had been dug. But there was nothing to it; it looked as if the project had been abandoned.

What had Michael Holt been doing out here? What had he been digging for, if not that mine? That story Bethany Graves had told didn't ring true. He'd never heard it before. There were lots of tales and legends about ghosts and murders in The Hollows. Some of them were true, some weren't. But Jones was pretty sure he'd heard them all.

His phone rang then. He pulled it from his jacket pocket and answered. He didn't have to look at the caller ID to know who it was. No one ever called him except Maggie.

"Hey," he answered.

"Where are you?" Her voice broke up, the line full of static. Cell phone reception was bad out here. Sometimes there was no service at all.

"On my way home," he said. It wasn't a lie; he was about to leave. There was nothing for him to do here. He didn't have the tools with him to dig more out of the hole. But he figured Chuck Ferrigno would like to know about it. Jones walked to the edge of the hole and shone his light down. Nothing to see but dirt. He'd need equipment and manpower to find out what was buried there.

"So I understand you didn't make it to your appointment today," Maggie was saying. He only heard the sentence in chops. But he didn't need to hear the words. He heard the tone. She was angry with him.

"No," he said. "I rescheduled for next week." That was a lie. He hadn't rescheduled. But he would. Probably. His answer was greeted with silence.

"Reception is bad," he said. "We'll talk when I get home."

Still nothing.

"Maggie. Did I lose you?"

But the line was dead. He didn't know if they'd gotten cut off or if she'd hung up. All the service bars on his phone were gone; he couldn't call out. He felt angry then—angry at her for being angry with him. It wasn't her business—was it?—if he went to therapy or not. She couldn't control *everything* about him. He was a man, after all, not her kid, not Ricky. And *he* was the one who would decide if he needed to keep seeing a shrink.

It was fully dark now. He stuffed his phone back into his pocket. He made his way to the car, moving fast, not looking back.

chapter eighteen

It wasn't as though she was *in* them. She didn't feel what they felt, exactly. But her empathy to their various plights was so total that she took on a bit of the terror, the sorrow. Her own adrenaline would start to pump. She couldn't read their thoughts, didn't see through their eyes. She was the watcher. But she was neither omniscient nor omnipresent. Eloise had always felt, though she couldn't say why or by whom, that she was shown a particular perspective. And sometimes this perspective was partial, and sometimes she was front and center. Oh, it was frustratingly inconsistent. She had no control over it. She was a spectator to some twisted game. She was forced to watch but unable to choose her view.

And in the case of Marla Holt, or supposedly Marla (because sometimes what she thought was one person was actually someone else), there was sound and blurry, distant visuals. Eloise could hear her ragged breathing as she raced through trees. Above her a night sky was riven with stars, visible above the reaching branches of dead trees. There were voices, male voices in the distance. But Eloise couldn't hear the words. She could just pick up on the anger and fear in their tones.

Then the woman was bursting through a line of trees into a clearing. A large, sagging structure loomed ahead. She stumbled and slowed, as if she couldn't run anymore; she was gripping her side against a cramp. Then she limped, casting a terrified look behind her, into the wide mouth of the structure. Was it an old barn, a dilapidated church, or a schoolhouse? Eloise couldn't be sure.

Then there were two men. In the clearing they came to blows, and one of them was left lying on the ground, still and dark. The other man entered the structure. There was silence, silence until a wild scream tore open the night. Then it was quiet again. And when it ended, it was like waking from a dream.

She had to talk fast, write things down, because the details faded quickly. The edges started to curl back, and it lifted away in the air like burning bits of paper. What was left behind was fear and sadness, pain, loneliness—a little bit every time. Every time a little more, until after years of accumulation it filled her. And now it was all she was. She was like a miner who disappeared into the bowels of the earth, and every time she came back up into the sun, she brought a little bit of the blackness up inside her. It coated her lungs, her organs, her heart, suffocating her from within. And all the medicine in the world was only a stalling of the inevitable.

"The Holt house connects in the back to the Hollows Wood," said Ray when Eloise had told him everything.

"Yes," said Eloise. She remembered that from when she'd sat for Michael and Cara, too. Now the real-estate ads raved about how the properties backed up against state land. But people who had lived in The Hollows carried a superstition about those woods. Bad things happened out there. Everybody knew that. Of course, Eloise knew better than most that bad things happened everywhere—on a sunny tree-lined street, at the mall, at an office, at a Christmas party, in your home. But for most people it was easier to think that it could all be contained in the scary woods, in the dark of night. Bad things happened only in certain places, and if warnings were well heeded, they wouldn't happen to you.

"They searched the woods back then," Ray said.

"Yes," said Eloise. "Several days after her disappearance."

She remembered that a group had been organized; they walked the woods. But it was late in the game at that point. Eloise had not yet fully connected with her sight then, was still in denial. She didn't even try to get anything on Marla. She hadn't even known that she *could* try. Back then she thought if the visions didn't come, she couldn't seek them. And they were so painful and disorienting for her that she wouldn't have tried even if she *had* known.

"It was someone she knew," said Ray.

"It usually is."

She kicked the shoes off her feet, and they fell with a *thud-thud* to the floor. She wanted them off her feet. If there was more to see, she was too tired to see it now.

"Someone else was there, too?" he said. "Two men?"

"That's what I saw."

He leaned back, pinned her with his gaze. "You think she's dead."

"I think it's likely," she said. She was speaking strictly pragmatically. She never had any sense of these things. "Don't you?"

"I don't know," he said. "You never know."

It was getting late. She wanted to sleep, but she didn't want him to leave. She thought how nice it would be if he'd just sit there like a sentry in the chair as she drifted off. The thought surprised her, because she was used to being alone. As if reading her thoughts, sensing that she needed company, Oliver lumbered into the room and leaped heavily onto the bed beside her. He curled himself into a purring crescent, pressed against her leg.

"You know, I don't know if I ever really loved her." They were back to Karen. It had always mingled like this for them. They could talk about horror, about flight for life, about murder, and then chat about the weather, make love, have coffee.

"Isn't that sad?" he said. "I mean, we were together for twenty years, have two children. I like her, I respect her. But I don't know if I ever *loved* her. Not the way you loved Alfie."

He sat hunched, brow furrowed, his chin on his fist. *The Thinker.*

"You must have loved her once," she said.

"I don't know," he said. "I remember having the idea that she was the *right* one. She was pretty and sweet. But I don't think I really understood the whole marriage thing when we walked down the aisle."

Eloise smiled, offered an affirming hum. "They sell you the white dress, the dream of forever. It's the day-to-day that really surprises you. How much work it is."

"Exactly," he said. "But you never would have fucked around on Alfie, right?"

She shook her head. "No. Never."

"And what about Marla Holt? Was she cheating on Mack?"

"Maybe," said Eloise. "If she's looking for romance, excitement. The promise that life isn't just a couple of kids and a husband with a day job. Cooking meals, beauty fading, she wants more."

"But you knew her. You watched her kids," he said. "Was she having an affair?"

She remembered her conversation with Jones Cooper. "I wouldn't have thought so. She adored her children, spoke lovingly of her husband. But you never really know anyone, what's going on inside. I'm not sure where she went or with whom when I baby-sat. I never asked."

Ray chewed on the inside of his cheek when he was thinking hard. "So if she was fooling around at home that night, maybe Holt walked in on her. There was a chase out to the woods. The other man fights for her, gets knocked down. Holt kills her."

"That's one interpretation of what I saw. It's a possibility. But what happened to the other man? Did Holt kill him, too? And if so, where are the bodies? It's not easy to hide two bodies well, especially in a crime of passion."

"Or he ran," Ray said. "No one knew who he was."

"The neighbor said she saw Marla get into a black sedan, carrying a suitcase."

"That doesn't jibe with what you saw."

"It's just a moment. A moment I don't even understand. We can't know what came before or after."

Ray put his face in his hands and rubbed, released a frustrated grunt.

"It's late," she said. "Let's digest the information. You connect with Jones Cooper in the morning. I have a feeling he's a part of this somehow. He might be the one to connect the dots."

"If the Hollows PD reopens the case, we're out of a job," he said.

"We have a waiting list twenty people long," she said. "There are lots of people with unanswered questions, looking for justice, resolution. We move on to the next."

"I'm not like you," he said. Did he sound bitter? "I can't just move on."

"Sometimes we have to," she said. "You know that. We don't solve them all."

What was with him? It wasn't like him to be so *attached*. Dogged, yes. Determined. Relentless. But not attached. That was different. Attachment hurt, was in fact the source of all pain.

She sat up, and Oliver gave her an annoyed look.

"What's going on with you?" she asked.

He stood and walked over to the bed, sat down beside her. The mattress groaned beneath his weight, and the cat jumped away, left the room with an angry meow.

"I've been talking to this kid trying to find his mother, searching through that awful mess of a house, going over old interviews, newspaper articles, talking to folks who knew Marla Holt. But nothing's jelling. Something just doesn't feel right."

Eloise didn't say anything, only put a hand on his shoulder. It felt nice to touch him. His shoulder was round and powerful beneath the cotton of his shirt.

"And I just keep thinking that I'm losing it. I'm not good at this anymore. And if I'm not good at this, then what? I was a bad husband, a mediocre father." He turned to Eloise. "I'm not even an especially good friend. Look at you. You're drained dry, and here I am asking for more."

She put her hand to the back of his neck.

"We gave everything to this, didn't we?" he said. "Everything."

"Yes," she said. "We did."

She didn't say that she had already lost everything when she came to this. That it had been thrust upon her. She hadn't chosen it, as he had. The fact that she'd frightened Amanda off, that Amanda kept Eloise's grandchildren far away from her—that was collateral damage. That was Amanda's choice; Eloise was powerless against it. She'd have shut it off if she could have. She'd have rejected her sight, the work, all of it, for the love of her family, if only the choice had been offered. She didn't say any of that.

"It's okay, Ray," she said. "You've done a lot of good in your life. You've helped a lot of people."

He gave a slow, uncertain nod. She looked at the hard ridge of his forehead, the broken line of his nose. When he leaned in to kiss her, she didn't push him away. She let his soft mouth touch hers, tentative and slow at first, then deeper. He had this way of holding her that she'd always loved. He wrapped his arms around her back, enveloping her completely. She put hers around his neck and took him all in—the wide expanse of his chest, the stubble on his jaw, the fading scent of the cigar he'd deny having smoked.

"Ah, Eloise," he whispered. "It's been so long."

Once upon a time, making love was about flesh and beauty. It was about his muscles and his thick head of hair. It was about the heat between her legs. Her desire for Ray had been guilty and breathless. They'd rip at each other's clothes. He used to enter her in a desperate rush, and she'd cry out in her pleasure. Tonight it was something else. Something slow and quiet, something they'd earned rather than something they'd stolen. She reached for the light, but he stopped her.

"I want to look at you."

And he was right. She wanted to be seen, even though her beauty had faded and life had worn her down. And she wanted to see him, how the hairs on his chest had gone gray and the lines on his face had deepened into valleys. And it was all so imperfect—*they* were so imperfect—that she knew it was real. It wasn't gauzy or indistinct like her visions; she wasn't dreaming as she sometimes did about her life before. And after they were done, lay curled up in each other, Eloise found that for the first time in years she was hungry.

chapter nineteen

There was a warm scent to the room, something earthy and sweet. And there was a golden quality to the light. The sofa was plush, with big, soft pillows that Willow could hold upon her lap and hug with both her arms. And when she walked through the door, these things— as well as Dr. Cooper's warm smile and how she always offered something warm to drink—caused the tension to leave her shoulders. She felt like she could breathe more easily in here than anywhere else in her world.

Willow told that to her mother. Even though her mother had said she was glad, her voice got that tightness. Willow knew she'd hurt Bethany's feelings somehow by saying that. Willow couldn't imagine why that would hurt her mother's feelings. It had *nothing* to do with her. And Bethany wondered *why* Willow never wanted to talk.

Willow sank into the couch and fought off the urge to curl up and go to sleep. Here she had the sense that everything that was wrong with her would wait outside the door, unable to enter until she had rested. She could just *be* for an hour; she could just be honest.

"I hear you've had a rough couple of days," said the doctor.

Dr. Cooper had already made her some hot chocolate and settled into the chair across from Willow. She had a way of talking, a softness to her tone. Like she knew all about it but didn't judge. Which was new, because Willow felt like she was *always* being judged—by her friends, by her teachers, even by her mother. Judged and coming up short. She didn't feel like that here. Not that Dr. Cooper ever let her off the hook for bad behavior. She bored in, wanting to know why and what Willow was thinking and how she might do better next time. It was exhausting sometimes to look so closely at the things she'd done. Willow was often angry and frustrated, sometimes embarrassed. Sometimes here she cried. But she never felt judged.

"Yeah," she said. "I guess."

"Want to talk about it?"

She relayed the events of the last couple of days. And Dr. Cooper listened in that careful way she had, nodding, making low, affirming noises. She didn't interrupt, as Willow's mother did with pointless questions that confused Willow ("Why did you think that was okay?") and exclamations that shamed her ("Oh, my God, Willow!"). And so Willow found herself opening up. If she cried, Dr. Cooper didn't fawn over her, just handed her a box of tissues, told her it was okay to let her emotions out.

"So what was going on with you inside, Willow? It seems to me like you've been doing a lot of running away—cutting school, leaving the library to go out to the graveyard with your friends. What are you running from? Or to?"

Willow shrugged. She hadn't really seen it that way before. "I was trying to get some space, I guess."

"What does that mean to you?"

"Like, you know, when your backpack is too heavy or your pants are too tight. That feeling you have when you put the bag down or unbutton your jeans, that relief. Like that. I just wanted that feeling."

"I know exactly what you mean."

There was a crystal prism hanging in the window. The afternoon light shining through cast rainbow flecks on the far wall. Willow wanted to walk over and spin it, make the rainbows dance like fairies.

"You said something similar when we talked about the events in New York," observed Dr. Cooper. "You said you just wanted to step out of your skin, you wanted to be someone else."

Dr. Cooper was the first person to whom Willow had ever told the whole truth about what happened in New York. She was the only person Willow had ever told about that dark, angry, dead feeling she had inside sometimes. How she'd just wanted to get *away* from herself.

"It's not quite the same," the doctor went on. "But it has a similar essence."

"No," said Willow. "It wasn't as bad as that."

In New York it was about the lie that grew and grew. It took on a life of its own, getting more complicated, harder to manage. At first it made her feel good, powerful—the story about the concert and the boy she met there. Then it started to make her feel sick. But she still needed to do it, almost couldn't stop herself, even when she wanted to. The lie just kept getting bigger, until it became a monster that ate her whole life. When she ran away in New York, she hadn't planned to come back.

"It's just that school, this town, everybody's expectations," Willow said when the doctor stayed silent. "I just wanted not to have eyes on me for a little while."

They'd wanted to meet him, asked about him every day. This boy, her imaginary boyfriend. She'd made up a whole story about him: He went to Regis; his mother had died when he was little (so sad); his dad was a workaholic (they all knew about that). He took his little cousin to the Britney Spears concert (so sweet). His name was Rainer, after the poet (so cool). She bought herself gifts from him—a pretty ring, a teddy bear. She set up a fake e-mail account, sent herself notes from him that she could show her friends. Once they even had a fight.

But then it all got to be too much. She thought about staging a breakup—something dramatic. Another girl. Or maybe she'd discovered that he was into drugs. *I could not handle that,* she'd say. And everyone would heartily agree. And then she could just go back to being Willow. Except she couldn't. She didn't want to. Who was she without the fiction of Rainer? She couldn't remember. And she was smart enough to understand how pathetic this was. She'd made him up; he didn't exist. And she was lost without him.

She might have talked to her mother about it, if things were normal. If her father—if *Richard*—hadn't moved out. But her mom was a wreck. Every night when she thought Willow was sleeping, Bethany cried. *I fucked up our whole world,* Willow heard Bethany say to someone on the phone. What did that mean? Willow didn't know.

Then one day that dark feeling settled in and she started thinking things she'd never thought before. She thought her mother might be better-off without her. If it hadn't been for the fight Bethany and Richard had over the concert, they'd probably still be married. And if her friends ever found out that Rainer wasn't real, they wouldn't be her friends anymore. They'd hate her.

The night when she told her mother she was spending the night with Zoë and she told Zoë she was seeing Rainer, she didn't even know *what* she was going to do. She just wanted to go away, like she told the doctor. She wanted to get out of her own skin, to be someone, anyone else.

And she was. After she walked out of the lobby of her building and turned off her block, for the first time in her life no one knew where she was or what she was doing. She wasn't with her parents, in school, with her friends, or with a baby-sitter. She was totally and completely free. She could get on a train or a bus. She could go anywhere she wanted. But it wasn't exciting the way she thought it would be. Within ten city blocks, it was lonely and terrifying.

The city that was so familiar to her suddenly seemed loud and intimidating. Strange men leered, and car horns blared. The hundred dollars she had in her pocket suddenly seemed like nothing. The buildings were taller and harder, and she felt so small. She walked from the leafy airiness of the Upper West Side all the way down Broadway— through the chaos of midtown, the hip quiet of the Village. Eventually she found herself in the bustle of Chinatown, with icy cases of dead fish and duck carcasses turning on spits in windows, tables of Buddhas and crystal lotus flowers glinting. In SoHo the hundred dollars in her wallet wouldn't even buy her a pair of sunglasses.

She probably wasn't even five miles from her home, but she might as well have been a thousand miles. If she didn't go back, she realized, no one would find her in that city. That was the thing about New York—you were never alone and you always were. You were lost in plain sight.

But scared and sad as she was, she couldn't go home. She couldn't call her mom or her friends and tell them all how she'd lied. It wasn't the biggest thing in the world; it wasn't the worst thing she could have done. It was just that it revealed so much about her, how pathetic and sad she was, how lonely, how not okay inside. That dark anger in her started to grow and spread, until it wasn't only a part of her, it was all of her. And she thought it would just be easier to be gone.

After hours of wandering, she wound up in Washington Square Park. It was late, and the park was closed; you could walk through but not hang out. She stopped at the playground where Bethany used to take her and laced her fingers through the black bars of the locked gate. She didn't remember swinging on the swings or playing on the seesaw, bouncing on the little spring horse. But there were pictures of her there. And she wished that she were that small again. Which was strange, because usually the only thing she ever wished for was to be grown up, on her own, in charge of her life. Here she was with all of that and now she just wanted to be little again, playing with her mom on the playground.

"Willow."

At first she thought it was a hallucination, that she had finally and truly lost it. Her mom was standing there, eyes red from crying. And the next thing Willow knew, she was in her mother's arms, crying, too.

"How did you find me here?" she asked. She clung to her mom's red wool coat, unwilling to let go. Her mom didn't answer right away, just kept crying. She walked Willow over to a bench, and they sat. Bethany took Willow's face in her hands. Willow could see how scared and sad her mother was.

"When you were small," Bethany said, wiping her eyes, "I always told you if we somehow got separated in the park, you should come to this gate and wait for me and stop the first policeman you saw. I've been looking for you all night. I went everywhere we go together. This was the last place I thought of. I couldn't think of anywhere else to go."

Dr. Cooper had wanted to know if Willow remembered her mother's instructions, if on some subconscious level that memory had led her to the playground gate. Willow wasn't sure she knew the answer.

"What were you *doing*, Willow?" her mother had asked. "What were you going to do?"

"I just wanted to be gone from this place," she'd said. Really it was a wail, all her sadness and anger coming out of her in a roar.

"What place?" Bethany asked. "What are you saying, baby?"

After that, things just went haywire. Willow was ostracized at school. There was a battalion of shrinks, one worse than the last. Everyone thought Willow was suicidal. And then finally the announcement that they were leaving New York City, moving to a place called The Hollows. Her mother was right about their whole world being fucked up. It was just that it had been Willow's fault, not Bethany's.

"If it weren't for the things I'd done, we wouldn't even be here," Willow complained now to Dr. Cooper.

"And what's so bad about this place?"

"It's not New York City. The kids are all cretins. Suburban losers."

The doctor smiled. "No, it's not New York City. I grew up here, you know. I remember that it seems like kind of a snore. I didn't really fit in with the 'cretins,' either."

This piqued Willow's interest. It was hard to imagine Dr. Cooper as a kid who didn't fit in. "So what did you do?"

"I expressed myself in the ways that I could. I studied hard and made good grades. When I grew up, I moved to New York City. I lived there for a long time."

"And then you came back *here*? Why?"

"I fell in love with my husband. His job was here; my mother still lives here. We wanted a family, and I wanted that family to be safe. So we settled in The Hollows. Your mother wanted to come here so that you would be safe. So that she could protect you better."

Willow released a little snort. "So that she could *control* me better. So that she had to drive me everywhere."

The doctor shrugged. "Parents and children often disagree on the difference between protection and control."

Willow sank back into the couch and thought of Jolie and Cole, how free they were to do what they wanted to do, and what Willow knew about freedom now. The world was impossibly complicated. How did anyone ever figure anything out? How did you ever know what was the right thing? How could you ever tell what would make you happy?

"I hate it here," Willow said. "The Hollows sucks."

Usually this statement caused Bethany to lose it. But the doctor just offered her patient smile. "Wherever you go, there you are," she said.

Willow thought about this a second. "I don't get it."

"You might be in New York City. You might be in The Hollows. You might be on the moon. But you'll always be Willow. When you can be happy *there,* you'll be happy anywhere."

Dr. Cooper was smiling as if she were enjoying herself. And Willow found herself smiling, too, even though she wasn't sure she agreed. After all, New York City was cool. And The Hollows was *not.* What did that have to do with her?

She finished telling Dr. Cooper about Jolie and Cole, about the graveyard and how they never found what she'd been looking for out there, how Jolie thought she was lying, and how she was grounded forever now.

"You know, I don't agree with your actions. But I think it's progress that even though you felt the urge to lie, you stopped yourself," Dr. Cooper said when Willow was done. "I think you can be proud of that."

Dr. Cooper knew, too, that the lying had started long before the lie about Rainer. For years Willow had been telling little lies to her friends and her parents about meaningless things. How a cute boy on the subway had winked at her or how she was having recurring nightmares. Once she made up a story about having almost been mugged, how she ran from three thugs on the train when they tried to take her backpack. She didn't even know why she did it. She liked the thrill of it, the making up of events, coming up with details to make it more real. She liked the reactions she got. It wasn't so different from what her mother did, was it? *Okay, Willow, sure,* her mother had said to that. *The difference is, I'm not passing my fiction off as truth. If you want to tell stories, write them down.*

Dr. Cooper had said in one of their early sessions, "It's almost like you're creating a fictional Willow. Willow who boys like. Willow who escapes from muggers. A character. But I think the real Willow is pretty cool—smart, creative, adorable. Maybe you should try to get to know *her.*"

"Yeah," Willow had said. "I guess."

But isn't that what they always told you? Be yourself? Do your best? How could that be true for everyone? Not everyone was nice and kind, talented, pretty, intelligent. Sometimes your best was not good enough to achieve what you wanted. What happened then? Were you just stuck with yourself, your life just whatever sad product of your "best" effort?

They talked then about her plans to do better in school, to stay focused and not run off.

"When you feel like running, call me," said Dr. Cooper. "We can talk it through."

Willow agreed. "But what do I do about Jolie? She's my only

friend, and even if she doesn't hate me now because she thinks I lied, I'm not allowed to hang out with her anymore."

The truth was, she wasn't *that* upset about it. Everything had an unhinged quality when she was around Jolie, as if they could just go right off the rails.

"Be honest with her. Tell her you're being punished and that you promised to be more focused on your schoolwork. If she's a real friend, she'll understand that."

Willow almost laughed out loud. Jolie would definitely *not* understand that. It all sounded so easy in here, in this safe, warm space. It seemed like everything could be talked out and worked out. There were no variables in this room, no wild cards. No heady emotions, no swell of anxiety, no pressure to be something she wasn't. But it wasn't like that out there in the real world. Out there the moment could sweep Willow into its current. And all her good intentions and heartfelt promises would be washed away like broken branches in a rushing river.

chapter twenty

Jones didn't like it when Maggie was mad at him, but it wasn't going to keep him from going about his day. This was one of the things he hated about The Hollows, one of the things he'd *always* hated. Someone was always watching, itching to pick up the phone and start chattering. Because of Maggie's conversation with Henry, she knew that he hadn't gone to his scheduled appointment with Dr. Dahl. Their argument this morning was still ringing in his ears.

"What bothers me the most is that you know how important it is to me that you continue your therapy. I sat right here and told you." She tapped the dining-room chair for emphasis. "And you just don't care."

"I didn't *stop* therapy, Maggie," he said. "I just rescheduled an appointment. You're overreacting." It was a lie. He hadn't rescheduled.

She put her hands on her hips, gave him a flat look. "When? When's your appointment?"

"Tomorrow."

"What time?"

"Four."

She gave him a quick, skeptical glare.

"I have a patient," she said. She took the cup of coffee on the counter and moved toward the door that connected their house to her office and waiting room.

"I do care," he called after her. "It's important to me, too."

She turned back to look at him. He didn't like the look on her face—sad, disappointed. He could have handled angry and annoyed. That he was used to; wives were always annoyed with their husbands, weren't they? Her angry frown might easily melt into a smile or a little laugh. But sad? That was dangerous.

"You know what?" she said. "I'm not sure I believe that. I think if you start getting work like this from the department, you'll let it swallow you back up. You'll forget that you have work to do on yourself."

She was right, of course. He could feel already the blessed relief of being busy with work. All the navel-gazing was getting old. "I thought you wanted me to do this. You said it would be good for me."

She rolled her eyes at him like he was some kind of moron.

"Not if you use it as an excuse to avoid everything else. And P.S.," she said. "Dr. Dahl's office called to ask when you wanted to reschedule the appointment you'd *canceled.*"

He didn't say anything, tried for a sheepish grin. She didn't melt for him.

"So now we're lying to each other?" she asked.

But she didn't wait for an answer. The door closed behind her, and she was gone. She was one to talk about disappearing into work.

He was remembering their encounter as he pulled up to the Holt house. He could see Holt's truck parked in the drive. The house had an aura of abandonment. Even the For Sale sign in the yard looked hopeless, stranded in a sea of weeds.

He'd already talked to Chuck about the hole in the Hollows Wood. Chuck would need a warrant to bring a team back there, but there wasn't much to go on. And that would mean officially reopening the Marla Holt case, which he wasn't ready to do.

Jones suggested that it was private land and if they could get the Grove family to let them dig, that might be the way to go. Just quietly send a couple of guys with shovels back there. If there was nothing there, then no harm done. They hadn't made a ruckus for no reason. But if there was something, it wouldn't look as if they'd put convenience before crime solving. Chuck had been skeptical; he couldn't imagine the Groves cooperating with the Hollows PD.

Jones had pulled one of their cousins from a mine shaft a year back, and the family never forgot a kindness.

"Should I call in a favor?" he'd asked Chuck. Chuck had wanted Jones to talk to Holt first, catch the vibe. Was he a dog with a bone? Or did Jones think the kid was just going to give up and leave town once the estate was settled? In other words: Would this go away?

In an understaffed department, Chuck didn't want an open cold case cluttering up the board. If Jones were still heading the division, he'd feel the same way. Mainly because that was how Chief Marion Butler ran the department. She liked the board clean, cases solved or closed. She frowned upon reopening cases, unless a wrong could be righted, an injustice reversed.

But as a free agent, Jones didn't have any of those concerns. And though he wouldn't have said the Marla Holt case bothered him, now that the questions were being asked again, he wanted some answers. He was starting to remember the uneasy feeling he'd had while investigating. Like a rotting smell of unknown origin, something that couldn't be cleaned or aired out, something that lingered. But the younger Jones Cooper didn't always follow his instincts.

He got out of his car and walked up the drive. In his pocket his phone started to vibrate. He took it out to see Paula Carr's number flashing on the screen. He hit the "ignore" button. He had some feelers out for Cole Carr's mother but hadn't heard anything back. He couldn't talk to Paula Carr and focus on what he was doing now. He wasn't a multitasker and didn't know how people ever concentrated on anything with something always beeping and ringing in their pockets—e-mail, text messages, that idiotic Spacebook or MyFace or whatever it was that

Ricky seemed to like so much. *Dad, you and Mom need a page. It's a great way to stay in touch. . . . How about we just talk on the phone, son?*

His son's generation seemed to think that everyone needed to know what you were doing, thinking, feeling, every single second. He couldn't figure out if it was narcissism or fear—the idea that everyone *wanted* to know you were on your way to the mall or the idea that if you are alone in your own head with your own thoughts and plans that you are somehow invisible, dispensable. If you are not part of the wild, rushing current of information, then you are swallowed by it whole, you disappear. When Jones was a kid, there was none of this. There wasn't even a cordless phone in his house, growing up. If he'd wanted privacy, he stretched the long cord from the phone to the headset and stood in the pantry. Even then sometimes he could hear his mother quietly pick up the extension in her bedroom. Abigail could never let him have an inch of space to himself.

As he walked up the driveway, he thought about how he could have called before he left the house to reschedule that appointment. But he didn't. There was a mean, stubborn place inside him that wouldn't allow it. He *would* reschedule—when he was good and god-damn ready.

He lifted his hand to knock on the Holt door and found it ajar; it drifted open with a creak under his hand.

"Hello? I'm looking for Michael Holt."

He steadied the door with one hand and knocked with the other. Still, when he let it go, the door swung open until a hallway, lined with stacks of newspapers, lay ahead of him. He found himself reaching to rest his hand on the gun he wasn't carrying. It was his training to do this when entering a building where an unknown threat might be lurking. But he didn't carry his gun every day anymore, as he had when he was on the job.

Ricky would have been proud of his old man. Jones had Googled Michael Holt last night, interested in what Henry Ivy had said. Jones had found an elaborate website, designed by Holt himself, detailing various mine locations, histories, lots of photographs of tunnels and abandoned entrances. The site offered Michael as a tour guide, a guest speaker, and a "consultant for filmmakers, novelists, and television producers." Everybody wanted to be a star these days; it was never enough merely to be good at what you did. But maybe that was just Jones being a cynic, although on this point Maggie agreed with him. You couldn't simply have an interest in mines, do the work you loved, and try to make a good living. You had to have your own reality television show. Kids badly behaved? Need a new house, want to be a rock star, a supermodel, want to protect the whales? They'll make a show about you, and people will watch.

Michael Holt had dedicated the site to his mother: *Mom, we're still waiting for you to come home.*

"Hello?"

Jones could hear banging deep inside the house, and although he had no business entering, that's what he did. He followed the sound down the hallway; the space had been reduced to a narrow tunnel; Jones's shoulders touched on both sides as he made his way through. He was about halfway down the hall when the stench hit him, some stultifying combination of rotting food and urine. It stopped him like a concrete wall. There was a closed door at the end of the hallway, light shining through the bottom and sides.

"Hello?"

The banging stopped abruptly. Suddenly he felt like he was in another space and time. The light from outside seemed not to have followed him in. The place was dank and dark, and the air seemed to grow thin. Then the door opened and a huge form dominated the space. Jones found himself taking a step back.

"Who's there?" the form asked.

But Jones couldn't find his voice. Something—the dust in the air, maybe—had coated his throat. He started to cough and couldn't stop as the form approached. He turned and walked to the foyer, stepped outside into the cool air. When Michael Holt stepped out after him, Jones saw earnest apology on his face.

"I'm sorry. I'm in the middle of fixing up the kitchen, kicking up some dust, I guess," said Michael. "Can I get you some water?"

Jones held up a hand. Through the coughing he managed to get out, "I'm okay."

"Are you interested in the house?"

Jones glanced over at the sign on the lawn, which flapped lightly in the wind like a sad wave good-bye.

"No," he said. He'd found his voice. "I'm Jones Cooper. I was the original investigator on your mother's disappearance back in 1987. I'm doing some consulting for the police department, going over my old files."

"Are they reopening her case?" Holt asked. He looked so young, so nakedly hopeful, that Jones felt ashamed for a minute, though he couldn't have said why.

"I'm not sure yet."

"I think I remember you," said Holt. His eyes were no less startling than they had been. Jones remembered that the kid had been tall for his age, but as an adult Holt seemed huge, was massive about the shoulders. He'd let his hair grow long. It hung wild around his face. He had a smear of dirt on his cheek, presumably from whatever project had him banging away in the kitchen. There was something weird about him, a kind of boyishness in spite of his size. Not in a cute way.

"I just had a few questions." Jones forced a single hard cough to clear his throat once and for all. "Do you have the time?"

It looked to Jones as if Michael Holt had nothing but time.

Michael led him through the filth to the sitting room, an oasis in a sea of garbage. He offered Jones something to drink, and when Jones declined, Holt squeezed himself into one of the small chintz chairs, motioning Jones over to the couch.

"I'm sorry for the condition of the place. My father was a hoarder, I guess."

There was a show about *that* on television, too, wasn't there? People who collected and stored things, buried themselves alive in garbage? It was a condition, a mental illness or something. Jones had seen pictures of Holt climbing through tunnels and squeezing himself into narrow passages. Now he imagined Holt spelunking through mounds of garbage, sifting through the debris in his father's house. Hard hat, headlamp, waders.

"I've been going over my notes from back then. You were at a sleepover the night your mother left, as I remember," said Jones.

"That's right," Michael said. Jones noticed a sheen of sweat on the other man's brow. Michael wiped it with his sleeve.

"But you came home about ten. Rode your bike from the neighbor's place. Is that how you remember it?"

Michael looked out the window, up at the ceiling. Anyplace, apparently, but at Jones. When Jones had first arrived, Michael, in spite of the striking nature of his physical appearance, seemed open, engaged. In this room, in that chair, surrounded by his mother's things, Michael seemed to be drifting, closing off.

"Did you see your mother then?"

"No," he said. "I just went to my room and went to sleep."

"Why did you come home?"

Michael was staring at Jones. Some people might have found the young man's gaze menacing. But Jones could sense its vacancy. Michael was looking in, not out.

"I just did that sometimes, you know," he said. He ran his hand through his hair. "Wanted to be in my own bed, you know what I mean?"

"Of course."

Jones had no idea what he meant. As a kid he'd slept away from home as often as possible. He jumped at any opportunity to spend time away from his mother, from her need and criticism, the constant litany of her complaints and worries. He didn't recall Ricky ever coming home from a night away, either, or making weepy calls from camp, like so many kids did.

"Do you remember anything about that night?" he asked. "Things you didn't want to say then?"

Michael picked up a snow globe that held a New York City scene, turned it in his hand. After a few moments, it became obvious that he wasn't going to answer. Jones cleared his throat. And Michael looked at him, startled, as though he'd forgotten that Jones was there.

"I noticed that your desire to reopen your mother's case coincides with your father's passing," Jones said eventually. "I just wondered about that."

Holt still stayed quiet, kept turning that snow globe.

"Did you find something here?" Jones asked.

Finally Michael seemed to come back. "I heard voices that night. They were fighting, I think."

"Did you leave your room to investigate?" Jones asked.

"No. I never did. They weren't happy with each other. They had a terrible marriage, always fighting."

"What did they fight about?"

Holt blew out a breath. "I don't know. What do married people argue about? Money—she spent too much, he didn't make enough. He was always gone, leaving her alone with us. Like I said, they just weren't happy together. She didn't love him. All those arguments, whatever they were about, were about that, I think."

Holt tapped out a staccato rhythm with his right foot. Jones kept quiet.

"Coming back here," said Holt, "seeing this place, looking at her things—I just want to know what happened to my mother. We've hired people over the years. No one has ever found a trace of her. I feel like if there are answers, they're here in The Hollows."

"That's why you hired Ray Muldune and Eloise Montgomery?"

Holt leaned forward in that too-small chair. His face had taken on the open expression again, the normal one.

"The Hollows PD kind of blew me off. Eloise knew my mother, used to baby-sit for me and my sister. She's got this ability, supposedly." He lifted his shoulders, looked out the window again. "She tried to talk me out of it. Did they tell you that? She said that sometimes people don't like what they find when they start asking old questions. She said maybe I should just consider letting my mother go. But I insisted, and they agreed to take the case. Well, Muldune did. But they don't seem to be getting anywhere, either."

"Is that why you were digging back in the woods?"

Michael Holt turned those eyes on Jones. Jones couldn't say what he saw there now, but he didn't like it.

"Where did you hear that?" Michael asked. His voice was flat.

"There aren't too many secrets in The Hollows," said Jones. He kept his answer purposely vague, not wanting trouble for the girl. "And that's private land."

"It's my work to study and record the mines in this area." Holt recounted the legend that he had already shared with Bethany Graves. Again, even in Holt's retelling, it didn't ring true. And Jones had not been able to find anything about it on the Internet.

When Holt was done, Jones asked, "Is there a mine where you were digging? I didn't see a shaft head or any other evidence of a tunnel."

A slow, easy blink. He could see Holt processing the fact that Jones had visited the dig site. "I didn't find anything," he said.

"But why there? I'm curious."

Michael shifted in his seat. "I don't know. Just a feeling."

Jones nodded. "I get those, too. So your work—you're a historian, a tour guide?"

Michael Holt picked at a fleck of something on his pants.

"I guess I'm both of those things," he said. "I'm trying to record a fading history. The earth, soil, is like a slow-moving liquid. It falls and flows like water; it covers things and washes them away, buries them deep. I'm trying to photograph what I can, write down the lore and legend, make a record. I have a website. I'm working on a book."

Jones offered a slow, considering nod. The guy was in his late thirties, unmarried, crawling around in mines, still looking for his lost mother.

"So there's a living in that?" That's the kind of comment that would have drawn a frown from his wife. Invasive, belligerent, that's what she'd say. You're not a cop anymore, she'd remind him.

"I get by," Holt said vaguely.

I can see that, Jones thought but didn't say. He bet if he started digging into the guy's financials, employment history, credit records, he'd find that Michael Holt didn't have a penny to his name. This house and whatever he had inherited from his father were probably the total of his assets.

"My father and I were estranged," Holt said. "I've always believed he was hiding something from us about my mother's disappearance. Now that he's gone, I want to know what it was."

Jones opted for silence again. People didn't like silence. They rushed to fill it.

"I don't think she would have run off on us," Michael went on. "Maybe him. But not us. She always told me that I was the center of her world, that she couldn't live without me. And for her never to contact us in all these years? It's not right. She wouldn't. She *couldn't* have left me."

Jones heard the pitch of petulant rage, the anger of a young boy. It was right beneath the surface, eating this guy alive. Jones found himself remembering Michael's lurking form back in 1987, how he hung at the top of the stairs. He was big, powerful, even then.

He didn't ask, wouldn't have asked him. But Holt said, "I think she's dead."

"Do you think your father killed her? Is that why you're back? Now that he's dead, you want to answer that question?"

Holt covered his eyes and shook his head. He didn't reply, and Jones regretted asking. The words were harsh. Even if Holt was toying with the idea himself, he wasn't necessarily willing to say it out loud. Jones had a feeling that the conversation was going to come to an abrupt end. Not being a cop, he'd have no right to press. When Michael Holt looked up again, all Jones saw was a desperately sad young man.

"I'm not feeling well, Mr. Cooper. If there's nothing else, you can see yourself out."

Holt got up then and left the room. A minute later Jones heard more banging from the kitchen. He saw himself out.

Once in the car, he called Chuck.

"It's my advice that you get someone out there to start digging. I'll call Bill Grove and get you permission, no problem."

He heard Chuck shuffling papers on the other side. "Really? What do you think is out there?"

"No idea." That was a lie. He had an idea.

Chuck was eating something now, chewing unapologetically into the phone. "What are you thinking, Jones?"

Between whatever Michael Holt was hiding (and he *was* hiding something), Ray Muldune's obsessive nature (they went way back), and Eloise Montgomery's visions, this thing was not going away. Jones told Chuck as much. What Jones didn't say was that he didn't want it to go away. He wanted to know what had happened to Marla Holt. He wanted to know what was back in the Hollows Wood.

As a young, ambitious cop, he'd been eager to clear the board, to move on from cases that couldn't be solved. He didn't always follow his instincts. It wasn't that he let things slide. It was just that he relied more heavily on what he saw than on what he felt. And what he saw back then when he looked at the Holt case was a beautiful and unhappy woman who'd had an affair and run off on her family. Even though there might have been a few details that nagged, he'd relied on the facts and maybe a little on his preconceived ideas about women, about people.

The years had taken plenty from him. But he'd learned a few things, too. He'd learned patience, for one thing. Not much, Maggie would argue. But he had more than he used to, certainly. He'd learned that people had many facets, each of them true. And just because you saw one face clearly most of the time, that didn't mean there wasn't another one right behind it. But more than anything, he'd learned that when he felt that nagging discomfort (he had it now that he was looking back on the Marla Holt case), there was something to it. He wasn't arrogant enough anymore to imagine that he knew what it was.

"We didn't talk about renovating, Michael. We just wanted to clean up the place." Tammy, the real estate agent, sounded exasperated.

"Right. But wouldn't putting in new cabinets help us sell the place better?"

Tammy issued a sigh on the other end of the phone. Michael could just see the parting of those perfectly glossed lips, the wringing of her manicured hands. She was one of those women, tight-bodied, waxed, painted, hair-colored. He wasn't sure he'd seen any part of her in the raw. Everything from eyebrows to toenails was in check.

"Michael, you're not getting it," she said. There was a new harshness in her voice. "The kitchen cabinets are *not* the problem. The house is a teardown. Someone will *demolish* it and build a new structure on the land. Putting in cabinets is a waste of your time and money. Did you call those cleaning crews I told you about? Get some estimates? We need to remove that *junk*."

He didn't tell her he'd already taken a sledgehammer to the kitchen. It always looked so easy on those home-repair shows. But the real world didn't yield so easily; it splintered in some places, held on tight in others. It came off in great chunks or refused to budge.

"Let's just get back to basics, Michael." She had this really annoying habit of using his name all the time. As if he were a hyperactive child and she was always struggling to keep his attention. "Call a crew. Start having the junk hauled away. You can't do this work by yourself. And forget about those cabinets."

He didn't say anything. For whatever reason, her advice reminded him of Eloise Montgomery. "Just let this go," she'd said. "She's gone. She has been for many years. It never does any of us any good to live in the past."

"Are you hearing me, Michael?" asked Tammy.

He wanted to answer her, but he couldn't find his voice. This happened to him when there were too many competing thoughts, or sounds, or demands on his attention. Something in him just froze. He stood in the semidemolished kitchen, phone in one hand, sledgehammer in the other, and he just couldn't manage to get any words out.

"Michael?"

Then, "Oh, for crying out loud." And Tammy hung up. He stuck the phone back in his pocket.

He felt it then, that terrible tide of rage. It came up from within him, filling his ears with the sound of rushing blood. He hefted the sledgehammer and used all his strength to put it through the drywall, releasing a mighty roar. A plume of white-gray dust rose into the already cloudy air. Next the counter. It splintered but didn't collapse. Then the floor. He felt the impact rocket through his arms and into his back. The pain sobered him. Concrete. The floor must be concrete beneath the linoleum. He sank to the floor, let the dust settle on his hair, his body. He wished it could bury him, like snow. He felt a little better, the terrible rush of anger passing, receding, then gone.

But what kind of advice was that from Eloise Montgomery? Most people could recognize that a child would want to know what had happened to his mother, even if that child was nearly forty and his mother had been gone for more than twenty-five years. This is not something that a person moves on from. It defines him.

His sister seemed to have more peace with it, periods in her life where she was busy with school, career, later her husband and children. But she was so young when Mom had disappeared. Cara admitted that she hardly remembered their mother at all. She did suffer bouts of depression related to their mother's disappearance, went through a phase where she'd hired a private detective. When that endeavor turned up nothing, she started to see a shrink. But it had been a long time since they'd talked about Mom; Michael sensed that Cara had given up, moved on in a way he could not. In some sense, Cara thought of their aunt Sally as her mother, with whom Cara had gone to live in the year after their mother vanished. Michael stayed with his father. He wanted to be there, waiting, when his mother came home.

Cara had been upset that he'd hired Ray Muldune and Eloise Montgomery. She hadn't come back to say good-bye to their father or to help Michael settle the estate.

"A *psychic*? Really, Mike? Really?" She said it in that flat way that people do now. *Really.* A way that manages to imply disbelief and disdain, an air of superiority.

"I wanted this to be the closing of a door," she'd said to him. "Why do you have to keep prying it open?"

"The door will never close until I know what happened to her. And I feel like this is my last chance. He's gone. Whatever he was guarding, hiding here, is mine now."

He heard her breathing. When she was little, Michael had liked to watch Cara sleep. She was so peaceful, so solidly asleep, as though nothing could wake her. The sound of her breath used to make him happy, relax him.

"Take it all, okay?" she said. "Whatever money he had left, the house, whatever you find. It's all yours." She didn't say it with heat. "But when you've found what you're looking for—or if you don't— promise me you'll stop focusing on Mom and use whatever money is left to start focusing on yourself. Promise me."

"I promise." But the line between them crackled with uncertainty.

"I'm a mother now, you know," she said. "I understand how hard it is, how unceasing are the demands, how mundane and just frustrating it can be day after day. There's no break from being a mother, no weekends or holidays. You're on call twenty-four/seven. When you're not with them, you're thinking about them."

He'd never heard her say anything like that. He always thought of her as the perfect mom—carpooling, baking cookies, making Halloween costumes.

"What are you saying?" he asked.

"I'm just saying that I never wanted anything else, you know. Not like my friends. I never had big dreams. I just wanted to have a house, a family—you know, to be a mom. So it's good for me. I love it. But if I didn't? If I had wanted something else and got this instead, and if I didn't love my husband? Maybe I *could* just walk away and not come back."

"She didn't," he said.

"I'm just saying. And then you wouldn't—*couldn't*—come back. Even if you hated yourself, regretted it, missed your children. How could you face that shame, face the pain you'd caused, answer those questions? *Mommy, why did you leave us?*" Her voice broke on that, and she started to cry.

"I'm sorry," he said. He didn't know what else to say.

He listened to her take a couple of deep, shuddering sobs. He wanted to hold her, comfort her. But even if they were together, he wouldn't be able to do that. He couldn't handle physical closeness like that, not with her. Not when she looked so much like their mother. In fact, though they talked every month at least, he hadn't seen his sister in three years.

"I have to go," she said. "I love you. Take care of yourself, okay?"

She'd hung up before he could say anything else, and they hadn't talked since. She'd sent flowers to Mack's grave. The card read, *We hope you have found peace.* Did she really hope that? he wondered. Or was that something people just said? These niceties that people uttered—

blanketing a well of anger and resentment or masking apathy—they were so confusing.

Now he looked around at the mess he'd made. The kitchen was bad before. He'd cleaned out all the decaying organic matter, and the smell *was* better. At least to him—when he was wearing a mask. But in taking down the rotting old cabinets, he'd managed to turn the space into a demolition site. And the fact was, Michael realized, he had no idea whatsoever how to install new cabinets or floors. He wasn't even sure that's why he'd done it. Did he decide to renovate and then begin demolition? Or did he decide to renovate after he'd already picked up the hammer and started destroying? He honestly couldn't remember. He'd never really even painted a wall. Tammy was right. He needed to call in that cleaning crew.

But the thought of that—strangers stomping through this place, taking everything that was left of her and putting it in a Dumpster—filled him with dread. Holding on, even to these wrecked remains, was so much easier than letting go. Maybe he was his father's son after all.

He heard another knock at the front door and moved quickly from the kitchen. He was afraid that Tammy had gotten into her car and come to see what he'd done. Or that Jones Cooper had returned with more questions that Michael couldn't and didn't want to answer. He'd found Cooper's visit unsettling, mainly because he recalled so little about that night, had so many questions himself. And he remembered Jones Cooper, with his hard, analytical stare. Jones Cooper saw things, no matter what you said. He saw things in you that you didn't know were there.

"Michael, are you home?"

It was Ray Muldune, carrying the brown paper bag that Michael knew contained his mother's running shoes. Ray stayed in the foyer, had his hand over his mouth.

"I've been trying to call you," Ray said.

The older man had an odd look on his face. Michael really liked Ray. Ray said what he meant, even if it was rude, insensitive, or ugly.

"Did it work?" Michael asked.

Ray gave a noncommittal lift of his shoulders, a quick bob of the head. "She saw something. I don't know what it means."

"Tell me."

Michael had never wanted to be away from her. Even when he was too old to want to be with her all the time, he did. At sleepovers he'd often slip out and ride his bike home, causing much commotion in the morning at his friend's house when he was discovered missing. He didn't like to sleep away from his mother. She needed him. She'd said so. More than Cara, more than his father, she needed Michael. Or maybe she hadn't said so; he couldn't remember when she had. But somehow he just knew. That's why he didn't understand, could *never* understand, how she would have left him behind.

That night she'd wanted him to go. He remembered *that*. "You're too old for this, honey. Most kids love sleepovers—scary movies, pizza, candy till you drop. You don't want to sit home in your room while all your friends are having fun."

Were they really his friends, though? He and Brian *used* to be friends in grade school. They used to play in the woods behind Michael's house, explore the abandoned structures, climb into the forbidden mine heads, and walk the dark tunnels. But now that they were in middle school, things were different. Michael still wanted to do those things. But Brian wanted to play baseball, talk to girls. They didn't really hang out anymore, even though their mothers were still friends. In the hallway the other day, Michael had heard someone call him a freak. When he turned around to see who it was, he saw Brian standing in a group of jocks. Brian wasn't looking at him, but the other guys were laughing.

These sleepovers were really just about baby-sitting: I'll take Brian this Saturday; you'll have Michael next week. But he went, because she wanted him to go. He knew that his father wouldn't be home until late. Cara would have Mom all to herself. Sometimes he wished he were small like Cara, could still fit into his mother's lap, that she still brushed his hair and buttoned up his coat. *Why can't I go on a sleepover?* Cara had wailed as he left on his bike. The irony of it.

There *was* pizza, candy, and a scary movie. But Michael and Brian barely exchanged a word that whole night, skulking around each other, both sullenly enduring what had been demanded of them. And when everyone was sleeping, Michael crept out the front door, climbed onto his bike that tilted in the driveway, and drove home. That ride, the high white moon, the strips of gliding clouds, the smell of skunk and cut grass, the chill of the air. That was all he remembered, really. He didn't remember letting himself in, or creeping up to his bedroom, or going to sleep. But that's what he must have done, because he woke up in his bed the next morning.

It wasn't until this afternoon, talking to Jones Cooper, that he remembered the raised voices, the fighting he'd heard. He *did* remember that now; it had been coming back since he'd talked to Mrs. Miller. But that was it. Maybe it was clearing up the clutter that was jogging his memory. He'd heard about that, how cleaning out your house could cleanse your mind and your spirit, change your life. The clutter represented trapped energy, a repressed past. Not that this was his house. But in a way it was, because he'd never made another home for himself, not really—just a string of dorms, rooming houses, and studio apartments. In a way he'd never really left this place.

Ray told him about Eloise's vision, about men chasing a woman through the woods—two men, voices raised, calling behind her. Hearing Ray talk about it, Michael felt his stomach start to wrench and cramp.

"Eloise wants me always to be careful to say that these visions might not be related to your case," said Ray. "But she saw these things while wearing your mother's shoes."

They were standing outside on the front step. Ray didn't like to come into the house. Michael didn't blame him.

"So what does it mean?" Michael asked. "What happens now?"

Ray had a way of looking at Michael that sometimes made him uncomfortable. It was a calm and searching gaze, a careful examination of what stood before him. He always looked slightly mystified, as though he couldn't quite believe his eyes.

"Sometimes her visions deepen, meaning that she'll see greater detail over the next couple of days. And if she does, then we might have more to go on; she might see faces, or the voices might become clearer, or maybe she'll hear a name. But right now it sounds to me that the area she described is about a mile into the woods behind your house. There's a clearing with an abandoned building. The locals call it the Chapel. Do you know it?"

He knew it. Of course he did. Inside, he heard a kind of white noise. A lightness welled up from his stomach, and he started to feel so hot. Beads of sweat trailed down his back. He sat on the step and put his head in his hands, willing himself not to throw up.

"Michael. Are you all right?"

No, man, no. I am really not all right. My father is dead. My mother has been missing for so long, and I cannot stop looking for her no matter what I do. And I'm starting to remember things, ugly things about the night she left. Christ.

"I'm fine," he said instead. "Just overheated, I guess, or breathing in some bad air. I'm trying to renovate the kitchen."

Ray was quiet, sat down beside Michael. Michael told him about Jones Cooper's visit, about how he remembered raised voices in the house that night.

Mikey, be a good boy for Mom, okay? I love you more than anything. Those were the last words he remembered hearing from his mother. He'd replayed them, the quick kiss that followed, the feeling of her hand patting him on the back as he left. She always said that: *I love you more than anything.* Her tone was light, harking back to when he was small, and she'd say, *I love you more than all the stars in the sky and all the fish in the sea and all the flowers in all the fields.* And he'd say, *I love you more than all the ladybugs and dragonflies and butterflies.* She'd say, *I love you more than all those things, times ten. I love you more than anything.* He'd heard her say it to Cara, too. Which hurt in a way he knew even then that it shouldn't. He turned back once as he got on his bike. But she wasn't standing in the door waving as she usually did; she was tending to Cara's misery. If she had known that it was their last moment together, he would have felt it. But it was a parting like any other casual parting, quick and perfunctory and see you in a bit, honey. There was no charge to it. It was this moment, more than any other, that made him think that something had happened to her, something not of her choosing.

"It was your parents' voices you heard?" asked Ray.

"I think so." He hadn't considered that there might have been someone else in the house. He still had his head down. The world was wobbly; it could tilt on its side and dump him into space.

Michael knew he should say something about Jones Cooper's seeing him out there, digging in the very spot where Eloise had had her vision. But he didn't. For the first time, he allowed himself to consider that he wasn't back there digging for that lost mine. After all, it was a shot in the dark. He had no idea where that mine was. No one did. The story was folk legend; he'd never found anything about it in all his research. It was just a story his father had told him.

Michael's father was fascinated by the idea that men thought they could blow great veins in the earth and take what they found there. And they left these massive scars, these deep valleys in the ground. If you looked carefully, if you observed them, Mack believed, you could learn about the planet and about the people who were its current inhabitants. *We will seek to take whatever we want, not for one second worrying about the damage we do,* his father told him. *And the earth, this patient mother, slowly heals herself of the wounds we inflict. But one day, she will tire of us, her incorrigible children. There's going to be a cosmic time-out. The earth will reclaim herself.*

"Are you sure you're okay, son?" Ray asked again.

Michael made himself lift his head and look at Ray. "I'm just not feeling well. Everything is starting to get to me."

Ray put a hand on his arm. He glanced over at the neighbor's yard. "Your neighbor, Claudia? She won't talk to me. I've tried twice."

"She's a bitch," Michael said. Ray's face registered surprise, and Michael realized he'd said it with more heat than he'd intended. "She always has been."

Ray laughed a little. "I picked up on that. The mean old lady next door."

"I'll try to talk to her," Michael said. "One more time."

A red van drove slowly down the street. It pulled in to a driveway, then turned around and headed back more quickly. Someone lost, finding his way. Michael couldn't see the driver as the vehicle passed them by.

"Mike, look," said Ray. "I'm at a bit of a dead end here. I don't have anyone else left to talk to. None of the database searches, the classified ads we've run, or the people I've interviewed from back then have led us to anything new. Unless Eloise gets any closer, I don't know what's left for me."

Michael felt a wash of fear. He didn't want to be alone with this. Ray was the only person who didn't think he was crazy for wanting to find his mother. "Are you quitting?" Michael asked.

"No. I'm just being honest with you about where I'm at."

"I was thinking of putting up a website, you know, with pictures of her from back then, details about the case. I could get it up on the search engines. Maybe I'll even make a Facebook page."

"And you'd do this because . . . ?"

"Because everyone's online these days, maybe even her if she's still alive," he said. He felt a welling of excitement now. This was a good idea. "Maybe one day she searches herself on the Internet and she sees everything we've done to find her, and she'll know we want her to come back to us, that we're not angry, we just want to understand."

Ray wasn't good at hiding his feelings. Michael pretended not to see the unmasked pity in the other man's eyes.

"That's a good idea," Ray said even so. "You never know what can break a case. It's the little things that do it sometimes. All it would take is for her or someone she knows to sit down at a computer and enter her name."

"Right," Michael said. "That's what I was thinking."

"So we'll wait on Eloise a day or so and revisit. Okay?"

"Okay," he said. Then, "I'm sorry. I'm not going to have the money to pay you until I sell this house."

"I know," Ray said. "Don't worry about it. We'll work it out."

There were two mourning doves cooing on the telephone wire above the street. And the day, coming on noon, seemed unseasonably warm to Michael, even though he noticed that Ray was wearing a dark wool jacket and a knit cap. The leaves on the trees around them were turning from gold to brown. His mother had always hated autumn. *Everything dies,* she said. *But it comes back in the spring,* he'd remind her. She'd nod, as though she weren't convinced. *Of course it does, darling.*

chapter twenty-one

J olie wasn't in school the next day. But that wasn't unusual. Some-times it seemed she was out more than she was in. Jolie skated by on C's, though Willow thought that maybe she could do better. Jolie didn't care. If Willow got a C, her mother would flip out. She'd be happy with nothing less than a B. *And you shouldn't be happy with anything less, either, young lady.* Willow thought this was pretty funny, because her mother was so much the "rebel," the "artist," and had al-ways taught her to ask questions and not bow to authority. But when it came to grades, she was as conservative as Laura Bush. *Your educa-tion is your ticket to anywhere. Do well in school, learn as much as you can, and the world belongs to you.* Was that true? she wondered. Had all those homeless people in the parks and subways of Manhattan just not paid attention in class? Wasn't there more to success in life than algebra and biology?

Willow slogged her way through the day. She didn't see Cole, ei-ther, though she kept looking for him in the hallways. Maybe Cole and Jolie had cut together, she thought. They probably had. They'd probably hooked up after her mother humiliated her and dragged her home and grounded her forever. She really hated her life so much.

Mr. Vance was no longer her friend. Even though he was just as nice to her in class and complimented her on her essay, she knew that she was no longer invited to linger after the bell and talk about her thoughts on what they were reading. *A Separate Peace* by John Knowles. Seminal coming-of-age tale. Intense adolescent friendship gone awry. Having to face yourself because of your own ugly deeds. Did Gene bounce the branch on purpose? Of course he did. Whether he realized it or not. No one else in class wanted to believe it.

"It was an accident," the pert and pretty Jenna said. She sounded almost desperate. "He couldn't. He just wouldn't. They were *friends*. Friends don't hurt each other. Friends don't *lie*."

Willow saw Mr. Vance looking at her, waiting for her to play the devil's advocate, to say what she was thinking. But Willow didn't say a word. She knew all about why people do bad things, why people lie. She knew all about that dark place inside, that angry storm cloud. Inside the storm you were capable of anything.

It wasn't until the end of the day when she'd given up on seeing Cole that he appeared beside her locker.

"Hey," he said. He had dark circles under his eyes. His shirt was wrinkled.

"Hey," she said. She felt her heart start to do a little dance in her chest. "What's up?"

"Just wondering if you wanted a ride home from school." He leaned against the locker beside her and kept his eyes on her.

Oh, yes!! I would love, love, love a ride home!!!

"I can't." She looked away from him. There was a river of kids moving past them, shouting, laughing, horsing around. All the pent-up energy of the day was crackling in the air. "I'm grounded. My mom would kill me."

He looked down at his feet. "That's cool." She liked that he didn't push her, the way Jolie would have.

"You could come over later, if you want." It just spilled out of her. It was so stupid and lame. What were they going to do, play *Barbies*? "I mean—you probably don't want to."

When she could bring herself to look at him again, he was smiling a little. Was he laughing at her?

"Would it be okay?" he said. "I mean, with your mom?"

"Yeah," she said quickly. "She said I could have people over, just not go out." Bethany hadn't in fact said that. She'd said they'd work something out if Cole called.

"I'm sorry about that," said Cole. "About you getting in trouble."

"It's my fault," she said. "I knew I should have gone right back."

"My mom's pretty strict, too," he said. He wrapped his arms around his middle, rocked back and forth slightly. "So I'll come by at four?"

She felt a rush of giddy excitement. She was embarrassed to feel heat rise to her cheeks. Was she blushing? Please, no.

"Do you know where I live?" she asked. She turned back to her locker to hide her face.

"Jolie told me," he said.

"Oh," Willow said. She closed the locker door. "Where is she today?"

"Dunno."

And then he was gone, disappeared into the mob of students rushing out the doors to the buses. A moment later she drifted out, too. Floated, glided, danced. If her mom didn't let him come over, she was going to totally *die*.

chapter twenty-two

The Groves weren't hillbillies. Bill Grove was a general contractor, had a thriving business building gigantic homes for the people moving to The Hollows from the city. But you wouldn't know it by looking at his own house, the same place Bill's parents and grandparents had lived. It had gotten bigger, was improved inside. He'd built other structures on the land—his office, a house for his son's family. But as Jones came up the long drive, it still somehow just looked like the run-down old place that had sat there since he was kid.

As he brought the car to a stop, he saw Bill come out the front door. Today Bill was all smiles and outstretched hands. He was dressed in a pressed denim oxford and khakis, work boots. His belly was so big and protuberant that he might have been hiding a medicine ball under his shirt. He was the very picture of upper-middle-class comfort and success. But Jones had seen other versions of him, too. Jones had wrestled Bill, red-faced with rage and booze, from a drunken brawl at the Old Mill Bar. He'd watched the man collapse in wailing grief when he thought his youngest son had died after a fall down a well back in the woods. Jones had endured Bill's powerful, weeping embrace of gratitude when Jones delivered his son from the hole, with a broken leg but alive and ultimately well.

"How are you, Cooper? Good to see you."

"Good, man," said Jones. "How's that boy?"

"Keeping him out of trouble—best I can." A hearty laugh.

"Glad to hear it."

They exchanged the usual handshake and niceties, asking about the usual things—the family, work, plans for the holidays. How was Ricky doing at Georgetown? Did he still have that crazy ring in his nose? What was wrong with these kids today? They were like aliens sometimes, weren't they?

Then right to business. "So what brings you out, Jones?"

Jones glanced around the property. Once upon a time, the place had been littered with all manner of rusted-out vehicles, dead appliances, a tilted, rusted old swing set—it had been a virtual junkyard. Now there was a row of three white Dodge pickups, the doors bearing the neatly printed business name: GROVE AND SON GENERAL CONTRACTING. Bill's shiny new black Mercedes preened in the sun. Jones knew that particular vehicle cost about a hundred thousand dollars. He didn't assign any special value or judgment to this. He just noticed these things. Every little detail told you something about a person.

"You remember Marla Holt?" said Jones.

Bill squinted. "I guess I do. Young woman ran out on her family about half a lifetime ago? Mack Holt died just recently, right?"

The sun was high in the sky. And Jones put a hand up against the glare as he told Bill about finding Michael Holt digging back by the Chapel, and the legend Holt had told Jones.

When Jones was done, Bill wore a deep frown.

"I want you to give the Hollows PD permission to dig where he was digging," Jones said. "We want to know what's back there."

Bill rubbed his forehead. When he took his hand away, the frown was still there.

"You know I'm not crazy about that fellow from New York," Bill said.

Chuck had referred to the Grove land as a "compound." And the word had gotten back to Bill; he hadn't appreciated it.

"Chuck's all right, Bill. He's a good cop."

"In my book there's no such thing." Bill cleared his throat. "Present company excluded, of course."

"Of course," Jones said with a smile. "Besides, I'm not a cop anymore."

Bill let go of a breath.

"Fact is," Jones said, "I can't keep them from getting a warrant and going back there anyway. I just wanted to pay you the respect of getting your permission. It would mean a lot to me, since this is my first consulting gig. You're going to make me look real good if you say it's okay."

Jones was certain the other man was going to tell him no, to get on. But people were always full of surprises.

"How can I say no to you?" Bill said finally. "After what you did for my boy? But you tell them to watch their way, respect the land."

Jones called Chuck as he backed out of the drive, asked him to keep it small, just a few men. He told him to ask the boys to tread carefully, to treat any watching landowners with courtesy and gratitude. Chuck agreed, but he didn't sound as if he liked the advice. The idea of finesse was a bit lost on Chuck; that was city people for you. Before Jones got on his way, he made another call. He rang Dr. Dahl's office and made himself an appointment for tomorrow afternoon.

As he pulled down the drive, the rain came. It was just a drizzle, really, a few drops glinting on the windshield. He didn't even bother with the wipers. The blue sky was still peeking out from the low, gray cloud cover. But the sun had disappeared. Jones thought that they'd better start digging soon.

part two

faith

Before birth; yes, what time was it then? A time like now, and when they were dead, it would be still like now: these trees, that sky, this earth, those acorn seeds, sun and wind, all the same, while they, with dust-turned hearts, change only.

—Truman Capote,
Other Voices, Other Rooms

For those who believe, no explanation is necessary. For those who do not, no explanation will suffice.

—Joseph Dunninger
("The Amazing Dunninger")

chapter twenty-three

Eloise didn't remember that Marla Holt had been a smoker. And yet there she was in a pair of navy pedal pushers and a crisp white top, smoking a cigarette. She sat on the chair by the fireplace that Eloise hadn't used in years, her legs draped over the arm like she owned the place.

"Do you mind?" Marla asked. She held up the cigarette in two slim fingers.

"Not at all," said Eloise. There was no use in fighting these things. Better just to ride it out. She'd been vacuuming. Now she was talking to Marla Holt. That's just the way it was some days.

"Can I help you with something?" asked Eloise. She took a seat on the couch.

"You were always so kind to me," Marla said. She offered that warm smile Eloise remembered. Smiles like that, genuine and open, were truly rare. "So kind to the children. Thank you for that."

"It was my pleasure," said Eloise. "They're lovely children. I hear Cara has two girls now, twins."

Marla looked distant. "Yes."

That's how Eloise first knew that these types of encounters weren't supernatural, exactly. Meaning that Eloise was quite sure she wasn't talking to a *ghost,* in the traditional sense. Marla was more like a hologram, a facsimile, something Eloise's mind did to translate energies for her consciousness. Eloise was certain that if she'd been talking to a real ghost—in other words, Marla's disembodied spirit—Marla would have been more animated about her granddaughters. This was more like a broadcast, a message; today it happened to take the form of Marla Holt. From whom or what the message came, Eloise had no idea.

"What happened to you, dear?" Eloise said. "Where did you go?"

Sometimes it was that easy. Sometimes they just told you. Of course, it wasn't always the truth. Or it was some kind of riddle. This was a very confusing business.

Marla took a drag of her cigarette, crossed her legs. Her long hair was lustrous and thick, falling in waves over her shoulders. Her body was equally lush, full at the breasts and hips.

"When you're young, you only think about *getting* married, you know. The white dress, the flowers, the honeymoon. You never think about *being* married, what that means." She looked up at the ceiling. "Do you have any regrets, Eloise?"

Marla's words echoed Eloise's recent conversation with Ray. This was another reason Eloise didn't think the Marla in her living room was a ghost. There were always these subtle links to whatever was going on in her own life.

"Some days I'm not sure I have anything *but* regrets," said Eloise.

"So you know what I mean." Marla tossed the cigarette into the fireplace. A fine line of smoke wafted up toward the ceiling. Of course, there was no scent of tobacco in the air.

"I wasn't happy," Marla said. "And in that unhappiness I made mistakes."

"You had an affair?"

"There were dalliances. I wouldn't call them affairs. Flirtations?" She pressed her bloodred lips into a tight, thin line.

"He knew I was a flirt," Marla said. "He liked that about me at first. He was so quiet, reserved. With me he could be that. My personality more than made up for it. And he kept me centered, kept my feet on the ground."

"I can see that." Eloise had found that it was better to agree with them, to be encouraging.

"Isn't it funny, though, that the things we love about each other at first become the things we hate later on? I was flamboyant. He was staid and professorial. I wanted to spend. He wanted to save. We were so different. And in the beginning, that was okay. And then, suddenly, it was oppressive."

"So what happened? Did he catch you with someone?" Eloise said gently. If she didn't try to move it along, it could go on forever. And the longer it took, the more exhausted she'd feel afterward.

"That would be easy, wouldn't it?" Marla said with a mirthless laugh. "Husband catches me in the act, kills me in a jealous rage. Or miserable wife runs off on her husband and two kids, disappears forever."

"Then what? What happened?"

Marla got up and started walking toward the door. Then she turned to look at Eloise with a pleading expression.

"I was wondering if I could convince you to let this one go," Marla said.

It was little phrases like that that disturbed Eloise the most, so familiar but off the mark. Let this one go? She'd let them all go if she could. *She* wasn't the one who couldn't let go of the people who had passed. It was everyone else.

"It's Michael who can't let you go," Eloise said.

"I mean, it doesn't matter anymore," Marla said, as if Eloise had argued the point. "Mack's gone. He suffered the most with all of it. If the truth comes out now, it's only going to cause more pain."

Eloise lifted her palms. "What can I do?"

But Marla wasn't listening. They never did.

"You know what my biggest mistake was?" she said. She was crying now. "I let him love me too much. I catered to it. I loved how much he loved me."

"Mack did love you," Eloise said. She wasn't sure what Marla meant. "I always saw love there."

She shook her head. "No, Eloise. Not Mack. Michael."

Eloise was lying on the floor then. The vacuum cleaner was still running beside her. She reached over to turn it off and then lay back down in the silence that followed. Her head ached, presumably from the fall, which she did not remember. She'd met a woman, another so-called psychic, who'd taken to wearing a helmet at home, where most of her visions occurred. *So many blows to the head cannot be healthy for the living. The dead have no regard for us whatsoever, so we must protect ourselves.*

Prior to her accident, Eloise had had little faith and less religion. She didn't believe in the Catholic God she'd been raised with. The concepts of heaven and hell, a divine system of punishments and rewards, seemed overly simplistic. The world, life, was so complicated. How could the afterlife be any different? She'd been firmly agnostic for most of her remembered life. Her visions and encounters, the sight she had after her accident, did nothing to change her position.

In the industry there were plenty of psychics who claimed to talk to the dead, to know the geography of the world beyond. Some of them were quite convincing—millions bought their books, attended their seminars; some of these people had appointments scheduled for years with the grieving who had unfinished business with the dead. And Eloise couldn't say for certain that they *weren't* doing what they said they were. Maybe souls did linger, to say good-bye, to offer an apology, to seek justice—all those things we don't always get in life. And the living do cling, unable to face the possibility that after death there is nothing. That sometimes there is no forgiveness, no resolution, no justice. It just ends, it just goes dark.

What Eloise did believe in was energy. Energy cannot be destroyed; it can only change its form. So life, as the ultimate form of energy, must find another shape, another dimension, when the body dies. She believed in a net that connected everyone in the universe to everyone else, living and dead. Something had happened to her during the accident, or in her coma, or maybe in the moments where she'd been closest to death, that altered her biochemically, turned her into a receiver of energies. She still did not necessarily believe in God or the afterlife. People often found that odd. Coming to her for solace, they didn't get what they expected. They found her cold, left her disappointed. Maybe that's why she wasn't a regular talk-show guest.

"Eloise?"

Ray was standing over her. He was accustomed to finding her in odd places—once in the shower with her clothes on, once in the basement closet, often on the kitchen floor. *You're like a cell phone. Sometimes you have to move around to get the best signal,* he'd said once. That probably made sense.

"I saw Marla Holt."

Ray gave her a hand up from the floor. She was wobbly on her legs for a second, so he helped her over to the couch.

"She asked if I'd let this one go."

"Maybe we should." This was not like him, a complete reversal from their last conversation. Ray was not one to let things go.

"I'm at a dead end," he said. "The next-door neighbor, Claudia Miller, was the last person I had to talk to, but she's not talking."

Eloise remembered what Marla had said about her "flirtations," her "dalliances." She recounted this for Ray.

"What does that mean? Did she have an affair or didn't she?" He sounded irritated with Eloise's apparition. Which was irritating to Eloise.

"How should *I* know?" she asked.

He released a long breath, leaned against the couch, and tilted his head back. "I had one last idea," he said.

Oliver sauntered into the room and made a graceless leap onto the coffee table, nearly slipping off the other side and then catching himself with a last-minute shift of weight. The magazines on the table—*Time, Newsweek, TV Guide*—all fell softly to the floor. Eloise let them lie. Oliver regained his composure quickly, began glaring at Ray.

"That cat is fat," said Ray. Ray was a powerfully built man, big in the shoulders and the middle. No one would accuse him of being svelte. Eloise suppressed a smile.

"Beauty comes in all sizes," she said. Oliver started to purr, daintily licking his paw. The clock on the mantel chimed the quarter hour.

"Let's go to the Chapel," Ray said. He turned to look out the window.

She followed his gaze. "It's raining."

"Wear a raincoat," he said. "When's the last time you left the house?"

It *had* been a couple of days since she'd gone to see Jones Cooper. Sometimes this happened; she didn't leave the house for a while. Then she didn't want to leave. Then she was almost afraid to leave, couldn't think of what to wear that would be acceptable to other eyes. Sometimes she was afraid she had forgotten how to talk to people, real people, not ghosts or holograms or whatever they were, or herself.

"Last-ditch effort," he said. "If you don't get anything out there, you're off the hook. I'm going to tell Michael Holt he's going to have to keep pushing the Hollows PD. I don't have those files, so I don't know what other leads they had back then. Your visions are vague at best. We move on, like you said. There are other people waiting who maybe we could help."

It had been raining since the early afternoon. It was coming down harder now. On the news they'd said it wouldn't let up for the next three days. She rose from the couch and went to the hall closet, with Ray and Oliver following behind. She put on her hideous yellow slicker and matching rain boots.

"Good," said Ray.

The only thing that was motivating her to do this was the hope that it would be their last involvement in the case. Marla Holt had asked her to let it go, and she wanted to do that. She didn't want to tell Ray what Marla had said about Michael. She didn't know why. But if there was one thing she'd learned in her old age, it was to follow her instincts.

chapter twenty-four

Jones walked into his house and closed the door. He felt a heaviness settle on him, a low-grade despair. The Hollows PD was probably re-opening the Marla Holt case, on his advice, and that left him where? He didn't know. Chuck hadn't said, *Okay, I'll call you and let you know what we find.* He'd said, *Thanks for doing this, Cooper. Stop by and we'll get you a paycheck.* Jones knew that it was nothing personal. Budgets had been slashed. They could afford a few hours from him, but probably not much more. Still. He was itching to get up to that dig site, had half expected to be invited.

He hung his coat in the closet, heard Maggie making lunch in the kitchen. This had been their habit for many years, even when he was on the job. They met in the kitchen for lunch, if they could. Unless one of them was busy with work. Or unless Maggie was mad at him. He hadn't expected her to be waiting for him today. But there she was.

He walked into the kitchen. When she didn't look up at him from the soup she was stirring on the stove, he went to the pile of mail on the counter, starting sorting. Bills, catalogs, advertisement postcards. Was there ever anything good in the mail anymore? Seemed like everything important or timely came over the phone or by e-mail. No one wanted to wait days for letters to be delivered anymore. Everything was now, now, now.

He walked over to his wife and wrapped his arms around her, kissed her cheek. "Still mad at me?" he asked.

He felt her body soften against him. In the glass of the microwave oven door, he could see her reflection, the reluctant smile tugging at the corners of her mouth.

"Yes," she said.

"I'm sorry I lied to you," he said. "I'm struggling with this, Mags." He held her tighter.

"I know you are," she said. She still stirred the soup. "I'll try to be more patient."

He breathed onto her neck; she'd always loved that. "I rescheduled my appointment with the doctor."

She put down the spoon in her hand and turned in to his embrace, wrapped her arms around his neck.

"I'm so glad," she said. It sounded like she might cry. "Thank you."

But when she pulled back to look at him, she was smiling. It was *that* smile, warm and proud, which had always motivated him to be a better man. It was the gold medal, the mark of highest personal achievement. When they were younger and first in love, he saw it every time she looked at him. She could see something in him then that he hadn't seen in himself. And he strove every day to be that man. In the years they'd shared, he hadn't always succeeded. Sometimes he'd failed miserably.

He made the salad while she finished the sandwiches and poured the soup into red stoneware bowls. Then they sat at the kitchen table as the rain tapped at the window beside them. Over lunch he told her about everything that had transpired that day, even how he was feeling about it.

"So go up there," she said when he was done.

"They didn't ask me," he said.

"So? You're the one Bill Grove trusts. He asked *you* to make sure they respect the land. It's your responsibility to make sure they do. If you're going to be doing this kind of work here in The Hollows, people need to trust your word."

He loved his wife. "Good point," he said. "You're right."

She gave a quick, self-satisfied nod and got up to clear the table.

"So do you think you might hang out a shingle?" she said from the sink.

"What? Like a private-detective kind of thing?"

He came up behind her with the glasses, put them in the sink.

"Yes, something like that."

He gave a little chuckle. "It's a small town. I'm not sure how much call there would be for my services."

"You'd be surprised."

He thought about Paula Carr then and the call he'd seen on his phone. When he'd checked his messages, he found that she hadn't left a voice mail. His old buddy at the credit bureau hadn't gotten back to him yet. Hands down, that was the fastest way to locate someone. If you had the right contacts, you could find out someone's last charge and where. In a culture where people used their cards for virtually everything, it was almost impossible to hide unless you went off the grid—lost your cell phone, switched to cash.

"Anyway," said Maggie, "part-time wouldn't be bad."

"I'll think about it." He was trying for nonchalant, but he kind of liked the idea, and he could tell that Maggie knew he did, too. She gave him a fast kiss on the cheek, a light squeeze around the middle.

"I have a patient," she said.

And then she was gone, slipped through the door that took her to her other life. Dr. Cooper. He used to have another life, too. Detective Cooper, local cop, former jock, hometown boy. He'd been those things for so long he didn't know how to be just Jones Cooper, husband, father, retired (not by choice). He thought about what Maggie had said earlier. *What you were before, what we were, it's gone. We have to find a new way forward together, as the people we are now.* He was starting to understand what she meant.

There was a list of phone messages on the counter: The plumber apparently hadn't been paid; the Andersons were going out of town, so could Jones feed their cats? And then another, which gave him pause. Kevin Carr had called. Paula's husband. Could Jones please call him back?

Jones took out his cell phone and scrolled through the numbers to find Paula's, then quickly hit "send." He'd get in touch with her first before he called her husband.

"Hello?" It was a male voice, presumably Kevin Carr. Jones toyed with the idea of hanging up. But with caller ID there wasn't much point in doing that anymore. Jones stayed silent.

"Is this Jones Cooper?" The voice on the other line was edgy, nervous.

"It is," Jones said reluctantly. "Who's this?"

"This is Kevin Carr. I saw your name and number on my wife's cell phone bill. Has she been talking to you?"

What was he going to do, lie?

"That's right," he said. He put on his cop voice—distant, almost, but not quite to the point of rudeness. "What can I do for you, Mr. Carr?"

"I want to know what you've been talking to my wife about."

Jones didn't like the sound of the other man's voice. He heard insolence and anger in Carr's tone. He remembered what Paula had said: *Kevin cares about what he cares about, and that's it.*

Jones kept his voice light and level. "I think that's something you should discuss with her, Mr. Carr."

There was a long pause on the line. "My wife's gone," Carr said finally.

"Gone?" Jones felt his blood pressure go up a bit.

"She left me yesterday," he said. Carr could barely contain the heat of his rage; Jones could feel it. "She assaulted me. Then she took my two youngest children and left. She *kidnapped* my children."

Jones couldn't imagine Paula Carr assaulting anyone—unless she had no choice. He *could* see her defending herself, her children. He was always suspicious of men who accused their wives of kidnapping the children. When a woman like Paula Carr left her home and took her kids, there was generally a damn good reason. Usually that reason was her husband.

"Why did she leave, Mr. Carr?" Jones asked. "Why did she assault you?"

"Look," said Carr, his voice going peevish and high-pitched. "I'm calling you because I want to know who *you* are and why you were talking to *my wife.*"

Jones noticed that Carr hadn't used Paula's name once. He'd referred to her as "my wife." That said something to Jones about Carr, about how he viewed Paula.

"At the moment I'm not willing to discuss that with you," said Jones. "Have you called the police to report the assault or to report your children missing? If you have, they can get in touch with me and I'll answer any of their questions."

Jones heard Carr take a deep breath. When he spoke again, the guy was crying. Jones really hated it when men cried. It made him extremely uncomfortable.

"Look, Mr. Cooper," Carr said. This time his voice was soft and pleading. "My wife is not well. I don't know what she told you, but she's unstable, has a history of depression." Carr paused to take a shuddering breath. "I'm afraid of what she might do—to herself, to the kids."

Jones felt the first trickle of fear for Paula Carr and her children. Had Carr hurt them? Was this call a setup, a play to make himself look innocent when things got ugly?

"I can't help you, Mr. Carr," he said. "But what I will do for you is contact the police."

"No," Carr said quickly. "I don't want to get her in trouble. It's against the law, right, to leave the home with the children without· your spouse's permission?"

Or was Carr trying to set her up as unstable, as someone who had kidnapped and might harm the children, when what she was doing was fleeing an abusive marriage?

"That depends upon the circumstances," said Jones.

There was another heavy silence on the line. Jones could hear the other man nearly panting.

"You're a private detective, right?" Carr said. Why did everyone think he was a private detective? Jones chose not to respond.

The other man went on. "It doesn't matter why she was talking to you. Just . . . can you help me find my wife? All I want is for her to come home so that we can work things out."

Jones stayed silent, as if he were considering it. But he had no intention of helping Kevin Carr. On the other hand, he had promised to help Paula. And he was a man of his word.

"Okay, Mr. Carr. I'll help you find her," he said. "I will need some information from you, like her parents' hometown, her maiden name."

Carr got all mushy with gratitude. A moment later he was firing off the information.

"I'll be in touch this afternoon, Mr. Carr," said Jones when he had what he needed. "Just do me a favor until then. Stay put and wait for my call."

"And you won't call the police?"

"At this point I can't see why I'd have to do that." Maggie had accused him of being the king of noncommittal answers. It was a cop thing.

What he did first after he hung up was call Denise Smith, the receptionist at Hollows Elementary. He and Denise had known each other since they'd attended kindergarten together at the same school where she now worked. After the standard pleasantries had been exchanged, he asked her who had picked up Cameron Carr from school yesterday. It was an unusual request, probably information she wasn't authorized to give. But Jones had found that so many people were used to him in his role as cop that they answered his questions as if they *had* to answer.

"Well, it's normally his mom. But I can ask his teacher," Denise said. "We hardly ever see the dad. I think he works in the city." He heard her fingers clattering on a keyboard, then a pause.

"You know," she said after a second, "I don't need to ask. It *was* Paula. She stopped by the office to say Cameron was going to be out the next couple of days. They were going away."

"How did she seem?"

"Oh, busy, rushed, like everyone these days."

"Did she say where she was going?"

"No," she said. She drew out the syllable, as if she were thinking about it. "No. She didn't."

"Thanks, Denise."

"Is everything all right?" She'd lowered her voice to a whisper. He'd always liked her. She was one of the few people in The Hollows who could be counted on to keep her mouth shut.

"I hope so," he said. "Not a word about this, okay?"

"Of course not," she said. "You know me better than that."

When he hung up with Denise, every nerve ending in his body was buzzing. If he were still a cop, he'd know what to do. There was a very clear protocol to follow: have someone file a missing-persons report, access phone and banking and credit-card records, put her license-plate number in the system, hope she got pulled over or that someone found her abandoned car. But he was a civilian now; he couldn't do any of that. He could report her missing. But he didn't want to do that. If she had fled for good reason, he'd only be helping her husband track her down.

He put in a call to the contact at the credit bureau he'd reached out to about Carr's ex and left a voice mail. Jack Kellerman. They'd been drinking buddies forever, meeting every couple of months in the city or here in The Hollows when Jack was back visiting his parents. Jack was always broke, so Jones always picked up the tab. Jack returned the favor by putting Jones's requests ahead of everyone else's or keeping them quiet when they were trying to get around a subpoena.

"I thought you were out of this game," Jack had said when they'd spoken yesterday.

"I guess you're never really out of it, somehow," said Jones.

"It does get a hold on you," Jack said. "You know you can count on me anytime."

On the job Jack had been Jones's most valuable contact. It was nice to know that the relationship was still there. If Jones *did* decide to go private (which he had not), it would make a big difference. Once you had access to someone's credit-card charges, you could easily track that person—hotels, gas stations, tollbooths, ATMs. Everyone used plastic. If someone stopped, he was either dead, off the deep end, or trying to get lost.

Next he phoned Chuck, ostensibly to tell him about Paula Carr and the odd call from her husband.

"You think there's reason to be concerned for her safety?" asked Chuck when he was done.

"Possibly," said Jones.

"You want to report her missing?"

"I'd stop short of that."

"Why?"

Jones told him about the call to Denise Smith.

"So what *do* you want me to do?" Chuck sounded annoyed. Overworked. Underpaid. Hassled by bosses and civilians, probably his wife, too.

"I guess I was just wondering what you think," said Jones. This wasn't strictly true. There was silence on the line; Chuck had stopped typing.

"If it were me," Chuck said, "I'd call the parents. Feel them out if you're concerned."

"That's what I was thinking," said Jones. Jones could tell that Chuck was flattered that Jones had sought out his opinion. He was getting into it. No cop could resist a good mystery, or the idea that someone wanted to know what he thought about it.

"If she hadn't picked up the kid," Chuck said, "I'd be more inclined to tell you to fill out a missing-persons report, get the ball rolling in case we're looking at foul play. I mean, if she really had assaulted him and taken the kids, why wouldn't he have called the police and filed a report? If he was a good guy, truly concerned for the safety of his kids, no matter how much he loved his wife, he'd have filed charges last night. He'd be frantically looking—and so would we."

"Exactly," Jones said. "It's suspicious."

"Yeah, I'd call the parents," Chuck said. "Chances are she went to them."

"That's good advice. In the meantime can I give you her tag number?" he said. This was the real reason he'd called Chuck. There was new license-plate-recognition software. Using security and CCTV cameras that were all over the place, cops could track plates now. It was something that was happening very quietly, under the radar of the media and civil-rights groups. As a civilian, Jones didn't have access to that anymore, and the technology was so new that he didn't have a private contact. "Maybe you'll get a hit on her vehicle somewhere?"

Another pause. It was a favor he was asking Chuck, something not quite aboveboard. Jones waited.

"Yeah, sure," Chuck said finally.

Jones had taken down the make, model, and plate number of Paula Carr's SUV when he left her house the other day. Force of habit.

"Since I have you on the phone . . ." said Chuck.

"What's up?"

"Want to take a ride up to the dig site? The Grove boys are giving my men a hard time. Things might go easier if you were there to mediate."

"I thought you'd never ask," said Jones.

Chuck gave a little laugh. "It's nice to be working with you again, man," he said.

Brother, you have no idea.

chapter twenty-five

When Eloise glanced in the visor mirror to check her reflection, she saw Marla in the backseat.

"It has changed so much here," Marla said. She sounded wistful and far away, a voice broadcasting from another time and place.

Eloise ignored her. This was new. She was still aware of herself, of Ray, the car interior. She felt the heat of Ray's thigh pressed against hers. She could smell the stale cigar smoke that had made a home in the upholstery. The car was old; he could afford better. There was a crack in the beige dash, an ash burn on the seat. Outdated pictures of his kids were fastened with rubber bands to the driver's-side visor. Drive it till it dies, that was Ray's philosophy about cars—about cases, about relationships, about shoes, too, for that matter. The odometer on the old Caddy (bought used) read ten thousand miles, having turned over last year. She reached out a finger to touch the crack.

"What?" said Ray. "It's a piece of shit. I know."

"I didn't say anything."

"I'm old-school, El. I'm not buying into the mass-consumer bullshit. Everything doesn't have to be newer, better, brighter, shinier. What about the good-enough stuff rotting away in landfills? I'm about using as little as possible."

"Old-school is new-school," Eloise said. She held back a smile. "You're preaching to the choir." Eloise looked in the mirror again, hoping Marla had gone. But no.

"Nobody ever loved me like Michael," she said. "Not even Mack.

Even as a baby, Michael never wanted anyone else. I thought he'd out-grow it, but he never did."

Eloise remembered how Michael used to cry when his mother left, even when he knew she was just running out for groceries or going for a jog. It wasn't normal. Little Cara was so easy. She might fuss for her mama, but eventually she settled in after a bit to color or have some animal crackers. Michael sulked, sitting by the window until Marla came home. He was eleven or twelve the last time Eloise had watched him, far too old for that kind of behavior.

"He was fourteen that night," Marla said. "Too big, too tall for his age. Taller than Mack already by then. He never made friends easily. He was happy to stay home with me. And I was so lonely in my marriage to Mack that I was happy to have him. Is that wrong?"

Eloise saw the dark purple necklace of handprints on Marla's throat then. She brought a hand to her own neck.

"What are you staring at?" asked Ray.

"Nothing," said Eloise. She glanced down at her knees. Her legs looked like tree branches, thin and knobby, jutting out from her yellow slicker.

"He can't let me go," said Marla.

When had she started to let it waste her like this? Even her doctor wasn't sure what was wrong with her. She took something for the pain and weakness in her joints. One doctor had posited that her visions were something like ministrokes or TIAs. So she took something to prevent those episodes—which clearly it didn't. She wasn't supposed to drive, and she did only when something was really important, like her visit to Jones Cooper the other day. There was something for her stomach pains, diagnosed as IBS. Then there was the pill to help her sleep through the night. Her cholesterol was through the roof, even though she hardly ate. They gave her more medication for that.

"Mom? Are you taking all these pills?" Amanda had asked last year. She'd come to visit Eloise—without the kids. Her obligatory visit, which was actually worse than if she didn't visit at all. Eloise could hardly stand to see herself through Amanda's eyes. But her daughter was so kind, so vigilant about gifts and cards and flowers on Mother's Day. The children sent Eloise crayon drawings. And it was unspoken between them that Amanda endured her visits to Eloise the way she did her yearly trip to the dentist, something anticipated with distaste, obligatory, and mercifully brief.

But yes, she was taking all those pills on her little schedule or as needed. Lately she'd been wondering what would happen to her if she just stopped taking them. Maybe the legion of things wrong with her would march in and sweep her away.

She looked into the mirror and saw that Marla was gone. She was aware that they were on the access road into the Hollows Wood. It was narrow, barely a road at all, just a rut between trees. Ray brought the car to a stop.

The road ahead was wet, the dirt turning into thick, gooey mud. The rain was coming down, just a drizzle. But the sky was that kind of gray that looked as if it would never be any other color again.

"We have to go on foot the rest of the way," said Ray. He regarded her with a worried squint. "Can you do it?"

She didn't bother being indignant. "I think so."

"It's not far. But the old girl isn't going to make it through that muck." He patted the steering wheel. "Or if she does, she won't make it out again."

As soon as they exited the car, they heard voices. They followed, Eloise holding on to Ray's arm over the wet and unstable ground. Her yellow rain boots were ugly against the brown, made a slurping noise in the mud. By the time they reached the clearing, they saw four men in uniform digging into the earth. A few other men in heavy black slickers stood around watching. With the dead trees and the rain, the scene was as grim as a funeral. Eloise shuddered.

"Cops," said Ray. He said it like one might say "termites"—with surprise and dismay and a dread of things to come. One could forget that he'd been a cop himself. "What are they looking for?"

"I bet they're looking for Marla."

"No," he said. "How would they know about the Chapel?"

There was a flash of something in the trees across the opening. And then she saw him—too big, too tall, as his mother had described him. Clad in black, his long, dark hair hanging wet and ropy, fists clenched at his sides, he looked ghoulish. When he'd first come to see her, he'd looked sweet and bookish. He'd had his long hair back in a ponytail, wore those cute wire-rimmed glasses, was dressed neatly in jeans and a blue T-shirt. He was much like she'd remembered him as a boy, quiet, soft-spoken. The man she saw through the trees made her heart thud with fear. Eloise was about to point him out to Ray. But she was interrupted.

"I got something." The voice rang high-pitched with alarm. It disturbed the air. Some large-winged birds above them flapped away. Then Jones Cooper was coming up behind them, clearing his throat so, Eloise guessed, as to not take them by surprise. Ray turned around to look at the other man.

"All of a sudden, it's Grand Central around here," said Ray. He didn't even bother to conceal his dislike, which took the form of a sneer. Eloise couldn't remember what it was with the two of them. And she didn't much care—two old dogs with a bone between them.

"It has been a while, Muldune," said Jones. Eloise noted how he did always try to be polite, even when he was annoyed. She wasn't sure if this was a good trait or a dishonest one. She looked again across the clearing in time to see Michael slipping away into the dark between the trees. She still didn't say anything; something held her back.

The three of them started walking toward the group of men who stood around looking down at the ground. As he approached, Jones asked, "What did you find there, son?"

The man in uniform was just a boy, with a smooth, unlined face free from stubble. He looked pale and stricken.

"Detective Cooper," the boy said. Did everybody in this town know Jones Cooper? "I think I found bones."

They all looked at the hole in the earth and saw the shock of white against the dark of the soil.

"Okay," said Jones. He put up his hands. "Step away and stop digging. Call Detective Ferrigno and get some crime-scene techs out here."

"Don't tell them, Eloise. Please." Marla again. Just her voice, loud inside Eloise's head.

"It's too late," she said. And everyone turned to look at her with grim faces. That was her last awareness of the scene.

Marla sat up from the dirt and brushed herself off. For someone who'd been buried for more than twenty years, she looked remarkably well coiffed. Except for that throat, which was a mottled black and purple.

"He was supposed to spend the night with a friend. I should have known he'd come home. Cara was asleep. You remember how she slept like the dead, don't you? Once that child was asleep, I had a solid twelve hours before she'd open her eyes again. Mack was working late, grading term papers in his office at the university. I had been looking forward to that time to myself all week."

She stood up. "That's what you lose when you're a mother and a wife. You lose time to yourself. Your time is never yours again, is it? Not really."

She sighed. "Anyway, it was nothing, what he saw. I had a friend over. As I confided in him about my life, I cried. My friend moved to comfort me. That's what Michael saw. That's all, I swear. But the *rage* in that boy, like all his life it had just been simmering, waiting for a reason to blow. My God. Why was he so angry at me?"

But then Marla was running and Eloise was high above her. It was like a satellite image she couldn't zoom in on. She couldn't get closer as she watched Marla darting through the woods. Two large forms gave chase, until one of them gained on her and took her to the ground. The other form came up behind, and there was a fight. Marla ran again, disappeared into the Chapel, while the two men engaged in a vicious physical battle that left one of them lifeless on the ground. The one who remained standing went after her again.

But that was all. Eloise came to on her back in the field with Ray and Jones looming over her.

"Eloise, are you okay?" asked Jones.

Ray helped her up, less concerned. "What did you see?" he asked.

"She said there was someone else there that night. A friend, not a lover," Eloise said to Ray. She didn't care about Jones, what he thought of her, whether or not he believed her. She leaned against Ray.

"He was here, watching the dig, Ray. Just now, in the real world."

"Who?"

"Michael Holt. I saw him run off. Go after him." She pointed in the direction she'd seen him run, and Ray took off, leaving her alone with Jones.

"Are you okay?" he asked again.

"I'm okay."

He looked after Ray, seemed to consider giving chase himself. But he stayed rooted. Others had arrived. She saw more men moving into the clearing.

"It doesn't seem like this whole thing, whatever it is you do, is very good for your health," said Jones.

She didn't know how to answer him. No one who wasn't another psychic, or her daughter, had made that observation before. *This is killing you, Mom. You need to walk away from it.* In fact, no one seemed to notice her at all. For most people it was only about what she could do for them.

"He's using you," said Jones. He was still looking off in the direction where Ray had gone. "You shouldn't let him anymore."

She was about to protest. But she found she didn't have it in her. "He's my friend."

She sensed that he was about to make some kind of comment, but then he moved away from her and toward them, the other men, with a quick glance back. She turned and exited the clearing, heading back toward the car. There was nothing left to do for Marla Holt; she wouldn't visit Eloise again. Eloise couldn't help her anymore.

chapter twenty-six

Michael ran through the wet woods, branches slapping at his face, roots tugging at his feet. His chest was tight with effort, his heart an engine running too hot, too hard. When he finally came to a stop at the mine head, he was sobbing. Then, in the next moment, everything in his stomach came up in one heaving orange gush. The sound of the splatter against the ground made him dry-heave until he could hardly breathe. Then he sank against the wooden frame of the mine entrance. After a while his breathing slowed, his nausea subsided. The cool air from the mine shaft seemed to wash out and over him, soothing him.

He'd been coming here his whole life. His father had shown him the way. It was here where he went below the first time, first ventured into that always dark and cool and quiet place. There was no chatter, no traffic, no one else to look on him in judgment, to take stock of him and find him wanting.

It was Cooper who had led them all to that place, brought the police. And Eloise and Ray had been there, too. If it hadn't been for that stupid girl, tramping about where she didn't belong, no one ever would have known about him digging out there. Now the site would be lost, or someone else would take credit for it. But no, that wasn't it, was it? That wasn't why he couldn't stop crying.

He pulled himself to his feet and stood at the entrance to the mine. When he first returned here after his father had died, the mine head had been boarded up. There was a city sign on it that declared it condemned. DO NOT ENTER, the sign warned. DANGER. He'd brought a crowbar down and pried it open. The boards lay off to the side, a jagged pile of broken wood and jutting rusted nails.

"What did you do to her?" he yelled into the darkness. It was a wet, solid thing, that darkness. It could come out and grab you, drag you down into the earth.

"What did you do to her?" The question bounced back at him, echoing off the mine shaft's walls. His words sounded desperate and grief-stricken, his voice distorted and foreign, even to himself.

His own memories of that night were boarded up like the mine. Do not enter. Danger. And there was no crowbar strong enough to break through. All he could remember was the bike ride home through silent suburban streets, the moon high, the houses dark. He left his bike on the lawn, carelessly let it twist and fall to the ground. He climbed the porch step and put his hand on the knob. But that door wouldn't open, not in his memory. He couldn't get it to budge. And he was tired of trying.

"All the answers are down here," his father had told him about the mines and caves. "Down here you can hear yourself think, finally."

Maybe that's what he needed to do. Go down. Maybe his father was right. Maybe the answers were there.

"Michael!"

He looked up through the trees. The voice was familiar. Ray Muldune. He was making his way slowly, unsteadily closer.

"Michael!"

Ray was a good guy, but Michael didn't want to talk anymore. Not to Ray, not to anyone. He lifted his pack from the ground and hefted it onto his back. He stooped his head and stepped inside, into the blessed quiet.

chapter twenty-seven

When Cole pulled up to the house, he knew that something was wrong. He just knew. His dad's car was in the driveway, and his father was almost never home before Claire and Cameron went to bed. Paula's SUV was gone. And there was something else. He realized as he sat and watched the house that he'd never seen it without the outside lights burning. Paula always had all the lights on, inside and out. *I hate the dark,* she'd told him. *It makes me sad.* His dad was always complaining about lamps burning in empty rooms. But Cole liked it. He didn't like the dark, either.

He forced himself to exit the car, even though he just wanted to keep driving. He should have gone straight to Willow's. He'd wanted to. But he'd promised Cam that they'd play a game when he came home from school. And Cole didn't like to break promises to his brother. He closed the car door behind him, and the sound of it echoed on the quiet street. He didn't pull into the drive in case his father needed to get out or Paula needed to get in.

Cole walked in through the open garage and up the three wooden steps into the laundry room. There was none of the usual chaos to greet him. Usually Cam's shoes, coat, and book bag were lying on the floor until Paula ran around cleaning everything up. He'd hear the television blaring, Claire crying, or Paula talking on the phone. He'd smell something cooking on the stove.

Tonight he stood in the doorway that led to the empty living room, feeling an uneasiness. It was like the feeling he had when he'd called his mother and found that the line had been disconnected. Or when his birthday came and went and she didn't call or send a card. It wasn't like her. He couldn't imagine that she had some new boyfriend and didn't want him around, as his father said. But his father wouldn't lie, would he? Why would he lie?

Cole closed the laundry room door behind him. Again he thought about just leaving. No one tracked him. As long as he left a note for Paula, and as long as he was home by eight to do his homework, she wouldn't be mad. Instead he walked to the foyer.

"Paula?"

Nothing.

"Dad?"

He had that nervous stomach that he'd had on and off since he went to the apartment he'd lived in with his mother and found it empty. All their stuff—all his stuff—was gone. He hadn't wanted to cry in front of his dad. He couldn't remember the last time he'd cried about anything, really. But it had rushed out of him in a wave, like vomit. He'd just started sobbing.

"Where is she?" he'd asked. He knew he sounded like a little kid; he couldn't help it. "Where did she go?"

"Cole, I'm sorry, son," his dad had said. "I don't know. It's okay, though. You'll stay with us until we find her."

Except that horrible, sad sinking feeling had stayed. Sometimes he was able to ignore it, like when he was getting high with Jolie and Jeb, or when he was thinking about Willow Graves, or playing with Claire and Cam. But whenever it was dark or quiet, that ache just spread from his belly and swallowed him whole. Maybe that's why Paula didn't like the dark. Sometimes he looked at her when she thought no one was watching and he wondered if she had that spreading sadness inside, too.

On the staircase he picked his way over Cam's robot dog, a fire truck, a caboose from his train set, and headed up. He heard Kevin's voice. There was a sliver of low light coming from the door left ajar to his office. Cole stood and listened.

"I'm sorry, baby. I'm sorry. I'm stuck at work. I'll make it up to you."

Cole knew that Kevin wasn't talking to Paula. That was not the tone he used when he was talking to her. Cole pushed the door open. His father was sitting on the big walnut desk with his head in one hand, cell phone in the other.

"Dad?" Somehow the word never quite rang true for Cole. He'd wanted to call his father "Kevin." But Kevin insisted on "Dad." Cole complied, just to be polite.

His father looked up at him startled but then tried for a smile. He raised a finger.

"Look, honey," he said. "I have to go. Let's talk about this later."

Cole heard whoever it was get shrill and loud on the other end. But Kevin just hung up. Cole remembered how his mother used to yell at his dad, when Cole was small. He could see her standing at the kitchen counter crying. He didn't remember what they were fighting about. Just that for the longest time he thought that was why his father never came to see him, because his mother was always screaming her head off at the guy. He had recently started to wonder if that was true. And why it was that she'd been screaming at him.

"How was school, pal?"

Kevin looked terrible, pasty in the light of his computer screen. There was some kind of mark on his face, a dark line under his eye that trailed to his mouth. Was it blood?

"Dad, what's wrong?" asked Cole. "Where are Paula and the kids?"

His father didn't answer right away, looked at him with an odd, frozen smile.

"Uh, Cole," he said. He pointed to the chair across from his desk. "Take a seat, okay?"

Cole sank into the chair. The clock on the bookshelf behind Kevin said that it was almost four. He was going to be late to see Willow.

"Paula and I are taking a little break."

"A break?" Cole felt that ache in his stomach. He wished his father would turn on a light.

"She has taken the kids and, um . . ." His dad didn't seem like he could finish the sentence. Kevin looked down at fingers that he had spread wide across the blotter on his desk. "The truth is, I don't know where she is."

"What happened to your eye?"

Kevin lifted a finger to his face. "Oh," he said. The smear from his face had transferred to his finger. "I hit my head on a cabinet door."

Cole didn't know what to say. It was obvious his father was lying. He remembered what his mother had said to him the day he left to go spend a few weeks with Kevin. *I know you love your dad and I'm happy that you're going to have some time with him. But remember, all that glitters isn't gold. . . . Whatever, Mom. See you in a couple of weeks.*

He hadn't even been sad to leave her. He hadn't, in fact, given her a backward glance; she was too strict, too paranoid, always on his case about homework and who he was hanging out with. And when she found that joint, he thought she was going to have an aneurysm. Then, on the computer, he'd discovered that she'd been looking at those discipline summer camps. He'd *wanted* to get away from her and stay with Kevin. His father, Cole had thought, was smart and cool and had money. Not like his mother, who could barely make ends meet.

"Are you okay?" Cole asked

Kevin blew out a breath, tried for a smile. "I'm sorry, son," he said. "This is not what I had planned for your visit."

His father had been full of promises about the kind of summer they'd have together. But Kevin was often gone before Cole got up, sometimes didn't get home until very late. They'd played golf once. He had also, once, taken Cole and the kids to the beach. But Kevin was just on his phone the whole time, while Cole took care of the kids. Since school started, he'd hardly seen his father at all.

"It's okay, Dad. Don't worry about it."

Cole wanted to ask more about Paula, but something told him not to. Kevin's cell phone started ringing then. He glanced at it, his nose wrinkling as if he'd smelled something foul.

"I have to take this, okay?" Kevin said. He picked up the phone and looked down at the desk. "Hey, Greg. What's up? . . . I know. I know. . . . You'll have it tomorrow."

Cole rose and moved to the door. He stood there a minute, not knowing whether he should leave or not. He wanted to turn on the light, so Kevin wouldn't be sitting there with just the computer screen on. There was something really depressing about that. But instead, after a moment, he simply closed the door and left.

Cole walked into Cameron's room and sat on his little brother's bed. He looked around at Cam's mounds of toys and shelves of books. Then Cole put his head down on the sheets that were covered with planets and stars and smelled of Johnson's Baby Shampoo.

Cole remembered how he'd lied to Willow about his mother being in Iraq. He didn't even know why he'd done that; it was such a stupid lie. He'd have to keep it up if he went to her house. She'd ask about it, and he'd have to keep lying. And he'd have to pretend that everything was okay, that he was cool and in control. He couldn't tell her that he was nearly sick from wondering where his mother had gone. And now Paula, Cameron, and Claire had gone as well. Something wasn't right. Lots of things weren't right. But he had no idea what he was supposed to do about any of it. He hadn't realized how exhausting it was to be sad all the time. He was thinking that as he fell asleep.

He didn't come. Not at four. Not at five. At five fifteen Willow moved away from the window and threw herself in front of the television. Her mother was making dinner in the kitchen.

In a way Willow wasn't even surprised. She started to wonder if she'd imagined the whole thing—him appearing at her locker, the excited and surprised lift in her heart. She wasn't the girl that boys liked; she was the weird one with the orange hair and the poky elbows. She wasn't the pretty one with long-lashed eyes and big boobs. She was just Willow. He was probably only making fun of her. He went back to Jolie, and they had a good laugh.

"Where's your friend?" her mom asked. She stood in the doorway wearing an apron dusted with flour. She held a dishcloth in her hand. Willow's mother was beautiful; everyone said so. Willow knew that she herself looked like her father, who, honestly, was not her mother's equal in the looks department. In the pictures they had, he looked skinny and goofy. She wondered what Bethany had ever seen in him. *He was a wonderful man. He wasn't like any of the other men I've known.* So he was a freak. Maybe that's why Willow was such a misfit; it was hereditary.

She thought about lying—telling her that Cole had called and said he had too much homework, or that he got called into work, something responsible that didn't make him a screwup who broke his promises like Richard. But she didn't.

"I don't know," she said. She stared at the screen, some stupid cartoon. She didn't even know what she was watching. "He stood me up, I guess."

She tried not to cry, but a big tear escaped from her eye. She batted it away.

"Oh, Willow," said her mom. Bethany sat next to her, and Willow fitted herself into her mother's arms. "I'm sure he had an important reason."

"He could have called," said Willow.

"Maybe his car broke down or something like that. Just give him the benefit of the doubt until you know better."

"I guess," she said. But already she was feeling that dark place growing, that angry, disappointed hole in her middle.

"I know how hard it is to be your age, Willow. I remember."

"When does it get easier?"

Her mother issued a little laugh. "It gets *different*. Let's put it that way."

"Great."

Her mother switched off the television with the remote. And they sat like that, listening to the rain hit the windows. Her mother rubbed her back, and Willow closed her eyes. The room was warm, and the couch was soft.

She must have dozed off, because when she woke up, she was alone on the couch and she could hear her mother on the phone. Her voice had a funny tone, soft and sweet.

"No, I don't think it's inappropriate," she said. "I think it's fine."

Bethany laughed then, and she sounded so light and happy that it made Willow angry in a weird way. *How can she be happy when I'm so miserable?*

"That sounds nice," Bethany said. "Okay."

When Willow walked into the kitchen, the table was set for three. Bethany had made pizza from scratch. As her mother hung up the phone, Willow cleared the third place. She didn't need to eat dinner reminded that she'd been stood up.

"Who was that?" she asked when her mother hung up the phone.

Her mother was using the pizza cutter to make slices in the pie. The kitchen was a disaster—sauce and flour everywhere. Bethany was not a tidy cook.

"I thought you were sleeping," said Bethany, not looking at Willow. But she had this big smile on her face.

"Who was it?" asked Willow. "Not Richard? He's not still coming this weekend, is he?"

"No, it wasn't Richard," said Bethany. "And I don't know if Richard is still planning on coming this weekend. Do you want him to? You guys haven't talked in months."

"I really couldn't care less," said Willow. She brought the salad to the table and flopped down in her seat.

"Well, I told him he could come if he wanted to," she said. "Either way, we'll do something fun. We should check out that old cider mill. It's supposed to be really cool."

"Oh, yeah," said Willow. "It sounds like a blast."

They spent the rest of the meal talking about school—her classes, Mr. Vance, how maybe she should try out for drama next year. Then, after dinner, Bethany helped Willow answer her essay question about *A Separate Peace*: "Did Gene purposely knock Fin from the branch? Why or why not? If he did, what does it say about Gene and the friendship he shared with Fin?" Mom thought that was such a great question. But Willow just thought it was a cheat, since they'd been discussing it all week in class. Plus, she'd already read the book in seventh grade. But Mr. Vance said he liked to teach it again because the themes were so "complicated."

It wasn't until hours later, when Willow was lying in bed thinking about Cole and trying to go to sleep, that she realized her mother had never answered the question about who was on the phone.

That night she dreamed that Cole called her and told her how sorry he was for letting her down, for not being there when he said he would. He told her he loved her and that he couldn't wait to see her again. But then she woke up and realized that she'd only been dreaming, and the crushing disappointment she felt was almost too much to bear.

chapter twenty-eight

"I have to be honest. After our last session, I didn't think you'd be coming back."

Dr. Dahl was well pressed as always, looking particularly dewy and flushed, as though he'd just come from his daily workout. An open bottle of water, half empty, sat on the table beside his chair.

Jones shifted in his seat. "Well, to be honest, I wasn't sure I would."

The doctor looked at him with an open, expectant gaze. He seemed hopeful. Maybe even a little smug? No, not that. But there was something about his expression that annoyed Jones.

"So what are we doing here?" Dr. Dahl said.

Jones started to say how it was about Maggie, how he was afraid of what might happen to their marriage if he didn't keep coming to therapy. And even though this was part of the reason, it wasn't the whole reason.

"I realized that you were right," he said, even though it practically killed him. He cleared his throat. "That I've been holding back, afraid to move forward into the next phase of my life."

The doctor gave him an approving nod, which made Jones want to get up and leave again.

"What have you been afraid of, do you think?"

You had to love the guy. He went right into it. No foreplay at all. The headache was already starting.

"Well, I guess I've been afraid that there *is* no next phase," said

Jones. "That there would just be this puttering around for the next however-many years, taking pointless classes and mowing lawns. We'd take a few trips, go on some cruises. You know, I've been afraid that this was *it*. The only thing left was a kind of slow, inevitable trek toward the end. I mean, I don't even play golf."

"But you're a young man. Plenty of law-enforcement folks retire young, take their pensions, and find other work."

"I guess I don't feel that young sometimes," said Jones. "But anyway, some things have happened over the last couple of days."

He told the doctor about the cases he was working on, about Maggie's suggestion that he might hang out a shingle.

"And you're happy to be engaged in this type of work again? It gratifies you?"

"It does. I guess I originally came to police work as a kind of penance," said Jones. "A way to make up for wrongs I'd perpetrated."

"And has that changed?" The doctor took a sip from his water bottle.

"It has."

"What does it mean to you now?"

Jones thought about it a moment. But he didn't have to think about it much. He had a strange clarity on the subject.

"You know, I think I'm a little lost unless I'm helping people."

Part of Jones expected the doctor to praise him for his selflessness. But Dr. Dahl was quiet a moment, seemed to be turning over Jones's words.

Then, "You know, I think that's fine, Jones. As long as you don't use the work of helping others to hide from things inside you that need tending. I guess we both know you did that for a long time, first with your mother, then in your profession."

What was it with these guys? Was there some kind of manual they were all reading from? Maggie had said almost the same words. Jones didn't respond, really, just mimicked that affirming noise the doctor often made.

"But we can talk more about that next time," said the doctor. "Our time is up."

This was the other thing that always irked Jones about therapy. When your time was up, you got booted. It was like you were just getting comfortable, getting used to confiding in someone, and then you were asked to leave.

Back in his car, he turned on the cell phone; he expected messages. But there was nothing. Nothing from Chuck about the bones they'd found, which were being analyzed, or about Michael Holt, who'd apparently disappeared into the mines and had not yet emerged. Nothing from Paula Carr's parents; he'd called them twice, only to get voice mail. Nothing from Jack at the credit bureau on Paula Carr, or on Cole's mother, Robin O'Conner.

This was the thing about investigative work that people just didn't get. There were all these dead, waiting spots: waiting for DNA results—or in this case dental records—for contacts to wade through a river of other requests just like yours, for people who didn't want to talk to you to call you back. That's why cops drank after hours and overate on the job. How were you supposed to deal with the agitation, the urgency in the spaces where you had no control whatsoever? You went and got some food, scarfed it down in your car.

While he was still holding the phone, staring at it in frustration, it started to ring as though he'd willed it to do so. Ricky had set Jones's cell so that it sounded like the ringing of an old rotary phone. The tone was oddly comforting, that solid clanging of a bell, that sound of a real mechanism working—even though it wasn't that. The world had gone so quiet, all the noises that machines made now were soft and ambient, musical.

"Okay," said Kellerman. "Here's what I've got."

"Great," said Jones. He felt the relief that always came with action.

"Paula Carr hasn't used her credit cards or made any bank withdrawals in forty-eight hours." Kellerman paused to issue a hacking cough. The sound of it made Jones cringe.

"Sorry," Kellerman said. "One interesting thing. I did a little digging and found an account under her maiden name, husband not listed as an account holder. Last week there was a large withdrawal. Ten thousand."

Jones thought about this, and it made sense. She was planning a flight. She wanted to find Cole's mother before she left with her kids; that's why she'd called him. Something had happened to force her hand. Or maybe something worse.

"That's interesting," said Jones.

"Looks to me like she wanted to get lost."

"Maybe."

"Something else notable. Paula Carr hasn't made any ATM withdrawals in years. Her paycheck from a small company was direct-deposited into a joint account. But that account only had one ATM card, and that was for the husband. Her credit-card purchases are strictly mom-type charges. I'm talking about grocery and big-box stores, kids' clothing stores, online book retailers. There's not a charge on there over a couple hundred dollars."

"So her husband had her on a leash," said Jones. "Controlling her spending."

"I wish I could keep my wife on a leash," said Kellerman. He started laughing, but the laugh turned into that horrible cough again.

"You all right, man?"

"Ah, got this cough," Kellerman said. "I'm seeing a doctor on Friday."

"I'm sure it's nothing," said Jones. "Allergies, probably." The cough sounded bad, rattling and deep.

Controlling the money was a way of controlling the relationship. Jones thought about how Carr had referred to Paula only as "my wife," how the house was spotless, no pictures, how nervous and apologetic Paula had been throughout the visit. Jones was starting to get the picture. Kevin Carr was all about control.

"If I find anything on her, I'll give you a call. People get sloppy or careless after a while. Think no one is paying attention. Or they run out of cash."

"I'd appreciate it."

"The other woman, Robin O'Conner," Kellerman went on. "She's broke. She was recently fired from her job. She's got five maxed-out cards, about ninety-five dollars and change in her account. She's been evicted from her apartment, with two months owed in back rent."

"When was her last charge?"

"She tried to use her card yesterday at the Regal Motel in Chester. It was a charge for twenty dollars and twenty-three cents, and it was declined."

Chester was about an hour from The Hollows, another small working-class town, but one that hadn't developed in the same way as The Hollows had. He looked at his watch. He could go out there, try to find Robin O'Conner, as Paula had asked. But why? He didn't have a client, really. He wasn't a cop. He wasn't even a PI. At this point it was costing him money to fulfill his promise to Paula Carr—the drive, the dinner he'd owe Kellerman for these favors—and his buddy could pack it away. Maggie would not approve.

"Want me to keep tabs on her, too?" Kellerman asked.

"I'd appreciate it."

"I'll text you if either of them pops."

They made arrangements to get together for dinner the following week. Once the call had ended, Jones put the car in drive. He almost didn't realize he was heading to Chester until he'd pulled onto the highway. *Why not?* he thought. It was the only real lead he had on any of the three missing women. What was he going to do, go home and reflect on the future course of his life, his marriage, all the "work" he had to do on himself? He wasn't going to do that. He just wasn't. The very thought of it was suffocating.

As he drove, he found himself wondering what he would need to do to get his private investigator's license. He wondered, too, if he should start carrying a gun again.

chapter twenty-nine

The rumor swirling around the school office was that the police had found human bones up by the Chapel, suspected to be the remains of Marla Holt. At first this news landed softly, like a false whisper in Henry Ivy's ear. Something that could easily be denied and pushed away. But as the day wore on and the rumor spread and five separate people said to him "Did you hear?" he started to feel as if he were being buried alive under concrete blocks. By the late afternoon, the weight was crushing him. Was she up there? Had she been up there all these years? When he and everyone else had thought the worst of her? Had she been lying rotting in a shallow grave not a mile from where he worked every day? Had he stayed with her that night, as she had wanted him to, would she be alive right now?

All day he went through the motions: morning announcements, going over attendance records, disciplining the usual out-of-control students, chatting with his assistant. And all the while there was this terrible hum in the back of his head. He had plans that night with Bethany Graves. He felt like he was being punished for trying to be happy. There was something cosmic, wasn't there, that just wouldn't allow it.

"I can't go out," Bethany had told him. "Not with so much happening with Willow. Not with her being so unhappy."

"I understand," he'd said, trying to keep the disappointment out of his voice. He figured it was just a polite blow-off.

"But you can come here," she'd said. "For dinner? Tomorrow night?"

He felt a happy lift in his heart, the lofting of hope. "You don't think it's . . . inappropriate."

"No," she'd said. There was a smile in her voice. "I don't think it's inappropriate at all. I think it's fine."

When he woke up in the morning, he'd felt light and happy. He'd blasted through his 6:00 A.M. workout, had a power breakfast of egg whites and a fruit smoothie, gotten to work early to get a jump on some of his teacher evaluations. But by 9:30, after the office started to fill and people were talking about the rumors, he felt a kind of gray veil of grief and sorrow descend.

What he'd never told them was that he had loved her—in a way. It was not in the way he had loved Maggie Cooper. Once upon a time, he'd had a real hope that Maggie would love him, too. When they were teenagers, he'd imagined that one day their friendship would turn into something more, that one day they'd get married and have children. Of course, that had never happened. But their friendship had endured. And he had taken that as a kind of consolation prize.

He had loved Marla Holt like you love a movie star, never imagining that there could be anything between you. She was older than he was, seemed wise and worldly. And she was so beautiful that he almost didn't believe she was real. Even her imperfections—the tiny laugh lines at her eyes, the beauty mark on her lower right cheek (her witch's mole, she'd called it)—only made her more gorgeous. When she spoke to him, he was transfixed by her . . . by the way her mouth moved, by the way her hands danced to her throat, by the blinking of her eyes.

The night she'd disappeared, they were supposed to jog. He'd called her to ask what time, and she'd said she couldn't go. That Michael was at a sleepover and she had Cara. Mack would be late at work. But he could come by for a bit, couldn't he? Just to talk. Because that's what they did on their jogs. They talked and talked about everything.

At first he'd hesitated, because it seemed inappropriate. But she'd said, *Please, Henry. I so look forward to our time together.* And he had agreed. He enjoyed their time together, too. He looked forward to being with her, even though he knew he'd never touch her and that she was so far above and beyond him. Every instinct in his body told him not to go, that it was wrong, that it could lead someplace unseemly. But he did go, because she'd asked him to go and she had sounded so sad when she did.

He'd wanted to tell Jones about it that night in the woods. When they were out there, maybe feet from where they'd found those bones. He'd wanted to say, *I was with her that night, Jones. I held her in my arms. She was so unhappy with Mack, with herself, with the life they'd made. She told me that she'd made mistakes, that in certain ways she'd been unfaithful. I held her, and I wanted her so badly. I could have had her. I didn't care that there was someone else, someone not her husband. She was already opening up to me like a flower.*

Henry had wanted to tell Jones how it had taken every ounce of restraint in his body not to kiss her, not to feel the softness of her lips on his. His whole body had ached with desire as she wept in his arms. What would have happened if Michael hadn't come home and found them there, holding each other, swaying in the dim light of the living room? Would he have been able to walk away from her? Would he have been able to hold himself back? He knew that nobody thought of him as someone with the same drives and needs as any man. *Henry's so sweet. Henry's so kind. Henry's such a good friend.* But he did have needs, desires, always ignored and repressed. And he'd been alone so long.

"Mom?"

The word had rocketed through both of them, sent them reeling back from each other like an electric shock.

"Michael," she said. It sounded more like a breath exhaled, shocked and afraid. "What are you doing here?"

"Mom," the boy had said. "What are you *doing*?"

There was something strange and electric about the moment.

"It's nothing, sweetie," Marla whispered. "Henry's just a friend."

Henry's just a friend. The words sliced him, even though he knew in his heart of hearts that it was true. That's what he was to women. Just a friend. Even though he'd been burning with desire, she'd only been seeking comfort in her misery.

"I'm sorry," he said. "I'm very sorry."

And he'd moved quickly past the boy, who was already taller and thicker than Henry, with his face burning. The kid was panting like an animal. He was only thirteen, or maybe fourteen already. He was still in middle school, not yet at Hollows High.

"Don't, Henry." Her words followed him out the front door. And then he was running. He'd come over in his jogging clothes, because he hadn't expected to stay long, because he didn't want anyone to see him going to her house wearing street clothes. He ran and ran, did hard, sweaty miles through the neighborhood and out onto the road that led to the more rural areas of The Hollows, past the grazing fields and dairy farms. Later, when questions were asked, people had seen him running, as he did most nights. They had seen him running alone, not with Marla Holt. When he got back to his house, he saw that the Holt house was dark. And Mack's car was in the driveway. And that's when Henry saw Claudia Miller, standing in her upstairs window, a black silhouette against a glowing yellow light, watching, always watching.

The bell rang, and he snapped back to the moment. He wondered if he should cancel with Bethany Graves. What kind of company would he be with all this on his mind? He'd spent so much time wondering about that night with Marla. What would have happened if he'd stayed, hadn't run like a coward? Maybe she'd be with him right now, be *his* wife, instead of running off with whomever she'd finally chosen.

Honestly, he'd never believed that she had fallen to harm. He believed as everyone else had that she'd tired of her life in The Hollows and moved on without her children. She'd as much as told him that she'd been seeing someone else. Claudia Miller had watched her get into a black sedan, carrying a suitcase.

Maybe that night was just the last straw. Michael told Mack that another man had been in the house, and they'd fought. Maybe Marla had called her boyfriend and finally left, as she so desperately wanted to. She'd taken her beauty and her charm and left her suburban hell. If Henry had been a different kind of man, he'd have been the one to take her away. If he weren't Henry Ivy, bully bait–turned–high-school teacher, living in his parents' house, he'd have been the man to take her to New York City or Hollywood. But he *was* Henry Ivy, and try as he might, he had never been able to make himself into anything else.

Now he had to consider the idea that if he hadn't left her that night, he might have saved her life. He wasn't sure if he could live with that.

He forced himself to concentrate on the screen in front of him. He scrolled through the absences listed on the spreadsheet and saw that both Cole Carr and Jolie Marsh had not been in school for two days. Willow Graves had been in class—focused and attentive, if quiet, according to her teachers. He was glad for that. Henry knew that Willow was having a hard time, having problems adjusting to her parents' divorce, her new school. But he didn't think she was troubled, or at risk like Jolie Marsh. They could lose Jolie Marsh, as they'd lost her brother, Jeb. He'd make a call to each family. Neither absence had been explained with a phone call or an e-mail.

Thinking about the three young people made him remember their afternoon in the woods. He and Jones had discussed the legend told to Bethany Graves by Michael Holt. Henry had offered to research it, but he hadn't done anything more than a cursory Internet search that had, not surprisingly, yielded nothing. He'd even looked up Mack Holt online, wondering if some of his papers or research had been digitally archived at the university. But he found nothing except the man's obituary, sad and perfunctory. He'd died alone, estranged from his

children. The only reason Michael Holt had returned at all, according
to the endless Hollows rumor mill, was that he was still asking questions about his missing mother—questions that might be answered
now, by the discovery of human bones in a clearing in the woods.

Henry reached for the phone to call Maggie. But he couldn't bring
himself to dial her number. Maybe he should talk to Jones, tell him
what he hadn't told them years ago. But how could he say it now?
That he was there that night, holding Marla Holt? How could he explain keeping that secret all these years, revealing it only now, when
her bones turned up? How could he expose his terrible cowardice?
He'd always wondered why Michael Holt had never mentioned that
he was there, had never told the police or his father. Then he'd heard
that Michael had no memory of the night and what had happened to
his mother.

When the boy started high school, Henry feared that Michael
would recognize him, that it would jog his memory. But the boy had
never even seemed to notice him. He'd never had Michael in his AP
history class. When they passed in the hall, the boy only glanced at
him in blank unrecognition, even though they had lived in the same
neighborhood for years.

But this was all so long ago. A lifetime, it seemed. Until that afternoon in the woods with Jones, it had been years since he'd thought
about Marla. She was just another woman he'd wanted who remained
out of reach.

His intercom buzzed.

"Mr. Ivy, Bethany Graves on line one." He almost told his assistant, Bella, to take a message. But he couldn't do that. He wouldn't.

"Thanks, Bella."

He took a deep breath and picked up the phone. "Ms. Graves?
What can I do for you?"

She giggled a little, and he felt a warmth rise inside him.

"You sound so . . . like a principal," she said.

He glanced over at the door. Bella was on the phone, probably talking to her boyfriend, who was a rookie cop with the Hollows PD. Bella was the one with the inside information about the bones found at the Chapel. And the girl, sweet and efficient as she was, never stopped talking.

"Sorry," he said. He allowed himself a smile. "I'm looking forward to tonight."

"Me, too," she said. "I was just wondering about allergies. Or if there's anything you *hate*."

"Nope," he said. "I'm wide open."

He wasn't going to tell her that he was nearly a vegetarian, eating meat less than once a month. He didn't love spicy foods; they made him sweat unattractively and go red in the face. He tried to avoid dairy. Certain wines gave him heartburn. Women didn't like it when you were fussy about food.

"Good," she said. "Food is life."

"So true," he said. He liked that; he did think it was true.

"I had another reason for calling." Her tone dropped, went more serious. He prepared himself for whatever disappointment was coming. "Oh?"

"Do you know Cole Carr well?" she asked. "The boy from the woods the other afternoon?"

"He's new to the school," Henry said. "But he does fine. All of his teachers seem to think he's a good kid, if a little reticent and withdrawn. Why?"

"Well, he stood Willow up last night. He was supposed to come by and never did. She's crushed."

Henry glanced at the boy's name on the screen, the two red absence marks by his name. "I was just about to call his family. He's been out of school for the last couple of days. Maybe he's sick. Or there's some family emergency. The parents haven't called."

There was a pause on the line.

"Willow said she saw him yesterday. That's when they made plans."

He heard worry and disappointment in her voice. And even though he knew that it didn't have anything to do with him, he felt responsible.

"He might have been here but not attending class," he said. "He has a car."

"I'm sure he was," said Bethany. She didn't sound sure at all. "I really don't think she was lying."

Henry knew all about Willow's issues with the truth. Lots of teenage girls lied; it was a self-esteem thing. They generally grew out of it.

"I'll be reaching out to the family in a while," he said. He wanted to make her feel better somehow. "I'll let you know what I learn."

"Okay."

"Try not to worry, Beth." He liked the way her name sounded on the air. There was a beat where he wondered if he had been too familiar. When she spoke again, he heard that warmth in her voice.

"You're a good man, Mr. Ivy," she said. Somehow when she said it, it didn't feel like a punch to the gut.

The Regal Motel wasn't the worst place Jones had ever seen. Some motels like this—a depressing concrete U of shabbily appointed rooms—were nests of illegal activities, drugs in one room, prostitution in another. Recently a place like this closer to The Hollows had burned to the ground after the explosion of a small methamphetamine lab.

But the Regal was at least clean on the outside, with a fresh coat of paint. There was a decently maintained pool area, chairs and pool covered for the winter. The shrubbery along the sidewalk was trimmed. Someone was taking the time to keep the place in order, which meant management was also keeping an eye on the guests. The sign could use a little work. The *g* was missing, so from a distance it read THE RE AL MOTEL.

A little bell announced his entry into an orderly, quiet office. It was cool, the heat not yet on. A large woman with a head of tight gray curls tapped on a keyboard behind a desk. She didn't look up to acknowledge him right away. So Jones glanced around the room. Fake plant. A dingy love seat and coffee table. A magazine rack with overused, outdated women's magazines. The dark, wood-paneled walls were inexpertly studded with photographs of children in various poses of play, certificates from various agencies announcing compliance or excellence. There were some amateur line drawings of area sights. The carpet was stained, and a path was worn thin from the door to the desk.

"Help you, sir?"

She still hadn't looked up from her computer.

"I'm looking for a friend. I heard she was staying here. Robin O'Conner."

She lifted her eyes from the screen then, pushed her glasses up to the bridge of her nose, and gave him a cool once-over.

"Cop?" she said. She had the aura of proprietorship; she was not an underling or a worker. She had authority here, wouldn't be worried about her job. This could be a good thing or a bad thing.

"No," said Jones.

"Retired," she said. She wasn't asking.

Jones offered a slow shrug. With a woman like that, it was better to stick to the truth. "I'm doing a favor for a friend. Robin's got a boy who's missing her."

"You can leave a message. I'll see that she gets it." She turned back to the screen. He could see blue and white reflected in the lenses. She was on that social network. It was weird how into that everyone appeared to be. More into it than the real world, it seemed.

Jones waited. He walked over to the wall, peered more closely at the certificates. When he was a cop, he'd do things like that to unsettle. If the documents were fake or out of date, people would get nervous, start chattering.

"I run a clean place here," she said. When he looked back at her, she was staring at him hard. He was annoying her. She wanted him to leave. Good.

"I can see that, ma'am," he said politely. A little too politely, almost but not quite mockingly so.

"What time is it?" she asked.

Jones glanced at his watch, an old Timex he'd had since college. "Just before noon."

She gazed toward the window. Jones looked to see a small diner across the road. "She'll be headed over there soon, if she's not there already. She works the lunch shift."

Robin O'Conner must have been working off the books, or it would have popped on her credit report. The woman hefted herself from the chair, and it hissed with relief. She had a slight limp as she moved through a door behind the desk. Jones took this to mean that he'd been dismissed. He could just have left, but curiosity got the better of him.

"Her card was declined here yesterday," he said. He raised his voice a bit so that she could hear him in the next room. There was silence, and he didn't think she would come back, but then she filled the doorway.

She wore a deep frown. "I thought you said you weren't a cop."

"I'm not."

She took her glasses off and rubbed the bridge of her nose. He could see the red impression of her frames.

"Sometimes people need a break. Don't you think?" she said.

"I do," he said. "But in this business I wouldn't think you could afford to give too many of them."

"True. And I don't. But Robin's a good girl. She's not our usual patron."

"Care to elaborate?"

"Why don't you go see for yourself?"

This time when she disappeared through the doorway, he knew she wouldn't come back. He liked people like that, solid, sure of themselves. They were good judges of character, good witnesses. He remembered what Paula had said about Cole, that he was a good boy, that someone had loved him and done a good job raising him. It jibed with the old woman's assessment of Robin O'Conner.

He knew her right away, because her son had inherited all her beauty, the raven hair and almond-shaped eyes. She looked tired and too thin, her collarbone straining against the skin, the knobs at her wrists too prominent. Something about that made him think of Eloise, then in turn about Marla Holt. And he wondered how he had wound up with all these missing and injured women in his sights. *You never could resist a damsel in distress,* Maggie had said. Maybe she was right.

Robin O'Conner was working the counter. There was one trucker there, with more food on his plate than Jones had eaten in two days— eggs, hash browns, bacon, sausage, and two biscuits drowning in gravy. And yet the guy, stooped over his meal and eating with gusto, was about the size of one of Jones's legs. Was there any justice in the world?

She came over and leaned on the counter with a sweet smile. "Help you?"

"Just a coffee," he said. "Thanks."

"Are you sure? You look hungry."

Jones glanced over at the trucker. "I'd have what he's having. But I'd drop dead on the spot."

"And just look at him," she whispered. "I bet he looks better in a skirt than I do."

"I doubt that." But he said it in a gentle, fatherly way. Non-intimidating, nonsuggestive.

"Charmer," she said with that same sweet smile. "I'll get you some egg whites and toast."

"Sounds good."

When the trucker left and Jones had finished his meal, they were alone in the diner, except for whoever was cooking in the back. He could see why she couldn't make rent. There were no businesses in the area to attract a lunch crowd. The diner was perched across from the motel on a lonely two-lane road. Truckers pulling off the highway, motel guests, the stray tourist heading up to the mountains for camping or hiking—that was probably the extent of their clientele.

"Can I get you anything else?" she asked.

"I'm not here just for the meal. Can we talk?"

Fear pulled her face long. She looked toward the back, stepped away from the counter.

"Don't be afraid," he said. He lifted a hand. "Paula Carr asked me to find you."

She still didn't say anything. He decided to go on. "The best I can figure is that she wanted to get away from her husband, but she didn't want to leave your boy behind."

He watched her eyes fill with tears.

"But now she's gone. I don't know where."

"And where's Cole?" Her voice was a tight whisper.

Jones hadn't considered that point. Stupid. "I'm assuming he's still with his father."

"He wouldn't have left his dad," she said. A single tear fell down her cheek, and she batted it away. "He loves Kevin." He heard sadness and not a little bitterness in her voice.

"I saw Cole the other day," he said. "He seemed healthy, well cared for."

She offered a relieved smile. "I miss him so much."

"Kevin told Paula that you had asked him to take Cole because your new boyfriend couldn't be bothered. He implied that there were drug and alcohol problems."

She started to sob in earnest then. "No," she managed. "No, never."

He motioned for her to come sit at one of the booths, and she came around from the counter and sank into one of the red vinyl seats. No one came from the back to see what was happening. The parking lot was empty of cars.

"I have to pull myself together," she said. She took a napkin from the dispenser and wiped her eyes, blew her nose. She was pretty even while crying. "Who are you?"

"I'm Jones Cooper," he said. "I'm an investigator hired by Mrs. Carr."

The words felt like a lie, even though they were as close to the truth as possible. She seemed to accept his answer without question. He guessed he fit the part.

"It was just supposed to be for the summer," she said. She stopped then, laced her fingers, and seemed to consider how to go on. "Cole and I were battling constantly. He was hanging out with thugs at school. I found a joint in his backpack. We were fighting every day. It was terrible. I was thinking of sending him to one of those discipline camps."

Jones found himself watching her body language, the lacing and unlacing of her fingers, rubbing at her forehead. The inside points of her eyebrows turned up in the middle. She was stressed and sad.

"Then Cole told me he'd gotten in touch with his dad, even though we hadn't heard from him in years. He wanted to spend the summer away. Away from me."

"And you agreed?"

"Cole wanted to go. Kevin showed up in his shiny car and laid on the charm. Said all the right things, like how he'd been an absent father, maybe that's why Cole was so out of hand. Maybe a summer together would straighten him out. He wanted the chance to be a better dad, for Cole to know his half brother and sister. After all, I couldn't really afford to send him to one of those camps."

She stopped, looked out the window. "And honestly, I was *tired*. Working so hard just to meet our bills, fighting every day with him. Cole is smart, wants to go to college. I had no idea how I was going to pay for that. Kevin said *he'd* pay. He always knew how to say what I wanted to hear. I should have known. In my heart maybe I did."

"Known what?"

"That either you go along with Kevin when he's being nice or he gets ugly and you go along the hard way."

"Meaning?" But Jones had a feeling he knew exactly what she meant.

"At the end of the summer, the day Cole was supposed to come back, Kevin came alone. He said he wanted Cole to finish school in The Hollows. And if I let him do it, Kevin would pay for college."

"I said no. I wanted my boy back. Even though it was a relief in some ways to have him gone for the summer, I missed him terribly. It was like an ache in my heart to walk past his room and see it empty." Her eyes filled again, but she seemed stronger.

"You have kids," she went on. "I can tell. You love them so awful, don't you? It takes everything to raise them well, but, man, that love fills you up."

"So true," he said. And it was. "Did he get ugly with you when you said no?"

"Not at first," she said. "He implied he'd come alone because Cole was so happy in The Hollows. He loved Paula and the kids; they had such a stable, loving family. He said it like he was trying *not* to hurt my feelings, but that's what he was trying *to* do. And he did. It cut me deep. I thought about letting Cole stay. But no, that was my son. Plus, we'd been talking and e-mailing. He'd said he missed me, was ready to come back and do better at school. I knew my boy. We fought, but we always had a good relationship at the core. Lots of love."

She told him how Kevin had seemed to accept this, left a while later, and said he'd come back with Cole tomorrow. But he didn't. She started calling Kevin's office, his cell phone that night, but the calls went straight to voice mail. Then strange things started to happen. First Cole's cell phone number was disconnected. And her e-mail messages to him bounced. She figured he was avoiding her.

But then *her* phone was disconnected. She called from a neighbor's house, and the phone company told her that records showed she'd called to have her service turned off; the caller had had her Social Security number and password. It would take a few days for service to be restored.

"That's when I started to get scared," she said. "I got in my car to drive to The Hollows. I was going to get my son back. I had legal custody, and I would fight for my boy. I remembered what Kevin was, why I'd left him. He was cold. Cold at his center. I mean, he doesn't feel. People don't change. How could I have forgotten?"

"We always want to think the best of people," said Jones. "It's normal."

But she didn't seem to hear him. Her face was pale with anxiety, her words rushing out as though she'd been holding them all back for too long.

"Next my car wouldn't start. When the mechanic came out to tow it, he told me that the motherboard, the main electrical component that controlled the car, had been fried and that it would take days and thousands of dollars to fix."

She shook her head as though she were still incredulous about it.

"I was in a state of pure panic. For three days I had to call in sick to work."

Jones thought of what he already knew about Robin O'Conner. "So you lost your job."

He thought she would start to cry again. But she didn't. "I'd already missed so much time because of my problems with Cole. I was on thin ice. I think Kevin knew that. I think I'd even told him."

"So there you were with no job, no phone, no car."

"My credit cards were already close to the limit. I didn't have much money saved. I've never been good with finances, you know? I've been living paycheck to paycheck for as long as I can remember."

So many people were on the edge like this; it just took a single push to send someone's life into free fall.

"I knew I wasn't going to be able to make my rent that month. I'd already missed payments over the last couple of years. The management company said they wouldn't make any more allowances."

"So . . . what? You left your apartment and came here?"

He looked out the window at the motel, then at the woman sitting across from him. She was a good mother, a hard worker—at least that's how she seemed to Jones, just as the motel owner had said. He didn't like to see it. Jones, same as everyone, wanted to believe that people who fell on hard times deserved it, had made mistakes that led them to a place like the Regal Motel.

"Kevin came to see me. Just when I was at my lowest. Just when I was about to get a ride from a friend and make a scene at his house, call the police."

"Why wasn't that the first thing you did?"

"What—call the police? Make a scene?"

"Yeah."

She looked at him as if he were a moron. "Because of Cole. I didn't want him to see me freaking out like that. He chose his dad."

"Or so Kevin said."

She blinked at him, then looked down at the tabletop. It was clean—spotless, in fact—as though it had just been wiped.

"He asked how I could take care of Cole now with no job and no car. Didn't I want to see him with a good family, living in a nice house? Didn't I want to see him go to school? I did. I do want those things for Cole."

"So you just let Cole go? Even though you had every reason to believe that Kevin had your phone turned off, destroyed your car?"

She didn't say anything. But she straightened up a bit, turned her dark eyes on him.

"Listen," she said. "I don't have anyone. My mom is in a nursing home in Florida; I haven't been able to afford to see her in over a year. She was a single mother, had nothing to give me but love and encouragement. That didn't get me into college. If I'd had the money for an education, I might not have spent the rest of my life drifting from one stupid job to another. I wanted Cole to have better than this. He's smart, way smarter than I am. He deserves a leg up."

He heard the logic in her words. But he thought they weren't the words of a fighter. She'd given up on herself. She didn't think much of herself or her abilities. Perfect prey for someone like Kevin Carr. The sun moved from behind the clouds, and a milky light shone in on them. She turned her face to the window, a flower seeking the sun.

"He was Prince Charming until I got pregnant, every girl's dream. Handsome, wealthy, intelligent. Beyond that, you never see until it's too late. It's not until you get older that you realize only kindness matters, the courage to love and be loved. All the rest of it is a lie."

In all that time, not a car had passed on the road. No one peeked out from the back of the restaurant to see what she was doing. She seemed small and young. He wanted to take her home and tuck her in somewhere, bring her some tea.

"You want your boy back?" he asked.

She drew in a sharp breath, looked at him with some mingling of hope and fear. "I do."

He told her about what Paula Carr had said, how she knew that the things Kevin said about Robin couldn't be true, because Cole was such a good boy. He told Robin how Paula said that Cole was so sad, missed his mother so much.

"It was more than just letting Cole go," she said. She wiped tears from her eyes with the napkin folded on the table.

"You were afraid of Kevin."

"Yes."

"Did he hurt you?"

She shook her head. "It's not like he gets physical. There's a strange blankness to him, like he'd be willing to do anything to get what he wants. When he was in my apartment, I was terrified. I couldn't tell you why. He never threatened me, never put his hands on me."

Jones knew that it was the blankness that terrifies. When you look into the eyes of the sociopath, either you see the mask or you see the abyss. That's what's so frightening, just the absence of anything warm or familiar, anything human.

"Paula was afraid of him, too." Jones said.

"And now she's gone," she said.

Jones felt that angry rise he fought so hard to control. He thought it might be time to pay a little visit to Kevin Carr.

"How long can you stay here?" he asked.

"I don't know," she said. She wiped her eyes again. "I'm already living on Patty's good graces."

"Well, the service here is excellent," said Jones. He had a hundred dollars in his wallet, his weekly "allowance." He gave it to the girl; his wife would find this annoying, but not out of character. Besides, he knew she'd do the same thing.

"I can't take this," she said. She pushed it back across the table. But he stood up.

"Just stay here until I call you. This should keep you a couple of nights, right?"

She looked at the money sadly. "Thank you," she said. "Thank you so much."

"I'll be in touch," he said, and moved toward the door.

"Are you going to bring him back to me?"

He didn't like to make promises. The world conspired against the heroic statements he often wished he could make. "I'm going to try."

They both knew it was the best he could do.

chapter thirty

Mercifully, the children slept. It wasn't late, not yet seven thirty. But they were exhausted. Claire was in her portable crib in the corner of the large room, and Cameron sprawled, belly exposed, on the double bed beside her. The room was okay. Not hideous, clean. She had the shades drawn and the light beside her bed on dim, and she just lay there, looking up at the ceiling. Her parents wanted her to come back home. But she couldn't do that. She'd taken the children. Legally it was kidnapping. She'd left the family home. There was no evidence of physical abuse. In fact, in their final conflict Kevin had borne the brunt of the injuries. He could say that she'd assaulted him and taken their children. Technically he was right. She had the gun.

It was possible that he had called the police, that even now they were looking for her car. But a kind of numbness had settled over her. She'd been weeping at night after the children went to sleep. The days were hard, drifting from one restaurant to another, finding playgrounds so Cameron could play, nursing Claire in the backseat of the car while Cameron whined and complained in his car seat: *Where's Dad? I want to go back to school. This is the worst vacation ever. Why can't we go to Disney World again?*

But tonight she didn't have the energy to cry. She had to get strong, think about where they were going. She had a friend in Maine, her old college roommate. They'd reconnected on Facebook last year. *Come by and see me anytime you're in the area!* Paula wondered if she'd meant it.

The blue truck had taken Kevin's right leg out from under him and sent him crashing to the floor. The gun had sailed through the air and landed harmlessly on the couch. She ran for it, but he turned and grabbed her ankle, bringing her heavily to the floor as well, landing hard on her right knee. She heard a snap, ugly and loud, then a rocket of pain up her thigh. He straddled her, sitting on her hips, holding her hands over her head, immobilizing her.

"Paula, let's talk about this," he said. The words came through gritted teeth, a horrible grimace.

She turned her face away and started to weep. He was so strong she couldn't even move her arms.

"Okay," she said. She took a deep, shuddering breath. "I'm sorry."

He looked at her a moment, suspicious. She tried for a sad smile. And after a moment he released her left arm to wipe the sweat from his face.

"Okay, good," he said. "I don't want it to be like this."

She couldn't believe how rational, how normal he sounded, as if this were any old argument a married couple might have. He smiled down at her, pitying, sympathetic. She felt a lash of rage, and it was over before she realized that she'd clenched her fist and slammed it against his face, purposely aiming her big diamond ring for his eye. She was thrilled to hear him wail in pain, his weight reeling off her. She ran for the gun. When she turned around with it in her grasp, he was right there. He stepped back, put his hands up. A thick line of blood ran down his face; his eye was red and already swelling. She'd hit him hard. But not hard enough.

"Paula," he said. "Be reasonable."

Her voice came out in an unintelligible shriek. *"Get away from me!"*

She backed up the stairs; the baby's wailing had reached a fever pitch. It was like a siren in Paula's head. In slow motion they moved up the stairs, her backing up one step at a time, him pacing her.

"This is not good, Paula," he said. His voice was a warning. "What are you going to do, huh?"

She took a deep breath, willed her voice calm. No more screaming; it made her feel out of control. She held the gun; *she* had the power now.

"Don't make me kill you, Kevin," she said. "Please. I don't want to. But I will."

She wasn't even sure what he saw on her face or heard in her voice but he stopped in his tracks. She *would* kill him; he knew it. And he knew she *could,* too. She knew how to use a gun; her father had taught her. She knew she had a Glock in her hand, a semiautomatic without a safety feature. She knew there was a round in the chamber and nine in the magazine. She was a good shot; she knew to aim at center mass.

He stood in the doorway of the nursery while she gathered the baby in her arms. Claire stopped crying against Paula's chest, started rooting, rubbing her mouth against Paula's breast. Her chest ached with engorgement.

"If you let me leave here, I'll call the bank once I'm safe, and give you access to that account. You can have the money if you let me leave with the kids."

He blinked at her, considering.

"My mother is the beneficiary on that account," she said when he didn't answer. "If you kill me, it will go to her."

That part wasn't true; it wasn't even possible. She'd tried to do that at the bank, and they'd told her that she'd need written consent from her husband. All assets transferred to the spouse in the event of her untimely demise. But maybe he didn't know that.

He lifted his palms, offered an appeasing smile. "You're overreacting, baby. Let's talk this through."

What was weird was, even in that moment she could almost believe that she *was* overreacting, that *she* was acting like a crazy person. He'd come after her with a gun and she'd effectively defended herself, and now she was wondering if she'd lost her mind. That's how good he was. Or how weak she was. At this point who could tell?

Everything was in the car. She'd packed enough for all three of them. It had been sitting there for months. Stroller, portable crib, toys, clothes, diapers, wipes, even a breast pump. She backed her way there, holding the baby in one arm, the gun in her free hand. He trailed her slowly, talking to her softly.

"I love you, honey. Don't do this. Look at me. I'm bleeding." He started to cry. "Don't take my children from me."

"Don't call the school. Don't call the police," she said. "And when I'm safe, I'll get you access to that money."

Inside her was a hurricane of terror and guilt, hatred and sorrow. But when she caught sight of herself in the mirror, her face looked hard and cold. She didn't even recognize herself.

Getting the baby into the car seat was tricky with one hand, but she did it. Mothers could do almost anything with one hand. Once the doors were locked, she stowed the gun under the front seat and backed down the driveway slowly, as if it were any other afternoon and she was off to get Cammy. She pressed the button on the visor to close the garage door. It came down, erasing the sight of her monster of a husband, who was no longer crying but smiling.

The baby shifted in her sleep, sighed. Paula wanted so badly to call her mother. It had been three days and three nights that they'd been traveling. She'd read on the Internet that you should avoid using credit cards and cell phones, because that was how the police tracked people. So she'd been using the cash she had stashed in the car. She'd been very careful—until tonight. Tonight she'd had to use her card to book the room in this hotel. It was much nicer than the dumps they'd been staying in, horrible motels off the highway. Last night she'd stayed up all night with the gun under her pillow, listened to people walking by, voices raised in the other rooms, a television blaring. The police probably weren't looking for her. After all, she'd made her deal with Kevin. A deal she had no intention of keeping.

This hotel wouldn't accept cash without a credit-card guarantee.

She'd offered a cash deposit for incidentals. But they said it was their policy to allow check-in only with a card, even though she could pay in cash when she left. And she *had* to get a good night's sleep. She was frayed and edgy with the kids. So she'd used her old card, one she hadn't used in years. Maybe it wouldn't show up until she checked out, though she'd seen them run it through a machine. And maybe no one was watching after all.

She fought a few more minutes and then picked up the phone to call her mother collect.

"Paula," her mother said. "Honey, where *are* you?"

"We're okay, Mom. Has he called you?"

"No," she said. "He hasn't. But a man named Jones Cooper has been leaving messages."

She'd forgotten all about him. How had he gotten her parents' phone number? Why was he looking for her? There was only one explanation: Her husband had seen his number on her cell phone records and called him. Now Jones Cooper was looking for *her*.

"Don't tell him anything," Paula said. "He's a private detective."

"He said he wanted to help you. Do you think Kevin hired him?"

"I don't know."

She was getting that panicky, confused feeling she'd had on and off for days. They'd been driving in circles; she probably wasn't more than two hours from The Hollows. She had no idea where she was going to go or what she was going to do.

"Paula," said her mother. Her voice was stern now. "You need to come home to us with those children. I've been making some calls. I found a lawyer, a good one who specializes in situations like this. He says you need to come home and file for divorce, get emergency temporary custody of the children, and file a complaint and a restraining order with the police. Let's work this out the proper way."

It sounded right, a good course of action. But she was so afraid.

"But what if he comes after us? Like that man in California. He came to the house during that Christmas party and killed all those people."

Her mother was silent on the line for a minute. Then, "At least we'll all be together. I can't have you out there by yourself with Cameron and the baby. I'm sick with it. Let us help you and protect you. We're your parents, for God's sake. We *have* to be safer together than you are alone."

Paula didn't say anything. She wanted to go home. She needed to go home. The truth was, she wasn't equipped to run with her kids, to stay in some shelter, hiding from her husband. She felt a wave of relief.

"Okay, Mom," she said. "I'll come home in the morning."

She heard her mother release a long, relieved breath. "We'll come get you right now. Where are you?"

"It's okay. I need to get some sleep, and then, first thing, I'll load up the kids and come home. Maybe you can make an appointment with that lawyer for tomorrow afternoon?"

"Are you sure?" her mother said. "We'll get in the car right now."

She looked at Cameron and Claire, sleeping so peacefully. They needed to rest, and so did she. She couldn't stand the thought of waking them up.

"I'm sure."

She told her mother where they were staying, so that her mother could call if she wanted to, if she got worried in the night. Then she hung up, feeling better, as if everything somehow was going to be all right. She got up and checked the locks on the door. Then she placed the desk chair under the knob. She kept the light on but got under the covers and closed her eyes. For the first time in three nights, she slept, the gun in the drawer beside her.

chapter thirty-one

Just when it seemed to Willow as if her life couldn't get any worse, Mr. Ivy came to dinner. Really? *Really?* Was she really supposed to put up with this? Once upon a time, wouldn't it have been socially unacceptable, morally wrong, for your mother to be dating? Widowed, divorced—why didn't she just *give up?*

And to have it sprung on her like it was nothing. *Oh, Willow? Did I tell you I invited Mr. Ivy to dinner? . . . What? When? . . . Um, tonight.* And then Willow noticed that her mother was wearing a dress and not her usual leggings and big sweater. That her hair was down, not up in a bun. And she was wearing makeup! *Oh, my God—do you like him? . . . I'm not a teenager, Willow. It's just nice to have a friend. . . . So he's your friend. . . . He's not anything right now. . . . Then why are you wearing perfume?*

And now he was sitting across from Willow. Eating. Slowly, deliberately—as of course he would. He was probably chewing everything twenty bites, just the way every mother in the world told you to do. He was that kind of guy. At least he'd lost the argyle sweater. He wore a denim shirt that was halfway cool. His hair wasn't completely dorky. Maybe this was his *date* look, not his *principal* look. Because it *was* a date. They didn't talk about Willow or how she was doing in school. The conversation wasn't focused on her, though they had tried to include her.

But he was *literally* hanging on her mother's every word, leaning forward, laughing, smiling. Oh, they were having a grand old time.

Over salad she could still convince herself that this was a big nothing, that her mother was just trying to be sociable. By the time they were finished with dinner (Bethany's special Chilean sea bass in hoisin sauce with baby bok choy, which was so good that even Willow liked it), she knew. Willow realized by the blush on her mother's face—and an interesting smile that Willow wasn't sure she'd ever seen before—that Bethany did in fact *like* Mr. Ivy. By dessert Willow wanted to be sick. She couldn't take it anymore.

"So what time is Richard coming this weekend?" she asked. "Didn't you say he was coming? That he might spend the night?"

Her mother looked at her with a cool smile. They knew each other so well.

"Richard's my ex-husband, Willow's stepfather," Bethany said to Mr. Ivy, who had stopped chewing. "And no, he won't be spending the night. Nor has he ever, as Willow well knows."

Bethany and Mr. Ivy exchanged a look, a kind of knowing smile.

"It was her second marriage," said Willow. "Did you know that?" Oh, she felt it, that dark meanness, that black hole inside her. She was chastened for a minute by the look on her mother's face. It wasn't anger; it was pain.

"Um," Bethany said. Her mother looked down at her plate for a second. She had a death grip on the napkin in her hand. Willow noticed that Mr. Ivy had leaned back in his chair and looked down as well.

"My first husband," Bethany said finally, "Willow's father, died when she was three."

He looked up at her, but she didn't meet his eyes. "I'm so sorry," he said. "That must have been . . . really difficult."

Bethany issued that little embarrassed laugh she had when things weren't funny but she was trying to make light. "It was a long time ago."

"Yes," said Willow. "She's forgotten *all* about him."

When Bethany looked up again, Willow saw her awfulness reflected in her mother's eyes. Willow knew she was a terrible girl for saying that; her mother missed her father every day. She knew that; Bethany talked about him all the time. How he had a beautiful singing voice, how he loved to clown around and make them laugh, how he could cook, how he loved to read and always believed that Bethany would be a successful writer, long before she'd finished her first novel. Willow knew all this, and she couldn't stand to see that look on her mother's face.

I'm sorry, she could have said. *I'm sorry, Mom.* And her mother would have accepted her apology and put on a good face for the rest of the meal. Then she'd come to talk about it all later. But Willow didn't apologize. She just looked down at her plate, pushed around the bok choy she had no intention of eating. She wouldn't put a bite of her mother's food in her mouth, even though she liked it and was really hungry.

Outside, the rain that had been threatening for days with an on-and-off drizzle had finally committed. It was hitting the roof and windows so hard that it sounded like the pounding of feet.

"Wow, that rain is really coming down," said Mr. Ivy. He cleared his throat and rubbed his forehead. He probably had a sinus headache.

"Isn't it?" said Bethany. She jumped on the sentence like a drowning person looking for a lifeline. Her voice sounded tight and faint.

Willow let her silverware clank to the plate, and she pushed her chair back loudly. "Can I be excused?" she asked.

Her mother looked at her darkly. "Please, Willow, be my guest."

She made as much noise as possible stomping from the room. She pretended to storm up the stairs, but then she snuck back down to stand in the hallway outside the door to listen.

"I'm really sorry, Henry," said Bethany after a minute.

"No, don't apologize. Really," he said. "I get it."

"It's my fault. I did kind of spring it on her," she said. "I don't know what I was thinking."

"Maybe you were thinking we'd all have a good time," he said. His voice was soft and comforting.

"I was hoping."

"Should I go?"

Willow heard her mother sigh.

Yes! Yes! Go! Get out and don't come back.

"You know, Henry, I can see why you'd want to. And probably I should tell you yes, for Willow's sake. But I don't really want you to go. And I'm not sure Willow should act that badly and get what she wants. I think it might be time, though I know things have been hard for her, that she grows up a little."

There was a moment of silence. They were touching; she could feel it. Maybe they were holding hands. Or, God forbid, kissing!

"I'd like to stay," he said. "Can I help you clear the table?"

If Willow could have shrieked with rage, she would have. Instead she went quietly back upstairs. Inside her room she flung herself on her bed and started to weep. She couldn't even say why she was so upset. Eventually she cried herself out and lay spent on the bed, hating her mother, hating The Hollows, hating her whole miserable existence. Was there anyone on earth more miserable than she was right now? She doubted it.

The rain was hammering on her window. The sound of it was frightening and depressing, so she turned on the television but found that the cable was out. Of course it was. She threw the remote across the room, and it landed harmlessly on the basket of laundry she was supposed to have put away before dinner. She sat on the edge of her bed, feeling trapped and sorry for herself. Then at the window a flashing light caught her eye. A rhythmic flashing—light, then dark. Light, then dark.

She walked over to the window and looked down. In the glow from the front porch stood Cole and Jolie, under a large umbrella. Cole was flashing the light, and Jolie was holding the umbrella. She had that smile on her face, the one that Willow just couldn't resist. It promised a good time, no matter how awful everything else was. And then there was Cole. His smile promised something else altogether. She waved to them both and held up a finger. She grabbed her raincoat from her closet and moved quietly down the stairs. She could hear her mother and Mr. Ivy laughing. She didn't feel the slightest twinge of guilt as she slipped out the front door.

"How is it that you've never married, Mr. Ivy?" She'd been alternating between calling him Henry and Mr. Ivy. He liked the way his name sounded from her mouth. Usually the question would bother him, make him feel self-conscious. But there was something about her, something so wide open and nonjudgmental that he found himself really thinking about it.

"I don't know," he said. "Always in the wrong place at the wrong time or never in the right place."

He'd successfully pushed back his thoughts about Marla Holt to come to dinner. He'd decided after he hung up the phone with Bethany that whatever cosmic force had decided he wasn't allowed to be happy could just fuck right off. He liked Bethany Graves, and she seemed to like him. And he'd be damned if he was going to go home and brood over what had happened to Marla and what he might have done to prevent it. What good did that do now?

Then, on the way over, he'd heard on the radio that the medical examiner had confirmed that the bones found did in fact belong to Marla. She was up there. She had been up there all this time. Even that he'd managed to put into a box within himself. He'd look at it later.

"Have you ever been in love?" Bethany asked.

He'd had too much to drink, which for him was more than two glasses of wine. He was on his third, and he had that warm, light feeling. From the flush on Bethany's face, he'd say she was feeling the same. They'd been touching since Willow went upstairs. He'd dared a soft caress to her arm. There was a quick lacing of fingers while she told him about her husband who'd died so young, leaving her with a small child. Since they'd moved from the table to the couch in the living room, the desire to kiss her was almost an ache. The air between them was electric.

"I have been in love," he said. "Yes."

She frowned when he said it, put a hand to his face. "Love shouldn't make you look so sad," she said.

It was something about that sentence. Or maybe it was her tenderness, the openness of her expression. Everything that he'd been tamping down rose up inside him.

"It's not that," he said.

The music playing in Willow's room, something predictably raucous and angry, drifted down the stairs. He looked around the living room—the tall shelves of books, the flat-screen television, the warm amber recessed lighting. They sat close on the plush sectional, her leg pressing against his. He could sink into this place, this moment with her. If only he could shut off his mind.

"Tell me," she said. "Really, tell me. It's not like we can do anything but talk, with Miss Willow in seek-and-destroy mode."

Her smile was wide and trusting. She was expecting him to tell her about his unrequited love, or the one he'd lost, or how hard it was to meet someone in a small town. Something normal.

"Did you hear about the bones?" he said. "Back in the Hollows Wood."

A shadow crossed her face, like she was recalling something that disturbed her. And it was then that he remembered. It was Willow, really, who had found Marla Holt. If Willow hadn't run from school that day, made her way home through the woods, she would never have stumbled on Michael Holt near the Chapel. She never would have brought her friends back there, leading Henry, Bethany, and ultimately Jones Cooper to that place. If Jones Cooper hadn't gone back there and alerted the police, those bones might never have been discovered by anyone other than Michael. It struck Henry as almost funny, even as a blistering headache debuted behind his eyes.

"The bones?" she said. "What bones?"

It was almost too much for him to get his mind around. Marla and Bethany. Michael and Willow. It *was* some kind of cosmic joke. Here he was with this smart, beautiful woman, with the first romantic feelings he'd had in so long. And because Bethany Graves's child and Marla Holt's child had crossed paths, he couldn't simply sit here, maybe kiss her, tell her how pretty he thought she was and how much he enjoyed just talking with her. That it was enough. It was more than enough. He wasn't allowed even that simple thing.

"The police found bones back by the Chapel," he said.

She took in a breath. "Back where Willow was?"

He nodded, and the frown she was wearing deepened. He told her everything.

chapter thirty-two

Ray came in from the rain, soaked and cranky. Eloise took his jacket and hung it in the laundry room. Then she put on a pot of tea.

"Dental records confirm that the bones belonged to Marla Holt," he said. He sat heavily in the chair. She handed him a towel, and he used it to mop himself off.

She already knew that, of course. Not that anything was ever certain in her line of work. But she was as close to being sure of that as she was of anything.

"And Michael?"

Ray shrugged. "It's my second night out there looking for him, walking through those goddamn woods calling his name. Tonight I finally convinced Chuck Ferrigno to send some men out. After all, Marla Holt's body *was* out there, so there will have to be an investigation. Michael's a witness, at the very least."

Eloise sat across from Ray.

"Did he kill her, Eloise? He was just a kid. Did Michael Holt kill his mother?"

"I couldn't say."

"But what do you think?"

She didn't say anything. He knew better. She wouldn't speculate. She'd told him everything Marla Holt had said to her. It would be easy to jump to conclusions.

"How could I have missed it? It never even crossed my mind."

"Don't be so hard on yourself."

The kettle started to whistle, and she got up to pour the hot water into the teapot.

"He walked in on her with someone, went into a rage, and killed her. But he adored her, couldn't stand what he had done. So he repressed the memory."

Eloise knew that Ray was just talking, sounding it out.

"There was another man there, too," she reminded him. She looked at the steeping pot, the blue and white flowers on porcelain. It had been a gift from her daughter. Eloise missed her girl so much. For whatever reason, in that moment, the ache of it was almost unbearable. Eloise was going to call her. They needed to talk. Maybe *she* would go to see her daughter, invited or not; maybe it would help Amanda not to have to come to this house where so many ghosts lived and visited.

"Mack." Ray's voice brought her back. She wanted to be present for him, but somehow she couldn't stop thinking about what Jones Cooper had said to her. His words had wormed their way into her thoughts about who she was, about what she was doing, about her relationship to Ray, whom she really did love.

"He was working that night," she said.

"Maybe he came home? Maybe he covered for Michael all these years. That's what sent him over the edge. A fourteen-year-old boy wouldn't have the wherewithal to bury his mother."

"Maybe not." She didn't want to think about these things anymore tonight.

"Michael thought the answers were in that house," Ray said. "He also suspected that Claudia Miller knew more than she ever said."

"So maybe you should pay her one more visit," Eloise suggested. "Tell her about the bones."

"You think she'll talk now? Now that we've found Marla Holt?"

Eloise had no idea. She just knew *she* didn't want to talk anymore—

not about death, not about murder, not about pain and suffering and decades of lies.

"Maybe," she said.

He didn't need much more encouragement; he was in that agitated state. He wouldn't rest, wouldn't eat, wouldn't sit still until he knew he'd exhausted every avenue. And then he'd brood. Karen was right to have left him. He'd never cared as much about anyone as he'd cared about this work. Not even Eloise.

He was walking past her then, to get his coat from the laundry room. And then he was at the door. Before he left, he glanced at her.

"Are you okay?" he asked. His hand rested on the doorknob.

She took a step toward him. "You know, Ray, I'm thinking about taking a little time off. Maybe I'll go to Seattle to see Amanda and the kids."

Something played out on his face, a pull of sadness, a shade of regret. She expected him to argue, to remind her about their waiting list, about their responsibilities to everyone who needed justice and answers. But no.

"That sounds like a great idea, Eloise," he said. He gave her a warm smile, came back to hold her wrist lightly in his hand. "You *should* do that. It would be good for you. It would be good for Amanda."

"Ray."

He drew her into a quick, tight embrace and then opened the door. She was about to ask him if he'd consider going with her. But by the time she got the words out, he was gone.

"Did you hear?" said Jolie. "About the bones?"

Jolie was sitting in the front seat with Cole. The car reeked of stale cigarette smoke. It lived in the upholstery, tickled the back of Willow's throat, made her sinuses ache. Jolie lit another cigarette, let the smoke drift from her mouth into her nostrils.

"Crack the window," Cole said. She rolled her eyes at him but did as he said. Willow watched as the smoke was sucked out in a thin, flat line.

"What bones?" asked Willow. She was already there, in that place of regret she knew so well. It sat in the pit of her stomach. In the rearview mirror, she saw Cole staring at her, though he'd barely acknowledged her since she slipped out to meet him. She hadn't asked him why he didn't show up the other day. She wouldn't give him the satisfaction.

"Out by the Chapel," Jolie said. She had the ghost-story face. A gleeful, wide-eyed menace lit her gaze. "Where you saw that freak Michael Holt digging? They found bones."

Willow felt the tingle of curiosity. "Just like he told my mom."

"No," said Jolie. "The bones belonged to his mother. Everyone thought she'd run off ages ago. Turns out she was murdered."

Cole brought the car to a stop by the side of the road, and Willow saw that they were back at the awful graveyard. *Oh, no. What's wrong with me? Why do I do things like this?*

"What are we doing here?" Willow asked.

"Don't you want to see where he was digging?"

"No," she said.

"He's still back here," said Jolie. "He ran off when they found the bones. They think he went down into the mines, that he might be living down there."

"Yeah, like the mole people," said Cole. "Did you ever hear about that? People live in the abandoned subway tunnels beneath New York City."

"That's an urban legend," said Willow, even though she knew it wasn't. Her voice came out more sharply than she'd intended. She didn't like it when people who'd never lived there pretended to know things about New York City. He was still staring at her in the mirror, but she forced herself to look at Jolie.

"You don't want to go?" said Jolie. She seemed incredulous.

"Last time we were out here, you thought I was lying," Willow said. "You didn't believe me."

"Well, I believe you now."

Cole turned to look at Willow; his face was pale in the dim light. He had dark shiners of fatigue under his eyes. If she didn't hate him, she'd have asked him if he was okay. But she did hate him, a little. The rain was drumming on the roof of the car. Out the window she could barely see the tombstones. Why would anyone want to go tramping through the dark woods in the pouring rain when a crazy murderous freak could be lurking out there? She asked Jolie as much, and Cole issued a laugh.

"That's what I said," said Cole.

Jolie started to get sullen. "That's the problem with this place. Everyone is so fucking dull, dull, dull. Where is your sense of adventure?"

Willow found that she didn't really care what Jolie thought of her anymore. The whole enterprise was asinine. It was stupid, and beyond that, she had been so awful to her mother and now she was out here in the middle of a huge storm with these two. She'd run off on her mother again, let her down *again*. She didn't have her cell phone. When her mother discovered she was gone—and it wouldn't be long—she was going to be terrified.

"Those kids are lost," her mother had told her. "No one's looking after them. You might think that's cool. But you're wrong. It's sad." In this moment Willow finally understood what her mother meant. But it was probably too late. Her mother was never going to forgive her for this night. She looked at Cole in the rearview mirror.

"Can you take me home?" she asked.

"Sure," he said. He turned on the ignition.

"What?" said Jolie. Her voice went shrill, her eyes narrowing to two small points of anger. "You guys are *such* pussies."

And in the next second, Jolie pulled on her hood and stepped out into the rain. Willow saw the bouncing of her flashlight beam in the night as she stalked off.

"She's crazy," said Willow. She rolled down the window. "Jolie!" she yelled. "This is nuts! Come back!"

"Fuck you guys!" Jolie's voice sounded small and childlike in the rain, barely a whisper on the air. Willow brought the window back up when the beam disappeared into the trees. Cole was looking out after Jolie, too.

"Let's go get her," said Willow, yanking up her hood.

"Hold on," he said. "She's going to be back in like *one* minute. Trust me."

She didn't say anything, watching the night, willing Jolie to come back. Otherwise Willow knew they were going to have to go out after her. They wouldn't leave her out there. And Jolie knew it, too.

"I'm sorry," Cole said after a moment.

"For what?" Now he was looking at her over the seat. Willow tried not to stare at him. Those eyes thick with lashes, that nice soft mouth.

"For not coming to your house the other day," he said. "I wanted to, but . . ." He didn't finish the sentence. He just blew out a long breath, looked down at his nails.

"But what?"

For a second she thought she was dreaming. Sitting here alone with him, the rain beating down outside—it felt like something she could make up.

"I lied to you," he said. "About my mom."

Willow knew that. She remembered that she thought he was lying. "She's not in Iraq?"

"No," he said. "I don't know where she is. My dad said she's living with some guy and doesn't want me around for a while. She wants me to finish school here, stay with my dad's family."

"I'm sorry." She *was* sorry. She knew what it had felt like when Richard went off to live with that stripper, even though he and her mom were divorced. She knew what it had felt like when her mom was having a good time with Mr. Ivy. It felt like a betrayal. It hurt, made you unsure of your place in your family, in the *world*. She reached a hand over the seat, and Cole took it. She felt the heat move into her body.

"But now my stepmom and my half brother and half sister? They left, too. I guess Paula ran off on my dad. He *said* she hurt him, took the kids." He leaned away from her, against the driver's-side door.

"But?"

"But she's so *nice,* such a good mom," he said. "I just can't see her hurting anyone."

She couldn't quite see his face, obscured as he was now by the seat. She climbed over the center console and came to sit beside him in the place Jolie had occupied.

"You think he lied?"

He shook his head. "Maybe. I don't know. And if he lied about that, did he lie about *my* mom, too?"

"Can't you call her?"

"Her phone got disconnected. She got fired from her job. She hasn't answered any of my e-mails."

Willow found herself thinking of her own mother, how she really had to get home. But then she saw that he was crying. A single tear trailed down his face. He wiped it quickly away. She reached out for him, and he moved easily into her embrace.

"It's okay," she said, even though she had no reason to believe that was true. Everything about him felt good—his arms around her, his face on her neck, his hair against her fingers. "Where's your dad now?"

He pulled away from her suddenly, turned around to peer out into the darkness. "Did you hear that?"

Willow's heart started pounding as she listened past the beating rain. Then she heard it, too, faint and far away, the sound of someone screaming. Maybe. They both exited the car at the same time, into the buckets of falling rain. Willow came to stand beside Cole. They looked in the direction of the woods but didn't hear anything more. There was only darkness and rain, as far as Willow could see. Maybe it was their imagination. Maybe they hadn't heard anything at all. But Willow knew she wouldn't leave her friend out there alone.

"Let's go get her," said Willow.

"Okay."

The thin beam of Cole's flashlight was the only light they had.

Michael heard yelling. A woman's angry voice ringing out over the rain, and he moved toward it. He'd been wandering in a kind of fog for so long, he didn't know how long—dwelling in the mines, dozing there. There were some PowerBars and a few bottles of water in the knapsack he had with him, and he'd lived on those. He was happy where it was dark and quiet, where there were no eyes looking and no mouths talking. The darkness didn't judge him or want anything from him. It didn't care what he did or didn't do; it didn't care what he had done.

He heard more shouting; it sounded like the calling of birds. From the same direction, the rushing of the river seemed impossibly loud. He kept moving toward the voices. How long ago had it been since he had broken through the mine entrance and gone down, down, down into the world beneath? A day, two days—a week? Time had no meaning in there, just as he remembered when he used to go with his father. They'd descend in the day, and return in the night. It seemed as if they'd gotten into a spaceship and landed on a distant moon.

On his website, Michael called himself a caver and spelunker. He claimed that he gave tours and was a consultant. But, honestly, he wasn't any of those things, didn't do any of that. He was willing, of course. But no one had ever contacted him via the site he'd built. He didn't have any formal training, other than following Mack on his research journeys. Michael was just a drifter, a loser. He could never get a hold on anything, could never build a life in the world up above—or down below.

Since college, Michael had been drifting from one meaningless job to the next. First he worked as an admin at a website development company, which is where he learned how to develop and maintain sites. He was competent enough, but he just couldn't get the social stuff. He couldn't talk to people. He sometimes just blanked out in meetings, went catatonic in his boss's office. And, then, one day he found he just couldn't go back.

He attempted other kinds of work. He was a custodian in an office building for a while, then a grocery store stocker. The longest job he'd held was as a night watchman. He didn't have to see or talk to anyone, other than fielding the occasional call or visit from his supervisor, who'd seemed just as reluctant to have a conversation as Michael was. He could simply wander long, dim, empty hallways and feel something akin to peace. He had time to work on his website, the place where he was all the things he couldn't be in real life. And the night was suitable cover, wasn't it?

As he had entered the mines, with Ray chasing after him, he didn't have any plans to return. But after so many days wrestling demons, he had to come up for air. Now, in the woods, he was lost—in every sense of the word. He could still hear something, more faintly, and he followed. He had to tell someone what he had done. It was time for confession now, and punishment.

The dark had spoken to him. It whispered that it was safe to remember, that it was time. And then he was back, on his bike riding through the old neighborhood. He was a wraith, quiet and fast. And the night was silvery and slick. On reaching home, he dropped his bicycle on the driveway, and left it where it twisted.

Inside, he could feel that the energy was different and strange. He heard music. He heard his mother's voice. He felt powerfully that he didn't belong there in that moment and that he shouldn't have come home. But he was drawn toward the unfamiliar sounds . . . a man's tender voice, a strange cadence to his mother's words, a song he'd never heard before. And when he moved toward the light of his mother's drawing room, he saw her in the embrace of a man, not his father.

Inside him something shifted, went black and ugly. Why? He didn't know. But he went to that blank space he had within him— where there was just the rushing of blood in his ears and the sound of his own breathing. The man, a faceless stranger, left in a hurry. And Michael was left alone with his mother.

"Michael," she said. "Why are you looking at me like that? He was just a friend."

"You sent me away," he said. He knew his tone was bitter, vicious. "So that you could be with him."

He saw the shame on her face. But there was also anger.

"Michael," she said. "I am your mother. You don't speak to me that way."

Then there were the lights of his father's car in the driveway. And inside Michael, a familiar slow, simmering rage was starting to brew. He knew it well—he'd felt it before tantrums as a child, before fights at school, during screaming battles with his father. But he'd never felt it for his mother, never directed it at her. She'd always been the one to talk him through those rages. *Breathe, sweetie. Breathe.*

She was backing away from him when his father walked in.

"What's going on?" Mack said. He laid his briefcase and coat on the couch. He looked weary.

"She had a man here," said Michael. "She was in his arms. She's a whore just like you always said."

And Mack *had* said that so many times. Michael heard his father yell it during arguments and whisper it at the dinner table. And Michael had railed against him, always defended her and protected her. But Mack was right.

The stinging slap his mother landed on his face sent a shock through Michael. It was white lightning, electrifying him. Then she was running up the stairs, with Mack bounding after her. Michael heard her shrieking.

"I hate you! I hate this place! I hate this life!"

Michael stood there stunned, feeling the heat on his face, listening to them screaming at each other. What were they saying? He didn't even know. He was in that place where all the anger seemed to build from inside his belly, boiling and rising up into his brain. She'd *hit* him. She'd taken all her love away from him. She was going to leave them, leave *Michael*.

Marla came down the stairs with her packed suitcase. He knocked the bag from her grasp and the clothes spilled out on the floor . . . her lacy underthings, a pair of shoes, a few skirts and blouses. He knew he had to stop her, and he grabbed her hard by the shoulders.

"Don't leave me," he said. He was sobbing, sounding just like a child.

"Michael," she said. Her eyes were wild and desperate. "Let go of me. I'll come back for you and your sister."

But she was lying. He *knew* that. She'd come back for Cara, but not for him—now that she knew what he was inside, now that she knew that his rage could be directed at her. He outweighed her by fifty pounds at least, was already much taller at fourteen. She could never control him.

"Michael," she said. Her voice was just a jagged inhale. "You're hurting me."

Mack stepped in. "That's enough, Michael."

But Michael couldn't. He wouldn't let go of her. His grip on her grew so tight that she cried out. Somehow, in a struggle among the three of them, she broke away. She ran out the back door and into the Hollows Woods, the place where he now wandered.

She had been fast. All those years of trailing her on his bicycle, he knew how fast she was, even though she thought of herself as slow and clumsy. He was after her. There was no thought in his head at all, no malice really. He just wanted her, needed her to stay with him.

She turned into the clearing, and he was right behind her. But Mack caught up quickly. His father caught ahold of Michael with strong arms, tried to keep him back.

"Stop it, son," he'd said. His voice was a cough. Mack was panting, sweat pouring down his face and neck. "What do you think you're doing? You need to calm yourself."

Mack had a hard lock on Michael's wrist. But then Michael punched him mercilessly in the stomach, and Mack doubled over, falling. He moaned and writhed on the ground as Michael ran into the chapel. In the total darkness, he could see nothing. He could only hear her weeping.

"Mom," he said. "Mommy. Don't cry."

He thought of all those nights he'd slept beside her while Mack was working, or sleeping on the couch after they had been fighting. And Michael would lie there and listen to her crying, pretending that he was asleep. She would hold onto him, seeking warmth and comfort from him. And he cherished those moments with her, because she belonged only to him. He could see that she didn't need Cara in the same way, that Marla didn't draw the same kind of comfort from her that she did from him. She needed him. She couldn't leave him. What was he? Who was he without his mother?

He might have come back to himself if she hadn't tried to run from him again. But she burst from a hidden corner and tried to make it to the door. He caught her easily and his hands wrapped themselves around her neck. It was so small, so delicate under his powerful fingers.

From another place, another world, he watched himself. He watched her flail and struggle. He listened to her horrifying rasp for air, felt her weak pounding at his arms and kicking at his legs. He watched her eyes go wide, bulge, redden. And then he watched them go blank. Her body slackened, and all the fight, all the life, drained out into his hands. But it hadn't happened to him. It didn't happen at all. It was a dream, a terrible dream. It happened to someone else, another Michael—one who didn't even exist on a normal day.

He didn't remember anything at all after that. Even now, wandering in the rain, carrying the memory of what he had done to his mother, he remembered nothing else of that night. What had his father done? Why had Mack hidden it all from the police, from Michael himself? Why? He could never answer those questions for his father. He could never make amends to his mother. There was no more chance of his ever living in the light again.

It was then that he saw her running.

"Don't go," he said. "I just didn't want you to go."

He walked out into her path, and she stopped short, stared up at him with blank, nearly uncomprehending terror. On some level, he could see that it wasn't his mother. It was just some girl, a stranger who couldn't hold a candle to Marla because no one could. She issued a panicked scream that sent a jolt of fear through him. And she started to flee, nearly tripping once in her panic to get away from him. But this time, he didn't give chase. He wouldn't. He'd let her run, just like she had wanted so long ago.

"Heavy rainfall in the region tonight," the radio announcer said. "We have reports of flooded streets. Some local roads are washed out completely."

Jones hated the way newscasters always seemed to enjoy giving bad news. They had this faux-somber delivery that wasn't in the least bit sincere. "It's been thirty-five years since the Black River overflowed its banks. But authorities say the levels are rising. Folks, I'm sure I don't have to say it, but I will: If you don't have to go out tonight, stay home."

Jones brought the SUV to a stop in front of the Carr house and sat. He remembered the hours spent waiting and watching, sometimes alone, sometimes with a partner, the endlessness of it. Though often, when Ricky was young, he'd cherished the silence and solitude of it. But sometimes being alone with his own thoughts was the last thing he wanted. It was in those quiet, empty spaces that all the things you didn't want to think about paraded before you, demanding to be noticed.

Maggie had already called twice, first to ask him when he'd be home. She was worried about him out in the weather. Next she called to ask him to look in on her mother. Cell phones were working, but some of the landlines in the older parts of town were out. Elizabeth's phone was always one of the first to go in a storm. And of course, like the stubborn old mule that she was, she refused to get a cell phone—because that would make things easier on Maggie and Jones.

"No problem," he told Maggie. "I got it covered."

"And don't fight with her."

"I won't." And he wouldn't—unless Elizabeth started with him. Jones had always had a somewhat contentious relationship with his mother-in-law. But since the events of last year, it had gotten much worse. They could barely make it through a meal without arguing. It was another thing Maggie was angry with him about, even though he didn't think it was entirely his fault.

"Even if she starts with you, Jones," she said. "And see if she'll come back to the house with you."

"She won't."

"Just ask," she said. "And where are you now?"

During their last conversation, he'd told her about Robin O'Conner and the money he'd given her. *You old softie. Was she cute?* He'd told her about his trip to the doctor, what the other man had said about Jones finding his father. *It's true we don't talk about your father much. Maybe he's right—it bears looking into.* Now he told her that he was sitting in front of the Carr house. It was a dark, empty space in a street of warmly lit homes. In other houses he saw open garage doors, television screens flickering. Somewhere he heard the faintest sound of a ringing phone.

"What are you going to do?" she asked.

"I haven't gotten that far. It doesn't look like anyone's home."

"What would Columbo do?"

"Columbo? Really? All the sexy, tough-as-nails television detectives out there, and that's who I remind you of?"

"I don't watch much television. Besides, I always found him kind of appealing," she said. "Do you have your gun?" His wife, the pragmatist.

"No. Just the Maglite." On the job you had your gun, your blackjack, and your Maglite, the favored flashlight of police officers everywhere. About three pounds of metal, including D batteries, it could do some damage in a pinch.

"Hmm," she said, sounding uncertain. He watched the house for movement in the windows. There was nothing.

"Just be careful. Okay?"

She used to say that to him every time he left for work. Even though he was only a small-town cop in a place where things were quiet most of the time, she'd always worried about him. She'd get mad at him back then if he didn't call when he was supposed to or if he got hung up with overtime and came home late. *Don't worry,* he'd tell her. *They'll come to the door if there's really something wrong. . . . Is that supposed to make me feel better?* He'd liked it that she worried. He liked it now that she wanted him to come home.

"You mean you still love me?" he said.

"Don't be silly." She had that warm, flirty tone in her voice.

"You were pretty mad at me the other night."

"Not mad," she said. *"Concerned."*

"No. Mad."

"Okay," she said. "Angry. Upset." He remembered that she didn't like the word *mad.* That it implied insensibility, something out of control. "But I do love you. You know that, don't you?"

He did. He did know that. He told her so.

"This is the part where you tell me you love me, too."

He had a hard time with those words. They felt so awkward, so inadequate on his tongue. Abigail had demanded that he say it over and over to her, day after day. *I love you, Mommy.* It was like she'd used the words up. He'd said them so many times, not meaning them, saying them only to appease and escape, that the words seemed fake. And they were never enough for her. Nothing was ever enough for Abigail.

"I do," he said. "You know I do."

Maggie understood. She never hassled him about it. She didn't need him to say it. What Maggie needed was a lot of touching, a lot of holding. He hadn't always been good at that over the years, either.

"Seriously," she said. "What are you going to do?"

"I guess I'm going to ring the bell and see if anyone's home. Go from there." He'd been sitting and watching for the better part of fifteen minutes now. He'd come to believe over the years that an empty house had an aura; you could tell somehow when no one was home. It was more than just a lack of the lights and movement. It was like a lack of breath.

"Hmm."

"I know. Brilliant, right?"

"Just be careful," she said again.

There was no answer at the door. Jones went around back through the heavy rain and was bold enough to walk up onto the deck, peer into the living room. The light was on over the stove in the kitchen. Nothing out of place, no furniture overturned, no blood on the walls. Good. Another light shone in an upstairs window. He tried the sliding glass door, but it was locked. Not that he'd have entered, maybe just called inside. He reminded himself that he had no right to be there. He was not a cop; he was a trespasser.

He walked around the side yard. It was thick with trees, sparing him a little bit of the rain that fell. There were no cars in the driveway; he'd seen that on arrival. He cupped his hands and peered into the narrow window on the side of the house that looked in on the garage.

There were no vehicles there, either—not the Mercedes SUV he knew that Paula Carr drove, not the old BMW the kid had with him, either. He didn't know what Kevin Carr drove.

He tried the knob on the side door, and when he found it unlocked, he pushed his way inside. He wouldn't have done that as a cop, unless he had line-of-sight, meaning he saw something that looked incriminating or dangerous or had reason to believe that someone was in danger inside. Though he supposed he could make that argument if it came down to it. As a cop he'd always stuck to the letter of the law. Otherwise what was the point? As a private investigator, he wouldn't have that obligation—he wouldn't have to think about warrants and inadmissible evidence, cases thrown out of court because of evidence gained illegally. Of course, now he could also be arrested for illegally entering a home.

The garage was organized and tidy. Bicycles hung on a wall rack, sports equipment—tennis rackets, boxing gloves, roller skates in various sizes and colors—all sat orderly on shelves. The floor was painted a slate gray, free from the dirt and dust that would have been normal. Jones felt his heart thump, bent down to see if the paint on the floor was wet. But it wasn't. It was dusty, in fact, and dirtier than it had looked. He noticed that he'd left a trail of water from the door as the rain had sluiced off his jacket.

When his phone rang, he practically had a heart attack, adrenaline rocketing through him. *Note to self:* When illegally entering a home, turn off the cell phone. He didn't recognize the number.

He walked outside to answer, started making his way quickly back to the car. The rain had let up for a minute, slowed to a fine drizzle.

"Jones Cooper," he answered.

"Jones, it's Henry Ivy." He sounded upset. "Sorry to bother you, but we have a problem."

Henry told him about Willow Graves running off.

"I'm kind of in the middle of something here," Jones said. It wasn't exactly true. There was no one home at the Carr house. He had no other leads on Paula Carr. He was at another dead end. At this point he'd go check on Elizabeth and then go home.

"This is my fault," said Henry. He'd lowered his voice, told Jones about his night with Bethany Graves and Willow's unhappy response. As soon as Jones got back into his car, the rain started coming down hard again.

"You think she ran off on foot in a storm like this?" he asked.

"Maybe not."

"She has friends with cars?"

Then Jones remembered that Willow Graves knew Cole. Cole had a vehicle, and he wasn't at home. Jones wasn't a big fan of coincidence, but here he was again. He *was* looking for the kid. It would be a good thing to find him away from the father, have a word with him in private about his mother.

"Beth called Jolie's mother, who said that Jolie was out with Cole Carr. We think they all might be together." Jones heard Bethany say something in the background. But he couldn't make it out. "We checked around at some of the local spots like Pop's Pizza and the Hollows Brew. No one's seen them."

"Okay," said Jones. "You don't think they'd have gone back there? To the Hollows Wood?"

"Maybe, if they heard about the bones," said Henry. "Bethany seems to think it's possible. We're headed there now."

"All right," said Jones. He looked at his watch. It was still early, just after eight thirty. "I'll meet you at the graveyard."

"Thanks, Jones."

"When did I become the guy to call?" Jones muttered to himself. Of course, if he was honest, he had to admit he liked it. Anyway, it was at least a detour from dropping in on the old crank. As he pulled out, he thought briefly about Eloise, her predictions for him. But he pushed them quickly and totally away. By the time he reached the main road, he'd forgotten about them completely.

———

She was swimming, and the water felt good. When was the last time she'd been submerged in water? Dipped her body into crystal-blue pool water or tasted the salt of the ocean? She and Alfie used to take trips to the beach, lie on the sand beneath a big blue-and-green striped umbrella. They'd drink beer from the cooler and listen to the gulls and catch up on their reading. Then they'd jump into the cool, gray Atlantic waves. That was before the kids, when it was just them. When they could just sit and be quietly together.

The water was cold, murky. She found that she didn't need to surface for air, that she could just drift beneath, her fingers grazing against stones and drifting ribbons of weeds, branches. River water, that's what it was. If clean had a feeling, light and cold against her skin . . . It had been so long since she'd done anything that gave her pleasure. Why had she been punishing herself all these years?

The other psychic she'd known, the one who'd taught her everything, had warned her. *You must not forget to live. Spending all our time with the dead, something about it drains the life from us if we let it. Be out in the world, Eloise. Don't bury yourself for them.*

But she hadn't listened, had she? She pitied Ray for giving up everything for their work. She thought because she'd already lost everything that she had nothing left to give. But she'd given herself, all of herself. She used to love to garden, to feel her hands in the earth, to bring fresh flowers and vegetables into the kitchen. She used to read. And knit. She'd made almost every blanket, scarf, and hat in the house. When was the last time she'd made *anything*? She didn't even cook anymore, living on salads and cans of tuna fish.

Ahead of her, she saw the reedy form, long and black, floating. She swam faster, but the form floated away just as quickly, as though her own movements were pushing it farther from her. She fought harder, and found herself against a swift current. Now she was getting breathless, her chest tightening, painful.

Eloise could see her then. It was just a girl, her hair spread around her. A mermaid with opalescent skin, long arms spread like wings. It was just a girl, so young and pretty, just like her girls had been; prettier yet because they didn't know their own beauty. She was still—eyes sleeping, mouth slack.

It's just a girl. There was that voice in her head. *That's why. He'll have no choice but to save her.*

She felt afraid then, personally. She'd inexplicably come to like Jones Cooper. *And he'll die saving her?* she asked without speaking. She had never asked anything of the voice before. She'd asked things of the dead who came to visit. But never of the voice in her head. And now she knew why. It didn't answer. It would never answer.

She woke up drenched in sweat, sitting in a bathtub dry of water. How she'd gotten there she didn't even know. The last thing she remembered was saying good-bye to Ray.

She lifted herself from the tub and headed downstairs, took her raincoat from the closet, took her purse from the table by the door. She walked out into the rain.

chapter thirty-three

Bethany felt numb, even as beneath that numbness there was a whir-ring panic, like a siren in the back of her head. She didn't know why Willow punished her like this. She could hardly love her child more. True, she'd made mistakes. Even now Richard was calling and calling on her cell phone, after she'd asked him not to. She'd alerted him on the off chance that Willow would go to him, knowing that the stripper had left him. *Why can't you keep track of her, Bethany?* he'd asked. It was cruel, ridiculous. How could she ever have married someone who would dream of saying something like that? She'd hung up on him.

"It's okay," Henry said. "We'll find her."

They saw the Beemer sitting by the side of the road, the headlights burning. For a second she thought they were all sitting in the car. And she nearly fainted with relief. But they weren't. Henry pulled over, and they both got out in the rain, started shouting.

"Willow!" Her voice broke, and she started to cry. She remem-bered that night still so vividly, racing around New York City, looking in Willow's favorite places, calling her friends. She'd been so frantic she'd felt unhinged. But this was so much worse somehow. Willow gone in this dark, wet place where the rain took Bethany's voice and the beam of Henry's flashlight was eaten by the impenetrable darkness.

She wouldn't hate herself for inviting Henry to dinner, even for springing it last minute on Willow. Her mistake here was that Willow thought she had a right to act like that, to abuse Bethany and then to run out into the night. Bethany had been too soft on her, too yielding and ready to take blame for Willow's unhappiness. That was going to change.

She didn't realize until Henry came up and put his arms around her that she was sobbing. They were both soaked to the skin. The wind had picked up, but she leaned into him, was grateful not to be alone this time.

"We *will* find her," he said. She let herself believe him.

The lights of an approaching car had them both moving toward the road. Bethany saw Jones Cooper in the driver's seat as he brought his SUV to a stop. He stepped out wearing a dark raincoat that was already wet.

"Mrs. Graves," he said. That natural air of authority had put Bethany, irrationally, at ease. "I'm going to ask you to wait here with the car."

"No," she said. "I can't just sit here."

"Someone needs to be here if they come out of the woods," he said. He put a soothing hand on her arm.

"Mr. Cooper—"

"It's just that Henry and I grew up here," he said. "We know these woods. It'll be faster if we go alone."

She wanted to argue, but he was shepherding her toward the car, telling her to keep her cell phone on her lap. They'd call as soon as they found anything. "Lock the doors. If anyone but the kids approaches the vehicle, call the cops and lean on the horn."

"What do you mean?" she asked. "Like who?"

"Like Michael Holt."

Bethany took a deep breath and did as she was told. She watched Henry through the window. He lifted a palm in an "it's okay" gesture. Then they were gone, swallowed by the trees. The wind was picking up, bending the tips of the pines against the night sky, whistling around the car. Bethany wished she were a religious person. She wished that she could pray.

The clearing at the Chapel was empty. The crime-scene tape around the hole had blown away and wrapped itself around a nearby tree. They walked the perimeter, calling out for the kids. But only the wind answered them. Henry returned to Marla's grave, stood at the edge peering down into the emptiness. It looked to him like the loneliest, coldest place on earth. Jones came to stand beside him.

"I heard tonight that the ME confirmed the bones were Marla Holt's," said Henry.

"I heard, too. On the radio," Jones said. "I wish I'd known back then. I wish I hadn't let her lie out here all this time."

Henry was surprised to hear Jones say something like that. Henry turned to look at the other man. Rain was making rivers down his face. The wind was getting wild, whipping at their slickers.

"I was her friend," Henry said. "I should have known she wouldn't run off on her children. I believed the worst of her, like everyone else."

Jones didn't say anything, started to move away from the site. Henry grabbed his arm, and Jones turned back toward him.

"I was there that night, Jones," Henry said. He cast his eyes to the ground. The words felt like the release of a breath held too long. "I'm sorry I never told you, or anyone. I loved her."

When Henry could bring himself to look at Jones, he saw that the other man was staring at him. Jones Cooper had a chilly, assessing gaze that made people question themselves. What did he see when he looked at Henry? A coward, surely. A fool. Henry squared his shoulders, told him about the night and what had happened.

"I never touched her, except to hold her as she cried that night. She told me that she was unhappy, that there was someone else beside her husband. Michael came home and caught us in an embrace. It was very awkward. I left."

Henry paused to breathe. "I never thought . . . she was in danger. I wouldn't have left her if I had."

Jones glanced around the clearing, scanning the night with his flashlight.

"Why now?" Jones said. "Why are you telling me this now?"

Henry had a thousand answers. *I thought she'd run off with someone else. How could I admit to loving another woman who would never love me? I was ashamed. I was angry. I never thought she'd come to harm.* He issued some jumble of those things, couldn't even bring himself to look at Jones.

"It doesn't much matter at this point." Jones had to raise his voice over the wind.

"But would it have mattered then?" Henry asked. He was practically yelling. "Would you have looked at her case differently had you known?"

Jones rolled his head to the side, seemed to ease some tension out of his neck. "I might have looked at you a little harder."

"But not at Michael. Or Mack?"

"It's hard to say," he said. Jones started moving back to the path.

Henry followed. "After my run I went back. I saw Mack's car in the driveway. Claudia Miller was sitting in her window, watching. Whatever happened that night, she must have seen it. Maybe she lied about the sedan."

"Why would she lie?"

"That's what I thought then, too. But who knows why we lie? A hundred reasons big and small."

"We'll talk about this later," said Jones. "We're wasting time. If those kids are out here in this weather, we need to get them home."

Jones was walking more quickly now, with a sudden purpose.

"Where are we going?"

"To the river."

"The Black River?" said Henry, even though there was no other river he could have meant. "Why?"

"Don't ask," said Jones. "Just move faster."

Jones felt as if he were dreaming. Was he? A year ago he'd found himself in the woods on a night like this one. Back then he was trying to bury his past, to protect an awful secret he had hidden for decades. To-night he was following the path of predictions he didn't even believe. He could smell the rotting vegetation, slick in the rain, beneath his feet. The rain falling on his hood, the rushing river off in the distance, it all created a cocoon of sound around him. Even though Henry trailed behind him, Jones could believe he was alone in this place. He could turn around at any time, say to Henry that they needed to call the police, conditions were too harsh, the night was too dark. Those kids could be anywhere. And no one would have questioned that. But he didn't. The irony, of course, was that if Eloise hadn't come to him, it might never have occurred to him to check the banks of the river.

The Black River wasn't normally deep or fast. But tonight it could be, according to the news, a full two feet over its normal depth. The river worked its way through a glacial ravine lined with hemlock and pine, its rocky bed studded with boulders. Even in the summer, the water was cold.

As Jones crested the rise, he saw that the river was high. And down below on the banks, he saw the beams of two flashlights bouncing like fireflies. The path before them, the one that would switch back all the way to the riverbank, was washed away with rainwater. It would be faster, possibly safer, to cut down through the trees.

But it would be treacherous; he thought about telling Henry to go back and call for help. But then he was making his way down the side, gripping onto wet trees, feet slipping beneath him. He crashed his knee against a rock. He heard Henry making a similarly graceless descent.

The voices below, raised and frantic, carried over the sound of the river. But Jones couldn't hear what they were saying. He cupped his hands around his mouth and yelled at them to stay where they were. But then he saw the flashlights start to move downriver fast. They were running.

The bank of the river was gone; he had to make his way through the trees that usually stood high above. Up ahead he saw the flashlight beams bouncing, and he and Henry followed. Henry pulled ahead of Jones. He was lighter and stronger. Jones was already panting with effort, feeling the fact that he was as out of shape as his doctor kept telling him. *Did you know,* his doctor asked, *that survival in extreme circumstances can come down to how long you are able to hold your own hanging body weight? How many pull-ups do you think you can do?* Three, Jones could do three pull-ups, maybe four if he'd had a light lunch.

As they drew closer, he saw the three slender forms. He heard Henry yell something, but Jones couldn't make it out. And what happened next seemed like a memory, as though he had already been there so many times. And each time the events unfolded in exactly the same way, no matter what he did to try to alter them. He had the thought that maybe that's just what life was, after all. Maybe you repeated it over and over again until you finally did the right thing—even though it was never really clear what the right thing was. He moved closer to them, called out to them again. But his voice was lost.

He watched, helpless, as the smallest form moved too close to the water and lost her footing. He watched her cling for a second to a thin branch, which broke off in her hand. The other two forms bent toward her like reeds, arms outstretched. He watched her fall into the cold, rushing water. And then, a second later, while everyone else stood stunned and rooted, sound and distance isolating them all from one another, he raced down what was left of the incline and jumped in after her.

The cold hit him like a freight train, sending a shock through his body. The rushing water churned around him, then pushed him toward the surface, where he gulped at the air before going down again. He could hear her yelling in front of him. He tried to swim, but the current carried him along, knocking him against the rocks. He wouldn't have thought this river could be so powerful, that his physical strength would be nothing against it. *There are things more powerful than your will.* Isn't that what Eloise had said? He still didn't believe it, even now when it proved to be true.

And then everything suddenly seemed to quiet. The girl had stopped yelling, the current slowed. He could still hear voices on the bank. He dove below the surface. At first there was nothing but a rushing flood of cold. Then he saw her floating up ahead. Or rather he saw something darker than the rest of the darkness. He used all his strength to reach her, to be faster than the water that pulled her along, too.

Finally he was able to put his hand on her; her arm was impossibly thin and cold, her fingers so small. He tried to pull at her, to take her up with him. But something held her fast. He grabbed hold of her leg and dragged himself down to where he could feel that her foot was wedged between two large rocks. He yanked at her calf, his chest growing painful with his held breath. When he realized he wouldn't be able to free her, he started working on the laces of her thick leather boots. He could only feel them beneath his fingers. He could see nothing now. All he wanted to do was surface and take the air into his lungs, but he knew if he did, the current would take him and he'd never find her again in the dark water, never be able to fight his way back to her.

When he finally untied the lace, her foot drifted free. Just as it did, there was a flood of light. And she seemed to lift away from him, pulled from the water by unseen hands. Was it the current taking her down the river? Where was the light coming from?

He let her go because he didn't have any strength left, and he was bone tired suddenly, numb with cold. And it was so easy to just *stop* moving. He'd always heard that drowning was a peaceful way to die, though that seemed like a strange idea. How could anyone ever know such a thing? But as the darkness closed around him in a cold embrace, he knew it was right.

chapter thirty-four

It was the light that brought him back. It was not a soft and heavenly light, beckoning him to the great beyond. It was the harsh white of a floodlight. There was someone pumping mercilessly on his chest and then breathing hard down his throat. He choked up a river of water and bile, took in a ragged breath that felt like swallowed razor blades. When he opened his eyes, he didn't see the face of God. It was Chuck Ferrigno, looking like some combination of determined and desperate. Behind Chuck stood Eloise Montgomery, holding a gigantic police-issue flashlight. Her expression was serene, as though the outcome of everything were already well known to her. Or possibly she just didn't care. It was hard to tell which.

"Jones," the other man said, kneeling back. "Christ. You are too old to be jumping into the river like that."

All Jones felt was cold. "Where's the girl?"

"She's here," said Chuck. "She's okay."

The kids sat under the tree, all three of them wrapped in a blanket. Willow Graves was soaking wet. She leaned her head on the shoulder of the other girl, who held her tight. Cole Carr just looked lost beside them, blank and staring off at nothing. The rain had slowed to little more than a drizzle.

"You pulled us out?"

Chuck, too, was soaked and shivering. "You wouldn't have thought I had it in me, right? I wouldn't have been able to do it without Henry and the kid. They held me. I grabbed the girl, then you."

"How did you find us?" Jones asked. But he supposed he already knew the answer. Chuck glanced back at Eloise.

"Eloise came to my house. She said there was trouble."

"And you believed her?" Jones was irrationally angry at this. How could someone like Chuck, so grounded and pragmatic, listen to Eloise Montgomery?

Chuck offered a quick lift of his shoulders. "Hey, I'm a New Yorker. Nothing surprises me. Anyway, she wouldn't leave unless I came with her, said I'd have to arrest her. I'd rather go out in a storm than spend all night filing paperwork against the town psychic."

Jones looked at Eloise in her giant yellow slicker and big flashlight. He supposed he should thank her. But he couldn't bring himself to do it. Wasn't it her fault he was here in the first place?

"I told you that you wouldn't be able to manage the risk," she said. She wasn't smug, but almost.

Up above them they heard voices, saw lights. Jones hauled himself to his feet, fighting nausea and light-headedness. He didn't want people to find him lying on the bank of a river. From where he sat now, it didn't look that wild. It certainly didn't seem like the churning, rushing nightmare to which he'd nearly surrendered.

"You called for backup?"

"I did. The kids said they saw Michael Holt up at the dig site. He chased them down here. That's why they were running along the bank."

"Where's Henry?"

"He went back to get the girl's mother," said Chuck. "And to call Maggie."

Jones made his way over to the kids. Cole had his arm around both the girls, and they leaned into him.

"Are you okay, Willow?"

She looked up at him, her eyes full of fatigue and sadness. "You almost died trying to save me. I'm so sorry. I shouldn't even be here."

He put a hand on her shoulder, and she pressed her cheek against it. "Thank you," she said again.

"Thanks for helping to get us out of there, kid," Jones said to Cole. Cole gave him a shy nod, looked down at the ground as though he were embarrassed.

"I've been looking for you," Jones said.

The boy glanced up at him quickly, startled. "For me?"

"I saw your mother today."

Cole leaned forward. Jones saw how young he was then. Teenagers looked like grown-ups sometimes. They occupied such an awkward, uncomfortable space between childhood and adulthood. In that moment, wet and scared, Cole Carr looked far closer to boyhood than manhood. "My mom? Where?"

"I thought you told us your mom was in Iraq," said Jolie. Willow shushed her.

Cole stood up. "Where did you see her?"

A young man walked up behind Jones and wrapped a blanket around him. The paramedics and other officers had clambered down the hill and were forming a group around Chuck. The dark night was filled with light and voices.

"Sir, you should have a seat," the paramedic said. Jones recognized him from his time on the job but couldn't place his name. He looked just like Ricky, with spiky dark hair and a ring in his nose.

"Okay," said Jones. "In a second."

Between breaths he told Cole about his mother, where she was and what had happened. Jones told Cole how much his mother missed him and wanted him to come home. He thought the boy would cry, but he didn't. He just looked at the ground and hunched his shoulders forward in a protective stance.

"Do you want to go back to her, son?"

"I do," he said. "I want to go back to my mom."

"I'm going to take you to her," Jones said. "Do you know where your father is?"

Cole shook his head. "I don't know. I think he went looking for my stepmother. She's been gone for a couple of days."

"Did he know where she was?" Jones felt a surge of fear for Paula.

"I don't know. He was watching her credit card online, to see if she charged anything."

"Did she?"

"I don't know."

Jones put his hand into a jacket pocket filled with water and retrieved his phone, which was ruined. He stared at it, helpless. Then he let the paramedic lead him over to a large, flat rock, where he sat while the young man shone a penlight in his eyes. Above him the thick cloud cover that had persisted for days preceding the rain was breaking apart, and Jones could see the white of the moon. He called Chuck over and told him about Paula.

"I'm going to get someone on it right now," Chuck said.

"I've got a contact at the credit bureau who's been watching her card for me," he said. Jones gave Chuck the name.

"I know Jack," said Chuck. "We'll find her."

"Find her fast," said Jones. He kept looking up at the path, expecting to see Henry and Bethany. But no one came. What was taking them so long?

"How did you wind up in the middle of all this, Jones?" said Chuck. "I thought you retired."

But Jones didn't get a chance to answer, because Chuck's call went through. He walked off, and Jones heard him inquiring about Paula Carr's credit-card charges. Jones heard Chuck say, "Jones Cooper said he was working with you."

Eloise walked toward him.

"You like it," said Eloise. "All of this. You're happier today, having nearly drowned, than you were the day I first came to see you."

He was about to argue with her. But what was the point? "I guess we all have our calling. This happens to be mine."

"I know what you mean."

He watched her then. She looked as small as a child in her big rain slicker. Her hair was matted with the wet. The lines on her face were as deep and dark as valleys. But he noticed for the first time that there was a light to her skin, an odd youthfulness. She seemed lit from within. He remembered the pictures he'd seen in her home from a time when she was young and happy. He could still see that prettiness in her. He'd Googled Eloise. He knew now that she'd lost her husband and child in a terrible accident, nearly died herself. He knew now that people from all over the world consulted her on their cases, for the sight that seemed to come after surviving the car wreck. He found himself with a grudging respect for her.

"Did you know," said Eloise—she was looking up at the clearing night sky—"that the oxygen in our lungs, the carbon in our muscles, the calcium in our bones, the iron in our blood, was created inside a star before the earth was ever born?"

He followed her eyes up.

"Do you know where Paula is, Eloise?" He hated himself for asking. But he would have hated himself more for not asking. She didn't say anything right away. She just looked up at the moon, shifting from behind the clouds.

Henry was moving fast, at a light jog in spite of the slick conditions of the path. Once Jones and Willow had been pulled from the river and Chuck arrived on the scene, Henry ran for Bethany and to call Maggie. He was halfway there when he stumbled on a rock and came down hard on his right knee.

He lifted himself up, and when he stood, Michael Holt blocked the path before him. It took him a minute to get his head around it. Jolie had told them that Michael Holt was out there. That he'd chased them from the dig site. But Henry figured he'd have run, knowing that more cops must be on their way. The guy was a giant, tall and wide in the night. And Henry found himself taking a step back.

"I know you," Michael said. Henry heard the other man's breath coming hard and fast.

"Yes," said Henry. "You do."

"You were there the night my mother died."

"I was," Henry said. Henry raised his palms. "But it was nothing more than what your mother told you. We were only friends."

"You were holding her."

"I was *comforting* her," said Henry. "Your mother was . . . unhappy. I'm sorry."

"Why?" asked Michael. His voice was desperate and childlike. "Why was she so unhappy?"

He wanted to sugarcoat it, to soothe Michael. But maybe there had been enough of that. Michael Holt needed the truth; he'd spent his whole life looking for it. And Henry felt at least partially responsible for that.

"I think she wanted more from life than what she had, Michael," said Henry. He had a voice that he used with troubled students. Firm but gentle, soothing but not yielding.

"More than us?"

Henry forced himself to breathe before answering.

"She loved you and your sister very much," Henry said. "But sometimes people have expectations of life, and life gives them something else. Most of us accept that. Some of us can't."

Henry saw Bethany then. She had come up behind Michael on the path and now stood behind him.

"She didn't leave you and Cara, Michael," said Henry. "She was *taken* from you. At least you know that now. She didn't run away."

"No," said Michael. It was a sad and desolate grunt, the beginning of a sob.

Michael's breathing came ragged then, and for a moment Henry thought it was rage. That he was going to have to defend himself against this concrete wall of a man. But Michael fell to his knees and started to wail, a horrible keening that filled Henry's head. Bethany put her hands to her ears and started to cry as well. It was primal, the very sound of sorrow. Henry didn't know what to do but kneel beside him and take Marla's son in his arms. Even as the truth dawned on Henry, he let Michael rest against him.

Michael whispered to Henry, "All these years I thought it was my father. That he was hiding this awful secret, and I was his accomplice in silence. I couldn't wait for him to die so that I could uncover his lies."

Michael's breath was foul; he reeked of body odor and rotting vegetation. Still Henry held him tight, for Marla. Even with what Michael had done, Henry knew that Marla would want him to help her son.

"Michael," Henry said. A part of him didn't want to hear the truth. Once it was said, there would be no more denial.

"All these years I thought he holed himself up in that house with all his garbage, that guilt was burying him alive. But it wasn't guilt. It was *grief*."

"Please," said Henry.

But there was no stopping the words now.

"I killed her." The words were a horrific howl, and they cut Henry to the bone. He heard Bethany sobbing. She was on her knees as well now. "When my father came home, I told him that there had been a man in the house. I was so angry. I felt so . . . betrayed. They fought, worse than they ever had."

Henry wished Michael would stop. The biggest part of him didn't want to know what had happened to Marla.

"I heard her slamming drawers in her room. She was screaming, *'I hate you! I hate this place! I hate my life!'* I couldn't let her leave. She must have known that."

Michael's voice dropped again to that hoarse whisper.

"I tried to stop her. Her suitcase spilled open. She ran from me, out the back door, into the woods. And I followed her. My father tried to stop me, but he couldn't. No one could have stopped me."

Michael took a deep breath. "And all these years, he kept that secret. He was protecting me."

He was sobbing again. Weeping like a child, he put his head to the ground. There were lights and voices coming up the path. And a minute later they were surrounded. Michael looked up, as if surprised by the crowd.

"It's over," Michael said. There was a glassy, unhinged quality to his gaze.

And Henry supposed that it was true, that it must offer Michael some kind of relief to know. However tragic and horrifying the outcome was, Michael had finally found his mother.

chapter thirty-five

The woman working the hotel desk was the wrong side of forty. She wore thick, dark-framed glasses, had her hair pulled back tightly, fanning out from a dramatic white part in the center of her head. There was a flurry of acne below her cheekbones. No ring on her finger. But Kevin Carr could see she still had hope. That was a good thing. All women react to a handsome man carrying an extravagantly large bouquet of roses. But a woman like that would react more favorably than most.

He had his overnight bag slung over his shoulder. Had made a point to keep his suit jacket off while he drove, so that he would arrive looking pressed. He wore a bright pink tie, a light smattering of cologne. He'd dressed to make an impression. He'd shaved and styled his hair for the first time since Paula had left. He hadn't been to work; hadn't even called. His partners were panicking, because he was the only one staffed with a client. And the client was *freaking*. He hadn't returned a call in days. Fuck them. Fuck them all. He'd been waiting for his bitch wife to make good on her promise. And, of course, she hadn't. She wasn't going to give him that money. But it was going to be his just the same.

Amelia, his girlfriend, was starting to get suspicious. His card got declined at dinner the other night; she'd had to pay. He made up some excuse about identity theft, but he could tell she wasn't buying it. He'd been pretending to have the flu, told her that's why he hadn't seen her for a few days. He wasn't sure she was buying that, either. She wasn't smart like Paula. That's what he'd liked about her. She was beautiful and desperate, not sharp. But even she was starting to wonder about him.

"Hey," he said as he approached the counter. He tried to sound a little breathless, gave the girl (WELCOME, I'M CAROLINE!) a bright smile. And the look. There's a look you can give a woman, a warm smile, a kind gaze. It's a look that says, *I find you so attractive.* Most of them smile back. The girl at the counter beamed.

"I'm *so* late meeting my wife and kids," he said. "She's gonna kill me."

"They're staying here?" she asked. Her hand fluttered to the heart-shaped locket at her neck.

"Checked in a few hours ago," he said. Idiot. He *knew* she'd use that card, that old American Express she still had open in her name. He'd been watching it, pressing the "refresh" button every hour or so. He knew she'd get tired of motels, want something nicer. She was a spoiled brat and had been since the day he met her.

The girl at the counter was too shy to hold his gaze for long. Her eyes drifted to the roses and then down to the screen in front of her. "What room are they in?"

"I was hoping you could tell me?" He pulled down the corners of his mouth, lifted his eyebrows. He was going for sheepish. "She told me, and I can't remember."

"If you give me her name, I'll call the room and let her know you're down here."

"Hmm," he said. He wrinkled his forehead a bit. "What time is it?" He looked at his watch and saw her noticing it.

"The kids will be sleeping," he said. "If you call up there, you'll wake them."

"I'm sorry, sir," she said. "I can't tell you the room number. That's our policy."

"Oh, I understand," he said. He made a show of trying to figure out a solution. He pretended to text his wife. They waited. He could tell that the girl wanted to please him, to help him out. But she was still clinging to that policy.

"You're too young to have kids, I'm sure," he said. He saw her blush; the red came up unattractively from her neck. "But when you do, and they're asleep? You'll remember this encounter. Trust me, I'd rather sleep on that couch right there than wake them up." He pointed to the lobby sitting area.

"My sister has kids," she said. She smoothed out her hair, which was thick and wooly, probably the bane of her existence. "I hear you."

He looked at the phone again. "Poor thing," he said. "She's probably sleeping, too. She's exhausted. I've been so worried about her lately. She's under so much stress with the kids."

He looked lovingly at the roses. "It's our anniversary. Ten years. Hard to believe."

"Oh," she said. "That's so sweet."

"Yeah," he said with a little laugh. He gave her a funny eye roll. "If she doesn't kill me for being late."

"What was the name?" she said. He'd made a point of staying at the counter, not sitting in the sitting area. The immediacy of the situation would help move things along. Nobody wanted some person with a need hovering around. And this girl was too much of a mouse to get rude, to call her manager.

"Paula Carr," he said.

She turned to smile at him, put a finger to her mouth as she made him a key card. "They're in Room 206."

He gave her a wide smile, pulled one of the roses from the bouquet, and handed it to her.

The woman started to giggle, girlish and sweet. "Oh!" she said.

"Thank you so much," he said. "I can't even tell you. You just saved my life."

———

The hallway was quiet except for the sound of someone's television, the volume up too high. That always aggravated him, people who kept the volume up too loud, like the people who put their seats all the way back on airplanes. Or the people who let the door close behind them in a public place without looking to see if there was someone there. What was wrong with those people? Inconsiderateness was a national blight.

She'd have the secondary latch on as well. But he'd found a video on YouTube about how to unlatch a chain with a rubber band. There was a tool that looked like a crowbar, which easily undid the folding metal latch. He had one of those, too. Something he'd fashioned himself in the garage.

He'd have the upper hand. She wouldn't hurt him in front of Claire and Cameron. And if she called the police, he'd accuse her of kidnapping the children, tell them how depressed she was, that he was afraid of what she'd do to herself and their babies. She'd get hysterical, and they would believe him. People always believed Kevin Carr. Not that he wanted the kids; they were a major pain in the ass. But it would be worth it to really zing it to Paula.

He stood at the door, put his ear against the cool surface, and heard only silence. He put the roses and his bag down on the floor and took the key from his pocket.

"What do you think you're doing, son?"

He didn't recognize the man at the end of the hall.

"Excuse me?"

The guy reminded Kevin of a side of beef, tall and solid. He wore a barn jacket and a pair of jeans, thick brown lace-up boots.

"I said, what do you think you're doing?"

"I'm not sure it's any of your business."

The other man smiled a bit. "I disagree."

Kevin lifted his palms. "I think there must be some misunderstanding."

"I don't think so," said the other man. He was moving slowly down the hallway now. "You need to step away from the door and keep your hands where I can see them."

He was one of *those* men, the no-bullshit kind. The one you couldn't charm or manipulate; he was the one who had no vanity to be flattered, no illusions to be bolstered. He was the guy who saw right through the mask. Kevin really hated people like that. Kevin didn't see a weapon on him. Was he a cop? Was that a police siren he heard off in the distance? His heart started to thump. He stepped back from the door.

"My name is Jones Cooper. You wanted me to find your wife," he said. "Well, I found her."

It took Kevin a second to place the name. He *had* called this dog. It seemed like a hundred years ago and he'd forgotten all about it.

"Look," said Kevin. He lifted the roses. "Thanks, but Paula and I have worked things out."

"No," said Jones. He had a kind of snide half smile on his face. "You haven't."

Kevin heard the siren grow loud and come to a stop somewhere outside. The door opened then, and Paula stepped into the door frame.

"This woman kidnapped my children," he said. He took his voice up an octave. "I'm here to get them back. She's suffering from postpartum depression. I'm terrified of what she'll do to herself and our babies."

Paula just stared at him. "You're a liar, Kevin."

"Where are my children?" he yelled. He even managed to force some tears down his face. A door opened up down the hall; a man with tousled hair stuck his head out and then disappeared quickly.

"They're safe," she said. Her voice was soft, almost a whisper. "I have a lawyer now."

He turned to look at her, but she was stone cold.

"I haven't done anything wrong," said Kevin. He turned back to Jones. "You can't call the police."

"You threatened me with a gun," said Paula. "I fled in fear for my life. And now you've come after me."

Someone had obviously coached her, told her what to say. Ever since she'd started having kids, she'd been so foggy and addled. She didn't seem that way now, more like she had when he'd first met her.

"That's a lie," he said. "She's the one with the gun."

"I have documented your affair." Paula went on as though he hadn't spoken. "I have printed copies of e-mails to your girlfriend and the lies you've been telling about me. I also know that you've been stealing money from your company to pay your debts."

How could she know that?

"Meanwhile, today I had a little chat with Robin O'Conner," said Jones. "I know what you did to her."

The elevator door opened then, and two uniformed officers stepped out, a bald and lanky black man and a petite blond female. Both rested their hands on the large semiautomatics at their waists. Behind them the girl from the counter emerged, along with a man who looked like he must be her manager.

"That's him," said Caroline. Her warm smile and goo-goo eyes were gone.

Jones stepped to the side.

"Everyone needs to keep their hands where we can see them," said the female officer.

Kevin had had moments like this before, ugly, dark moments when he was backed into a corner. The sinking hole in his center opened. It was the place where all the selves he created and put out there met. And there, where the real Kevin should have been, there was nothing.

chapter thirty-six

Ray was waiting for her in the driveway when she got home. She pulled up beside him and saw that he was sleeping. The car was running with the heat on, and he had his head leaned back, his mouth gaping open. He could have gone inside. The door was unlocked.

She got out of the car and walked over to his Cadillac, tapped on the window. He startled awake, looked over at her, and frowned. He rolled down the window.

"Where were you? Out partying with your new best friend, Jones Cooper?"

"Not exactly," she said. "Do you want to come in?"

He turned off the car and followed her into the house. Oliver greeted her at the door, immediately started purring and weaving himself between her legs. She'd forgotten to feed him.

As she opened up some food for Oliver and changed his water, Eloise told Ray about her night. He made some coffee while she did, even though it was way too late for coffee.

"I thought you were retiring," said Ray. He hadn't looked at her the whole time she was talking. He'd busied himself fussing with the cabinet door that always came off its hinge. He'd pulled a Swiss Army knife from his pocket and was trying to tighten the screw, his brow furrowed with concentration.

"Vacationing is not the same thing as retiring," she answered. She checked the lock on the back door and the window over the sink. "Anyway, what choice did I have? I couldn't just let him drown."

"I thought you had a policy about speaking your vision but not getting physically involved. You know, after what happened in Kansas."

She didn't like to think about Kansas. "I changed my policy," she said. "Just this once."

"Because of Maggie Cooper?"

A lifetime ago Eloise had given a prediction to Maggie's mother, Elizabeth Monroe. This prediction may or may not have saved Maggie's life—it was hard to say in the way that these things were. Other unintended possible results of her conversation were that a not-quite-innocent man had committed suicide in prison and Jones Cooper had built his life around a terrible secret. After living in the city and getting her education there, Maggie returned to The Hollows and married Jones. Eloise had always known that Maggie would one day come to her with questions. And last year she had. Since then Eloise had felt an odd connection to Maggie. And then she'd started having her vision about Jones. Ray knew all this. He knew everything about her, she realized.

Eloise sat down at the kitchen table, and Oliver rubbed against her before heading over to his food bowl.

"Maybe," she said. He came behind her and put his hands on her shoulders, began kneading at her tight muscles. She felt heat and release down her back.

"What about your visit with Claudia Miller?" she asked.

"She wouldn't talk to me. And the Holt house? I poked around in there some. The place is a nightmare. I couldn't get out of there fast enough."

"Some boxes stay locked."

She didn't know if he'd heard that Michael had confessed. She wasn't sure she wanted to be the one to tell him. She'd seen Michael sitting in the back of the patrol car as she left the Hollows Wood. For the first time since she'd known him, he didn't look haunted. Sometimes a confession is as good as an exorcism.

"I guess you heard," he said.

"About Michael?" she said. When he didn't reply, she said, "Yes, I heard."

"You knew all along, didn't you?"

"I suspected."

"She told you." He meant Marla. He was the only one who believed in her wholly and completely, without question.

"She hinted."

His hands moved down her arms, and she felt her body relax beneath his palms. "This is ugly work, Eloise."

She wasn't sure if she agreed with this. Death was life. Maybe it wasn't the end people thought it was. Maybe it was worse than that. People did horrific, unspeakable things to one another. And there was so much pain. But it was just one part of this gorgeous, hideous, chaotic, and wonderful mosaic they experienced from the moment they drew their first breaths until they drew their last and beyond. And wasn't it a gift, in some ways, to see all the colors, all the sharp and broken bits, the ones from which all others turned their eyes? According to the Kabbalah, every human soul is just a fragment of the great world-soul, just a tiny piece of the cosmos, linked to every other piece. Eloise liked the idea of this and felt that it could be true. And that was as close to faith as she thought she was apt to get.

"So," said Ray when she didn't answer him, "I've never been to Seattle." He cleared his throat. "I heard it was nice. Lots of rain, but good coffee."

For the first time in forever, Eloise smiled.

chapter thirty-seven

Claudia Miller watched them come, as she knew they would. She'd known as soon as she saw the For Sale sign in the yard. First there was a single patrol car. Then a black unmarked cruiser. Then more. Eventually the others, her neighbors with their too-loud, bratty children, came to stand on porches and stoops, watching, too. She could feel their nervousness, their excitement. Of course, none of them had even come to the window when the paramedics took Mack from that house. No one came to stand beside her at the ambulance while they'd wheeled him down his overgrown walk and carried him away. No one cared about an old man leaving his home for the last time.

The neighbors all stood. A group of them eventually gathered in the street. Finally the lawyer with the black Mercedes (the one who snuck a cigarette in his side yard at night when he was taking out the trash) walked over to the uniformed officer standing in the drive.

"Can you tell me what's happening, Officer?" His voice was strident in the cold, chill air. Now that the rain had stopped pounding on her roof and windows, the neighborhood seemed so quiet.

The officer lifted a hand and shook his head. But Claudia couldn't hear what he said.

"We have a right to know," said the lawyer. She knew he'd get peevish if he didn't get his way. She knew why the police were there. Claudia Miller knew lots of things.

She knew that the pretty blond girl (what was she? maybe sixteen?) climbed out her window some nights, using one of those rope fire-escape ladders that people keep under their beds. Her boyfriend picked her up on the corner, brought her back a few hours later.

Claudia knew that the big-chested woman at number 180 was having an affair. She was a popular area real estate agent, flitting in and out of her house all day like a bee bringing honey back to the hive. But every Wednesday at lunchtime, she met a man at her house. Claudia would watch as each of them went casually in, casually out. Sometimes the woman's husband didn't get home until after midnight.

Claudia knew that the cat Misty wasn't really lost, despite the sad signs on lampposts and pinned up on the supermarket bulletin board. It had slipped outside while the housewife at 183 got the mail. Later Claudia watched it get hit by a car, stagger up to the curb, and die. Later still, the housewife came out and saw it lying there and wept in the street. Then she carried the body gingerly and laid it on top of the trash. The truck came soon after. The kids were still looking for their dead cat, hoping Misty would come home.

Claudia knew their secrets. Each one was like a gem she locked away in a box. They belonged to her, because she was vigilant.

She'd been watching the night Marla Holt disappeared. Claudia had been waiting for Mack to come home. She waited every night to see him pull in to the drive in his sensible car. What was it that he drove then? She couldn't remember things like that anymore. He'd climb out slowly, retrieve his satchel from the backseat. She watched him mow the lawn on Saturdays, wash the cars on Sundays. She enjoyed it when he played basketball in the driveway with his boy (even though the sound of that ball almost drove her crazy). She liked to watch him stroll with the baby in the carriage on the nights she was fussy. With his broad shoulders and perpetually tousled hair, Mack reminded her of a man she'd loved once. The one her sister had married, if the truth be told. Married and then drove him to an early grave with her spending and demands for this and that. At least that's the way Claudia saw it, even if no one else did. She moved far away from all of them, rather than watch it unfold.

Mack Holt was the only person on the block to ever show her any kindness. He never failed to wave hello when he saw her, or to offer her a smile. He brought her newspaper to the porch from the sidewalk on rainy Sunday mornings. And so she kept an eye on things for him.

She was at her window that night. Mack was late in coming home. And instead Henry Ivy came walking up the drive. It was their night to jog. (Claudia thought it was unseemly for a married woman to flaunt herself around the neighborhood like that with another man. But she suspected Marla Holt of much worse.)

She saw the boy Michael come home, drop his bicycle in the yard. Henry Ivy left. And then the yelling started. Soon Mack came home. There was more yelling, the sound of something breaking. Then Claudia saw the woman run from the back door, the boy and husband chasing after her. She could have called the police, even put her hand on the phone. Nothing good could come of what she'd seen. But a woman like that, always putting on airs, flaunting herself, having men into her house while her husband was out working. Well, maybe she deserved what she got.

Later, hours later, Mack and Michael came back. The boy was sick, or drunk. Mack was practically dragging him. He brought the boy inside, and a few minutes later he returned to the back deck, leaned heavily against the rail, and looked out into the night. She could see him in the amber light over his kitchen door. But she had her lights out; he couldn't have seen her, hidden as she was behind the curtain.

Then he turned and looked over at her house, as though he knew she was watching. He looked at her house for a long, long time. And she knew that he wanted her to be quiet. And because Mack Holt reminded her of what it felt like to be young and in love, because he had shown her kindness when others couldn't be bothered, she made a silent promise to him that she would take what she'd seen that night to her grave. And she would, even though Mack was gone now. She'd keep their secret, no matter who came calling.

When the police knocked on her door all those years ago, she'd told them that she'd seen a black sedan, that Marla Holt had gotten into it and ridden away. She *had* seen that, many times. The vehicle would come to a stop outside the house, and Marla would run outside and climb in, always dressed up pretty. Once she'd had a small valise. Claudia had seen that, just not the night Marla went missing.

Among all her secrets, her little bits of stored knowledge, this had been her most precious. Watching from her window as the lights went on inside the Holt house, lights she hadn't seen burning in years, she knew that someone had discovered the truth. And she felt angry, bitter, as though something had been stolen from her.

She shut the blinds and went to bed.

chapter thirty-eight

THE HOLLOWS SUCKS. Willow wrote this in her notebook as Mr. Vance handed back their essays about *A Separate Peace.* She barely glanced at it as he put it on her desk. An *A*, of course.

"Nice work, Miss Graves." She looked up at him, and he smiled at her, the way he used to. And she smiled back. He leaned in to whisper, tapping on her notebook, "It's not that bad."

They spent the rest of the class talking about the essay question. Willow stayed silent until the end, when Mr. Vance glanced in her direction.

"Willow wrote an extraordinary essay," he said. "Would you care to share your thoughts about the book? You're uncharacteristically silent today."

Everybody was looking at her in the way they had been for the last couple of days. Everyone, it seemed, knew about her running away, falling into the Black River, being fished out by the police. They thought that she'd been chased by Michael Holt. (In fact it was only Jolie who claimed to have seen him. That's why she was screaming. But Willow wasn't sure it was true.) They'd really been chasing Jolie, trying to get her to come in from the rain.

In some rumors Michael Holt had confessed to Willow about murdering his mother. (She'd never even seen him. By the time her mother and Mr. Ivy got her back to the car, he'd been taken away already.) They all knew now that she'd been the one to see him digging in the Hollows Wood. They'd stopped sneering and laughing at her, for some reason. Everyone wanted to talk to her, to hear about that night in the woods. And Willow was happy to tell the tale for them. Finally she had something to say that was harrowing and extraordinary, and not a lie at all.

"I think Gene *did* knock Fin from the tree on purpose," said Willow. "He bounced the branch."

"But they were friends, *best* friends," said Mr. Vance.

"True. But sometimes we hurt the people we love, and we do it because something inside us is hurting," she said. "It doesn't even have to do with the other person. Sometimes there's just this ugly, unhappy place inside us. And everything bad—anger, jealousy, sadness—it all lives there."

Mr. Vance was looking at her so intently that she almost stopped talking. Everyone was looking at her.

"Go on," Mr. Vance said.

"And sometimes you go there—you live in that place. And when you're there, you might do and say terrible things. Because things that are good and happy and bright seem ugly and cause you pain. You want to smash those things. You want other people to hurt, too. So you hurt them, even if you love them."

"Very insightful, Willow," said Mr. Vance.

She shrugged. "It's just a book." When she glanced up at him, he was smiling, but he still looked sad. She was sad, too. He was one of the people she had hurt, and they couldn't be friends, not like they used to, anymore.

"Story is life, Miss Graves," he said. She'd heard him say that a million times. She finally understood what he meant.

Out in the hallway after class, Cole was waiting for her. He took her backpack and walked her to her locker.

"How was class?" he asked.

She held up her essay.

"Brainiac," he said. He leaned in to give her a kiss on the cheek. "Want a ride home?"

"I have to ask my mom," she said. She gave him a roll of her eyes.

"So call her," he said. "I'll wait."

"How was it today?" she asked him.

He shrugged, looked down at his feet. "Fine." He wasn't much of a talker.

It was his first day back at school since the night in the woods. His father had been arrested for embezzlement or something like that. And Cole had been reunited with his mother. They were both staying with his stepmother and his half siblings—which Willow thought must be the weirdest possible situation. She tried to imagine her and her mom living with Brenda the stripper. It would *not* be okay. But Cole seemed happy with it. His mom needed a place; he wanted to stay in The Hollows and be close to Claire and Cameron—and to Willow. So, for now, it worked. When his mom got a good job, they'd get their own place.

"Cole asked if he could give me a ride home," she said when she reached her mom. The hall was thinning out, people heading to the buses. They started moving toward the door, in case she said no.

"Willow."

"We'll come straight there," she said.

Willow had been sure she was going to be grounded for life after the woods. But instead she and Bethany had stayed up all that night talking. They talked about things they'd never really discussed—the night Willow first ran away in New York City, the lies she'd told that alienated all her friends, how lost she felt, and how much blame she had felt after Bethany's divorce from Richard. She'd just wanted to disappear, not die, not end her life. She wanted to dissolve, be invisible. It was hard to explain, but her mother seemed to listen and understand.

When Willow had chased Jolie in the rain, trying to get her to come back to the car, she'd slipped and fallen into the water. And after the shock of the cold, panic set in. And as the water took her away from Cole and Jolie, who chased her through the trees and finally fell behind, she screamed for her mother.

In her frightened mind, she believed that her mother could always hear her when she called and would always come for her. That her mother was just like the mom in that story she loved. And she'd realized she believed that because it had always been true; her mom was always there. Even if she did invite Mr. Ivy to dinner. But she also believed that she had to stay close by for her mother to hear her. And Willow had strayed very far. Her mother couldn't hear her calling for help.

And then her foot got stuck and she was pulled under. She didn't remember much after that, except opening her eyes on the bank, seeing Jolie and Cole looking at her in horror like they thought she was dead.

She told her mother all this. And her mother, *amazingly,* didn't cry. And because she didn't, because she seemed strong, Willow told her about that dark, angry place she had inside sometimes. The place that helped her understand Gene in *A Separate Peace.* She'd been in that place when she was so mean to her mom at dinner with Mr. Ivy. She had never told anyone about that.

They went to see Dr. Cooper together the next day and talked to her about what had happened, how they could move forward together in a better way, what they could do to earn each other's trust. Grounding for eternity was not on the list of things to do.

She was actually breaking one of her promises right now, by calling in to question a rule her mother had made. No riding in cars with boys.

"Sorry," she said. "I'll take the bus."

"He can meet you here," she said. "We'll bake cookies."

She was about to make some smart comment about how they weren't three years old and cookie baking had lost its charm. But she didn't. She still loved to bake cookies.

"I have to take the bus," she said to Cole. She stuffed the phone into her bag. "She said you could come over."

She felt that anxiety well up, that fear that he would think she was a giant dork and that he'd rather be with Jolie, who could go anywhere and do anything she wanted to do.

"Cool," he said. "See you there."

He read something on her face, gave her that quick, shy smile he had. "I'll be there this time. Promise."

And then he was gone. Mom thought he was too old for her. Next year he'd be a senior and she'd be a sophomore. Mom thought he had too many problems. *He's got a lot on his plate for a kid. His dad's in jail. His mom is out of work. I don't want his baggage to become yours.* What did that even mean? And then, of course, there was the big talk about sex. And how Willow wasn't ready, and how it was a special thing that she was too young to understand, and how she shouldn't make the choice to share herself that way yet. And that she had to promise to talk to Bethany if she was thinking about it, and not to do anything until she did. How disgusting was it to talk to your *mother* about things like that? Anyway, Willow *so* wasn't there. She didn't even want to think about *that*.

"Are you going to have sex with Mr. Ivy?" Willow had asked. She drew out his name into a playful taunt.

"Willow!" Bethany had said. Bull's-eye. Willow was off the hook. A high red blush lit up her mother's face. "Please! That is so not your business."

"Are you going to see him again?" she asked. Because that's what she really wanted to know.

"At the moment we're just friends."

"But you *like him* like him, right? You don't just friend like him."

Honesty, that was the other promise. No secrets and half-truths. No lies. Her mother looked away. "Yes, I *like him* like him. But there's no guarantee he feels the same way. Our first date did not exactly go seamlessly."

"He likes you," Willow said. "I can tell."

"Whatever," Bethany said. "Whatever it winds up being, it's going to be very slow. So you don't have anything to worry about. It's not going to affect your life at all."

Willow got on the bus and sat in the back. She put her earbuds in and listened to Lady Gaga as the bus wound its way home. They passed the silver-gray pond surrounded by trees losing their leaves. And the sky above was blue with high white clouds, and the light was already going golden. The days were growing short. As the bus pulled to a stop in front of her drive, a flock of birds startled and fluttered noisily away. When she stepped outside and the bus pulled away, she was left with that silence she'd grown to appreciate and the smell of pine, somewhere the scent of burning wood. Maybe Mr. Vance was right. The Hollows wasn't *that* bad.

chapter thirty-nine

Jones was behind on the leaves. The lawn was almost covered with them. Maggie wanted him to get a leaf blower, but he liked the exercise of raking. Going to the gym and logging miles on a machine seemed like a waste of time. Everyone was pounding away on some piece of equipment, staring at a television screen, with headphones in ears. That couldn't be healthy, could it? At least when he was raking, he was outside, taking in the air, accomplishing something. But it seemed like he'd been raking for hours. And he hadn't even scratched the surface.

To his dismay and annoyance, the mourning doves had made a nest in the upper corner of the porch roof. He'd heard them cooing when he came out to get the paper and looked up to see them nestled together in a small pile of twigs and scraps of newspaper on a little ledge that Jones hadn't even noticed before.

"Oh, leave them," said Maggie. "They're so cute, and it's going to be cold this winter. Maybe we should hang a bird feeder."

"No," he said. "No way. They have to go."

"Don't be such an old crank."

"They carry lice, you know."

"Oh, Jones."

Now the doves sat on the rail, cuddling together, looking sweet. They knew they had Maggie on their side, didn't they? If he got rid of their nest while they were out doing their mourning-dove things, he'd be in trouble. He leaned his rake against the tree, dropped his gloves on the ground, and walked inside through the garage so that he wouldn't have to walk past those smug little birds. He'd find a nice way to re-locate them, just *move* the nest somewhere. Maybe when Maggie was over at her mother's later.

Inside, on the old table in the kitchen sat a copy of the *Hollows Ga-zette*. There was an article in there about the discovery of Marla Holt's remains. He'd been mentioned in the article as the retired cop–turned–private investigator. He didn't know where the reporter had gotten her information. The phone started ringing a couple of hours after the paper hit the driveways. There was no mention in the article of the circumstances under which Jones had retired. And it seemed that no one remembered or cared.

Maggie had been taking messages. A woman wanted to find her sister who had been missing since 1985. A man wanted his wife followed—you know, just to be sure she was faithful. There were a couple of others—someone wanted a background check on his daugh-ter's boyfriend. One lady's dog had run away, and could he help? PI work was not glamorous.

"I told you you'd be surprised," Maggie had said after he'd read through the stack.

"I'm not taking jobs like that," he'd said.

"Jobs like what?"

"You know, following cheating spouses, checking up on boy-friends, tailing people collecting Workers' Comp. That's lower than I'm willing to go."

Maggie put her hand on his face, delivered a kiss to his forehead. "Just do what moves you."

Holding the newspaper in his hand, he thought about that sen-tence. What moved him? He wasn't sure he knew. Rather, he wasn't sure he could put it into words. He figured he'd know it when he found it.

A couple of hours later, he was in Dr. Dahl's office running down the week's events.

"So I guess we know what phase two is," said the doctor. "Is private-investigative work where you want to put your energies?"

Jones picked up on something from the doctor. Was it disappointment?

"Is there something wrong with that?" he asked.

"No," said Dr. Dahl. "Of course not. I just wondered if there was anything else you wanted to look at. You haven't made any firm decisions. We'd talked about woodworking."

Somehow Jones just couldn't see himself making bookshelves for a living. It's not like he had some drive to be a designer or any real passion for it. He had some native ability, enjoyed working with his hands. But it wasn't something that fascinated him, not in the same way that police work had. He told the doctor as much.

"Well, good," he said. He smoothed out his perfectly creased charcoal slacks, fixed Jones with a warm smile. "Passion is important. I just wonder if it's not the darkness of it all that calls you, Jones."

Jones didn't know what to say to that. Something about it smarted, made him feel the rise of that anger.

"It's gritty work," the doctor said. "There's danger. You said yourself you could have died."

"But I didn't," he said. "I saved that girl. If I hadn't freed her foot, she would have drowned. That means something to me."

"Of course it does," said the doctor. "Of course."

Since the night of his near drowning, the nightmares had ceased. He hadn't been waking up sweating, yelling, gasping for air in a full week. Maggie had moved back into the bedroom and stayed the whole night. He wouldn't say that he'd conquered his fear of death; it was a specter that lingered. It snuck up on him when he least expected, and he'd be struck wondering, what would it be? A slip in the shower? A car accident? Murder? Maybe he would be murdered by someone like that psycho Kevin Carr. But then it would pass. It was a specter that lingered for everyone, wasn't it?

Maybe the night terrors would come back. But maybe they wouldn't, now that he knew what he was supposed to be doing with his life. He was meant to be helping people—and not just checking their mail and watering their plants. He knew that as surely as he knew anything. And the fact that he knew with such clarity made him think that maybe, after all, there was something larger than himself. Maybe.

"When last you were here, we talked about your father," said Dr. Dahl. He was apparently looking to pick at some scabs. Maybe Jones seemed too happy today. The doctor was afraid he'd be out of a job. "Have you done any thinking about that?"

"Some," Jones said. "I've thought about it some."

He *had* thought about it some. But he wasn't ready to talk to the doctor or anyone about it, not even Mags.

"Would you care to share your thoughts?"

Jones looked at the clock. "I think our time is up, Doc," he said. It *was* up—a little over, in fact.

"Ah, yes," said Dr. Dahl. "Next week, then."

"Definitely."

At the reception desk, he paid his bill. As he waited for his receipt, Jones watched some other guy about his age walk into Dr. Dahl's office. He wondered what that guy's problem was. He looked depressed.

Jones had promised his wife that he'd keep seeing Dr. Dahl, and he would. He knew it helped him, kept him thinking about and working on the things that he might otherwise avoid. Maggie needed that, deserved that, and so did he. And more than that, Maggie was hot for him right now. She was digging the whole PI thing. She was proud of him for staying in therapy. She was sleeping in their bedroom. She wasn't mad at him, had stopped giving him *the look*. She was a smart woman, and he'd do what she wanted. If he knew what was good for him.

Out in the car, he reached over to the file he'd left on the passenger seat. He'd written the name on the protruding tag: Jefferson Cooper.

It had taken him only a couple of hours to find his father. All these years, and all he had to do was pick up a phone. He dug through some of Abigail's old papers and found his father's Social Security number. Jones gave Jack a call at noon, and by three that afternoon he had an address, credit and employment history. He hadn't decided what he was going to do with that. He hadn't allowed himself to have a memory of his father—ever. Maggie had suggested once that he try to think of three good memories he had of the time he, his father, and his mother were all together. Every time he did this, he felt that headache come on, had the urge to run for the nearest burger joint, anesthetize himself with fat and simple carbs. He'd be taking his time with this. He wasn't sure what he was going to do.

When he got back to the house, the sun was already low in the sky. The days were getting shorter. Ricky's car was waiting in the driveway. Ricky would be home tomorrow. They'd already made plans to go look at a new stereo for the car, something the kid wanted for Christmas. Jones knew that it would probably be their only time together. Ricky would be seeing his friends who were home for the weekend, too, including Charlene, his son's on-again, off-again girlfriend. At the moment they were only friends. She made Jones nervous, for a lot of reasons. Too much history there, like everything in The Hollows. Everything was tangled and connected across years and families. He wanted Ricky to get away, not be tethered here to this place as he was, as Maggie was now because of Jones.

Anyway, he'd make his time with Ricky count. He'd talk, wouldn't get all tongue-tied and silent. He'd written some things down, questions to ask about MyFace, and e-mail, texting, too. He'd ask about

Rick's music. Did he find a band? And what were his favorite classes? Had he met any girls? Maggie had helped him come up with some topics. *And listen when he talks. Try not to do any lecturing, even if you don't agree with what he says.*

On the porch he stopped to look up at the mourning doves. They both sat in their perch and stared at him. One of them issued an annoyed little chirp.

"Okay, fine," he said. "One more night."

He went inside. There was music playing, something classical (slow and depressing), maybe Chopin? He followed the sound and found Maggie in the kitchen, cooking—a rarity since Ricky had left home. She was making lasagna, their son's favorite.

"My last patient canceled today," she said when he walked in. "I thought I'd do something special, since Rick is coming home tomorrow." She'd been better about calling him that; their son didn't like "Ricky" anymore.

He walked up behind her and wrapped his arms around her, took in the scent of her hair, lavender and sage. And in the warmth of his own kitchen, with his wife in his arms, his son on his way home, his calling acknowledged if not exactly answered, Jones Cooper felt good. He felt alive, and grateful for it.

"Another call came in while you were out," she said. "Eloise Montgomery."

"Oh?" The sound of her name stirred something in him. It wasn't anxiety, exactly. But it was something close.

"She asked if you'd return her call. In fact, what she said precisely was, 'Will you ask him to please call, if he is so moved?'"

What had the doctor said? *I just wonder if it's not the darkness of it all that calls you, Jones.* The doctor was right. The darkness did call to him, didn't it? And he would answer. He spun his wife around and kissed her gently on the mouth. But he wouldn't answer tonight.

acknowledgments

I am continuously astounded by the wonderful, loving, and supportive people I have in my life—both personally and professionally. Over the years, the people I work with have become my dear friends, and the lines between life and work are happily blurred. I'll take this opportunity, as I always do, to shower them all with praise and thanks:

My husband, Jeffrey, and our daughter, Ocean Rae, are simply everything. Every day they bring immeasurable amounts of love and laughter into my life. My husband is a true partner in every sense of the word, making our world safe and secure so that I can find the time and the mental space to write. He's also hot. And he does the accounting. And, did I mention? He's a great cook. I am floored by the wisdom, beauty, light, and sheer power my daughter displays. Watching her grow from a little bean into my budding rose is the greatest joy and pleasure of my life. She has made me a better person, and a better writer. And she totally cracks me up daily. Really, she is so cool—cooler than I can ever hope to be.

My agent, the brilliant and fabulous Elaine Markson, and her assistant, the incomparable Gary Johnson, hold my entire professional world together. Elaine has been my unflagging supporter and champion for more than ten years, and she is also my cherished friend. Gary keeps me sane (though I'm quite sure I don't do the same for him) and keeps me laughing. I really can't begin to list everything they do for me, day after day. But, as I've said before (and it only gets more true each year), I'd be lost without them.

I am indebted to my wonderful editor, Shaye Areheart, and to the truly stellar team at Crown: Maya Mavjee, Molly Stern, John Glusman, Jill Flaxman, Whitney Cookman, David Tran, Jacqui LeBow, Andy Augusto, Kira Walton, Patty Berg, Donna Passannante, Annsley Rosner, Sarah Breivogel, Linda Kaplan, Karin Schulze, Cindy Berman, Kate

Kennedy, Domenica Alioto, and Christine Kopprasch. This is a long list, but believe me when I say that every single one of these people brings a unique and special talent to the team, and I am thankful to them all. Of course, I can never say enough good things about the amazing, top-notch sales force. They are on the front lines of an ultra-competitive business. I know that my books find their way into the hands of readers largely through their tireless efforts on my behalf.

My family and friends continue to cheer me through the good days and drag me through the challenging ones. Thanks to my parents, Joe and Virginia Miscione, and to my brother and his wife, Joe and Tara, for their love, support, and for endlessly spreading the word. I haven't published a thing that the dear, funny, and talented Heather Mikesell hasn't read first. Marion Chartoff and Tara Popick, my two oldest friends, have been with me on this journey every step of the way.

As always, I must thank the people who so generously offered their expertise to fill in the gaps in my knowledge. David Steinberg, author of *Hiking the Road to Ruins: Day Trips and Camping Adventures to Iron Mines, Old Military Sites, and Things Abandoned in the New York City Area . . . and Beyond* (www.theroadtoruins.com), was an invaluable resource in my research about abandoned mines in the tri-state area. His wealth of knowledge helped inform and ground the fictional mines of The Hollows. The photos and descriptions found on www.ironminers.com fueled my imagination, and my conversations with Mike Hetman (aka Miner Mike) had me thinking about mines in a whole new way. Mike said, during one of our talks, that he thought of soil as a kind of slow-flowing liquid. This idea stayed with me and found its way into the narrative of this book. It should be noted that Mr. Hetman was in no way the inspiration for the character of Michael Holt. The character and all his various flaws, as well as his name, were on the page long before my research into mines began.

My thanks to Special Agent Paul Bouffard (Retired), who continues to be my source for all things legal and illegal, and his wonderful wife, Wendy, one of my earliest and most important readers. Thanks also to Debi McCreary for her very insightful early read. There's a scene in this book that's just for you, Debi.

Sitting down to write these acknowledgments every year reminds me that I am truly blessed by the people in my life. I can't thank them enough for everything they do, but at least I can keep trying.

LISA UNGER is an award-winning *New York Times, USA Today,* and international bestselling author. Her novels have been published in more than twenty-six countries around the world.

She was born in New Haven, Connecticut (1970), but grew up in the Netherlands, England, and New Jersey. A graduate of the New School for Social Research, Lisa spent many years living and working in New York City. She then left a career in publicity to pursue her dream of becoming a full-time author. She now lives in Florida with her husband and daughter. She is at work on her next novel.

an excerpt from

heartbroken

BY

LISA UNGER

coming in June 2012

Birdie Burke stood on the edge of the rock and watched the first light of morning color the sky a dusty rose. As she perched on the cold, slippery stone shore, the lake water lapped at her toes. Other than the whisper of a light breeze through the trees, there was only the distant calling of a loon. She let her robe drop, and the cool air raised goose bumps on her flesh. No one could see her; the other islands were visible only from the north and south. Her husband had been asleep when she left him in the main house.

And even if anyone *could* see her, who wanted to look at the bathing-suited body of a seventy-five-year-old woman? Most people would avert their eyes in embarrassment, even though she was thin and fit. When fully clothed, she knew, she was very stylish. In fact, she still considered herself quite attractive. Even so, it seemed to Birdie that no one ever looked at her—not really.

Time had robbed her of the lushness of her body, her creamy skin, and the shine in her hair. And even though she didn't *feel* any different than she had when she was twenty, she was unrecognizable as the girl she was then. This was true for everyone, she knew. No one her age recognized the people they saw in the mirror. Most of her friends and acquaintances were engaged in a full-scale battle against the onset of old age, rallying teams of personal trainers, plastic surgeons, beauticians, aestheticians to hold back the clock. *How silly,* Birdie always thought. *If ever there's a battle you can't win, it's that one.* Not that she didn't take care of herself. Not that she didn't know about fighting losing battles.

The water was frigid as she inched in and then quickly submerged herself to her shoulders. Though she was well accustomed to the shock of the cold, her whole body seemed to seize in protest, her heart starting to race and her joints to ache. Then she began to move, placing one careful stroke after the next, her still-powerful legs pumping. Normally, she'd warm gradually, and the water would grow to feel bracing and crisp—refreshing.

But today was different. Maybe the water was just a few degrees too cold. Or maybe she was just old. She couldn't seem to get her rhythm. She hadn't gone far at all, and she was already thinking about turning back.

When she was younger, she'd effortlessly circle the perimeter once, maybe twice. She would enter, as she had today, to the west of the house at the only point that allowed for a safe plunge into the water. Then she'd swim out far enough to avoid being pushed back into the large, sharp rocks that surrounded most of the island. She used to relish the fresh water against her skin, the pleasure of her heart rate elevating, her lean, strong limbs pulling her past the dock, then around the east side, then another quarter turn back to where she began. The whole circle took her about half an hour when she was in good form.

She remembered the water being *warmer.* And the early morning was a stolen time, the time before the children woke and needed her. She used to wish it could last forever—the quiet, the freedom. Of course, now that it *could* last forever, now that she could pass an entire day without anyone needing a single thing of her, it wasn't nearly as pleasant as she'd imagined it would be. Birdie wondered why that so often seemed to be the case—once you had what you wanted, it was a shadow of what you'd dreamed it to be.

She'd made it to the dock, about a quarter of the way around, before she realized, frustrated, that she would need to go back. She couldn't manage the rest of the distance. Reluctantly, she turned around, swam to where she had left her robe in a soft pink pile, and stiffly climbed out. She was disappointed, even angry with herself, for not having what it took to complete the circle. She didn't like being reminded of her age. She was unbeatable once upon a time.

But maybe it was just as well; there was a lot to do. Everyone was coming on Sunday. There was so much required of her when guests were about to arrive. Her husband Joe was very little help; he fussed over details like the wine and the music, what games they should play. Meanwhile, all the heavy lifting—the shopping, the cooking, and the cleaning—were up to her. By sundown on the day after to-morrow, her children and grandchildren would be sitting at the long dining table for dinner. The blessed quiet of her island would be shattered. And the work would begin.

You do this to yourself, Birdie, her husband admonished regularly. *Why don't you just try to relax and enjoy? Everyone would be just as happy with hamburgers on the grill, baked potatoes in tin foil, and a green salad.* Yes—everyone except Birdie.

She was so deep in thought that she didn't see him until she'd fastened her robe, slipped on her shoes, and turned around to head back to the main house. For a moment the shock of a figure standing at the edge of the trees didn't register.

Without her glasses on, she couldn't make him out. Who in the world could that be? Not her husband. The figure was tall but narrow, not powerful like Joe. One of the neighbors? No, it wasn't possible; she'd have heard the boat approach.

"Who's there?" she called.

But he stood motionless, possessing an almost ethereal quality. Birdie couldn't quite bring him into focus. Even though she felt a flutter of apprehension, she moved toward him. She was never one to move away from a threat. Always take it head-on; that was her philosophy.

"Identify yourself," she said. She didn't like the sound of her own voice. *Do you really have to be so goddamn imperious?* Her husband's other favorite admonishment. *You're not the queen, for Christ's sake.*

"You are *trespassing* on private land."

He didn't answer. What was she seeing? Was there anything there at all? Was it just a trick of light?

She picked up her pace. As she drew nearer, he seemed to disappear into the trees. She hadn't realized her vision was so poor. When she got to where he'd stood, there was no one there, no trace of anyone having been there. But someone *had* been there. She wasn't crazy or senile. She *had* seen someone. Hadn't she?

She walked over the rocky terrain that comprised the west side of the island and headed down toward the dock. Today, because there had been little rain for the past week, the rocks were fairly dry above the waterline, though somewhat treacherous. Birdie was sure-footed, having tramped over them at every stage in her life. Her feet belonged on those rocks, just as they had when she was a little girl, a teenager, a young woman. She moved quickly, her feet knowing which stone was loose and which was too pointy and which was a good, level place to step. When the rain fell and storms made the water choppy, this side of the island would become impassable—too slick, jagged, and treacherous by foot, waves knocking against the steep island face. There would be no way to traverse the perimeter except to get into the water and swim.

Rounding the bend, she saw the light gray dock against the steel blue of the water. A formation of Canada geese honked overhead, heading south already. The temperatures were growing colder without ever having seemed to warm.

Their old skiff bobbed in the water. Their cuddy boat, too, was fastened securely to the dock cleats, the cabin covered against the weather. But that was all—no other boat was docked there, as it would have to be if someone had come to call. There was no place else along the coastlines of the island where anyone could come ashore without badly damaging his boat.

Directly to the south was Cross Island. Only two years ago someone had built a house there. For most of Birdie's life, it had been empty. As children, she, her brother, and her sister used to row a small boat across the narrow channel, and explore. Though their mother always called them back, when she caught them, anxious and angry.

"Don't go there," she'd say. "It's not our island."

They'd come back, sullen and complaining quietly to one another. No one dared argue with Mother when she had that look on her face. She was rarely angry, almost never raised her voice. But there was a look. And when you saw it, you hushed and did as you were told.

Looking at Cross Island now, Birdie could just see the house that had been built there, its brown-shingled roof peeking through the trees, its windows glinting pink in the morning light. She didn't like it. It felt like an intrusion. Plus, the island itself held bad memories for her. Most often she ignored it, pretended it wasn't there, as she did with many of the things that pained her.

She glanced back the way she had come, then to the north, where she could see the main house. From the dock, a narrow gravel path led up to the main structure, then wound around it to the guesthouse. Beyond that cabin, the path wound on to the bunkhouse. She saw no one. No shadow followed her, no interloper. Toward the mainland, thunderheads darkened the sky.

The surrounding islands were occupied by private homes. Though the nearby island hotels and inns had shuttles from the mainland, there was no water taxi service. If you wanted to get to the private residences, you had to have your own boat.

There had been a rash of thefts in the area. Many of the homes stood uninhabited for most of the year. Undesirables from the mainland had grown wise, and they had been taking boats out, breaking in, stealing valuables, vandalizing—even spending a few days partying. Birdie had been angry when she heard the news. It was typical.

They were always waiting, angry and entitled, to take or destroy the things for which you'd worked so hard. There was always someone with less looking at you with envy and resentment, just waiting for your back to be turned so they could steal from you. Somehow they always seemed to get away with it.

About a week after she'd learned this, Birdie had gone into town and purchased a small handgun. She was often alone on the island. Joe didn't cherish his time here the way she did, and he went back to their apartment in the city when he tired of the solitude—or was it her company that tired him? After all, it wasn't his place. Heart Island hadn't been in *his* family for three generations. *He* hadn't spent every childhood summer here, as she had. She refused to be afraid in this place. And she pitied anyone who tried to take anything from her. She kept the revolver in its case, in a high kitchen cabinet. When she was alone at night, she moved it to her bedside table.

Birdie picked up her pace as she walked the rest of the perimeter of the three-acre island and ended at its highest point, Lookout Rock, as it was named by the Heart children—Birdie, her sister, Caroline, and her brother, Gene. From this vantage point, she could see each of the structures, surrounded tightly by large rocks and trees.

The path was really the only way to get around the island now; it led from the bunkhouse to the guest cabin to the main house and then down to the dock, dimly lit by carefully spaced solar-powered ground lights. Once there had been only a single house, the one that was now the guest cabin. Then there was no path from the dock to the house, and everyone made his way up through the trees to the clearing. No one ever walked through the trees anymore, especially in the pitch-dark nights, preferring to keep to the path.

Up high and looking down, Birdie felt that maybe her eyes had been playing tricks on her, hard as it was to believe. But she didn't see a boat anywhere, run up ashore or tied off on a rock. There was no other way to get here. So logic dictated that she hadn't seen what she thought she had. Next time she'd bring her glasses or put in her contacts before the swim.

Her late sister, Caroline, would have claimed that Birdie had seen a ghost. Birdie's sister, and Birdie's mother, Lana, had both believed that the island was home to otherworldly inhabitants. According to them, there was a man who walked the edge, and a woman who stood at Lookout Rock. And something else she couldn't remember. It was sheer silliness. Birdie had never seen anything remotely like that. Caroline hinted that it was because Birdie, as a pragmatist, as a cynic, wasn't worthy of a ghostly appearance. Even though Birdie couldn't explain what she had just seen, she wouldn't turn to the supernatural to do so. She was wondering about her vision, her sanity, maybe, but certainly *not* spirits.

Birdie walked the whole island and ended up back where she'd started. The stand of trees was just a blurry line of black. She stared a moment, willing a form to appear from something—a shadow, a swaying branch—so she could explain to herself what had happened. But no, there were just her old friends the pines, the birch trees, the sugar maples, and their eternal whispering.

Finally, she walked back up to the main cabin to start her breakfast. Her mood, which had been fine, had turned dark. She felt rattled in a way she shouldn't have, as though she'd gotten some terrible news or remembered something she had been trying to forget.

New from Lisa Unger

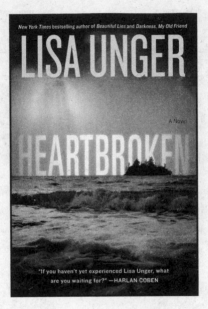

Heartbroken

A Novel

$24.00 (Canada: $28.00)

978-0-307-46520-7

On sale June 2012

Also by Lisa Unger

Fragile
A Novel
$15.00 (Canada: $17.00)
978-0-307-39400-2

Die for You
A Novel
$14.99 (Canada: $17.99)
978-0-307-39398-2

Black Out
A Novel
$14.99 (Canada: $17.50)
978-0-307-33847-1

Sliver of Truth
A Novel
$13.95 (Canada: $15.95)
978-0-307-33849-5

AVAILABLE WHEREVER BOOKS ARE SOLD

Want More Lisa Unger?

Use your smartphone to take a photo of the barcode below for exclusive **short stories, sneak peeks,** and **behind-the-scenes** access.

If you do not have a 2D barcode reader on your smartphone, download the software free at LisaUnger.mobi.

Don't have a smartphone?
Text THEHOLLOWS to 333888.